DEAD RECKONING

D0066202

Also by Clive Egleton

Orange Public Library

DEAD
RECKONING

Clive Egleton

PROPERTY OF THE
ORANGE N.J. PUBLIC LIBRARY
THE LIBRARY NEEDS & WELCOMES GIFTS & BEQUESTS

St. Martin's Minotaur
New York

DEAD RECKONING. Copyright © 1999 by Clive Egleton. All rights reserved.
Printed in the United States of America. No part of this book may be used or
reproduced in any manner whatsoever without written permission except in the
case of brief quotations embodied in critical articles or reviews. For
information, address St. Martin's Press,
175 Fifth Avenue, New York, N.Y. 10010.

ISBN 0-312-24102-X

First published in Great Britain by Hodder and Stoughton, a division of Hodder
Headline PLC

First St. Martin's Minotaur Edition: November 1999

10 9 8 7 6 5 4 3 2 1

This book is for Viola Norman and my sister-in-law, Daphne, who had to contend with my original spelling.

PROPERTY OF THE
ORANGE N.J. PUBLIC LIBRARY
THE LIBRARY NEEDS & WELCOMES GIFTS & BEQUESTS

Chapter One

The terraced house stood on the corner of Lansdowne Mews with Clarendon Road and was a convenient three-minute walk from Holland Park tube station. Behind the wrought-iron gate and railings, a footpath not much larger than a hearthrug ended at a solid oak door. A brass nameplate on the centre panel indicated that Dr Z. K. Ramash, MD, Clinical Psychiatrist could be found on the ground floor. In fact, Dr Ramash owned the whole building and lived directly above the front office and surgery. Much to the annoyance of the other residents in the mews, the top floor had been converted into a refuge for battered wives, which, the neighbours claimed, had reduced the value of each of their properties by at least a cool hundred thousand.

At £150 an hour, it was hardly surprising that the consultations Dr Ramash provided were not available to patients on the National Health. The people she treated belonged to the AB socioeconomic group, the wealthy top five per cent of the nation. All her patients were women, the vast majority of whom were going through the menopause; Mrs Virginia Hardiman was one of the few exceptions. A former model who had left school at sixteen without any academic qualifications, she had married a highly successful barrister and had felt out of her depth ever since. Lacking self-esteem, Virginia Hardiman had turned to chocolate for solace, developing an addiction for Cadbury's Dairy Milk, Bourneville, Fruit and Nut, as well as Terry's Old Gold. Some twenty pounds overweight for her height, she had gone to Dr Ramash on the recommendation of a girl she knew at her old model agency who'd faced a similar problem. After four consultations she had stopped eating chocolate and had succeeded in losing approximately seven pounds.

There was no sign of Amanda, the twenty-three-year-old receptionist, when Virginia Hardiman walked into the waiting room a good five minutes early for her ten fifteen appointment. It was customary for Amanda to provide her with a cup of coffee and two digestive biscuits when she arrived, a service which Virginia regarded as no more than her due, considering how much Dr Ramash charged for a consultation. Somewhat miffed, she rang the bell on the counter outside the cubbyhole which served as an office, and was even more displeased when after a minute Amanda had still failed to appear.

Virginia glanced at the array of magazines on the round table in the centre of the room. *Tatler* and *Harpers & Queen* were delivered to the house but the latest issue of *Homes and Gardens* had arrived here since her last visit and she settled down to read it. Ten fifteen came and went, then ten thirty. At a quarter to eleven, Virginia decided enough was enough and tapped on the communicating door. Getting no reply, she opened it and walked into the consulting room.

Dr Ramash was at her desk, which faced the waiting room. Amanda was sitting bolt upright on a ladder back chair, arms stiffly by her sides. Neither woman answered when Virginia said 'hello'. Near-sighted and unable to use contact lenses because they made her eyes water, Virginia Hardiman was also too vain to wear glasses. Consequently, it wasn't until she moved a lot closer that she noticed the rope around Amanda's neck. Thereafter everything began to register in her mind like a camera on auto. Dr Ramash looked darker than usual, her eyes bulging, the tongue sticking out as if she was making a rude face at her receptionist.

The shutter clicked again and registered another image, this time of a wrist lashed to a chair leg. Then the eye lit on a high-heeled shoe lying on the carpet near the leather-upholstered chaise longue. And behind the couch the body of a third woman, a bloody halo surrounding the head. Suddenly Virginia Hardiman was conscious of the nauseous smell of excrement and she gagged on the bile that immediately rose in her throat.

2

Turning her back on the gruesome scene, she fled the room and ran out of the house into the street. There she leaned against one of the horse chestnut trees that lined the pavement at regular intervals like guardsmen on parade.

The street began to revolve and she hung on to the tree like grim death. She retched, then doubled up and vomited on to the pavement. An elderly couple, exercising their French poodle gave Virginia a wide berth and continued on their way towards the park as if they hadn't noticed her. A small voice inside Virginia's head told her to call 999 but her Cellnet phone was in her handbag which she had left behind in the house, and nothing on God's earth could make her go back inside to retrieve it. The only alternative was to go knocking on doors.

There was no answer from the adjoining house nor from the next two and she was halfway down the front path, having given up on the fourth, when a woman with a lilting voice called out to her from the doorstep. Virginia turned about and stared at an elderly Indian lady in the primrose-coloured sari. Traumatised by what she had just seen, the power of speech momentarily deserted her.

'Yes? What is it you want from me?' the woman asked softly.

'The police.'

'The police? They are not here, surely you can see that?'

'Dr Ramash, Amanda . . .' Virginia pointed to the end house. 'They are dead. Strangled . . . You understand?' Reaction set in and her whole body began to shake as if she had suddenly gone down with malaria. 'There is another woman but she has been shot.'

'What is your name?'

'Mrs Ralph Hardiman.'

'Good. Then we will phone the police together.'

Lansdowne Mews was located within the boundaries of the Met's B District. Within a matter of seconds the divisional station on Ladbroke Road had dispatched a mobile to the address of the reported incident. Once it was known that the 999 call was not a hoax, officers from the scene of the crime team descended on the neighbourhood. As Virginia Hardiman was still in shock, one of the battered wives from the refuge on the top floor of the house identified Dr Ramash and the receptionist for the record. Nobody, however, had seen the third victim before but the desk diary indicated that a Mrs Harriet Ashton was due to see Dr Ramash at nine fifteen that morning and there was nothing to show that she had cancelled the appointment. From the clinical notes pertaining to Mrs Ashton, the police were able to discover her address and phone number.

Roy Kelso had been promoted to Assistant Director a week after his thirty-ninth birthday. Despite the fact that he had always been in the Administrative Wing of the Secret Intelligence Service and had never held an operational appointment, he had convinced himself that he was destined to go right to the top of the tree. It had taken him all of ten years to realise that he had reached his ceiling and wasn't going anywhere. Disappointed and thoroughly embittered, Kelso had let it be known to all and sundry that he couldn't wait for his fifty-fifth birthday to arrive when he would be eligible for early retirement. When, earlier in the year, severance had been only a few months off, the thought of leaving the SIS before the age of compulsory retirement had so dismayed Kelso that he'd written to Victor Hazelwood, the Director General, asking if he might be permitted to withdraw his original application.

It hadn't been the easiest of letters to write. Kelso could not forget that when he had been promoted in 1979, Hazelwood had been a Grade I Intelligence officer in charge of the Russian Desk. Furthermore it had taken Victor eleven years to catch up with him and, in his opinion, he would never have done so if the Assistant Director in charge of the Eastern Bloc Department hadn't suddenly dropped dead in the office one morning. Thereafter Hazelwood's rise to power had been positively meteoric. Eighteen months after Hazelwood had taken over the Eastern Bloc Department, the newly appointed Director General, Stuart Dunglass, who'd spent most of his service in the Far East, had invited him to become his deputy. The onset of cancer of the prostate had forced Dunglass into early retirement and with the reluctant blessing of the Foreign and Commonwealth Office, Hazelwood had stepped into his shoes.

It was hard to ask a favour of a man who knew you disliked

4

him intensely, harder still when flattery and obsequiousness only aroused his ire. In the end, Kelso had simply told Hazelwood that he couldn't afford to retire on a reduced pension and Victor had said the job was his for as long as he wanted it.

As the Admin King of Vauxhall Cross, his empire consisted of the Finance Branch, the Motor Transport and General Stores Section plus the Security Vetting and Technical Services Division. Among his many duties Kelso was responsible for control of expenditure, internal audits, Boards of Inquiry and liaison with the public. Since the SIS didn't believe in freedom of information, it was his job to field all enquiries from 'outsiders'. In practice this meant that callers who didn't know what extension they required were automatically routed to the Admin Wing by the switchboard operator.

Shortly before twelve o'clock, Kelso received one such call from Detective Chief Superintendent Orwell of B District who wished to get in touch with a Mr Peter Ashton. Kelso gave him the stock answer, told the Chief Superintendent that Ashton wasn't available at the moment and asked if he could take a message.

'Who am I talking to?' Orwell demanded.

'My name is Mr Roy,' Kelso said blandly. 'I'm a chief personnel officer in the civil service.'

'Yeah? Which government department?'

'May I suggest you call Whitehall 1212 and talk to Commander, Special Branch, on extension 3899, then call me back?'

'I get it,' Orwell said, and hung up.

Ten minutes later the Chief Superintendent was back on the line. As a result of what he had to say, Kelso decided it was essential to brief Hazelwood as soon as possible.

In accordance with Government health regulations, the whole of Vauxhall Cross was a no-smoking area. The ban on smoking had originally come into force while the SIS was still using Century House in Westminster Bridge Road but Hazelwood, being the man he was, had persuaded the then DG to make an exception in his case. Consequently an extractor fan had been installed in his office, the bill for which had been passed to Kelso for settlement out of the contingency fund. A second bill for an extractor fan had found its way to the Admin Wing when the SIS had moved across the railway tracks to Vauxhall Cross and a view of the Thames. To fill his cup of bitterness to overflowing, Kelso had been landed with a third bill the day after Victor Hazelwood had changed offices, having been confirmed in the appointment of Director General.

The extractor fan was not the only personal stamp Hazelwood had put on the DG's office. As the equivalent of a permanent under secretary of state, he could have chosen a Canaletto, a Turner or an Utrillo from the list of original oils and watercolours held by the Property Services Agency. Instead he had selected a signed print of Terence Cuneo's *The Bridge at Arnhem*, a picture showing a battered-looking corvette on a storm-tossed Atlantic entitled *Convoy Escort* and *Enemy Coast Ahead*, which depicted a vic of three Wellington bombers on a moonlit night approaching a smudge of land on the horizon.

There were two other items which Kelso thought reflected Victor's somewhat jingoistic tastes. One was the ornately carved wooden box on his desk which he had bought on a field trip to India many years ago. The other, a more recent acquisition, was a cut-down shell case, which had probably come from a junk shop in the Portobello Road, that served as an ashtray. At that precise moment it held four cigar butts but not for much longer; as Kelso tapped on the door and walked into the DG's office, Hazelwood opened the wooden box and took out a Burma cheroot.

'What can I do for you, Roy?' he asked, and lit the cheroot with a match.

'I'm afraid I've got some bad news. Harriet Ashton is dead.'

'What?' Hazelwood stared at him in disbelief.

'She had been shot twice in the back of the head,' Kelso continued remorselessly.

'Who told you this?'

'Detective Chief Superintendent Orwell of B District. Harriet had an appointment to see a Dr Ramash, a clinical psychiatrist with a private practice in Lansdowne Mews. The good doctor was strangled, so was her receptionist; the police seem to think it was some kind of ritual killing. Obviously the killers were still around when Harriet arrived for her nine fifteen appointment and they must have decided she had seen too much.'

'There's no doubt that the dead woman is Harriet?'

'I'd like to think it wasn't her, Victor, but the description I was given fits Harriet to a T. Orwell told me the deceased was tall for a woman, had shoulder-length hair and must have been good-looking before most of her forehead was shot away.'

'Have the police made a positive identification? From a driver's licence, credit card or cheque book?'

Kelso was tired of standing in front of the desk like some errant schoolboy being taken to task by the headmaster. After he'd glanced pointedly at one of the leather upholstered armchairs which the Property Services Agency provided for visitors, Hazelwood finally caught on and waved a hand at the nearest one.

'They didn't find her handbag, Victor.'

'Well then, how do the police know the dead woman is Harriet? Just from the appointments diary?'

'And from the clinical notes Dr Ramash had made. That's how they got hold of her address in Chiswick and the BT phone number at 84 Rylett Close.'

Some fourteen months ago 84 Rylett Close had been one of the safe houses owned by the SIS. With the end of the Cold War and the consequent reduction in Intelligence gathering, the Treasury had attacked those high-spending government departments which were not politically sensitive with a hatchet. Although the armed forces had suffered the most, the SIS had been told to sell fifty per cent of their housing stock. In what Kelso regarded as rank nepotism, the DG had allowed Peter Ashton to purchase the house in Rylett Close at a knockdown price. But that was beside the point, which was that the phone the Ashtons used for personal calls was ex-directory with the additional caveat that the subscriber would not accept operator-assisted calls under any circumstances. Although the inference was obvious, Kelso wanted to be absolutely sure Hazelwood had seen it.

'We both know Harriet was very responsible; she would only have disclosed her phone number to the family and very close friends. Bearing in mind the physical resemblance, I don't see how the dead woman could be anybody other than Harriet.'

'The police phoned the house?'

'Yes. The Ashtons' daily woman gave them the number of this place.'

'What did she have to say about Harriet?'

Kelso gritted his teeth. Hazelwood was reluctant to face the facts; he wanted every i dotted, every t crossed before he would accept that Harriet was dead. In a few brief sentences, Kelso told him the daily had arrived at eight thirty and that Harriet had left a quarter of an hour later, saying she was going to shop at the local supermarket. She hadn't taken Edward, her sixteen-month-old son with her and the Ford Mondeo was still parked outside the house.

'I have to admit it doesn't look good.' Hazelwood left his cheroot to burn out in the brass shell case. 'I assume Peter hasn't been informed yet?' he added.

'I thought you would want to break the news to him, Victor.'

'Quite so.'

'The police would like Ashton to go straight to the mortuary at Notting Hill General. They want him to identify the body.'

'They would.' Hazelwood swung round in the swivel chair to gaze down at the river. 'Lay on a car and driver for him, will you, Roy?' he said quietly.

'Right.'

'Send Brian Thomas along as well.'

Brian Thomas was an ex-detective chief superintendent of the Metropolitan Police and a bit of a hard nose. Now employed as a Grade II Intelligence officer in the Security Vetting and Technical Services Division, he was responsible for clearing personnel who needed to have constant access to Top Secret and codeword material. He would be a crutch to lean on should Ashton need one. More importantly, Thomas would get a lot more out of the police than anybody else at Vauxhall Cross.

Ashton was a fourth-floor man with an office on the wrong side of the building. Instead of the Thames, he had an unrivalled view of the railway tracks leading to Waterloo, which was one reason why he didn't spend much time looking out of the window. The SIS consisted of four operational departments each headed by an assistant director. The largest and most unwieldy was the European, which embraced the old Soviet Bloc as well as the NATO countries. The Middle East was the tidiest, the Asian won the prize for the least active while the Pacific Basin and the Rest of the World was nothing short of a dog's breakfast. Ashton belonged to none of these departments; on paper he was a Grade I Intelligence officer, General Duties [supernumerary to establishment], a job description dreamed up by his old mentor, Victor Hazelwood.

There were two schools of thought about Ashton. Those who liked him maintained he'd had a raw deal and instanced how he had been put out to grass in the Admin Wing four years ago because the then DG had decided, without any justification, that he'd got too close to a lieutenant colonel in the GRU and had become contaminated in the process. They also believed he had been sent into Russia far too often for his own good. His detractors regarded him as a loose cannon who did more harm than good and a source of embarrassment to the Foreign and Commonwealth Office. He was, they said, Hazelwood's Rott-weiler. There was some truth in the allegation but in fact he was supposed to work under the direction of the Deputy Director, Clifford Peachey, which was precisely what he was doing at that moment.

When Ashton had been on the Russian Desk their primary role had been to ascertain Soviet political and military strategy in the long term. With the demise of the USSR, priorities had changed. Nowadays the SIS was concerned to know who was likely to replace Boris Yeltsin should his heart condition ulti-mately prove fatal. While Peachey had asked for his thoughts on the subject, Ashton reckoned it was even money he'd also asked Rowan Garfield, the Assistant Director in charge of the Eur-opean Department, for his thoughts.

Knowing Rowan Garfield, Ashton believed the Russian Desk would approach the task by digging out the profiles they'd compiled on politicians, civil servants, and senior army, navy and airforce officers who had come to their notice. Then they would

9

try to assess the amount of support each one could command. He attacked the problem from a different angle and looked at just one man, the erstwhile Deputy Head of the Russian Intelligence Service, Pavel Trilisser.

Rightly regarded as a brilliant officer, Trilisser had received accelerated promotion to lieutenant general in the old KGB and, at the age of forty-six, had been the youngest ever second in command of the First Chief Directorate when he had been appointed in 1987. His career had suffered a setback when the hardliners in the Communist Party had turned against Gorbachev in August 1991. Although internal security was the responsibility of the Second Chief Directorate, a number of Yeltsin's supporters reckoned he should have intervened much earlier than he had. They believed that Pavel Trilisser had waited until it was evident the coup was going to fail before he arrested his own chief and sent word to the Minister of the Interior, Boris Pugo, that he should surrender himself to paratroops of the Ryazan Division who were about to surround his apartment building. Boris Pugo hadn't accepted his advice; instead the Minister of the Interior had put the barrel of a Makarov pistol in his mouth and squeezed the trigger.

Two years later, Trilisser had been involved in another power struggle, this time against Yeltsin. By skilfully misappropriating funds, he had raised a secret private army of 325 officers and men recruited from Spetsnaz personnel who had been made redundant. Organised into teams of five, their task was to eliminate the President; the Chief of Police, Moscow District; the Minister of Defence and to seize control of all TV and radio stations as well as the more important government buildings.

As usual, Trilisser had held back until he could see which way the coup was going. When T80 main battle tanks from units loyal to Yeltsin had opened fire on the parliament building, he had switched sides. With the aid of the militia, he had shot down his second in command, Vasili Petrovich Urzhumov, in a gun battle in one of Moscow's nuclear deep shelters. In recognition of his supposed loyalty, Trilisser had subsequently been appointed to the post of Special Adviser to the President on Foreign Affairs.

If Yeltsin died without nominating a successor, Ashton believed Trilisser would make yet another bid for power. He wouldn't do it openly but would shelter behind some stalking horse whom he could eventually remove without too much difficulty. The trick was to discover the people Trilisser had been cultivating in recent months. To help him in this search, Ashton resorted to the stand-alone computer-based information system. As its designation implied, it was purely an in-house facility; it was also crypto protected, which meant hackers couldn't get into the system. As a further safeguard, the visual display unit was tucked away in the corner of the room out of sight from the window. The possibility of anyone having binoculars powerful enough to read what was on the screen from a tall building on the far side of the railway tracks was remote, but the SIS didn't believe in running unnecessary risks.

It was because Ashton was tucked away in a corner with his back to the door, that he wasn't aware he had company until Hazelwood spoke his name. When he turned round and saw the look on Victor's face he knew something was terribly wrong. 'It's Harriet', he heard him say and suddenly his whole world was shattered.

Harriet shot and killed in the consulting room of a psychiatrist he'd never heard of? She hadn't told him she was having therapy and they didn't have any secrets from one another. So what if the police had found her name, address and phone number in some diary? It had to be a mistake. Harriet was alive.

'Has anybody phoned the house?' he asked huskily.

'I have,' Hazelwood told him. 'Your daily said that soon after she arrived at eight thirty, Harriet left the house to go shopping.'

Ashton couldn't accept what Victor was telling him; lifting the receiver, he obtained an outside line and rang the house. An irrational hope that Hazelwood had got it wrong was destroyed when he spoke to Mrs Davies. He felt drained, and there was this physical pain in his chest as if he had swallowed a pebble. He gathered the police were anxious for him formally to identify the body and it seemed Roy Kelso had laid on a car for him. They were showing their concern for him in other practical ways because there was good old Brian Thomas waiting outside in the corridor, ready to hold his hand if things started to get on top of him.

Dead inside, Ashton walked towards the bank of lifts like a robot. Everything passed in a blur – the descent to the basement garage, the drive across town. He saw Harriet in a series of cameos that flashed before his eyes beginning with the day he'd first met her when she walked into his office at Benbow House and introduced herself, the bright young officer from MI5, the Security Service, on secondment to the SIS. A tall girl, half an inch under six feet which made her the same height as himself. A good figure too, long tapering fingers to go with the long tapering legs. But it was the perfect symmetry of her face that had really claimed his attention and had remained firmly implanted in his mind afterwards . . . Another place, another time: the surgical ward of St Thomas's Hospital on the Müllenhoffstrasse in Berlin. Harriet had been caught up in a riot in the Kreuzberg District where the *Gastarbeiters* lived, and had sustained a fractured skull when one of the Turkish workers had thrown a rock at her, believing she was one of the Neo-Nazi Demonstrators who'd been making life hell for the community.

Harriet had looked awful, there had been no other word to describe her appearance. Her face had been the colour of marble and had resembled a skull, the skin stretched tight as a drum, cheeks sunken. The woman he loved had been just a mess of tubes, drips, and wires. Her hair, or what had been left of it, was concealed under a white turban. She had come through all that to die violently in a consulting room. It wasn't bloody right. What the hell did God think he was doing?

'We're here, Peter,' Thomas said, and touched him lightly on the arm.

Still functioning like a robot, Ashton got out of the car and followed Thomas. He didn't know where he was and didn't care. He didn't look at Orwell when the Detective Chief Superintendent introduced himself, didn't shake his hand when it was proffered to him. Walking into the mortuary was like entering a cold store, which he supposed it was in a way. He saw a body covered by a white sheet on the raised slab and steeled himself when the attendant removed the covering and Orwell motioned him to come forward. Ashton took one quick look and stepped back.

'That's not my wife,' he said, and came alive again.

Chapter Two

Ashton wasn't sure who looked the most stunned, Detective Chief Superintendent Orwell or Brian Thomas. Both men had their mouths open but Orwell was the first to recover.

'Let's go outside,' he said. 'I could do with a breath of fresh air.'

It also became apparent that Orwell badly needed a cigarette. Government health warnings were like water off a duck's back to him; Ashton could tell from the way he drew the smoke down on to his lungs and slowly exhaled that smoking gave him a real buzz, and no matter what the risk of cancer might be, he wasn't about to forgo the pleasure.

'Have you ever seen that woman before, Mr Ashton?' he asked.

'No.'

'OK, does your wife have any friends that you haven't met?'

'Not that I know of,' Ashton told him.

'Was she seeing a psychiatrist?'

Ashton hesitated. Nearly twelve weeks ago, when four months into her pregnancy, Harriet had trodden on a drumstick which Edward had left on the landing and had miscarried after falling downstairs. To say that she had been upset about losing the baby would have been a massive understatement. For a time she had been racked with irrational feelings of guilt but she had come through that without the need for counselling. He liked to think he had been there for Harriet when things had started to get her down. 'You're my rock', she had told him, 'you are the one who gives me the strength to pick up the pieces and carry on.'

'Well?' Orwell said, prompting him.

'I'm quite certain Harriet wasn't seeing a psychiatrist.'

'Is there anyone in her circle she might confide in?'

'I don't think Harriet has any real friends; four or five acquaintances perhaps but nobody she actually bonded with.'

Ashton suddenly realised how it must have sounded to Orwell. The word picture he'd painted of Harriet didn't show her in a favourable light and he sought to correct it.

'Harriet was born in Lincoln and she may have spent the first eighteen years of her life there, but the friends you make at school are not the ones you keep up with when you go to university. Unless you settle in your home town you eventually lose touch. That's what happened to Harriet. She joined the Home Office as a graduate entrant straight from Birmingham University.'

But even before her probationary period was up, Harriet had decided she had made the wrong choice. She didn't have to go looking for a new job; a talent spotter for the Security Service had talked her into joining MI5. He had told her she would find greater job satisfaction and had been proved right. The only trouble with being in the Security Service was that you didn't get to make many friends. The Official Secrets Acts saw to that; you couldn't tell anybody on the outside what you did for a living, what sort of day you'd had at the office, which put a brake on the conversation.

If you were single or a stranger in town, London could be a pretty lonely place. Add the fact that you had been allocated an impressive government-owned flat in Dolphin Square at a peppercorn rent, as Harriet had, and your chances of meeting someone in your own age group were pretty remote.

'Does your wife have any money of her own, Mr Ashton?'

'What the hell do you want to know that for?'

'Dr Ramash charged her patients £150 an hour.'

'Well that rules out Harriet.'

'According to her case notes on Harriet Ashton, the woman who impersonated your wife always paid cash.'

'Safer than a cheque,' Ashton observed. 'I'm no expert but I would think tracing money back to the source is almost impossible.'

'The impostor said more or less the same thing to Dr Ramash. She was frightened of what her husband would do to her if he discovered she had been discussing their marital problems with a psychiatrist. Dr Ramash wondered if this meant she was frequently assaulted by her husband.'

'I'm not sure I like the inference,' Ashton said in an ominously quiet voice. 'Are you by any chance asking me if I knock Harriet about?'

'And I'm not sure if you haven't deliberately misunderstood me.'

'You'd better ask yourself why the hell I would bother to do that.' Ashton turned to Brian Thomas. 'Have you got a mobile on you I could borrow?' he asked.

'Yes, of course.' Thomas reached into his jacket and took out a Cellnet.

'You're going to phone the house?'

'That was the general idea, Brian.'

Ashton took the phone from him and walked away until he was out of earshot of the other two men. He punched out the area code and subscriber's number, then waited impatiently for Mrs Davies to pick up the receiver. When she did, there was no good news. Harriet still hadn't returned. After asking her to stay at the house until he returned, Ashton switched off the phone, collapsed the aerial and returned the Cellnet to Brian Thomas.

'Any news?' he asked.

'Only the negative kind,' Ashton told him.

Orwell took one last drag on his cigarette, dropped the stub on to the ground and trod on it.

'Look, Mr Ashton, I think maybe we got off on the wrong foot . . .'

'I think we probably did.'

'But the fact is I've got an unidentified victim who was masquerading as your wife and I need to know how much of what she told Dr Ramash was true, how much she had invented.'

Ashton couldn't believe what he was hearing, wondered how this moron could be so insensitive when he was worried sick about Harriet.

Oblivious of the offence he was causing, Orwell droned on: 'The more this woman knew about Mrs Ashton, the closer she must have been to her. If I'm right, then given a bit of luck it shouldn't be too long before we're able to put a name to this unknown woman.'

'Well, that's great. Now let me ask you a question for a change. How do I get to the nearest tube station from here?'

'Where do you think you're going?' Orwell demanded.

'Home,' Ashton snapped back. 'My wife has been missing for at least four hours, the daily says she left the house to go shopping at the local supermarket and so far as I know, nobody is looking for Harriet.'

'You'd better take the car,' Thomas said, 'I'll make my own way back to Vauxhall Cross.'

'Thanks, Brian.'

Ashton turned away and walked towards the waiting Ford Granada. He had almost reached the chauffeur-driven car when Orwell called out to ask him if he had a sixteen-month-old son named Edward. If it had been Orwell's intention to unsettle him, he couldn't have made a more telling Parthian shot.

There was no more formidable assistant director than the Head of the Mid East Department, Jill Sheridan. She also happened to be the youngest, the most physically attractive and in the opinion of many, had more balls than the other four assistant directors put together. Moreover, nobody could doubt her qualifications for the job. Jill's father had been an executive with the Qatar General Petroleum Corporation and she had spent most of her childhood and early adolescence in the Persian Gulf, with the result that Arabic had become her second tongue. Persian or Farsi was an additional language qualification she had subsequently obtained at the School of Oriental and African Studies.

Although she had never actually said so, it was common knowledge that Jill Sheridan was determined to be the first woman to be appointed Director General of the SIS. Currently she presided over the second largest department, which was reflected in the authorised establishment of typists, translators, archivists, cipher operators, code breakers, desk officers and Analysts, Special Intelligence. In total, she directed the activities of 137 men and women and did so extremely well. In her bid for ultimate stardom, she could count on the friendship and active support of Robin Urquhart, the senior of four deputy under secretaries at the Foreign and Commonwealth Office. She also enjoyed more than her fair share of luck, surviving a number of near disasters that would have permanently blighted the careers of her rivals had they sailed as close to the wind as she had.

Victor Hazelwood was not one of her admirers. Only too well aware of her devious nature and lack of moral scruples, it irked him that he was unable to do anything about it because she had the ear of Robin Urquhart, which meant she practically had a direct line to the Secretary of the Cabinet and Head of the Civil Service. For this reason, Hazelwood tried to ensure that any matters concerning the Mid East Department were dealt with at the daily conference with assistant directors, commonly known as morning prayers. In this he was not always successful and today was just one more instance when he had found it necessary to ask Jill if she could spare him a few minutes. For once Hazelwood was not smoking a Burma cheroot when she tapped on the door and walked into his office.

'Am I in trouble, Victor?' she asked in a voice that didn't sound the least bit concerned.

'Trouble?'

'You sounded worried on the phone,' Jill said, and promptly sat down before he could invite her to do so.

'Dr Z. K. Ramash,' Hazelwood said tersely. 'Does the name ring any bells with you?'

'Not immediately. What does he do? I mean, apart from practising medicine.'

'Wrong sex. Ramash was a clinical psychiatrist; she also provided a refuge for battered wives above her surgery in Lansdowne Mews.'

'Why the past tense, Victor?'

'The doctor and her receptionist were tied up and then garrotted. The police seem to think it was a ritual killing. In other words the two women were slowly strangled.'

In Hazelwood's opinion Jill Sheridan was the original ice

18

maiden. Her face betrayed no emotion whatsoever and she expressed no horror at the manner of their deaths; in fact Jill didn't even bat an eyelid. Hazelwood wondered why he should be surprised by her callousness considering the number of occasions he had witnessed her detached attitude.

'Why are we interested?'

'There was a third victim,' Hazelwood told her, 'a tallish, dark-haired woman who'd been shot in the head. It seems she had an appointment for nine fifteen. According to the case notes, Dr Ramash knew her as Mrs Harriet Ashton of 84 Rylett Close, Chiswick.'

'Peter's wife?' Jill raised a cool eyebrow.

'No. The deceased was an impostor.'

'Why should she have wanted to assume Harriet's identity?'

'I haven't the faintest idea.' Hazelwood opened the cigar box on his desk, took out a cheroot and lit it. 'However, I can tell you this: today was the fourth time the woman had been to see Dr Ramash. At least that's what Brian Thomas learned from the Chief Superintendent in charge of the investigation.'

'Is this information relevant?'

'Dr Ramash only counselled women. She also had an alarm system linked to the police station in Ladbroke Road. This enabled her to summon immediate assistance if some violent husband or partner tried to force his way into the house.' Hazelwood leaned back in his chair. 'Now what does this suggest to you, Jill?'

'How was the alarm activated?'

'By a press button. There was one in the consulting room, another in the office and a third in the flat occupied by Dr Ramash on the first floor.'

'What do the police have to say about this mystery woman who called herself Harriet Ashton? That it had been her misfortune to arrive for her appointment before the killer or killers had departed?'

'That was more or less their first assumption.'

'Then I think they were barking up the wrong tree. I have a feeling the mystery woman was involved in the murder of Dr Ramash and her receptionist. She checked the house out, learned about the alarm system and how it was operated during those previous sessions with the psychiatrist.' Jill wagged a finger at him. 'I'll go even further. Unbeknown to the good doctor and her receptionist she let the killers into the place and thereby signed her own death warrant. Now tell me I've got it wrong, Victor.'

'No, that's how I see it too.'

'And you want to know if we have a trace on Dr Ramash?'

'Yes.'

Jill frowned. 'You obviously suspect she hailed from some-where in the Middle East otherwise you wouldn't have sent for me. Any idea which country?'

'Your guess is as good as mine.'

'The Lebanon. Her name has been anglicised but for my money she was Lebanese.'

'Keep an open mind.'

'Oh, I will, Victor.'

There was a rasp of nylon as Jill crossed her right leg over the left. Whenever she did this, Hazelwood was never sure whether it was an unconscious act or if she was deliberately flaunting herself. Jill was undoubtedly pleasing to the eye but unlike Harriet Ashton she was aware of her physical attractions and made the most of them. Not that she dressed outrageously; all her clothes were designer label, reflected the latest fashion and fitted like a glove. They were also very expensive; the black suit with a thin grey pinstripe which she was wearing probably cost in excess of £500. But of course Jill could afford it; she had done rather well out of her brief marriage to Henry Clayburn, one-time whoremaster in chief to the ruling families of the Arab Emirates. Jill had kept the four-bedroom house overlooking Waterlow Park at the top of Highgate Hill, the Porsche 928 GIS that had been Clayburn's pride and joy, and had received a sizeable lump sum in lieu of maintenance . . .

'Victor?'

If that wasn't enough, she had come through a difficult subject interview following her change of circumstances which could have led to the withdrawal of her Top Secret security status had it gone wrong.

'Victor,' Jill repeated, in a louder voice.

'What?'

'Have MI5 been asked if they have anything on Dr Ramash?'

Hazelwood hated the omniscient smile which hovered on her lips. It said, you can't fool me, you've been peeking at my legs, you sly old thing.

'Clifford Peachey has that in hand, Jill.'

In addition, the Deputy Director was going to check with the Immigration Service at the Home Office.

'Do we know what the initials Z. K. stand for?' Jill asked.

'Not yet.'

'Any idea of her age?'

'Nearer forty than fifty. According to the Chief Super, Ramash is about five feet six and quite slender.' Hazelwood stubbed out his cheroot in the cut-down shell case. 'Having said that, we're unlikely to get an accurate description of her physical characteristics before the post mortem.'

'Remind me again, why did you think Ramash was of Middle East origin?'

'It was on account of her dark hair, brown eyes and sallow complexion.'

'Sounds almost racist,' Jill said jokingly, then stood up and moved towards the door. Just when it seemed her curiosity had been satisfied, a last-minute thought occurred to her and she turned about. 'What does Harriet have to say about her doppelgänger?'

'I haven't asked her yet,' Hazelwood said, poker-faced.

Jill nodded sagely as if this was exactly what she had expected to hear. Promising to let him know whether or not there was a trace on Dr Z. K. Ramash, she finally left the office and set off down the corridor. When he could no longer hear her muffled footsteps on the carpet, Hazelwood lifted the phone and buzzed Roy Kelso. What he wanted from Security Vetting was the present whereabouts of Henry Clayburn.

Harriet returned ten minutes after Mrs Davies had left the house. Observing her from the front room, as she walked up the path, Ashton thought she looked preoccupied, as if in a trance. Vulnerable was another adjective which immediately sprang to mind, triggered by the same wounded expression he had seen on Harriet's face in the weeks following the miscarriage. Ashton was very clear about two things: no way was he going to allow Orwell to question her before she was back on an even keel; nor was he going to ask Harriet where she had been all this time or what she had done with the shopping. Moving swiftly, he went out into the hall and opened the front door before she had time to find the key in her handbag.

'Peter!' Her face lit up. 'This is a nice surprise. What are you doing at home?'

'I thought I would take the afternoon off.'

'With or without permission?'

'I didn't stop to ask,' Ashton said, following on behind as she walked down the hall and entered the kitchen.

'Victor will have something to say about that.'

Harriet was not enamoured of Victor. She could not understand why her husband was so loyal to him when in her opinion it wasn't reciprocated to anything like the same extent. She also thought that Hazelwood used him to advance his own career but then Harriet was deeply prejudiced.

'I presume Mrs Davies was still here when you arrived?'

'Yes, she left ten minutes later.'

'Do you know if she remembered to feed Edward?'

Harriet was calm and matter of fact. She acted as though Mrs Davies had known that she would be late back and had agreed to give Edward his lunch at the usual time. Although Ashton had never met anybody in the throes of a nervous breakdown, it was all too evident that Harriet had lost touch with reality, which made his blood run cold.

'You know Mrs Davies,' he said cheerfully, 'she's very dependable.'

She had in fact seen to their little boy, spoon-feeding him Heinz baby food, much of which seemed to have ended up on his bib or around his mouth. Harriet hadn't told her to do it; she had done so of her own accord, she'd told Ashton, because Edward had been getting hungry and fractious with it. But Ashton didn't tell Harriet that.

'Where's Edward now?' she asked.

'Upstairs in his cot, sleeping it off.'

'Good. I think I'll have a cup of coffee. How about you?'

'I'll make it,' Ashton told her. 'You sit down.'

He filled the electric kettle and plugged it in, then found a couple of mugs and measured two heaped teaspoons of Maxwell House into each one.

'You ever heard of a Dr Ramash?' he asked casually.

'No. Why do you ask? I'm perfectly happy with the one we've got.'

'This doctor was treating a patient with the same name as yours.'

'What – Harriet Egan?'

'No, Ashton. You're married to me. Remember?'

Conscious that he was walking on eggshells, he tried to make it sound as if he was joshing her but he failed to hit the right note.

'So I am,' Harriet said in a distant voice.

'This patient gave our address and private phone number. She also knew we have a son called Edward.'

'How very curious.'

Same dead tone, same numb reaction. What the hell was wrong with the bloody kettle? It should have come to the boil ages ago. Of course, it would have helped if he'd remembered to switch it on at the wall. The truth was, he was prevaricating. Orwell believed the third victim was an impostor because he had Ashton's word for it that the dead woman was not Harriet. But what if Harriet had cancelled an appointment which she had made for nine fifteen and the third victim was somebody who had been fitted in at the last minute? God knows he didn't want to give Harriet the impression that he didn't believe her but the question had to be put to her.

'There's something I've got to ask you,' Ashton said carefully. 'Are you sure you don't know Dr Ramash?'

'Damn you,' Harriet said, and there was a catch in her voice.

As he turned to face her, he could see tears were running down her cheeks.

'What's the matter?' he asked softly, and moved to comfort her.

'My mother is dead.'

'What?'

'Mummy's dead,' Harriet screamed at him.

23

Margaret Egan – dead? She hadn't even been taken ill as far as he knew. 'When did you hear this, love?'

'This morning . . . Daddy phoned after you'd left. She choked on the words, swallowing half of them, 'to go . . . that stupid office of yours.'

He moved closer still and tried to embrace Harriet but she was sitting down at the kitchen table and he ended up cuddling her head.

'How? I mean what happened?'

'How?' Harriet struggled to her feet and started to pound his chest with a fist. 'Damn you to hell, she had cancer of the breast.'

The rest came out in dribs and drabs, some of it inaudible because Harriet was crying into his shoulder but he had no difficulty in piecing it together. Margaret Egan had kept the news from her daughter in the belief that Harriet had enough to cope with as it was, following her miscarriage. The specialist had decided the cancer was inoperable. Instead he'd proposed to kill the growth with chemotherapy and for a while it looked as if the treatment was doing the trick. So long as there was hope, Margaret had endured the usual side effects of the loss of hair and appetite, the nausea and listlessness with dogged courage and quiet dignity. But ultimately the cancer had spread and there had been nothing the doctors could do for Margaret except ease the pain.

'Mummy wanted to die at home, not in a hospice.'

Margaret Egan had also wanted to choose the moment but the medical profession hadn't been prepared to provide her with the means. But Harriet's mother had always been a singularly determined woman and she had managed to get hold of a large plastic bag. And this morning, soon after her husband had gone downstairs to make a pot of tea, she had somehow found the strength to put her head inside the bag and suffocate herself.

'Daddy told me there would probably be a coroner's inquest,' Harriet said brokenly.

'We'll drive up to Lincoln this evening,' Ashton told her.

'Can you get away?'

'I'd like to see anybody stop me.'

He could imagine how devastated Harriet must have been on hearing the news from her father. He could understand too why she felt she had to get out of the house and had then wandered around for hours on end, not knowing where she was or what she was doing. It was only much later that Ashton realised that she hadn't answered his original question.

Chapter Three

<hr/>

Clifford Peachey had started his career in the Security Service as an interrogator and had earned himself a reputation in that field second only to that of the great Jim Skardon who, in the 1950s had broken Klaus Fuchs, the Atom spy. Peachey was renowned for his tenacity and refusal to give up once he had scented his prey. His sharp terrier-like features mirrored this characteristic. At the height of the Cold War he had become one of the leading lights of K1, the section which was tasked to ferret out the KGB and GRU officers in the Soviet Embassy, Trade Delegation and Consular Service.

By 1993 he was in charge of both K1 and K2, the specialists who kept an eye on the home-grown subversives. Earlier on in his career he had twice refused promotion to the top strata, convinced that working on the ground was far more satisfying than being involved in the largely administrative chores associated with high command. However, once Yeltsin had firmly established himself in power, the workload of K1 and K2 had been drastically reduced and much of the fascination with the great game had evaporated with it. By the time Clifford Peachey had been ready to join the top table the opportunity to do so had long since passed him by.

However 'K', as the Director General of MI5 had always been known ever since Vernon Kell had formed the Security Service, didn't believe in allowing a valuable resource to go to waste. When Victor Hazelwood had suddenly been put in charge of the SIS, a vacancy had occurred at deputy director level which could not be readily filled. Aware of this, 'K' had persuaded the Home Office to back Peachey's candidature for the post.

In the event the MI5 officer had been handed the job on a platter. Of the five possible candidates within the SIS, Roy Kelso had no practical experience to offer, Roger Benton was inclined to panic under stress, while Rowan Garfield, who was in charge of the largest department, was considered too pedestrian. That had left Jill Sheridan, and William Orchard of the Asian Department, a man so self-effacing as to pass unnoticed in an otherwise empty room. Jill Sheridan had all the requisite qualifications for the post but she happened to be the youngest and most junior of the assistant directors and was seen by many to be overambitious. Her time would come, of that Peachey was certain. His was a stopgap appointment of a year to eighteen months, which suited him down to the ground. He was looking forward to occupying on a permanent basis the retirement cottage he'd bought at Helmsley on the edge of the Yorkshire Moors. Meantime he enjoyed life at Vauxhall Cross and knew he made a valuable contribution because, as Hazelwood had said often enough in his hearing, co-operation between MI5 and the SIS had never been closer thanks to him. In practical terms this meant that any request for information addressed to MI5 was answered the same day. Peachey just wished that on this occasion the Security Service could have come up trumps.

'No luck, I'm afraid, Victor,' he said, walking into Hazelwood's office. 'Five has never heard of Dr Z. K. Ramash.'

'Well, that's one avenue closed. What about the Immigration Service?'

'They're still checking and it will take them some time to go through their records. After all, they're dealing with thousands of people and we can't tell them when Dr Ramash entered this country or where she might have come from. It's possible she was born in the UK, in which case she won't show up.'

'Quite.' Hazelwood glanced at the green-coloured dossiers in his pending tray. 'Are you busy, Clifford?' he asked.

'Not particularly.'

'Good. I'd like to pick your brains.'

'Fine.'

'Well, the way I see it, there are two possibilities: either the third victim was an impostor or else Harriet was seeing Dr Ramash on a regular basis and had cancelled her appointment for this morning.'

'Where's Harriet now?'

'Back home. Ashton phoned me a few minutes ago.'

'And?'

'Harriet claims she has never heard of the psychiatrist. She went walkabout this morning after learning that her mother had committed suicide.'

'My God, poor Harriet. I really feel for her.'

'Yes indeed. The news that her mother had terminal cancer was kept from Harriet because both parents believed she hadn't recovered sufficiently from losing the baby to take another bad knock.'

'When exactly did Harriet learn about her mother?'

'Ashton thinks it must have been about seven forty, roughly ten minutes after he left the house.'

'Dr Ramash lived above the shop,' Peachey said reflectively. 'I suppose Harriet might have known her private number and could have cancelled her nine fifteen appointment as soon as she heard the news. Wouldn't have given the psychiatrist much time to fit in someone else though.'

'The third victim had no means of identification on her because she wasn't carrying a handbag. Now that wouldn't be quite such a mystery if she happened to be one of the battered wives from the refuge on the top floor and Ramash could certainly have fitted one of them in at short notice.'

'What about those battered wives?' Peachey asked. 'Have the police interviewed them yet?'

'I don't know, that's why I've told Brian Thomas to find out what he can from Orwell. I've also authorised him to answer any questions the Chief Superintendent has about Harriet. Without, of course, breaching security, which brings me to my next point.' Hazelwood removed the top file from the pending tray and placed it on the desk. 'No need to tell you whose this is?'

'I take it Harriet is still cleared for constant access to Top Secret material?'

Hazelwood nodded. Although Harriet had resigned from MI5 two years ago, he had subsequently employed her as a relief housekeeper. Theoretically this meant that at the drop of a hat, she could be sent to any one of the safe houses owned by the SIS. For taking on this commitment, Harriet was paid a retainer of ten thousand a year, an arrangement which did not meet with the approval of the Treasury. They had a point. To date, her services had only been required on one occasion and then only for a few days.

'So what are you suggesting, Victor? That we should withdraw her security clearance on the grounds that she is emotionally unstable?'

'No, but I think we should perhaps suspend it for the time being, otherwise we could be criticised for being unduly lax. The question has already been raised by Roy Kelso.'

'What is it you want from me then?'

'You know Harriet better than anyone else, Clifford.'

'Except Ashton.'

'Well, his opinion is certain to be biased.' Hazelwood patted the dossier. 'Ninety per cent of the enclosures in this security file were originated by MI5 before Harriet was seconded to our Security Vetting and Technical Services Division. You were one of the senior officers who was interviewed after she had completed her probationary service with MI5. You were asked for your opinion again at the quinquennial review of her PV clearance.'

'So?'

'So I'm asking you if you are aware of any character blemish which isn't on record in this security file?'

'No I do not,' Peachey said unhesitatingly.

'Good. Do you think there is a reasonable chance that Harriet will regain her equilibrium within the foreseeable future?'

'I'm not a psychiatrist, Victor.'

'All right, I'll make it easier for you: is she made of the right stuff?'

'Yes.'

'That's all I need to know. We'll suspend her clearance for now, subject to review in three months' time.'

Hazelwood opened the dossier and recorded his decision on the minute sheet on the inside of the front cover, then tossed the file into the out tray. He eyed the cigar box and, unable to resist temptation, helped himself to a Burma cheroot. Equally addicted to smoking, Peachey took out his pipe and filled it from the oilskin pouch containing Dunhill Standard Mixture which he kept in his jacket pocket.

'Let's look at the other side of the coin,' Hazelwood said between puffs. 'If the third victim was an impostor, she knew a great deal about the Ashtons. Agreed?'

'Yes.'

'So the question is how did she get this information and from whom?'

'I hope you don't expect me to answer that, Victor. I haven't been here long enough to venture an opinion.'

'Maybe not but you are a useful sounding board.'

'If you say so.'

'I think the source was Jill Sheridan. Not directly of course, but I wouldn't put anything past her ex. She could have told him about the Ashtons – pillow talk.'

'Why would she do that?'

'Jill was engaged to Peter at one time. Matter of fact they lived together, had a flat in Surbiton.'

'Really? You do surprise me.' Peachey leaned forward in the chair and knocked his pipe out over the cut-down shell case. 'Even so, it's a bit far-fetched, isn't it, Victor?'

'Possibly.'

Hazelwood froze, stared at the open doorway behind Peachey like a gun dog pointing. As if responding to a cue from a prompter in the wings, Jill suddenly materialised and tapped on the door.

'Oh, I'm sorry,' she said. 'I didn't know Clifford was with you. I'll come back later.'

'No, don't go away. What have you got for me?'

'Nothing, I'm afraid. I took the liberty of asking Bill Orchard to check his index to see if the Asian Department had carded Dr Z. K. Ramash.' Jill smiled deprecatingly. 'I thought there might be a chance she had an Indian or Pakistani background.'

'Better ask Roger Benton to do the same with his Pacific Basin and Rest of the World organisation.'

'It might be better coming from you, Victor.'

'You're probably right.'

'I'll leave it with you then,' Jill said gravely, then withdrew as quietly as she had arrived.

Hazelwood allowed the best part of a minute to pass before he left his desk to close the door.

'Do you think Jill heard what you said about her ex?' Peachey asked.

'Well, if she did, you can bet she will take pre-emptive action pretty damn quick.'

The knowledge that he had only himself to blame if Jill Sheridan had overhead their conversation annoyed Hazelwood. The husband of his PA had phoned in that morning to say that she had gone down with flu, thereby joining a growing sick list which included Clifford Peachey's own PA. With so many of the clerical staff off work he had decided not to call on the secretarial pool to provide a temporary replacement. Had he done so, the door to his office, which opened into the corridor, would have been closed and anyone wanting to see him would have been obliged to gain admittance through the PA's office as was the normal practice.

'Old soldiers never die, they only fade away': the same could be said of policemen. Although Orwell hadn't intimated as much, Brian Thomas had the distinct impression that the Detective Chief Superintendent wished he would do the same. The instructions he had received from the DG via Roy Kelso had been extremely succinct: live in Orwell's shadow, learn all you can, disclose as little as possible. It was easier said than done. Orwell had known there was an SIS involvement minutes after obtaining the phone number of Vauxhall Cross from the Ashtons' daily woman. Consequently whenever lack of knowledge prevented Thomas from answering a question, Orwell assumed he was deliberately withholding information, which was embarrassing because the Chief Superintendent had been very open with him.

After Ashton had left them outside the mortuary, Thomas had persuaded Orwell that it might be to their mutual advantage if he was permitted to see the clinical notes Dr Ramash had made. His anonymity had been preserved because nobody with an axe to grind had been present outside the house in Lansdowne Mews to ask him who he was. The press, who'd learned about the triple slaying soon after the police had received the 999 call from Virginia Hardiman, had dispersed when the bodies had been conveyed to the mortuary.

The clinical notes had made interesting reading. The impostor had known where Harriet lived, her phone number, how old she was, where she came from, the name of their daily woman and what sort of car they had. She had said nothing about Harriet's miscarriage, which university she had attended, or the fact that her brother had been an RAF pilot. The mental and physical abuse she had allegedly suffered at the hands of her husband, his violent temper and the bizarre sexual demands he had made upon her were pure fiction and he'd had no hesitation in telling Orwell so.

The information had only whetted the Chief Superintendent's appetite. Currently there were just two battered wives living on the premises, one of whom had left for work before the impostor had arrived, while the other claimed she hadn't heard anything or seen anyone. Initial house-to-house enquiries had yielded equally negative results. None of the neighbours recalled noticing anything unusual that morning. And that wasn't unhelpful enough, there was no apparent motive for the triple slaying which had all the hallmarks of a professional hit.

'I don't believe this is a drugs-related crime,' Orwell said.

'I wouldn't know.'

'And the real Mrs Ashton is either a spook herself or is married to one.'

Thomas had a pretty good idea of what was coming.

'So are we looking at a terrorist outrage?'

'Your guess is as good as mine.'

'I believe you can do better than that,' Orwell told him grimly. 'I want you to find out if this Dr Ramash is known to your organisation.'

Thomas punched out the number of Vauxhall Cross on his Cellnet and after a certain amount of argy-bargy with Roy Kelso was patched through to Victor Hazelwood on an open line. He wished afterwards he hadn't bothered.

'I can't give you an answer about Dr Ramash; they're still checking the various card indexes.'

'You do surprise me,' Orwell said tartly.

'I do have one piece of news, Harriet Ashton is no longer missing.'

'I shall want to interview her.'

'Well, I'm afraid that won't be possible,' Thomas said, then added, 'at least not for several days.'

'Somehow that's what I thought you would say.'

'Her mother died this morning and there's to be an inquest. Mr Ashton is driving his wife up to the family home in Lincoln.'

'Have you got the address?'

'Not on me.'

'I think you're dissembling again.'

'You're wrong.'

'OK, what's her maiden name?'

Thomas hesitated. Just how co-operative the police would be in the future depended on the answer. 'Egan,' he said reluctantly.

'Now we're getting somewhere.'

'But in your shoes, I wouldn't interview her without first clearing it with the Assistant Commissioner, Crime.'

Orwell stared at him. 'Now I understand what you people mean by mutual advantage,' he said, making no effort to hide his anger.

Urquhart gave the taxi driver a £5 note and told him to keep the change, then waited until the tail lights of the hackney cab had disappeared round a bend in the road before he turned about and walked towards Highgate High Street. This was the first time he had been to the house in Bisham Gardens which overlooked Waterlow Park and he had this guilty feeling that somehow he was betraying Rosalind. It was, of course, utterly ridiculous; he and Jill Sheridan were not having an affair and as for betraying Rosalind, the boot was definitely on the other foot.

Rosalind was county and he was the lower-middle-class boy who had made good. They had met when he had been in charge of the British Consulate in Berlin and she had come out to spend three weeks with her elder brother, a major in the Royal Green Jackets whose battalion had formed part of the British garrison. Luckily the midsummer holiday had stretched to a year when Rosalind had managed to wangle a job as PA to the brigade commander. And he had considered himself doubly fortunate when she had agreed to marry him.

Some marriages suffer from the seven-year itch; theirs had fallen apart after sixteen when he had been appointed to the European Community Policy Division in London and Rosalind had moved in with a junior but well-heeled partner in the biggest firm of commercial lawyers in the City. She had taken great delight in informing him that her lover was extremely well endowed where it mattered. Rosalind had always ridden to hounds and, thanks to the influence of the new man in her life, she had been invited to join the Withersfield Hunt. It proved to be the worst thing Rosalind could have done. One frosty morning in November 1989 she had put her horse at a six-foot-high hedgerow and paid the penalty when the animal had balked and thrown her headfirst over the obstacle. Landing awkwardly, Rosalind had broken two vertebrae, leaving her paralysed from the waist down. The well-heeled lawyer had broken off their relationship while she was still in Stoke Mandeville Hospital.

Urquhart was aware that in the eyes of his friends and acquaintances he was a saint for taking her back but for him it had been a matter of honour. 'For richer, for poorer, in sickness and health': he actually believed the vows he had made in church. They lived in a four-bedroom house in the better part of Islington which he had purchased and adapted to meet her special needs, which included a live-in nurse. It was, however, a fact that he couldn't have managed without Rosalind's private income to fall back on, something she never allowed him to forget.

Jill's house was called 'Freemantle', the significance of which escaped him. He opened the gate and was halfway up the front path when the sudden glare from the security light completely dazzled him. With his head down and shielding his eyes with his left hand, he managed to avoid tripping over the raised step under the porch, and rang the bell. He heard Jill remove the security chain and surmised she had been watching him through the spy hole. Her welcoming smile as she opened the door to him made the journey doubly worthwhile.

'Oh, Robin,' she said, 'am I glad to see you.'

'I can assure you the feeling is mutual,' he said, and stepped into the hall.

Urquhart had always thought that Jill had style but never more so than tonight. She knew what colours suited her best and her taste was impeccable. The striped shirt with its broad white lapels, double cuffs fastened with gold links, looked exactly right with the dark blue trousers which fitted like a glove and emphasised her flat stomach and taut buttocks. They were a tantalising sight and he tried unsuccessfully to avert his gaze from them as he followed Jill into the drawing room.

'What can I get you to drink, Robin? A malt whisky?'

'That would be very nice,' he said in a husky voice.

'Well, sit down, make yourself comfortable. I won't be a minute.'

He avoided the settee and chose one of the armchairs instead. The last thing he wanted was to give the impression that he was hoping to manoeuvre her into sitting next to him. He had been rebuffed by Rosalind so many times since the accident that he had no desire to court rejection from someone who was younger and infinitely more attractive than his wife.

'What do you know about the triple murder in Holland Park?' Jill asked.

'Only what I've read in the *Evening Standard*.'

'Apparently one of the victims was known to Dr Ramash as Harriet Ashton.'

'I don't remember seeing that in the paper.'

'The information wasn't released.' Jill gave him the malt whisky she had poured into a Waterford tumbler, then sat down on the settee, wedging herself into one corner with both legs tucked under her rump. 'As it happened Harriet Ashton was missing for several hours this morning which is why Victor Hazelwood believed the initial report and acted on it.'

'I've heard of Ashton and know something of his reputation.' Urquhart frowned. 'But Harriet?'

'One of our housekeepers, Robin, but not full time. Between you and me, it's a bit of a wangle. She gets ten thousand a year and in return the SIS can send her anywhere at virtually no notice. In my opinion it's money for old rope; Harriet's only been called out once and then just for a few days. We could get by without her but Ashton was, and probably still is, in financial straits and he and Victor go back a long way. I think our DG believed he owed him and to some extent that's true. Of course Victor has always had an eye for a pretty woman and Harriet is very, very attractive.

'And you aren't?' Urquhart said in a light bantering voice.

'There's a difference; Victor sees me as a threat which he is determined to remove.'

It had taken them some time to get there but Urquhart believed they had finally arrived at the crux of the matter and he was about to learn the reason why Jill had telephoned him that afternoon. Not that he was in a hurry to go home; he would be quite content to sit there all night nursing a good malt whisky while fantasising about the provocative-looking woman on the couch.

'Anyway, Peter was required to identify the body in the morgue and needless to say he was mightily relieved to find it wasn't Harriet. Furthermore, it seems Harriet denied she had ever consulted Dr Ramash but the fact is this impostor knew an awful lot about her.'

Jill paused, drank some of her whisky, then held the glass up to the light as if to see how much was left. It didn't take much acumen on Urquhart's part to realise that she was waiting for some kind of response from him.

'And?' he enquired dutifully.

'Victor believes the impostor got information from me or rather through Henry Clayburn, my ex.'

'That's ridiculous.'

'No, there is a certain logic in his thinking. I was engaged to Peter once so I know a great deal about him. And Harriet too for that matter. I am supposed to have discussed my past relationships with Henry; at least that's Victor's hypothesis.'

'And your former husband passed it on to the unidentified person?'

'I imagine that's what Victor thinks.'

'I've never heard anything so far-fetched in my life.'

'Well, to be fair to Victor, he is working in the dark and this was the only explanation which appeared to fit what few facts we have.'

There was another factor which Jill thought they should keep in mind. If the third victim hadn't impersonated Harriet she was convinced Victor would not have gone rushing in. It was only after Ashton had, *ipso facto*, identified the dead woman as an impostor that the situation had begun to get out of hand. Suddenly there was an SIS involvement and Dr Z. K. Ramash had been seen as the victim of a terrorist attack.

'The trouble is, MI5 has never heard of her and neither has the Immigration Service. She hadn't come to the notice of my department and her name hasn't rung a bell with any of the desk officers in Roger Benton's empire. I don't know about the Asian Department; Bill Orchard likes to do things himself and he was still checking their card index when I left.'

Urquhart didn't ask her where she had got her information or how it had been acquired. He took it on trust because past experience had taught him that Jill was not given to hyperbole. He had been opposed to confirming Hazelwood in the appointment of Director General; the man was a damn sight too aggressive, a risk taker bordering on the reckless who openly proclaimed that he liked to make things happen. But at the height of the Cold War Hazelwood had performed brilliantly against the Sovs and had found favour with the Thatcher government, or at least with the PM, a plus point that had done him no harm with the next administration. The Americans thought Hazelwood was a real go-getter and that had clinched his confirmation in post.

'If Bill Orchard finds that his cupboard is also bare, I'm hoping Victor will decide that what happened in Lansdowne Mews is none of our business.' Jill finished her whisky and left the glass on the low table in front of the couch. 'Actually, I'm sure he will,' she continued. 'The Conservative administration may say they want more open and accountable government but I don't believe they want this to apply to the SIS.'

Her view of the way the incident was developing and its possible consequences coincided with his. The newspapers had just been presented with three juicy murders to get their teeth into; for the SIS to be associated with the crime by the media was the last thing the Foreign and Commonwealth Office needed.

'Whether or not Victor will lose interest in this impostor is, of course, a very different matter, and therein lies the risk. If our continuing interest is known to the police there's a chance that some officer may tip off the press.'

'Quite so.'

'I'm not just thinking of myself here, Robin.'

Of course Jill wasn't, Jill was one of the most loyal people he knew. Urquhart finished his whisky.

'Don't worry about it,' he told her, and patted her leg. 'I'm sure the Cabinet Secretary will have a word with Victor.'

'Thank you, Robin. I really am most grateful.'

He left his hand resting on her thigh, wondered just how far her gratitude would extend.

'And I've kept you long enough. Rosalind will be wondering what has become of you.'

There was, he learned, a definite limit to the amount of gratitude she was prepared to bestow upon him.

Chapter Four

Ashton walked into the lift and punched the button for the fourth floor. Neither of the two women on the reception counter nor the armed policeman on duty in the lobby of Vauxhall Cross said anything so mundane as 'welcome back' or 'nice to see you again, Mr Ashton'. Although he had been away for almost a fortnight it appeared nobody had noticed his absence. For some people time had a habit of passing in the blink of an eye but as far as he was concerned, the last twelve days had seemed interminable. The tomblike silence of the house in Ferris Drive opposite Lincoln Cathedral where Harriet and her brother, Richard, had grown up hadn't helped. And the inquest had been something else. By the general tenor of his questions, the coroner had created the impression that he believed that Frederick Egan had assisted his wife to commit suicide.

The loss of his wife coupled with the hostile atmosphere of the inquest had knocked the stuffing out of Frederick Egan, and his son, the ex-Tornado pilot, had looked and acted as if he was in need of support. It had been Harriet who'd taken the strain, arranging the funeral, choosing the hymns, the readings and ordering the wreaths. In twelve days she had found and engaged a housekeeper to look after her father and see to his every need.

Mindful of her reaction when she had first heard the terrible news from her father, Ashton had watched Harriet like a hawk the whole time they were up in Lincoln. He had looked for signs of melancholia but his fears had proved groundless. Although Harriet had shed a few tears at the graveside, that had been the only sign of grief she had displayed. Two days after the funeral, she had turned to him and in a quiet voice had announced that it was time they went home.

Now Ashton stepped out of the lift, turned right and walked along the corridor to his office on the southeast side of the building. He barely had time to remove his raincoat and hang it up from the hook on the back of the door before the office intercom came to life with the dulcet tones of Victor Hazelwood's PA. The timing was so slick it was obvious that the receptionists in the lobby had been instructed to advise her when he arrived. The DG, he was informed, wished to see him before morning prayers at eight thirty. Although he hadn't opened the safe, old habits die hard and he looked round the room to make sure everything was secure before he went on up to the top floor and presented himself to the PA. There were two coloured lights above the communicating door, one red, which meant do not disturb, one green to signify the visitor was free to enter the inner sanctum. Neither bulb was illuminated but the green lit up the moment the PA pressed the buzzer on the underside of her desk.

Hazelwood was smoking what he called his first cheroot of the day, conveniently omitting the qualifying words 'in the office' because it was odds on that he'd already had one in his study after breakfast.

'How's Harriet doing?' he asked dutifully.

'Better than just holding herself together.'

'Good, I always said she was made of the right stuff.' Hazelwood lowered his head, frowned at the large blotter on his desk as if he'd made a notation on it in pencil which he was now unable to decipher. 'Orwell wanted to interview her about the impostor but I had a word with the Assistant Commissioner, Crime, and persuaded him this wasn't on in the circumstances.'

'Thank you,' Ashton said.

'It hasn't made us too popular with Chief Superintendent Orwell. Matter of fact he more or less sent Brian Thomas packing.'

'That doesn't altogether surprise me,' Ashton said cautiously.

'Have you been following the case in the newspapers?'

'Yes, what little has been reported.'

'Then you know as much as we do . . .'

Hazelwood left the statement hanging in the air and waited expectantly. Ashton knew what Victor was hoping to hear from him but there were limits to what he was prepared to do for The Firm.

'I'd like to build a few bridges,' Hazelwood told him eventually.

'In other words you're asking me if Harriet is up to being interviewed by Orwell?'

'I want to know whether or not the Ramash affair is any concern of ours.'

'And we don't have her on record at all?'

'No. Bill Orchard's Asian Department completed their check the day after you drove up to Lincoln.'

'Maybe some other Intelligence agency has Dr Ramash on its books.'

'MI5 has never heard of her.'

'What about the Defence Intelligence and Government Communications Headquarters?'

The Joint Intelligence Committee met every Tuesday morning at 09.00 hours under the chairmanship of the Deputy Cabinet Secretary and was attended by the Directors General of MI5, the SIS, GCHQ and the Head of the Defence Intelligence Service at the Ministry of Defence. Ashton couldn't think of a better time or place to raise the question but Hazelwood was being unnaturally reticent.

'Do I take it we haven't approached Defence Intelligence and GCHQ?' Ashton asked.

'Of course I haven't. Use your brains, Peter; what on earth could I tell them? That we were looking into the triple slaying in Lansdowne Mews because one of the victims had been passing herself off as the wife of one of my Intelligence officers? My God, for all we knew Dr Ramash might well have been treating your wife.'

'It didn't stop you from approaching MI5, did it, Victor?'

'That was different; Clifford Peachey did it on the old boy net.'

Whereas Hazelwood would have been forced to come clean had he raised the matter with the Joint Intelligence Committee, which would have been somewhat embarrassing for him. It was all a question of saving face.

'So what about Harriet? Is she fit enough to see Orwell?'

'What good will that do? Harriet has never heard of Dr Ramash before I mentioned her name. If she tells Orwell that, he's going to think she's deliberately withholding information.'

'You presume,' Hazelwood said tersely.

'There are only two ways the impostor could have acquired her information: from Harriet herself or from a source within the SIS.'

'If you are referring to Jill or her ex-husband, Henry Clayburn, you can forget it. I've already looked into that possibility.'

And got your knuckles rapped in the process, Ashton thought. At the first whiff of trouble, Jill would have gone running to one of her influential admirers and fluttered her eyelashes at him. The lady was a born survivor, blessed with the most sensitive nostrils in Whitehall.

'You haven't answered my question about Harriet,' Hazelwood reminded him.

'I'll have to ask her first how she feels.'

'Well, don't take all day about it.' Hazelwood glanced at the Rolex which his wife, Alice, had given him as a combined Christmas and birthday present. 'I'm going to be late for morning prayers,' he said pointedly.

'Right.' Ashton stood up and moved towards the communicating door.

'Come and see me again before the end of the morning. I'd like to know how we stand with Orwell.'

So far as Ashton was concerned, the Detective Chief Superintendent could get stuffed. So could Victor come to that. The leakage was here in Vauxhall Cross and Ashton was damned if he was going to put Harriet in the frame before every other possibility had been examined in depth. Leaving the PA's office he rode one of the lifts down to the Security Vetting and Technical Services Division.

When Ashton had been in charge of Security Vetting and Technical Services, the establishment had provided for a deputy, an appointment which Harriet had filled on secondment from MI5. In those days, Frank Warren had been responsible for the equipment held by Technical Services which was classified under two broad headings – hardware and software. Now he was in charge of the division, but, as part of the Treasury-led peace dividend, he had lost the services of a deputy and had seen his own former post abolished.

When Ashton walked into his office, he was playing with a desktop computer, his eyes riveted on the visual display unit. Frank was three inches shorter than himself and overweight. He had thinning black hair which was retreating from his forehead, a round face and a moustache which an old movie star like Clark Gable would have been proud of. He always had a faint smile on his lips which was one of the reasons why he was so well liked.

'Hello, Frank,' Ashton said. 'Since when have you been plugged into the stand-alone Intelligence data base?'

'I'm not,' Warren told him. 'The system you see here only serves the Security Vetting section of the division.'

'Yeah? What does it do?'

'Well, it's a sort of *aide-mémoire*. Suppose you wanted to know the date of the latest security report on Mr Smith, you'd phone me and I would call up his profile sheet and tell you.'

'OK, call up Harriet's.'

'Oh, come on, Peter, you know I can't do that. The rules clearly state that where a married couple or both cohabitees have been cleared by positive vetting, neither party can be allowed to see the security file relating to their spouse or partner.'

'I know the rules as well as you do; that's one thing which hasn't changed since I was sitting in your chair. Now call up Harriet's profile.'

'There are no exceptions, Peter.'

'Believe me this is important.'

'If it is that important, you should give your superior a list of questions you want answered and let him deal with it as he sees fit.'

'I'm not going to argue with you, Frank,' Ashton said, tight-lipped, 'but you are really beginning to piss me off. Now, just put the fucking profile on the screen.'

'OK, but on your head be it because I'll have to report this

43

breach of security to Roy Kelso and you can bet he will take it up with the DG.'

Warren tapped out the necessary instructions on the key-board. Moments later the extract of Harriet's file appeared on the VDU. The profile sheet gave her married, maiden and Christian names, next of kin, marital status, date and place of birth, home address and telephone number, educational quali-fications, particulars of children and a box showing the current security status. After the capital letters PV there was a dash followed by 'Sus 3' and the date.

'Does that mean what I think it does?' Ashton demanded.

'I knew I shouldn't have shown you the damn profile,' Warren said bitterly.

'Harriet's PV clearance has been suspended – for what? Three months?'

'Yes, subject to a further review in January '96.'

'And the decision was taken the day Harriet learned her mother had died?'

'Yes. I'm sorry, Peter, but don't take it out on me. I didn't make the decision.'

'You're right, and I'm sorry too.' Ashton rubbed his jaw. 'Tell me something, is this system crypto protected?'

'No, but then there is nothing higher than Confidential on the system. In fact the material only rates a Restricted classifica-tion.'

Since Ashton had been in charge of Security Vetting, the definition of Confidential had been changed. It now related to information whose compromise would materially change dip-lomatic relations, prejudice individual security or liberty; cause damage to the operational effectiveness or security of British or allied forces; or work substantially against national finances or economic and commercial interests.

'How long has this system been up and running, Frank?'

'About four months.'

The equipment had been offered up by the Department of Energy as surplus to requirements following an internal orga-nisation. The capital cost had been very reasonable and Roy Kelso had jumped at the chance to produce their 'in house' system. The programme itself had been designed by Ken

Maynard of the finance branch. A former warrant officer in the Royal Army Pay Corps, Maynard had joined the SIS straight from the MoD's Computer Services and Stats Research branch where he had produced the Master List of appointments in the navy, army and air force which required the incumbent to hold a Top Secret clearance.

'Who installed the equipment?'

'Ken Maynard.'

Ashton frowned. 'Why not Terry Hicks?' he asked.

Terry Hicks was the acknowledged expert on electronic warfare and countermeasures. At the height of the Cold War he had helped to build a plastic dome inside the British Embassy, Moscow. Shaped like an igloo with a hinged door, it was completely soundproof and therefore ideal for Top Secret briefings.

'Terry wasn't available,' Warren told him. 'He was away on a field trip to the Ukraine, checking out the British Embassy in Kiev.'

'I bet that made somebody's day,' Ashton said drily.

When Hicks descended on an embassy to clean it up, you could be damned sure the building was 'bug free' after he had swept the place from top to bottom. Unfortunately, there was a downside to Hicks, who had an uncanny knack of rubbing people up the wrong way. Kelso referred to him as 'that cocky, insolent little oik of a technician'; in turn Hicks's opinion of the Assistant Director in charge of the Admin Wing was unprintable. It was therefore hardly surprising that Kelso had been eager to get the job done while the electronic whiz-kid was out of the country.

'Tell me again, Frank, this is purely an in-house system?'

'Yes. No other department has access.'

'No outsiders?'

Warren hesitated. 'Well, I wouldn't call the commandant of the Training School an outsider.'

'Why the hell does he need to have access?'

'It was thought he might find it useful.'

'I don't see it,' Ashton said. 'If the commandant wants to know the security status of a student attending one of his courses, he has only to pick up the phone and come through on the scrambler.'

'Well, actually there was a spare terminal and Roy offered it to him.'

Ashton closed his eyes. He was willing to bet the commandant would never have asked for the facility off his own bat. However, few people would have turned down the offer because there was always the faint possibility that one day it might come in handy. But that was beside the point. The Training School was located at Amberley Lodge outside Petersfield and nobody was sending messages through the ether.

'Just how is the Training School linked to the system?' he asked.

'By a rented line from British Telecom.'

'Is it dedicated solely to us?'

'It's not Tornado protected, if that's what you mean. There's no crypto input at either end and the copper line is not encased in hardened steel.'

'Let's get Terry Hicks in here.'

Warren didn't like it. 'If you insist,' he said, and left the office. A few minutes later he returned, still very much out of sorts, with the electronics whiz-kid in tow. 'Would you like me to leave?' he asked petulantly.

'Of course not.' Ashton turned to Hicks. 'From a security standpoint, how do you rate this *aide-mémoire* system? Could a hacker get into it?'

'It wouldn't be too difficult.'

'Oh, come on,' Warren protested. 'He'd have to know the codeword.'

'Which is what?' Ashton enquired.

'Hamlet.'

'No problem,' Hicks said. 'Every self-respecting hacker has a gizmo.'

'A gizmo,' Warren repeated and looked blank.

'A gadget like a mini computer. The hacker picks up an impulse, locks in the gismo and in nothing flat, discovers the entry codeword. The only way you can fox the gismo is to have a codeword which is complete gobbledegook.'

Ashton smiled. 'You know any good hackers, Terry?'

'Can't say I do. Is there nothing else you want from me, Mr Ashton?'

'Not at the moment.'

'Mr Warren?'

'No, you've been very helpful, Terry,' Warren said, and tried to sound as if he meant it.

'See you then,' the electronic whiz-kid said, and left.

Warren started swearing as soon as they were alone. All of the invective was directed against himself and he had a choice vocabulary of four-letter words which surprised Ashton because Frank was not usually given to uttering obscenities, no matter how angry he might be.

'It's not the end of the world, Frank. You can put it right; just withdraw the facility from the Training School.'

'That's like shutting the stable door after the horse has bolted.'

'While you're at it, delete the home address and telephone number on each profile and replace them with a reference to the individual's security file. The Provos may have declared a truce but they are still targeting people and we don't want to make things easy for them.'

'Oh, Jesus Christ, the IRA.' Warren gave an agonised cry and punched his head with a clenched fist. 'I'll report it and tender my resignation at the same time.'

'Don't be silly.'

'I deserve to be sacked.'

Frank was right. He had committed a sackable offence but he was only two years away from early retirement on a full pension and he'd earned every penny of it. Ashton knew he shouldn't lift a finger to help him, never mind participating in a cover-up. He was also aware that in his shoes, Jill Sheridan wouldn't hesitate to carpet Frank but that was the reason why she was an assistant director on the way up the ladder and he was a Grade I Intelligence officer going nowhere.

'I should have spotted the inherent weakness of the system,' Warren continued miserably.

'Look, these things happen, especially when you're over-worked and understaffed.'

'Nice of you to say so, Peter, but who is going to believe it upstairs?'

'The DG for one after I've finished with him. One last question though: how are these security profiles arranged?'

'In alphabetical order,' Warren asked. 'How else?'

'OK, I'm a hacker looking for someone special. Now run the programme from the beginning.'

The end result was exactly what Ashton had privately anticipated. Harriet was logged under her married name and she was the first woman to come up on the screen. There had been nothing premeditated about stealing her identity, she had merely been selected at random.

Hazelwood had always regarded morning prayers as a tiresome business. The purpose of the daily meeting with assistant directors was to review any developments which had occurred during silent hours when only the departmental duty officers were on watch. In theory this was an eminently sensible drill, in practice it was a bit of a nonsense. All communications carried a signal precedence ranging from Deferred at the bottom end of the scale, through Routine, Priority, Op Immediate, Emergency to Flash, which was virtually a declaration of war. In all the years he had been in the SIS, Hazelwood could only recall three occasions when a Flash signal had been received during the hours of darkness – in 1968 when the Red Army had sent its tanks rolling into Prague to suppress the Dubcek government; in 1982 when the Argentinians had invaded the Falklands; and more recently when Saddam Hussein had decided to annex Kuwait in August 1990.

But even more to the point, he could not remember an instance when a night-duty officer had sat on an Op Immediate signal until normal office hours. The higher the signal precedence, the quicker the information was passed up the chain of command to the Director General himself via the appropriate senior desk officer, assistant director, and Deputy DG. As a result of this standing operational procedure there were never any major surprises at morning prayers. However, this did not necessarily mean that matters were dealt with expeditiously; without tight control from the chair, morning prayers could drag on interminably.

In the past, when the USSR had been seen as the number one potential enemy, with the People's Republic of China a close second, it hadn't been difficult to keep heads of departments focused; these days when there was no obvious threat, meetings tended to become far-ranging and rambling. This morning Hazelwood had been subjected to a long discourse on potential Islamic flashpoints by Jill Sheridan. She had covered Algeria, Tunisia, Egypt, and those good old standbys, Iraq and Iran. And he had just about had his fill of the Algerian Islamic Liberation Front, the Jamaa Islamiya group which was creating mayhem in Egypt not to mention Hezbollah and Hamas. Then to cap it all, Bill Orchard had delivered a not-so-short lecture on the Ananda Marg, a militant Hindu fundamentalist group which posed absolutely no threat whatever to the UK.

Instead of the usual thirty minutes, the conference that morning had lasted nearly two hours. Hazelwood knew that he had no one to blame for that but himself. As chairman he should have told both Jill Sheridan and Bill Orchard to get to the point. Leaving the conference room, he stopped by the PA's office to ask her to make him a proper cup of coffee instead of the usual sludge dispensed by the machine near the lifts, which had been installed a few months ago on the initiative of Roy Kelso. To his annoyance he saw that she had used some of his own private stock of Colombian beans to make a cup for Ashton.

'I hope you have done something to deserve that,' he said acidly.

'Only time will tell.'

'I take it you have spoken to Harriet?'

'No, that wasn't necessary,' Ashton said.

'You'd better tell me why not,' Hazelwood growled, and walked into his office. Leaving Ashton to close the communicating door behind him, he sat down and pressed the button on the underside of the desk to illuminate the red light in the PA's room. 'All right, Peter, let's hear it.'

'A hacker's been into Frank Warren's *aide-mémoire* system and looted it.'

Hazelwood's first instinct was to deny that such a breach of security was possible but immediately changed his mind when he learned that the Training School had access to the facility on an unprotected BT line. Although what Ashton had

49

suggested was perfectly feasible, the DG still had a number of reservations.

'I'm not sure I accept that Harriet was selected at random. By all accounts the impostor resembled her physically.'

Ashton shook his head. 'No, Roy Kelso was told the dead woman was tall and dark but lots of women have dark hair. Harriet's tall – she's half an inch under six feet – but the corpse I saw in the mortuary was a shade over five six, which might seem tall to Orwell but not to me. Harriet's name was down in the appointments diary so everybody assumed she was the third victim.'

'All right, Peter, I'll buy that. Now explain to me why this hacker should have picked on the SIS when he was constructing a false identity?'

'I can't.'

'Are you saying the hacker picked on us purely by chance?'

'I think that would be too much of a coincidence.'

'He had inside information?' Hazelwood frowned. 'Or she,' he added.

'Somebody could have talked out of turn to a fellow enthusiast.'

'You mean one of our programmers?'

'No reason why it shouldn't have been one of BT's work-force,' Aston said.

'Who put you on to this, Peter?'

'Frank Warren.'

'Really? You do surprise me. Frank's a good man, loyal, conscientious, thoroughly likeable but I never credited him with a first-class brain.'

He looked pointedly at Ashton, waited for him to make some sort of comment but the younger man wasn't going to be drawn. Peter was covering for Frank Warren; of that Hazelwood had not the slightest doubt. He was equally certain that he could rely on Ashton to take appropriate action to put things right.

'All right, Peter, first thing you do is square things with Orwell; then find me this damned hacker.'

'OK.' Ashton cleared his throat. 'Before I went up to Lincoln I was doing a profile for Clifford Peachey on a man who might succeed Boris Yeltsin.'

'Don't worry about it; this takes priority over gazing into a crystal ball.'

'You'll inform Clifford?'

'Of course I will.' Hazelwood waited until Ashton was about to disappear into the PA's office, then said, 'Incidentally, how did you know Harriet was the first woman to appear in the *aide-mémoire*?'

'I got Frank to run the whole programme from the beginning.'

'Then you will have seen that I suspended Harriet's PV clearance.'

'Yeah, the day she was told her mother had committed suicide.'

'Suppose you were sitting in my chair. What would you have done?'

'I'm not sure,' Ashton admitted.

'That's why you're still a Grade I Intelligence officer,' Hazelwood told him.

Chapter Five

It rapidly became evident to Ashton that Detective Chief Superintendent Stanley Orwell did not share Hazelwood's enthusiasm for building bridges. Although Ashton's appointment to see Orwell had been arranged for 2 p.m. at the divisional station in Ladbroke Road, the Chief Superintendent had left him to cool his heels in the public area for half an hour before sending a message via a detective constable to the effect that he was busy and would be another fifteen minutes. In the event, the DC reappeared some nine minutes later and showed Ashton into the Chief Superintendent's office.

For the second time that day, Ashton recounted the saga of the unknown hacker and the stand-alone system that wasn't. As a listener, Orwell gave a pretty good impression of a sphinx. His face was inscrutable, the pale grey eyes totally blank as if somebody had switched off all the lights. A feeling that nothing he'd said had registered with Orwell was confirmed for Ashton when the CID officer asked if Harriet was acquainted with a Lorraine Cheeseman.

'I don't think so,' Ashton told him.

'Her maiden name was Larissa Marchukova; maybe that rings a bell with you?'

'No. Are you saying that she is the woman who impersonated my wife?'

'That's the natural assumption,' Orwell said. 'I do know she was the third victim.'

'How did you discover that?'

'Through the Australian High Commission.'

Ashton took a deep breath before he exploded, and counted slowly up to ten, then exhaled. Prising information out of Orwell was like pulling teeth.

'Now look,' Ashton said, doing his best to sound reasonable, 'if you want us to check our records to see whether we have anything on this Russian woman—'

'Latvian,' Orwell said, interrupting him. 'She was born in Riga, lived most of her life there.'

Ashton wasn't going to argue with him. It didn't matter where the woman had been born or had spent her formative years or where she had been educated. With a name like Larissa Marchukova she was first and foremost a Russian. According to the 1989 census the population of Latvia numbered 12.7 million, of whom thirty-four per cent were Russians with the Belorussians and Ukrainians accounting for a further nine per cent between them. Of the ethnic Latvians, over 175,000 had been killed or deported by the Red Army when liberating the country from German occupation in 1944. In addition to the wives and families of Soviet military personnel stationed in the country, there had been an influx of migrant workers from nearby parts of Russia and neighbouring Belorussia as a result of the post-war industrialisation of Latvia.

Marchukova, Ashton had learned, had come west in 1991 in search of a better life. She had learned English and German at the University of Riga and had also qualified as a teacher. Berlin had attracted her like a moth to a candle and Larissa had fondly imagined she would have no difficulty in obtaining a teaching post, preferably at one of the high schools in the city. It was however one of the professions which was vastly oversubscribed, with a dozen or more applicants for every post that was advertised. It hadn't taken Larissa Marchukova long to realise that as a 'guest worker' she wouldn't even make the shortlist. After obtaining employment as a waitress, she eventually got a job with a travel agent's on Uhlandstrasse, which is where she had first met her husband-to-be.

'Roger Cheeseman was doing a postgraduate course on International Law at the University of Berlin,' Orwell continued. 'He had decided to spend Christmas with the folks back home in Melbourne. At least that had been his intention when he had walked into the travel agent's to get the necessary plane tickets but then he saw Larissa and changed his mind. Six months later, they were married.'

The couple had left Berlin in June 1992 when Roger Cheeseman, having finished his postgraduate course, went home to become a lecturer at La Trobe University. In March 1994 Mrs Cheeseman, who had changed her name to Lorraine by deed poll, returned to Europe ostensibly to visit her mother, who'd suffered a severe heart attack and was in hospital in Riga. Ten days after his wife arrived in Riga, Cheeseman received a cable from Lorraine to say that her mother had died and that she would be returning home after the funeral. She had subsequently telephoned him from Berlin, giving details of her flights via Heathrow to Melbourne via British Airways and Qantas.

'Cheeseman drove out to the airport to meet her but she wasn't on Qantas Flight QF10 which arrived on schedule at 06.20 hours on Tuesday the nineteenth of April.' Orwell paused to light a cigarette, then continued in the same monotone. 'He checked into one of the airport hotels and for the next three days haunted the arrivals hall but no Lorraine. Meantime Qantas had been in touch with their London office who'd no record of the lady booking a flight with them to Melbourne. By now, Cheeseman was getting frantic and the Australian national carrier was becoming rather perturbed as well.'

Following enquiries with British Airways and the travel agent's in Berlin, Qantas had learned that the airline had no record of a Mrs Cheeseman on any of their flights departing Tegel Airport for Heathrow on Saturday the 16th, while the travel agency was adamant that she hadn't made any flight reservations through them.'

Lorraine had subsequently sent a letter to her husband to explain why she hadn't returned to Melbourne. Covering two sheets of paper which looked as if they had been torn from a child's exercise book, her story simply hadn't made sense. Although the letter had been posted in Enfield on 6 July, the address she had given in North London did not exist.

'Nothing more was heard from her for a whole year,' Orwell said. 'Then ten weeks ago she resurfaced. Kensington appears to be a favourite haunt for Australians when they come to London.

Anyway, it was at the Kensington Palace Hotel in De Vere Gardens that a Mrs Irene Bell made her acquaintance. Truth is Lorraine Cheeseman stalked Mrs Bell, spent two days studying her before she pounced.'

'Cheeseman was staying at the same hotel?' Ashton asked.

'Mrs Bell thinks she was but the hotel can't find a registration card in her name. The fact is the night before Mrs Bell was due to fly home to Sydney, Lorraine produced a letter addressed to Cheeseman which she asked her to post when she was back home in West Ryde. Lorraine also told her that the letter contained her agreement to a divorce on the terms her husband had demanded but she didn't want him to know that she was now living in England. That was why she was asking Irene Bell to do her this favour.'

She had written a totally different story for Roger Cheeseman. Her mother had in fact died approximately thirty-six hours before Lorraine had arrived in Riga. On the day of the funeral, two police officers, who had been waiting outside the gates to the cemetery, had arrested Lorraine for currency speculation and had taken her into custody. After being held in cells overnight, she had appeared before an investigating magistrate, found guilty as charged and sentenced to six months' imprisonment with hard labour. According to Lorraine, the police officers had then offered her an alternative: work for them as a courier in Berlin and she wouldn't be locked up for the next one hundred and eighty days.

'Lorraine was involved in the drugs scene.' Orwell stubbed out his cigarette. 'It was about the only truthful thing she told her husband. She had a very fertile imagination did our Mrs Cheeseman. Spun a great story about how the men she had been forced to work for had smuggled her into this country and had got her deliberately hooked on heroin. It was a lie, of course; the pathologist who carried out the post mortem hadn't found any telltale tracks where she had been shooting herself up.'

Orwell believed that the whole purpose of the letter had been to get some dosh out of Cheeseman. She had wanted him to send a money order to an accommodation address so that she could buy a plane ticket and come home. Despite the way she had treated him, Cheeseman had wanted her back. He had been concerned for her safety ever since she had officially disappeared on 16 April 1994. In an effort to trace Lorraine, he had sent photographs of her to the Australian Consulate in Berlin and the High Commission in London.

'Cheeseman wrote to Australia House in the Strand again when he received the letter posted in Enfield and did so a third time when he got the one mailed in West Ryde. Australia House got in touch with us after her picture had appeared in the *Evening Standard* at our request.'

'I didn't read anything about that in the newspapers,' Ashton said.

'That's because we kept the fact that we knew the name of the third victim to ourselves.'

'One final question: what are you going to do about the hacker?'

'We'll ask BT for a rundown on their engineers in the Petersfield area; find out how many of them trawl the Internet in their spare time.' Orwell rested both arms on the desk and leaned forward, shoulders hunched. 'But I have to tell you that I don't believe you people were deliberately targeted. For one thing, I can't think why they should want to borrow the identity of an Intelligence officer. No, the way I see it the hacker latched on to your stand-alone system by accident. Now if that should be the case, we'll have a hell of a job tracing him, especially if what he did was a one-off job.'

Orwell was going down a different track. At one time he'd thought the triple murder had been some kind of terrorist outrage, but now all the evidence suggested it had been a territorial dispute over drugs.

'What evidence?' Ashton asked.

'We found a fair amount of cannabis on the property and there was 40 grams of crack in an envelope inside the three-drawer filing cabinet, taped to the back panel. We've also got a witness who saw Lorraine Cheeseman arrive at the house in a dark green BMW. The driver was a black man; he went into the house with her, came out alone, fifteen, maybe twenty minutes later.' Orwell smiled. 'I don't want you to get the idea that we aren't interested in your hacker but we do have other priorities. You understand what I'm saying?'

'Oh, absolutely,' Ashton said. 'In a roundabout fashion, you're telling me not to hold my breath.'

His name was Mungo Park but he was not related to the famous eighteenth-century explorer whose historic voyage down the River Niger had been recorded for posterity in his *Travels in the Interior of Africa*. There was no Scottish connection either; Park had been born in Plumstead, south of the river, and Bedford, fifty-two miles up the A6 trunk road from London was the furthest north he'd been. He was thirty-one years old and had all the brashness of a man who sought to compensate for his lack of height with an overabundance of self-esteem.

He had short blond hair, a rugged-looking face, as he liked to describe his features, and a well-proportioned, muscular frame which he kept in trim with regular workouts in the local gym. He was a martial arts buff and was into aikido and karate, two disciplines which should have curbed his natural aggressive nature but failed to do so. Since Park was quick to take offence and had inflicted grievous bodily harm on at least two occasions, the fact that he'd never come to the notice of the police was something of a miracle.

After leaving school at sixteen, Park had got a job as a trainee lineman with the General Post Office. With privatisation he had automatically become an employee of British Telecom and had begun to specialise in information technology. Five months ago, he had left the company to go into business on his own account undertaking computer repairs, upgrading of systems, providing support facilities and offering training courses. To keep overheads down to the absolute minimum, he had decided to run the enterprise from his flat in Westbourne Terrace near Paddington station. As it happened, this had been a wise move because the demand for his services had scarcely been overwhelming. To supplement his income, Park had branched out into the field of data acquisition, which was a euphemism for industrial espionage.

The firm which had got him started in this particular line of business was the Steadfast Enquiry and Research Agency in Shooter Place off Long Acre. Its managing director, principal shareholder and, for all Park knew, the sole operative, was Basil Wilks, a gaunt-looking man in his late fifties with grey hair, bad teeth, nicotine-stained fingers and a problem with dandruff. The clerical side of the business was looked after by a buxom, jolly-looking woman some five years younger than Wilks, who answered to the name of Mildred.

By second post that day Park had received a cheque for £250 from the agency signed by Mildred in her capacity as company secretary. She had also enclosed a compliments slip on which she had written 'In settlement of your account'. Park had news for her, the account was a long way from being settled; he had in fact been short-changed by some £750 and that was the reason why he was about to call on Mr Basil Wilks. Leaving Leicester Square Underground station by the exit nearest Wyndhams Theatre, he turned right, walked up Charing Cross Road, then turned right again into Long Acre and made his way to the Steadfast Enquiry and Research Agency.

The offices were on the second floor of the building directly above the two rooms occupied by a Miss Birch, her 'maid' and an unfriendly-looking Alsatian. The street door was kept permanently open to attract the passing trade. Park stepped inside the narrow hall and took the stairs two at a time. There were two doors on the landing, one facing the staircase, which was permanently locked, the other at right angles to it. The one to Park's right was the outer office which was Mildred's domain. Anybody wanting to see Basil Wilks had to get past her first and despite the ready smile and motherly appearance, she was not a lady he would want to cross. Mildred kept a steel-loaded rubber cosh in the top drawer of her desk together with a can of Mace. Strictly illegal, of course, but knowing that would be no comfort when the CS gas hit him in the face and his eyeballs felt as if they were on fire, and he was fighting to draw breath. Mad as he was about being short-changed, it was only prudent to bear that in mind.

'Mr Park,' Mildred said, and gave him a warm smile as he walked into her office, 'what a pleasant surprise.'

'The feeling's mutual,' Park told her, then asked if Mr Wilks was in.

'You've received our cheque?'

The question was a dead giveaway; it told him for sure that he had been gypped.

'Second post this morning.'

'No problem, is there?'

'No, I'm very happy.' He could lie with the best of them and keep a smile on his face. 'Just a business proposition I'd like to discuss with your boss.'

'You'll have to wait.'

'Why? Is he out?'

'Mr Wilks has got an upset tummy,' Mildred informed him primly.

The old bastard had got the runs. Too bad; but that would be nothing compared to the discomfort he would feel if he failed to come across with the rest of the dosh. He would be shitting through the eye of an needle by the time Mungo Park had finished pointing out the error of his ways to him.

'Would you like a cup of coffee while you're waiting, Mr Park?'

'No thanks. I've been drinking the stuff all morning; it's practically coming out of my ears.'

'Tea then?'

There was a sound of a chain being pulled, then the cistern emptied making a noise like Niagara Falls.

'Too late,' Park said with a grin. Before Mildred could stop him, he opened the communicating door and walked into the inner sanctum just as Wilks was emerging from the lavatory. 'Hello, Basil,' he said and surreptitiously locked the door behind him. 'I hear you're feeling a bit peaky.'

Wilks looked grim, cheeks pinched, face white as chalk.

'It's the egg sandwich I had for lunch. I'll be all right in a minute.' Wilks collapsed into his chair with a hollow groan. 'Anyway, what can I do for you, Mungo?'

'I'd like you to explain what this cheque for two hundred and fifty quid is for?'

'Final payment.'

'Think again, Basil. You told me the client had agreed to pay us two grand for the job.'

'That's right and you got seven fifty up front.'

'And your cut was twenty-five per cent of the bundle. Now where's the other five hundred?'

'You've got it wrong, son. It was always a three-way split, fifty per cent to you and twenty-five per cent each for Mildred and me. Mildred will tell you, she was present when we shook hands on the deal. Why don't I call her in here?'

Park leaned across the desk, shot out his left arm and jabbed the thumb into Basil's windpipe. 'Now you listen good. I took a hell of a chance doing that job.'

'You told me it was as easy as falling off a log.'

'Yeah, well, I've had second thoughts. If the people at Amberley Lodge ever discover that somebody's been into their system, I'm one of the men they'll be looking for, not you. So why should you and Mildred get fifty per cent for sitting on your backsides? Answer me that.'

'I can't,' Wilks spluttered, 'I'm choking.'

'OK, I'll ease the pressure. But just remember this, I've locked the door, so don't go yelling for Mildred because it won't do you any good.'

'I believe you.' Wilks massaged his throat as he took several deep breaths. 'And I'm not going to argue about the five hundred. I'll give you a cheque.'

'No, you open the safe.' Park pointed to the free-standing Chubb in the far corner of the room which was a good five feet high. 'I want to see what's inside.'

Wilks took a bunch of keys out of his jacket pocket and placed them on the desk. 'Look for yourself,' he said. 'The key you want is the large brass one.'

'And while I'm opening the safe, you trip the light fantastic, unlock the communicating door and let Mildred in here with her can of Mace? No thank you.'

'What a suspicious mind you've got.' Wilks picked up the keys, went over to the Chubb safe and opened it, then stood to one side. 'Take a good look, Mungo. All we've got in there are the company books for the last seven years and a lot of old files relating to individual credit worthiness.'

'What's the tin box on the top shelf?'

'Petty cash.'

'It's the petty cash I'm interested to see. Bring the box over here.'

It was a very flimsy-looking affair and no more secure than a child's piggy bank. Nevertheless, it contained a rolled bundle of £50 notes held in place with an elastic band. A quick check revealed that the petty cash amounted to a cool £1,200.

'I'll take that,' Park said and stuffed the notes into his pocket. 'You can have your cheque in exchange.'

'Except for fifty pounds, you'll have grabbed the whole two grand.'

'Well, let that be a lesson to you, Basil. Honesty is the best policy.'

Park moved round the desk, grabbed hold of Wilks by the left arm and lifted him to his feet. 'You can see me out,' he said.

Park walked him across the room, unlocked the door with his free hand and opening it, thrust the older man into the outer office and straight into the arms of Mildred. Released at close quarters, the jet of CS gas sprayed from the can hit Wilks straight in the face and burned his eyeballs. His high-pitched scream of agony was cut short as he inhaled the vapour and began to choke on it. Unable to see, he blundered forward, folded his arms around Mildred and clung on to her for support. Park slipped past him, wrenched the can of Mace from Mildred's grasp and turned it on her. When he walked out of the office, they were both crawling around the floor on hands and knees like two blind mice.

Today had been easily the worst Frank Warren had experienced since he had joined the SIS in 1965. People had often accused him of being unimaginative, and this comment had appeared more than once in his annual assessment but he had no difficulty in envisaging the extent of the disaster that would engulf the SIS should the IRA lay their hands on the material stolen by the hacker. All right, the stand-alone system hadn't been his idea and Roy Kelso had offered the facility to the Training School without consulting him. But dammit, he was Head of the Security Vetting and Technical Services Division and he should have foreseen the danger. He should have told Kelso either to pull the plug on Amberley Lodge or get the BT line Tornado protected.

Instead he'd placed too much reliance on the low-grade

security classification of the profiles. He had read what Michael Collins had done to the Secret Service during the early hours of Sunday, 21 November 1920, when members of his squad with the assistance of the IRA's Dublin Brigade had shot dead fourteen officers. Collins's informers hadn't been a hundred per cent accurate and most of the victims had had no connection with the Secret Service but now Warren feared he had made things easy for the gunmen who were following in the footsteps of Michael Collins. He had given them the names and addresses of every single officer in the SIS. Deep in thought, he did not hear Ashton tap on the door before entering the office and almost jumped out of his skin when he spoke to him.

'What did you say, Peter?'

'I offered a penny for your thoughts.'

'I'm surprised you should ask after our discussion this morning.'

'Have you started to amend the profiles?'

'Better than that, I've wiped out the whole bloody programme. But at the risk of repeating myself, that's like shutting the stable door after the horse has bolted.'

'That's something we'll have to ask the hacker.'

'And how the hell are we going to find him or her?' Warren demanded.

'Who installed the line at Amberley Lodge?'

'BT,' Warren said, and caught his breath.

'Exactly,' Ashton said. 'We wouldn't have let their engineers near the Training School without the necessary security clearance.'

The SIS would have submitted the names and personal details of the BT engineers to MI5 to see if any of them had ever come to the notice of the Security Service. They would also have asked the National Identification Bureau to take a look at the engineers for the purpose of ascertaining whether any of them had a criminal record. But even after the BT personnel had been cleared, the Commandant of the Training School would have appointed a watchdog to keep a friendly eye on them.

Ashton glanced at his wristwatch. 'Ten minutes to five, time enough for you to phone Amberley Lodge and get the names of those BT engineers before the permanent staff go home.'

'Right.'

'We're going to get that hacker, Frank.'

'And turn him over to the police?'

'Oh sure,' Ashton said, his voice chilly as the east wind, 'but only after we know what he did with the material he stole.'

Chapter Six

Wilks eyed the telephone, mentally debating whether or not to call the 'Go-Between'. Whatever decision he finally made, nobody could accuse him of being precipitate; Mildred had gone home long ago and the evening rush hour was winding down. His first instinct had been to pick up the phone and really stick it to Mr bloody Mungo Park. He hadn't done so because he hadn't been able to see a damned thing after the CS gas had hit him plumb in the face. Just feeling his way to the washbasin in the lavatory at the back of the office had been a major achievement. He'd coughed and hawked into the bowl, bringing up all the sputum the irritant had caused, then rinsed it away before washing his eyes under the cold water tap. By the time he had done the same for Mildred and made her a strong cup of tea laced with whisky, he had calmed down sufficiently to weigh all the pros and cons objectively.

Park was good at extracting information from a data base that was protected only by a simple entry code. No question about it, he knew what he was doing and the material he'd stolen had been just what the client had wanted. Before breaking into the system, Park had assured him that there was no risk of discovery and immediately afterwards had maintained it had been as easy as falling off a log. So why was he now saying he would be one of the men the authorities would be looking for if ever they discovered that a hacker had been into their data base? Was Park simply after more money or was he genuinely at risk? That was one of the conundrums Wilks had been trying to figure out for the past two hours or so. What complicated matters was the fact that Park was such an accomplished liar, it was difficult to know when he was telling the truth.

An inner voice urged him to assume the worst because it was safer than leaving things to chance and hoping for the best. If Park was identified as the hacker, the little bastard would go all out to get the best deal he could for himself. In other words, he would tell the police all he knew about the Steadfast Enquiry and Research Agency. And that presented Wilks with the second conundrum. What exactly did he hope the client would do about Park if he put the poison down? Persuade him to keep his mouth shut or make sure he wasn't in a position to open it in the first place? Wilks shied away from making the choice.

He lit yet another cigarette. His face still felt as if he was suffering from a bad case of prickly heat and it was this burning sensation more than any other factor that helped him make the decision. Hesitating no longer, he lifted the receiver, punched out the number of the Go-Between and depressed the record button on the answer machine. The area code related to subscribers in the Cricklewood area. Given the subscriber's number as well, Park could have discovered the name and address of the Go-Between for him but right from the start he'd decided it wouldn't be a good idea. At the back of his mind was the fear that Park would muscle in and deal direct with the client if he had access to Wilks's intermediary.

The phone stopped ringing and a voice he recognised informed him of the number.

'This is Basil Steadfast,' Wilks said. 'I need to see Mr V. J.'

'When?'

'The sooner the better, preferably tonight. Something's come up which he should know about.'

'Are you calling from your office?'

'Where else?'

'Ring me back in forty minutes,' the Go-Between told him, then added, 'from a pay phone.'

No flies on you, Wilks thought, and hung up in response to a dull click as the Go-Between severed the connection. He rewound the tape on the answer machine and played back the ·recording of their brief conversation. The definition was good, every word clear as a bell, but the substance was lousy.

There were no incriminating remarks on the tape which he could use as a bargaining counter if the need arose. The only thing which indicated it wasn't the usual exchange between two businessmen was the last four words when he had been told to call back from a pay phone.

Wilks extracted the tape, locked it away in the Chubb safe and left the office, switching off the lights behind him and securing the doors as he went. A low murmur of voices in the hallway below reached him as he stepped out on to the landing, and he was just in time to see a man in a dark grey raincoat scuttle out into the night like a frightened rabbit. Beatty, the old harridan who looked after the unfriendly Alsatian and entertained the punters until Miss Birch was free, called out to him.

'Working late tonight, Mr Wilks?'

'Yep, just following the example of your employer,' he said, and walked out into the alley.

It was never a good idea to seek an audience with Hazelwood towards the end of the day. In all the years he had known Victor, Ashton could not recall his guide and mentor ever leaving the office on time. It wasn't as if he didn't have a nice home to go to in Willow Walk near Hampstead Heath and God knows his wife, Alice, was hardly a difficult woman to live with. Ashton suspected that Victor couldn't bear to leave until he was reasonably sure that a crisis was not likely to develop somewhere out there in the big wide world during the so-called silent hours when only the duty officers were on watch. The trouble was Hazelwood was averse to keeping a lonely vigil and the last man in to see him during normal working hours was unlikely to get away much before Victor himself was ready to leave.

Knowing this, Ashton mentally kicked himself for not phoning Harriet to warn her he would be late home, something he should have done before going to see the DG.

'This won't take long,' he'd said optimistically.

'Take all the time you need,' Hazelwood had told him, 'I'm in no hurry.'

Ashton had needed only a few minutes to recount what he had learned from Orwell and summarise just where he thought

66

the police investigation was going. However, the moment Victor lit a cheroot and settled back in his leather-upholstered armchair it had been all too evident to Ashton that he was about to face a prolonged question-and-answer session. Inevitably, Hazelwood wanted to know if he had managed to patch things up with the Chief Superintendent.

'I was coming to that. It seems Dr Ramash kept a fairly large amount of cannabis on the property along with 40 grams of crack, which is why Orwell has his own agenda. He's convinced the good doctor was dealing and was murdered because she was muscling in on somebody else's territory. Naturally he would like to know if we have anything on Larissa Marchukova a.k.a. Lorraine Cheeseman but he's not interested in discovering why she had been passing herself off as Mrs Harriet Ashton.'

'Has he got a chip on his shoulder?'

'Orwell wasn't too friendly.'

'How long has he been a chief superintendent?'

'I didn't ask. I expect Brian Thomas could find out if you really want to know.'

'The rank is being abolished this year,' Hazelwood said. 'Maybe he hasn't been confirmed in his appointment yet and is feeling a bit edgy?'

'I didn't know you could be an acting chief superintendent.'

'What have you done about Larissa Marchukova?'

Sometimes it was hard to keep up with Hazelwood or see the way his mind was working. Larissa Marchukova was history and running a check on her could wait.

'Nothing as yet,' Ashton told him. 'I thought it was more important to identify the hacker.'

'Ah, yes, the crooked BT engineer.' Hazelwood shook his head. 'Well, even if he does find him I'm afraid Frank Warren will have to go. What he did wasn't merely stupid, it was criminally negligent.'

'In two years Frank is eligible to retire on a full pension.'

'I can't help that, Peter.'

'I think you can. What do we hope to achieve by dismissing him on the spot?'

'We're making an example of him; Jesus Christ, he has put every man and woman in the SIS at risk.'

'Before you do anything, why don't we wait until we've got our hands on this hacker?'

'How many engineers are we talking about?'

'I don't know yet; can't be more than three.'

'And what if your hacker isn't one of them?'

Hazelwood's use of the possessive pronoun did not escape Ashton. Suddenly the hacker belonged to him.

'I suppose that's a different matter,' he said reluctantly.

'I'm glad we agree about something. I was beginning to think your concern for Warren verged on the unnatural.' Hazelwood crushed his cheroot in the brass ashtray. 'How many other people know about this monumental cockup?'

'Terry Hicks will probably have guessed that there has been a serious breach of security. And of course Frank told the whole story to Roy Kelso.'

'Oh well, that does it, the whole damned world will know by now.'

'Kelso won't breathe a word because he's not above criticism himself.'

'And Hicks? Is there any reason why he should hold his tongue?'

'He has signed the Official Secrets Acts.'

'So has everybody else in this building. Give me another reason.'

'I can't.'

'I thought not.' Hazelwood opened the ornate cigar box and took another cheroot. 'What do you think people are going to say if I sit back and do nothing about Frank Warren? I've got a good few enemies in Whitehall who would seize any opportunity to bring me down. And then there are those who would see my removal as furthering their own career. I can name one in Vauxhall Cross.'

'You're referring to Jill Sheridan?'

Hazelwood struck a match and lit the cheroot. 'Who else?' he asked.

Ashton told him he was wrong. Whatever else she might be, Jill was a realist and knew her own limitations. Even in the eyes of Robin Urquhart, her most ardent admirer, she lacked the necessary experience to hold down the appointment of Director

General. At this stage of Jill's career it would not be to her advantage if Hazelwood was sacked.

'She's after Clifford's job. Of course, once Jill is established as the Deputy Director, it might not be too long before she is tempted to pull the rug out from under you.'

A ghost of a smile appeared on Hazelwood's face. 'I'd still be taking a risk.'

'You do that when you cross a busy road.'

'All right, Peter, I'll hold off for seventy-two hours. If you haven't wrapped it up by then, Frank is for the chop.'

'I'd better get moving.'

'Yes, you had. And while you're at it, look in on the European Department and get the duty officer to run a check on Larissa Marchukova.'

Ashton said he would do that and left before Hazelwood could think of yet another task for him.

The duty officer was employed on the Iberian Desk and knowing next to nothing about the Baltic States was reluctant to call up the relevant file on the stand-alone system without first obtaining permission from the appropriate head of section. He looked even more unhappy when told by Ashton that one way or another he'd better have the answer before morning prayers.

Frank Warren didn't look too happy either but then he had a lot on his mind. It also transpired that he hadn't had any luck with the Training School.

'They handed you a curate's egg?' Ashton repeated. 'What the hell does that mean?'

'Three engineers were detailed for the job. Unfortunately one of them went down with food poisoning, while another suffered a personal bereavement. Consequently they had to be replaced at short notice.'

BT had nominated a further two men with the necessary security clearance and had passed their details to the permanent staff at Amberley Lodge. Instead of getting the Security Vetting and Technical Services Division to validate the new personnel, the principal administration officer at the Training School had gone direct to MI5.

'The Security Service gave them the green light over the telephone. The two newcomers and the original member of the installation team were recognised by their photos on the BT Identity Cards.'

'So?'

'Well, this is where it gets embarrassing, Peter. The Training School didn't record the names of the newcomers and we weren't informed that two members of the original team had had to be replaced.'

'What about the watchdog who was detailed to keep an eye on the engineers? Can't he identify them?'

'Only by their first names.' Warren glanced at the memo pad on his desk. 'We've got a David, a Mungo and a Norman.'

'The director is right, this a monumental cockup.' Ashton ran a hand through his hair. 'We've got the particulars of the original team, including their home addresses. Right?'

'Yes.'

'So who amongst David, Mungo and Norman is the third man?'

'David, his surname is Arlott.'

'BT will have time sheets; they will know who did the work at Amberley Lodge.'

'I've already tried their personnel department,' Warren told him. 'Everybody's gone home.'

'What about their security organisation? You've got a hand-book listing the names of the chief security officer and his deputy of every major company quoted in the FT index which is engaged on contractual work for the MoD and other government ministries. Look up the BT man, ring his home number and get him to open up the personnel office.'

'He's not going to like it.'

'Do it, Frank. I want those names and addresses on my desk before eight thirty tomorrow morning.'

'He's still not going to like it.'

'If he gives you any old buck, ask him how British Telecom will like it when they lose every government contract to one of their competitors like Mercury.'

'Can we do that?' Warren asked doubtfully.

'I don't know,' Ashton admitted, 'but he sure as hell won't take any chances.'

70

Wilks turned into Piccadilly at the top of Regent Street, strolled past Hatchards and then on to Fortnum and Mason before finally ending the aimless walkabout by wheeling into Church Place, where there were several pay phones. To kill time after leaving the office, he had made his way down to the Strand and had stopped by the Irish pub to have a couple of beers. After that, he had simply wandered around for the remaining twenty minutes before he was due to contact the Go-Between.

Entering the nearest pay phone, he lifted the receiver, fed a 50 pence coin into the slot and punched out the contact number. The fly posters had had a busy day; everywhere he looked there were calling cards from girls with names like Michelle, Tina, Gaynor, Louise, or the more anonymous Coffee and Cream, French governess and Miss PVC. Presently the phone stopped ringing and the same neutral voice announced the Cricklewood number.

'It's me again,' Wilks said, 'Basil Steadfast. Have you got any news for me?'

'Ah, yes, where are you now?'

'In a call box just off Piccadilly.'

'Good. Mr V. J. will be pleased to meet you tonight at eight twenty-five.'

'Whereabouts?'

'In Kenton; that is near where you live, is it not?'

'Practically on the doorstep.'

'Then perhaps you are familiar with Rushout Avenue?'

Wilks frowned, tried mentally to place the street but had to give up. 'I don't think so,' he said.

'You get out at Northwick Park station, go down the pedestrian access, cross Northwick Avenue and you're there.'

'Right.'

'Mr V. J. will pick you up from the corner of Kenton Road and Rushout Avenue. I assume you know where Kenton Road is?'

'I've been down it in a number 183 bus often enough.'

'Eight twenty-five then, not a minute before, not a minute after.'

'Hang on a sec, how will I recognise Mr V. J.?'

'That's not a problem, Mr Wilks, he knows you by sight,' the Go-Between said, and hung up on him.

Wilks replaced the phone, scooped up his change and backed out of the box. Piccadilly Circus, Bakerloo Line to Baker Street, change to the Met. He knew the route to Northwick Park like the back of his hand but that was largely irrelevant. He had never met his client yet Mr V. J. would be able to recognise him, and the Go-Between appeared to know where he lived. There was only one explanation: the client had arranged to have him watched and fully documented probably for a number of days before he had initially contacted the agency by phone. Wilks didn't like the implications one bit. Entering Piccadilly Underground, he passed through the automatic gates and rode the escalator down to the Bakerloo Line.

He wondered if meeting Mr V. J. was such a good idea after all. He wanted him to do something about Mungo Park before the little bastard shopped them to the police, but V. J. wasn't vulnerable. Park had never heard of him, didn't know the Go-Between existed either. That meant Wilks himself was the only man who posed a threat which was stretching things a bit because all he knew about the damned Go-Between was his phone number. On the other hand someone who was as paranoiac as Mr V. J. might well assume he had got Mungo Park to discover the Go-Between's name and address. The thought made his blood run cold. Mouth suddenly bone dry, Wilks boarded the half-empty Bakerloo train and chose a corner seat where he could watch both sets of double doors.

So who is being paranoiac now? he asked himself. If he did have this abnormal tendency to suspect and mistrust people he'd been dealing with, Mr V. J. was largely responsible for it. Their business relationship had started with a phone call from the intermediary and he'd received his instructions in a call box on New Oxford Street. Had he not received a retainer of £500 in advance, he would have dismissed the initial phone call as a hoax but the money had arrived by first post the following morning, ten £50 notes in nonsequential order. All subsequent payments had also been made in cash through the post. In every case, the banknotes had been wrapped in a plain sheet of A4 paper so that if anybody did hold the envelope up to the light, the money inside couldn't be seen. There had never been any covering note, the packages had never been sent by registered post or recorded delivery and the franking had shown the envelopes had been posted in different areas of London.

The question he had to answer was what sort of behaviour by the client would he have wished for? Would he have been happier if V. J. had been less of an enigma? Bearing in mind the information he'd been hired to obtain, Wilks concluded that the less he knew about the client, the safer it would be for him. As things stood, there was no reason for V. J. to regard him as a threat.

Alighting at Baker Street, he climbed the stairs to the upper level for the Metropolitan Line. After checking the departure times for the next two trains to Uxbridge and Rickmansworth, he decided to give them both a miss. Eight twenty-five; not a minute before, not a minute after – it was less conspicuous to waste ten minutes in London than in the outer suburbs. He eventually caught a train to Watford and was the only passenger to get out at Northwick Park.

It had been drizzling all day on and off but now a northerly wind had got up, driving the rain before it. On such a miserable autumn night nobody in their right mind was out and about, certainly not on foot. Wilks found Rushout Avenue without any difficulty and walked towards the more brightly lit Kenton Road to reach the designated rendezvous. With incredible timing a dark blue Volvo 900 Estate pulled up beside him seconds after he arrived. Leaning across the passenger seat, the driver opened the nearside front door and invited him to get in.

'Mr V. J.?' Wilks asked.

'Indeed I am,' the driver told him, then apologised for the fact that the courtesy light was not working.

'No problem,' Wilks said, and clicked the seat belt into the housing near the handbrake.

V. J. pulled away from the kerbside and almost immediately turned right into a side road. Keeping to the back streets he made another two rights followed by a left to head back the way he'd come.

'So what is it you think I should know?' he asked in a voice that was only just audible.

73

'Mungo Park came to see me this afternoon; he's the former BT engineer who obtained the information you wanted. Before he hacked into the system, he assured me that if the Intelligence service did discover that some of their in-house records had been extracted, he would not be a prime suspect. Now he's saying he would be one of the men in the frame.'

'Do you believe him?'

'I can't make up my mind one way or the other.'

'Perhaps he is after more money.'

Wilks glanced sideways at V. J. It was difficult to judge the client's weight and height when he was sitting down. Not only that but he couldn't see too much of his face, only the profile. Dark, possibly of Indian extraction, very swarthy, one cheek pockmarked, black, bushy moustache.

'Well, Mr Wilks?'

'I suppose he could have been hinting for more money.'

'And what about you?' V. J. asked softly. 'Are you also dissatisfied, Mr Wilks?'

'My name's not Oliver Twist. I make a deal, I stick to it.'

'That pleases me greatly but what exactly is it you want from me?'

'If there is an investigation and Park ends up in the frame, he will turn informer.'

'He would betray you?'

'Yes.'

'And you, of course, know how to get in touch with my associate.'

Wilks felt his heart skip a beat. Although V. J. hadn't raised his voice or done anything to suggest he was angry, there was an air of menace in what he'd said.

'What are you implying?' Wilks said nervously.

'Nothing, I'm merely stating what is a fact.'

'I don't know who your associate is or where he lives; he's just a voice on the telephone. It's Park you need to worry about, not me.'

'Oh, I'm not worried, there's always a solution to every problem.' V. J. lapsed into silence and headed on through Kingsbury, tyres swishing on the wet road surface. 'I think we'll send him on a long holiday.'

'Good idea,' Wilks said.

'Make him disappear.'

'That's an even better one.'

'And you with him,' V. J. said, and chuckled.

Wilks looked sharply to his left and out of the corner of his eye, he saw something rear up from the floor directly behind him. In that same instant the significance of the failed courtesy light and V. J.'s quite unnecessary explanation suddenly dawned on him. Before he could raise a hand in self-defence, his head was completely enveloped in a heavily impregnated velvet bag. The sickly sweet odour was unmistakable: chloroform, he told himself, a split second before his brain ceased to function on a conscious level.

Chapter Seven

Yesterday had been grey and depressing – and not just the weather. Harriet had had every reason to be angry with him; he'd neglected to warn her he would be late home until he was on the point of leaving the office but she hadn't said a cross word. To be accurate, she'd hardly said anything to him. Distant, withdrawn, introspective: that had been Harriet last night and he hadn't needed to ask her why. In the space of a few weeks, she had lost their unborn child, then her mother, and had known real pain and grief. Nobody suddenly bounced back from a double blow like that; it was an uneven process, up one day down the next.

This morning things were different. The sun had come out of hiding to give a hint that maybe it wasn't too late in the year for an Indian summer to make a belated appearance and Harriet was definitely on the up.

With an obvious spring in his step, Ashton walked into Vauxhall Cross, showed his ID card to the security guard on duty in the entrance hall and made straight for the lifts. As he stepped into the first car to arrive, the guard called out to remind him he was supposed to wear the tag. Ashton slipped the chain on over his head so that the piece of plastic bearing his passport size photograph was prominently displayed on his chest. This fairly recent innovation was Roy Kelso's idea; it did not of course apply to assistant directors and above. Some of the junior grades thought the high-priced help should set an example but as Kelso had been the first to point out, rank did have its privileges.

The phone was ringing when Ashton walked into the office.

Certain that it had to be Frank Warren, he lifted the receiver and told him to come on up.

'You've got it wrong,' Garfield informed him. 'My office now, please. I've got a bone to pick with you.'

'Is this about Larissa Marchukova?'

'How did you guess?'

There were politer ways of ending a conversation and it was out of character for Garfield to act like a bear with a sore head. The stress of running what was undoubtedly the largest and most diverse department in the SIS was slowly getting him down. The break-up of the old Soviet Union had created more problems than it had solved. If anything, it had increased the workload, not diminished it. Before Gorbachev, foreign policy was dictated by Moscow and the republics towed the line. In those days there had only been one army, one navy and one air force to worry about and the Second Chief Directorate of the KGB had made sure there were no internal divisions. Now, in addition to the Russian Confederation, Garfield had to take into account the armed forces of the Ukraine and Kazakhstan, both of which had a nuclear capability. There was the ever-present threat that internal dissensions, the like of which hadn't been seen since the demise of the Romanov dynasty, could spill over and trigger a major conflict. Nor could he afford to ignore the lawlessness on the streets of St Petersburg and Moscow which could destabilise Russia and see some neo-fascist installed as president. Finally, his remit included the Balkans which was about as stable as weeping gelignite. If ever an organisation needed to have its charter revised to make it function more efficiently, it was the European Department.

Frank Warren had beaten him into the office and had left a note on his desk. It read: 'BT were very co-operative and gave me all the information I asked for. One dossier, is however incomplete. Would you give me a bell a.s.a.p.?' In this instance, Ashton decided that as soon as possible meant after he had seen the Assistant Director in charge of the European Department.

Although he had never crossed swords with Rowan Garfield, their relationship was not unlike a volcano which, despite having been dormant for a large number of years, was nevertheless still active and might erupt with little or no warning. More than anyone else, Hazelwood was responsible for that sorry state of affairs. He had gone all the way from junior desk officer to Assistant Director in charge of the Eastern Bloc and even when promoted to Deputy DG, had continued to act as if he was still Head of Department. This trait had in no way diminished after he had become Director General. Ashton caught the flak because Victor was forever using him as his personal foot soldier in operations that should have been conducted by Rowan Garfield.

But if Garfield was justified in feeling aggrieved so too was Ashton. In 1993, Garfield had sent a highly compromising signal to Riga in an effort to kick-start an operation aimed at ensnaring Pavel Trilisser, the Deputy Chief of the Russian Intelligence Service. However, instead of hooking Trilisser, the signal had blown Ashton's cover and he had ended up spending seventy-eight days in solitary confinement in Moscow's Lefortovo Prison.

'Larissa Marchukova,' Garfield said by way of greeting him when he walked into the Assistant Director's office. 'Would you mind telling me why you are interested in the lady? I'd like to know because we're only fifteen minutes away from morning prayers and the Director is bound to ask what I know about her.'

'She's the woman who was impersonating my wife and took a bullet in the head for her pains. Larissa was born in Riga and moved to Berlin where she met an Australian called Cheeseman whom she eventually married. That's all I know.'

'Which is a great deal more than we do. We've never heard of her.'

'Well, it was a long shot.'

'On the other hand,' Garfield said with obvious relish, 'we do know of a Major General Fyodor Aleksandrovich March-ukov, one-time commander of the 7th Air Division in Latvia.'

Marchukov had left the Soviet Air Force in 1987 at the age of forty-eight to manage the Aeroflot services in the Baltic States. When Latvia had become independent he'd headed up their national airline, Latvijas Avialinijas, which had been pretty remarkable because the Latvians usually had no time for the ethnic Russians in their midst.

'You could say they eventually put that right,' Garfield

continued. 'Gave him the old heave-ho when Baltia, a new airline offering direct flights to JFK New York, was formed in 1992. Didn't seem to do him any harm though; he still enjoyed the same standard of living.'

From personal knowledge Ashton knew that too was unusual. In Brezhnev's time senior career officers in the Soviet armed forces had been allowed to settle in the republic of their choice. Many of them had opted to retire in the Baltic States where food was more plentiful. Then the rouble had gone through the floor, Moscow had refused to increase their pensions and major generals like Marchukov had ended up as paupers. Aston had recruited one such veteran in Estonia, Leonid Nikolaevich Zelenov, Hero of the Soviet Union, holder of the Order of Lenin, whose hatred of Gorbachev and all he stood for had known no bounds.

'So how has Marchukov been getting by?' Ashton asked.

'He laid his hands on a couple of Tu-154Cs, the cargo version of the medium-range airliner, and set up as a freight carrier. He kept the planes just over the border in Russia, and ran the charter end of the business from an office in Riga. We lost touch with him in November 1993. Subsequently we heard from a low-grade, unreliable source that he'd upped sticks and gone to St Petersburg and was involved in the arms trade.'

'Is he married?'

'His wife's name is Alevtina.'

'What about children?'

'Come on, Peter, what do you think I'm running here? The Russian equivalent of the *Tatler*?'

It was possible that Lorraine Cheeseman was the daughter of Major General Fyodor Aleksandrovich Marchukov but the dates didn't fit. Lorraine had returned to Riga in March 1994 allegedly to visit her mother who'd suffered a severe heart attack and was in hospital. Marchukov, however, had left Riga some four months before his wife had been taken ill. Ashton supposed they could have split up but that was one assumption too many for his liking. Without a lot more information to go on, it was unsafe to make a connection.

'Could we ask the *Bundesnachrichtendienst* if they have anything on Larissa Marchukova? She had a job with a travel agent in Berlin.'

'I've got better things to do before morning prayers,' Garfield said curtly. 'Draft a signal and give it to the appropriate desk officer with my compliments.'

'Right.'

'And in future, please make sure the duty officer is properly briefed before you ask him. It would save us a lot of time and trouble.'

Ashton said he would be sure to remember that. What really angered him was the fact that Garfield was absolutely right. All the same, Rowan could have made the point without going off at the deep end. Maybe his wife, Eileen, had been giving him a hard time and he'd got out of bed on the wrong side this morning? It was an explanation Rowan would favour in preference to admitting the task of running a huge, unwieldy department was getting on top of him.

By the time Ashton had made his way down to the Security Vetting and Technical Services Division, he was in a much more equitable frame of mind.

'You should have rung me,' Frank Warren told him. 'I'd have come straight up and saved you the trouble.'

'It's not important, Frank. What's all this about one dossier being incomplete?'

'Oh, well, that's a guy called Mungo Park. Like the other four engineers he was with the Guildford Depot, but he left BT five months ago and moved away from the area.'

'I may have got it wrong but didn't you tell me the stand-alone system had come on line approximately four months back?'

'Yes, but the installation was completed some six to eight weeks before that. Everything was done on an ad hoc basis. We were short-staffed and unable to work full time on the project. I mean, Ken Maynard had to write and rewrite the programme in between doing his normal job in the Finance Branch. It's a miracle we got the show on the road when we did.'

Ashton smiled. 'I'm not criticising you, Frank. I just wanted to be sure this Mungo Park hadn't thrown up his job with BT before the installation work was completed.'

'I did wonder what you were getting at.'

'So what have you done about the four engineers whose names and addresses are known to us?'

The answer was quite a lot. Like MI5, the SIS had no powers of arrest and therefore operated in conjunction with Special Branch. Although they had less occasion to need their assistance than the Security Service did, contact was maintained through a liaison officer at Scotland Yard. Warren had already contacted Special Branch and made a bid for assistance with the Commander in charge of Operations. Except for Mungo Park, all the engineers lived in the Guilford-Haslemere area, which was policed by the Surrey Constabulary. Since they had a much smaller Special Branch than the Met, it was likely they would ask Big Brother to make up the numbers.

'I'm waiting to hear the final arrangements from Commander, Operations,' Warren continued.

'Who's going with the Special Branch officers?'

'Myself and Brian Thomas. I thought we could tackle two apiece.'

'And Mungo Park? What have you done about him, Frank?'

'Very little at present. I'm going to check with the Post Office to see if he'd arranged to have his mail redirected.'

'If you give me his old address in Guildford, I'll take Park on.'

'That would be a big help,' Warren said

'Better tell your friendly policeman that we will need an extra officer from Special Branch, preferably the Met. I've got nothing against the Surrey lot but I could be dodging about the country looking for Park and I'd appreciate a bit of continuity. OK?'

Warren said he would get on to it and let me know what had been arranged. Leaving the Admin Wing, Ashton returned to his office on the fourth floor and drafted a signal to the BND. He also drafted one to the British High Commission in Canberra. Specifically, he wanted to know what, if anything, Larissa Marchukova had told Roger Cheeseman about her father.

★   ★   ★

Office hours were nine to five. Mildred liked to arrive fifteen minutes ahead of time in order to deal with the post and listen to any messages which might have been left on the answer machine. The final part of her routine was to have a pot of tea ready and waiting to be poured when Basil Wilks walked in on the stroke of nine.

Although her eyes were still bloodshot and the lids sore from the CS gas, it had not occurred to her to take the day off. Arriving at the usual time, Mildred let herself into the building, collected the bottle of milk that had been left on the doorstep and then emptied the letter box. She didn't bother to look at the envelopes. The prostitute and her dreadful maid, Beatty, never received any letters or bills. Neither of them lived on the premises and everything was on slot meters – gas, electricity and telephone. Nose wrinkling in distaste at the faint smell of cheap scent which always seemed to permeate the hallway when she opened the front door in the morning, Mildred climbed the stairs and entered the office. Adhering to what was a well-established routine, she raised the sash window and placed the milk bottle on the ledge outside, then filled the electric kettle from the wash basin in the next-door office and plugged it in.

The Steadfast Agency specialised in bad debts, where the real money was, and credit ratings, which were semilegitimate but only a modest earner. Approximately ninety per cent of the letters addressed to the agency had to do with credit worthiness while the remaining ten per cent consisted of junk mail and bills. The debt collecting side of the business was conducted either face to face or over the phone. In all the years she had worked for Basil Wilks, Mildred had never known anything to be put in writing. The bad debts the firm was hired to recover were not enforceable in a court of law and she therefore assumed they were gambling losses.

She put the letters requesting assessments of credit worthiness on Basil's desk, retained the phone bill for payment and fed the junk mail through the shredder, then switched on the power point and brought the kettle to the boil. Nine o'clock came and went, then nine fifteen and still no sign of Mr Wilks. At half-past she rang his home number in Harrow and got his recorded voice on the answer machine regretting that he was not available at the moment.

Morning prayers had just finished when Frank Warren rang Ashton to say that the Met had assigned Detective Sergeant G. D. O'Meara to accompany him to Guildford. There had been a slight hiccup regarding transport because both Ashton and the Special Branch officer had left their vehicles at home and Scotland Yard's car pool was fully committed. Five minutes later Frank had rung back to say that the work detail had been rejigged and Eric Daniels was waiting for him in the basement garage.

Eric Daniels had spent twelve years in the Royal Military Police and had risen to the rank of sergeant before joining the SIS in 1979. He stood five foot nine and tipped the scales at a hundred and sixty-five pounds which meant he'd only gained a couple of pounds or so since becoming a civilian. Although a double chin was beginning to show, he had a full head of light brown hair and there was hardly a line on his moon-shaped face, which was not bad going for a man who'd turned forty-six.

He was a highly skilled defensive driver and the fact that a former Head of Station, Athens, was alive today was due in no small measure to Eric Daniels. In 1985 an active service unit of the Provisional IRA had attempted to ambush the SIS man on the way to the International airport. The terrorists' big mistake had been to open fire much too soon, thereby giving the former RMP sergeant plenty of time in which to execute a hundred-and-eighty-degree turn at speed. Familiar with this tactic, the IRA had sought to counter it by putting out a back stop. The gunman chosen for the job had been armed with a 5.56mm Armalite M16 fully automatic rifle and a totally unjustified belief in his own immortality. Instead of presenting the smallest possible target, he'd stood in the middle of the road firing short bursts from the hip which had gone all over the place. Hunched over the wheel, Daniels had told his passenger to get down on the floor, then whipped the gear lever into second and flattened the accelerator. He'd used the car as a guided missile, steering it straight at the terrorist and had crunched into the gunman before he could bring the butt up to his shoulder for an aimed shot. The impact had knocked the would-be assassin clean over the car roof, killing him instantly.

In Ashton's opinion, Daniels was everything a good army sergeant should be – cool, steadfast, a bit of a hard nose but just as tough on himself as he was with those under his command. Ashton expected Detective Sergeant G. D. O'Meara to be cast pretty much in the same mould. He could not have been more wrong.

The Special Branch officer who was waiting by the enquiry desk on the ground floor of Scotland Yard was black, the same height as Daniels but a good thirty pounds lighter. The sergeant was wearing a pair of dark greyish blue slacks and a thin roll-neck sweater under a thigh-length fawn-coloured jacket.

'That's right, I'm O'Meara,' she said. 'I bet you're surprised.'

'Not really,' Ashton said, then decided that trying to be politically correct was merely insulting. 'Well, maybe a little,' he added and smiled. 'I wasn't expecting G. D. O'Meara to be a woman. By the way, what do the initials stand for?'

'Geraldine Dawn,' she told him in a low voice. Her chin came up. 'Two names I dislike. That's why I answer only to O'Meara.'

'I'm glad we got that sorted out,' Ashton said.

As he rapidly discovered, O'Meara wanted to be treated the same as her male colleagues. When he went ahead and opened the near-side front door for her to sit up front with Daniels, she immediately got in the back. She was also very businesslike; no small talk for Sergeant G. D. O'Meara. Nobody had told her why he was anxious to locate Mungo Park and she expected to be properly briefed. Although in common with all Special Branch officers she had been cleared for constant access to Top Secret material, Ashton observed the golden rule of security and told her no more than she needed to know.

'Exactly when did this Mungo Park leave BT?' she asked when he had finished.

'Five months ago, on Friday, May the twenty-sixth.'

'And we're starting our enquiries at the sub-post office nearest his previous address?'

'That's right.'

'I wonder if they will have any record of him.'

'We won't know that until we ask the sub-postmaster, O'Meara.'

'Sure. It's just that if you get the Post Office to redirect your mail, it's usually for one or three months.'

'You can pay for longer,' Ashton said.

'Yes. Twelve months is the next option.' She paused then said, 'I wasn't suggesting we should give the post office a miss.'

In the event what they learned was purely of negative value. The sub-postmaster was keen to help but he didn't have any record of a Mungo Park of Flat 2, 468 Old London Road, nor did the name ring a bell with him. The delivery manager at the sorting office, whom the sub-postmaster insisted on phoning, was also unable to assist them.

Number 468 Old London Road was one of several million semidetached houses that had been built all over the country between the two World Wars. Whether in Guildford, Derby, Durham, Leicester or Nottingham they all looked the same. The house where Park had lived was on the outskirts of town, part of a 1930s ribbon development that had stretched hungrily towards London. Since those far off days, the property had been converted into two self-contained flats, each consisting of a kitchen/diner, bathroom/lavatory, bedroom and living room. Park had lived alone above the owner, a thin, sour-looking woman in her mid-sixties who appeared to have a soft spot for her former tenant, which seemed to be out of character.

'Such a nice, quiet young man,' she told Ashton. 'Very polite. I can't understand how he could have got himself into trouble.'

'He hasn't.'

'So why do you want to find him?'

Ashton groped for an explanation. The simplest questions were always the hardest to answer, especially when he couldn't give her the real reason. O'Meara came to his rescue.

'The Internet's being used to perpetrate an insurance fraud,' she said quickly. 'We need Mr Park as an expert witness. There are other engineers who could testify but he's the best.'

'Well, that's a relief. I'm glad he hasn't done something stupid.'

'Mr Park didn't leave a forwarding address with you, did he?'

'No, I don't know where he's gone.'

'Is the flat upstairs occupied?' O'Meara asked.

'Yes, but he won't have left his new address with her, she only moved in six weeks ago. Before that the flat stood empty for over three months.'

O'Meara thanked her for answering their questions and in almost the same breath apologised for the inconvenience, then turned away and went down the front path, leaving Ashton to make his own escape.

'There was no point in wasting any more time on her,' O'Meara said when he joined her on the pavement. 'She doesn't know anything and wouldn't tell us if she did.'

'How do you know?'

'I could tell by the way she treated me.'

Ashton wanted to tell her she was wrong but couldn't. The woman wouldn't look at O'Meara if she could help it and had answered her belligerently. The owner-occupier of 468 Old London Road was as racially prejudiced as any fully paid-up member of the National Front.

'For what it's worth I'd reached the same conclusion.' Ashton ushered her into the car, then got in beside Daniels. 'Question is, what's our next move? I know what I would like to do but you're the one with the warrant card.'

'I think we should start with BT and ask them how Park was paid. If it was by direct transfer they can give me the name of the bank. If he was paid in cash I doubt if he kept the money in a tin box under the bed. So I'll make the rounds until I find where he deposited it for safekeeping.'

Once it was known what bank Park had been using while he was living in Guildford, O'Meara believed it would be comparatively easy to find out the address of the branch to which the account had been transferred. Furthermore, no matter where the account was located the branch would have an address for the statements.

'There's no telling how long all this will take,' O'Meara continued, 'so if you would just drop me off at the BT office . . .'

'That's where we're on the way to now,' Daniels said, chipping in. 'Matter of fact we're nearly there.'

'How?'

Daniels surreptitiously adjusted the rear-view mirror so that he could see her better. 'That's easy, miss,' he said. 'I reckoned Mr Ashton would call in at the BT office so I looked it up on the street map before we left.'

'Eric used to be in the Military Police,' Ashton told her as if that explained everything.

'Really? I was about to say don't wait for me. I can make my own way back to London by train.'

'That hardly seems fair.'

'You know it makes sense.'

She was right, it did make sense. The warrant card would open any door for her and he would just be hanging around twiddling his thumbs and generally wasting time.

'There's a frequent train service to London,' she reminded him persuasively as Daniels pulled into the kerb outside the BT office.

'You win,' Ashton told her. 'Call me when you have something. I'm on extension 0028.'

'Thanks.' O'Meara moved across the back seat and opened the door. 'You won't regret this, Mr Ashton.'

'I know that.'

'I'll find this Mungo Park for you. He can't hide from me.'

'I know that too,' Ashton said.

O'Meara got out of the car, slammed the door and walked away, tall and proud.

'Now there goes a real cracker,' Daniels said appreciatively.

The phone rang for approximately twenty seconds before the answer machine kicked in. The familiar voice of her employer said, 'You have reached 3893. I'm sorry there's no one here to take your call at the moment, but if you would like to leave your name and number, I will phone you back later.'

Mildred hung up. She had rung Basil every half-hour since

arriving at the office and it was now two thirty. It was quite unlike him not to let her know what was happening and it was all very worrying. For all she knew, he might have been taken ill and was lying alone and helpless in his flat at Harrow. There was, she decided, only one way to find out. Leaving the office, she walked to Leicester Square underground to make her way out to Harrow.

Chapter Eight

Mildred got off the Uxbridge train at Harrow-on-the-Hill, climbed the stairs to the booking hall above and then made her way down to the bus station in College Road. No stranger to that part of London she knew that Basil Wilks had a one-bedroom apartment in a small block of flats behind St John's Church and the junction of Gayton Road with Sheepcote. She was also aware that he had a cleaner, a Mrs Bateman, who came in twice a week, on Mondays and Thursdays. However, today was Tuesday and the domestic help wasn't on the phone. What was her address now? Mildred frowned. Some road with a saint's name? Peter? Paul? John? Or was it a woman? St Joan? St Ann? No matter, if Basil Wilks didn't answer when she knocked on the door, probably one of his neighbours would be able to tell her where Mrs Bateman lived.

Mildred had started working for Basil ten years ago in the June of 1985 when she had replied to an advertisement for a secretary and bookkeeper which had appeared in the *Harrow Observer*. She had been living in Wealdstone at the time, had recently been widowed and was in a financial hole. The money wasn't very good, which was probably why she had been the only applicant. Had there been any competition, Mildred doubted if she would have got the job. In those days employers hadn't been interested in taking on women over forty, especially if, like her, they had little to offer.

Although she had learned elementary accounting procedures when a sixteen-year-old at secretarial college, she hadn't looked at a set of books for over thirty years until six months before her husband had died from a massive tumour on the brain. The work experience she had gained during those few weeks had not been something to shout about. For more years than Mildred cared to think about, the company secretary had been systematically milking Scarsdale Motors. If he hadn't suddenly done a bunk the fraud would never have come to light until her husband, Jack, had died. As it was, she believed the discovery that he was facing bankruptcy had hastened his death.

Wilks had conducted the interview in an office in Station Road he'd hired for the occasion. He'd told her a little about the agency, where it was located, the sort of work he undertook and had indicated that initially the successful applicant would only be required three days a week. As the business had expanded so had her salary and hours of work. Mildred wasn't so naïve that she didn't realise the books she kept were purely for the benefit of the Inland Revenue and merely reflected the tip of the iceberg. Moral scruples were for those who could afford them; when you had been faced with losing the roof over your head, cheating the tax man was something you could live with – and Mildred still could.

Mildred turned into Gayton Road and walked on past St John's Church. Gayton Court was the name the developer had bestowed with striking originality on the modest block of flats near the junction with Sheepcote Road. In all there were twelve apartments, four to each floor; Basil Wilks lived on the top floor overlooking the street. Instead of a lift, there were, to her chagrin, six flights of stairs which left Mildred feeling breathless by the time she reached the top floor. Even though she kept a finger on the bell for a full minute there was no reply from Basil. She had no better luck with the flat next door and it was the same story with the third apartment as she continued to move in a clockwise direction round the landing.

Her luck changed with the fourth and last, which was directly opposite Basil's. The woman who opened the door to Mildred was in her early thirties and obviously pregnant.

'I'm Mrs Scarsdale,' Mildred told her. 'I work for your neighbour, Mr Wilks. He hasn't been into the office today and he's not answering his phone. I wondered if you had seen him?'

'I can't say I have.'

'He has a cleaner who comes in Mondays and Thursdays, a Mrs Bateman.'

'Oh, you mean Carol. We often exchange the time of day.'

'Do you happen to know where she lives?'

'St Ann's Road, near the station. I've no idea of the number.'

Mildred thanked her, left Gayton Court and retraced her steps. Although she had rarely used the shopping centre opposite the bus station, she knew St Ann's Road was directly behind it. The one thing she hadn't bargained for was just how many doors she would have to knock on before finding somebody who'd heard of Mrs Bateman and could tell her exactly where she lived.

Mrs Bateman had three children under the age of ten, all of whom were home from school and decidedly hungry. No matter what Mildred said, she wasn't going anywhere until they had been fed. One demanded beans on toast, another wanted beefburger and chips, the third asked for fish fingers and spaghetti hoops. They all settled for Coca-Cola to drink. Cooking three separate meals took the best part of forty minutes; eating them in front of the TV was almost as time-consuming. After what seemed an eternity to Mildred, Mrs Bateman loaded her family into an old Ford Escort that had seen better days and drove round to Sheepcote Road. Making more noise than an army on the move, the children followed them into Gayton Court and clumped their way up to the top floor.

The flat looked spotless and about as lived in as a photograph in *Ideal Home*. They went from room to room but there was no sign of Basil.

'He didn't come home last night,' Mrs Bateman announced. 'The bed hasn't been slept in.'

'Are you sure?' Mildred asked.

'Of course I am. It only gets made properly when I come in. Any other morning he just pulls the sheets and blankets up. Sometimes he doesn't even bother to plump up the pillows.'

'Well, that seems to be that,' Mildred said.

'What are you going to do about Mr Wilks?'

'Report him as a missing person, I suppose. Where's the nearest police station?'

'There's a big one on the Northolt Road before you get to

South Harrow. Are you sure he's missing? Personally, I'd check with the family before I went to the police.'

'Do they live locally?' Mildred asked.

'I haven't the faintest idea.'

'I thought you'd know.'

Mrs Bateman steered her towards the door. 'I only see Mr Wilks now and again. Usually he leaves my money in an envelope on the hall table. On those rare occasions when he forgets, he comes round to my house on a Saturday morning.'

As she left the flat it occurred to Mildred that she hadn't seen any photographs in either the bedroom or living room to show that Basil was not alone in the world. Thinking about their long-standing relationship, she realised how very little Basil had told her about himself. She understood he had been born in Ormskirk but had no recollection of the place because his parents had moved down to Welwyn Garden City when he was a year old. She couldn't recall Basil ever mentioning a brother, sister, wife or girlfriend. He had, however, frequently spoken of his career in the Met and how it had been cut short on account of a duodenal ulcer.

'Can I give you a lift somewhere, Mrs Scarsdale?'

Deep in thought, Mildred missed half of what the younger woman had said. 'A lift?' she repeated hopefully.

'Yes. Where can I drop you?'

'That's very kind of you but I can catch a bus to South Harrow.'

'You are going to see the police then?'

'I don't think I've got much choice,' Mildred told her.

Ashton dug out the paper he'd been working on the morning Hazelwood had told him that Harriet was dead. Although Clifford Peachey hadn't enquired if he'd completed his analysis of the man most likely to succeed Boris Yeltsin, there was nothing else he could get his teeth into while he waited for O'Meara to come up with a result. Had Victor been in the office, he could have given him a progress report on the hacker but Hazelwood had been called to the Foreign and Commonwealth Office together with Bill Orchard, Head of the Asian

Department. Clifford Peachey had gone even further afield. He had flown to Washington DC that morning for one of his periodic liaison visits to the CIA.

Before leaving Guildford, Ashton had been tempted to stand down both Frank Warren and Brian Thomas, only to have second thoughts. Mungo Park might well be the hacker, but in the end Ashton had decided there was no justification for ruling out the other four engineers on the strength of what they'd learned about Park so far. Nor could he rule out the possibility that the hacker, whoever he was, had no idea why he had been hired to break into the stand-alone system. If that should be the case, they would be left with no alternative line of enquiry other than the late Lorraine Cheeseman.

In an attempt to discover a great deal more about her background, Ashton had rung the Defence Intelligence Service at the MoD with a list of questions concerning Major General Fyodor Aleksandrovich Marchukov. He'd also phoned Australia House and left a message for the Minister in charge of Administrative Affairs, the cover appointment for the Intelligence and Security Liaison officer.

Ashton put the finishing touches to the paper he'd written on Pavel Trilisser with a summary of conclusions and then gave the analysis a Top Secret classification because of the source material he'd quoted. That done, he marked the paper up for the typing pool and tossed it into his out tray. Nothing to do now but wait to hear from Sergeant O'Meara, the MoD, Australia House and Frank Warren. He looked at the telephone, willing it to ring and was visibly startled when it suddenly did. Lifting the receiver, he merely gave the number of his extension. The caller was a little more forthcoming and announced he was Defence Intelligence 3, brackets Air, then requested they went to secure speech. Ashton touched the button located on the cradle and a green bulb lit up to signify the scrambler was now activated.

'I'm all set to go,' Ashton said.

'So am I.' The squadron leader from DI3 (Air) cleared his throat, then said, 'About Marchukov. I'm afraid there's very little we can add to what you people already know about him. I should also warn you that what fresh material we do have to offer is almost entirely based on hearsay.'

93

Defence Intelligence acquired their information through the Signals Intercept Regiments, satellite aerial photographs and service attachés. Aerial photographs had no part to play in shedding light on the private life of Major General Marchukov. Signals Intercept had picked him up a number of times when he'd been commanding 7th Air Division but only in an operational context. What they had on his family had been gleaned by the Defence Attaché, Riga, and the squadron leader wanted Ashton to be aware that no such post had existed when Marchukov had been a serving officer.

'By the time our man arrived on the scene the General was running his own airline and was about to move to St Petersburg. What we have on his present life is how his Latvian colleagues saw him when he was in charge of their national carrier. I don't have to tell you what the Latvians think of the Russians so what they had to say about him should be taken with a pinch of salt.'

'I'll keep that in mind,' Ashton told him.

'All right. Well, first of all, his wife is said to be three years older than he and has a face like a lump of dough. She is also as wide as she is tall. Daughter Valentina takes after her. Fyodor Aleksandrovich married the woman because her father was a member of the Politburo and he was out to further his career.'

They had ceased living together as man and wife when he'd left the Soviet Air Force to head up the Aeroflot services in the Baltic States. By then, father-in-law had been dead for several years, which meant Marchukov had had nothing to fear from that quarter.

'He found solace with an Aeroflot flight attendant, a shapely blonde called Larissa who was reputed to be hot stuff in bed.'

A blonde, Ashton noted and was disappointed because that was the second thing which didn't tie in with his knowledge of Lorraine Cheeseman. In life her hair had been as dark as Harriet's. She had read German and English at the University of Riga and was a teacher not an airline attendant. In short, there was some fairly strong evidence to show that Lorraine Cheeseman, née Larissa Marchukova, was not the General's daughter or his mistress.

'I think that's about it.' There was a sharp click which suggested the squadron leader had snapped his fingers. 'Nearly forgot,' he said cheerfully, 'Larissa had one deformity, the top joint of the little finger on the left hand is missing. Apparently she lost it in some sort of industrial accident when she was working for Aeroflot.'

Ashton was back in the mortuary, the body on the slab covered by a sheet. He had been told the dead woman was Harriet and he was merely there to confirm the identity of the deceased. The attendant had folded the sheet back but only as far as the shoulders. Although her face had been badly shattered, Ashton had known at once that the corpse on the slab was not Harriet and that had been the end of it so far as he was concerned. He had looked no further and when they'd met again a fortnight later, Orwell hadn't mentioned the mutilated finger when he'd told him the dead woman was Lorraine Cheeseman née Larissa Marchukova. But why should Orwell have said anything? He'd no reason to suppose Ashton was in a position to help the police investigation.

'I don't suppose you happen to know her present whereabouts?' Ashton said.

'You suppose correctly,' the squadron leader told him. 'We only took notice of her when Marchukov left the air force to join Aeroflot. He was an outstanding major general and my predecessors in this appointment all thought he would end up as a marshal of the Soviet Union. They couldn't understand why he had turned his back on such a glittering career. They kept looking for some hidden agenda until finally it became blindingly apparent that there was no master plan. That's when his file went into the dead sack.'

Ashton thanked him, said he'd been very helpful and meant it.

'My pleasure,' the squadron leader said, and hung up.

The phone rang again a few seconds after Ashton had put it down and switched off the scrambler. Answering it, he found he had the Minister for Intelligence and Security at the Australian High Commission on the line.

'You wanted to know the date of Lorraine Cheeseman's birth, Mr Ashton?'

'Yes, please.'

'It was the eighteenth of April 1960.'

'She was older than her husband?'

'By over seven years. Anything else I can tell you?'

'Well, this has only just come to light but did she have any deformities?'

'Deformities?'

'Yes. Visible distinguishing marks.'

'If she had any, they won't have appeared on her passport.'

'I thought perhaps Cheeseman might have sent you a complete description of his wife.'

'Hang on a minute.'

Ashton heard a faint rustling noise and guessed the Australian was going through Cheeseman's papers.

'Yeah, here it is,' he said moments later. 'The top joint of the little finger on the left hand had been amputated. Is that what you were after?'

'It certainly is. I owe you one.'

'I might just hold you to that, Mr Ashton.'

He had made a connection. So, all right, DI3 (Air) reckoned their Larissa was a blonde and the one in the mortuary had had black hair but she could have dyed it at some stage in her life, and for two women to have the same mutilated finger on the same hand would be too much of a coincidence. Ashton hadn't the faintest idea what it meant or how far it would take him but at least two pieces of the jigsaw had interlocked which was something to be thankful for. He'd also learned that Lorraine Cheeseman was an inveterate liar and nothing about her background could be taken on trust. Although the questions he had put to Canberra were no longer relevant, he didn't cancel his request for information because there was no telling what they might uncover. The same applied to the signal the European Department had sent to the BND on his behalf.

The phone rang for the third time in under ten minutes. Answering it, he barely had time to give the number of his extension before Sergeant O'Meara cut in. She didn't have to say anything, the tone of her greeting did it for her.

'You've found him then,' Ashton said.

'Through his bank. Park is now living at 251B Westbourne Terrace, London W2. That's near Paddington station.'

'You've done a terrific job. Where are you calling from?'

'The Yard. I had to bring some big guns to bear before the new bank would disclose his account number and address.'

Ashton glanced at his wristwatch, saw it was ten minutes past five and calculated he could put a team together and be ready to move by five thirty. They would be battling against the rush-hour traffic but he couldn't afford to wait until things had quietened down. Whether the hacker had one or two names or a complete list of every officer in the SIS, any unnecessary delay would be criminally negligent.

'Have you got a search warrant?' he asked.

'I had one when we drove down to Guildford,' she reminded him. 'All I have to do is fill in the new address.'

'Good.'

'But I think you will need a more senior officer than me on the scene.'

'I want you,' Ashton told her, 'and there's an end to it. Of course it'll do no harm to have a backup when we take him into custody. OK?'

'Yes. What time are we going in?'

'Six o'clock. Whoever gets there first waits for the other.'

'Understood,' O'Meara said, and hung up.

In the next few minutes Ashton rang Harriet to warn her he would be late home again, told the Motor Transport Section to have Daniels standing by for 17.30, then went down to the Security Vetting and Technical Services Division to break the good news to Terry Hicks that he would be working overtime.

Mildred allowed four buses to go by before she finally plucked up courage and boarded a number 114 to South Harrow. To walk into a police station and report the fact that her employer was missing took a bit of doing. Much of what Basil did was illegal and it was no use her pretending to the police that she didn't know what was going on. She had two options: either she didn't see the police, which could prove even more tricky for her in the long run since she had already involved Mrs Bateman, or she told them no more than she had to.

'Well, here goes,' she muttered to herself, and walked into the police station.

The constable on the desk looked absurdly young to her eyes and he acted as though she was much older than her real age. Prejudging the situation, he assumed Basil was her husband, was in his mid-seventies, and like a great many old men was becoming forgetful. His faintly condescending attitude underwent a rapid sea change after she had described Basil and what he had been wearing when she last saw him. Before Mildred knew what was happening she was introduced to the duty sergeant who went through everything she had told the police constable, before showing her into one of the interview rooms. When the Inspector in charge of the station took over from the sergeant, Mildred thought she was in for much of the same and was immediately taken aback by his first question.

'Do you know if Mr Wilks has any relatives?' he asked.

'I never heard him speak of any,' Mildred told him.

'And how long have you worked for him?'

'A little over ten years.'

'In what capacity?'

'As the company secretary. I keep the accounts and pay the bills.'

'I see. How many people are employed by the Steadfast Enquiry and Research Agency?'

'That depends on how much work we have. Mr Wilks hires people as and when he needs them.'

'So how is business?'

Mildred sensed danger and went on to the offensive.

'What has that got to do with it?' she demanded. 'I came here to report a missing person.'

'Let me put it another way, Mrs Scarsdale. Did Mr Wilks have any financial worries?'

'Not as far as I know.'

'Was he depressed?'

'No. What's going on?'

'I'm sorry, Mrs Scarsdale, but a man answering to the description you've given us was found by the main line into London, roughly a mile from South Kenton station.'

'When was this?' Mildred asked in a hollow voice.

'At five thirty this morning. The body was taken to Northwick Park Hospital. There is every reason to suppose the deceased had committed suicide.'

'Mr Wilks would never do a thing like that.'

'I'm not saying your Mr Wilks did take his own life but this man most certainly did. He placed his head on the line and waited for a train to run over it.'

Mildred felt the bile rise in her throat and gagged. Little imagination was required to visualise what a diesel locomotive would have done to skin and bone. From what seemed a long way off she heard the Inspector ask if Mr Wilks had any abnormal features and was on the point of telling him that Basil had bad teeth when she suddenly realised that virtually nothing would have been left of the mouth. The bile rose again and she felt clammy and faint.

'Are you all right, Mrs Scarsdale?' the Inspector asked. 'Can I get you a glass of water or something stronger?'

'No thanks.' Mildred took a deep breath and recovered her composure. 'Mr Wilks had surprisingly small feet for his height. Had to buy his shoes in the children's department or have them specially made.'

'I think that about clinches it. Of course we'll need somebody to formally identify the body.'

'You mean me?'

'I don't know of anyone else,' the Inspector said quietly.

'I couldn't bear to look at his face . . .'

'You won't have to, just the hands and feet.'

Mildred nodded. 'All right,' she whispered, 'let's get it over with.'

The car journey passed in a blur. The driver went up Roxeth Hill past Harrow Hospital and turned left at the top. She remembered passing Harrow School and St Mary's Church before joining the Kenton Road and taking the third turning off the roundabout.

She spent less than five minutes inside the mortuary and had only to see the tiny feet and nicotine-stained fingers to recognise Basil. It did not, however, end there; needing a statement from her, the police took her back to the station.

'I presume there will be a post mortem?'

'You can depend on it,' the Inspector told her.

'And a coroner's court?' she asked.

'Yes, but it will be a formality.'

'Because all the evidence points to suicide?'

'Yes.'

'What about his wallet? Was that found?'

'It was on his person. The wallet contained forty pounds but no means of identity. There's nothing unusual about that, Mrs Scarsdale. You'd be surprised the lengths some suicides go to to hide their identity. It's almost as if they wished to deny their existence.'

'What about his keys?' Mildred asked, unimpressed by what the Inspector had just told her.

'There were four on the key ring which was found in his jacket pocket.'

'Would that include the one for the Chubb safe in the office?'

'I'm not sure.'

'You couldn't mistake it, Inspector. It was a large brass one which was always making holes in his pockets.'

'What are you suggesting, Mrs Scarsdale?'

No matter what the risk to herself, she had to put matters right. Basil Wilks had been very good to her and somebody had to pay for what had been done to him.

'I'm saying Mr Wilks was murdered.'

'By whom and for what reason?'

'By a man called Mungo Park. He came to see Mr Wilks yesterday afternoon, tried to make out he hadn't received all the money that was due to him. He was very angry.'

'Do you know where he lives?'

Mildred nodded. 'Oh yes, he has the top flat at 251B Westbourne Terrace.'

'Really?' The Inspector clucked his tongue while he thought about it. 'Well then,' he said eventually, 'I think we will have to look him up.'

Chapter Nine

———⟫·◦·⟪———

Westbourne Terrace was a run-down version of Eaton Square. The houses enjoyed nothing like the same frontage and most of them had not been well maintained. Finding somewhere to park in the street was not easy and Ashton had to settle for a space outside number 269, some twenty yards beyond the house where Park was living. He had in fact done slightly better than Sergeant O'Meara, who was even further away on the opposite side of the road, although this was not apparent until she flashed the main beams to attract his attention.

Ashton got out of his car, crossed the road and walked towards the Ford Sierra. O'Meara had brought two plain-clothes officers with her. As he drew near the police vehicle, she joined him on the pavement.

'A few ground rules,' she said. 'This isn't a raid so we are not going to smash our way in with a sledgehammer. We'll knock politely on the door, I'll introduce myself and if necessary, produce the search warrant for Mr Mungo Park's inspection.'

'Fine, it's your show, Sergeant.'

'Also we're not going to rip up the floorboards or generally mess up his flat without a very good cause. And by good cause I mean hard evidence that he has been up to no good.'

'Well, I don't know what counts as hard evidence in your book,' Ashton said affably, 'but a decoder would be good enough for me.'

'Yes, that would take a bit of explaining. Who've you brought with you, Mr Ashton?'

'Well, there's Eric Daniels, whom you've already met. He

used to be in the Military Police and is a pretty useful man to have around, and then we have Terry Hicks, the electronic whiz-kid of Vauxhall Cross. He's mustard; what he doesn't know about electronic countermeasures and information technology isn't worth knowing. Unfortunately, he has a knack of rubbing some people up the wrong way.'

'He'll rub me up the wrong way if tries to plant an incriminating bit of evidence.'

'That would be counterproductive,' Ashton said tersely.

'Right. So who are you going to leave behind? All six of us can't go traipsing all over his flat. We'll be falling over each other and we shan't know who has looked at what.'

Ashton had no quarrel with that and told Daniels to stay with the car and watch the street. The evening was drawing in and the lights were on in most houses. Some people hadn't bothered to draw their curtains yet and observed them openly from the windows as they walked towards 251 Westbourne Terrace.

The front door was locked. O'Meara pressed the buzzer for the flat on the ground floor and, speaking into the microphone above the two buttons, informed the householder that she was a police officer and would he kindly let her in. A harsh metallic voice told her to prove it and shortly afterwards a black man with a Rastafarian hairstyle appeared in the window of the front room on the ground floor. O'Meara sidestepped from under the porch and held out her warrant card. After staring at it for several seconds, his lips moved mouthing the words, 'What do you want, girl?' In reply, O'Meara placed a finger to her lips, then pointed to the upstairs flat and finally got an affirmative nod. The Rastafarian left the window; moments later the electronic lock was tripped and O'Meara pushed the front door open and walked into the hall. As she did so the Rastafarian stepped out of his flat to ask what the honky upstairs had been doing. Nobody felt inclined to enlighten him.

'Fucking racist,' Hicks observed in a voice that was a long way from being *sotto voce*.

'Too bloody right,' the Special Branch officer said. 'If Park had been one of the soul brothers he wouldn't have let us in.'

O'Meara didn't say anything, merely clenched her free hand and squared her shoulders, two gestures which signalled her anger to Ashton. By the time they reached the landing, she had mentally shrugged it off.

The battery powering the doorbell was on its last legs and could only produce a low, clattering noise. Nevertheless a stocky, well-built man with short blond hair opened the door as far as the security chain would allow.

'Mr Park?' O'Meara politely enquired.

'What's it to you?'

'I'm a police officer, sir. My name is O'Meara and I have reason to believe that you have in your possession certain classified papers which are the property of Her Majesty's Government.'

'Don't be stupid,' Park said contemptuously.

'This is a search warrant,' O'Meara told him, and waved the paper in front of his face. 'Now please open the door and let us in.'

'I'm going to phone my solicitor.'

'Mr Park, there's something you must understand. I can use whatever force I consider necessary to effect an entry. So let's not have any more nonsense.'

Park removed the security chain, opened the door and stepped to one side to make room for them. 'You're making a big mistake,' he said.

The flat consisted of a fairly sizeable living room, kitchen, bathroom/lavatory and two bedrooms, the smaller of which served as a study. Ashton and the DC took the bedroom, kitchen and bathroom/lavatory, leaving the other two to search the living room and study, where the sight of a top-of-the-range computer and printer had made Hicks positively drool. His enthusiasm guaranteed that O'Meara would be subjected to a nonstop discourse on every aspect of information technology.

'I'm warning you,' Park said aggressively, 'if you damage anything, I'll have the shirts off your backs.'

'I should phone your solicitor then, like you've been threatening to do,' O'Meara suggested acidly.

Ashton didn't wait to see if Park took her advice; beckoning the detective constable to follow him, he went into the bedroom.

'We're looking for a printout,' he told the Special Branch

officer. 'It could be A4 size or larger. It will be graded Confidential and will list the personal particulars of certain government officials.'

Ashton couldn't say just how many sheets they were looking for. In alphabetical sequence, Harriet was the fourth name on the file but whether the hacker had called it a day when her details had appeared on the screen was open to speculation. Everything depended on what instructions he had received and to what extent he'd complied with them. If the hacker had stolen the whole file, he had a total of four hundred and seventy-six sheets in his possession, which would take a bit of hiding.

The bedroom was furnished with a divan, wardrobe, tallboy, and bedside table with a couple of haircord mats on the linoleum-covered floor. They began by removing every drawer from the tallboy before laying it flat to see if anything had been taped underneath the bottom panel. They then checked the inside prior to emptying the contents of the drawers on to the divan so that they could see if anything had been hidden under the paper, lining the bottom of each one. That done, they examined the socks, shirts, pyjamas, sweaters and Y-fronts as they returned them to the various drawers. They did the same with the wardrobe and drew another blank. They took the bed apart, inspected the duvet, looked inside the pillowcases and under the bottom sheet, then turned the mattress. The bedside table measured thirty inches by twenty-four by eighteen; the drawer contained four loose contraceptives and a box of aspirins.

'I thought it was only women who pleaded a headache,' the DC mused.

'Never mind that, let's take a look under the linoleum. It's not nailed down so we can flip it back easily enough.'

The linoleum was laid in strips, the joins partially concealed by the furniture and the haircord mats. They started by the door and moved the tallboy, hanging wardrobe and bedside table to the opposite side of the room. It was also necessary to shift the divan bed a couple of feet nearer the opposing wall in order to lift the strip and expose the floorboards. Examining them to see if any of the nails had been drawn and then tapped back again was a time-consuming business that had to be done on hands and knees, side by side. There were no claw marks, none of the boards gave under their weight and there was no sign they'd ever been disturbed.

'Doesn't look good,' the Special Branch officer said when they reached the other end of the room.

'We're only halfway through,' Ashton reminded him.

'Even so, Park is too cocky, he knows we are not going to find anything incriminating.'

'Five pounds says he's bluffing.'

'You're on, Mr Ashton.'

They relaid the lino, put the items of furniture back in their original positions, then moved the divan a good three feet towards the bedroom door and repeated the process. They had only just started on the other half of the room when the Special Branch officer found the loose floorboard which normally would have been directly underneath the divan bed. Park had done his best to hide the claw marks made by the extractor, infilling the grooves made in the wood with boot polish. He'd also replaced the original nails with marginally smaller ones which were just as worn but the board had been lifted so many times, the outline was sharply defined. The Special Branch officer produced a penknife, slid the blade under each head in turn and raised the nails high enough to withdraw them with his fingers. Lifting the board, he placed it to one side and reached into the cavity. Instead of a printout there was a large manilla envelope containing twelve hundred pounds in £50 notes.

'I guess Park doesn't trust the High Street banks,' Ashton said drily.

The doorbell came to life with a low buzzing noise and the previous muted clatter inside the dome. The Special Branch man thought it was Park's solicitor, so did Ashton. Both of them were wrong. Drawn to the living room by the sound of several voices they found O'Meara conversing with a uniformed inspector and two plain-clothes men.

'What's going on?' Ashton asked her.

'These officers are from Q District, Harrow and Brent,' O'Meara told him.

'Mr Park is wanted for questioning in connection with the murder of Mr Basil Wilks.'

'What the fuck are you on about?' Park shouted.

'I'm about to inform you, sir,' the inspector said calmly. 'I believe you are acquainted with a Mrs Mildred Scarsdale?'

'Yeah. What's that old cow been saying about me?'

'Do you have a solicitor you'd like to phone, Mr Park? If you haven't, we can always arrange for one to be present when you are interviewed.'

'Excuse me a minute,' Ashton said, 'but where are you taking this man, Inspector?'

'I don't believe we've been introduced. Who are you?'

'My name is Ashton. I think we should have a quiet word, Inspector.'

'Oh, do you?'

'Yes, on a matter of national security.' Ashton returned to the bedroom and waited for the Inspector to join him. When the door was closed he said, 'I presume you are planning to take Park to one of your divisional stations?'

'Yes, to Harrow, and that's still my intention.'

'You'll have to stand in line.'

'What do you mean?'

'You're not the only one who wants to interview Park. Apart from you, there's also a Detective Chief Superintendent Orwell.'

'Park was involved in that triple murder in Lansdowne Mews?'

'He almost certainly provided Lorraine Cheeseman with a false identity stolen from government records.'

'So I gather there is an element of doubt?'

'We haven't found the printout yet. On the other hand we did find twelve hundred pounds under the floorboards.'

'Interesting. I've got a witness who claims Park was demanding money with menaces from her employer.'

'Yeah, well, Park is tied in with the provos, that's why I recommend we lodge him in Paddington Green.'

Park's only connection with the IRA was the material possibly in his possession which they would give their eyeteeth for if they knew of its existence. As a police station, Paddington Green had more in common with a fortress. Not surprisingly, it was the place where the majority of terrorists of every political persuasion were held while they were being interrogated.

Although every interview was conducted strictly in accordance with judges' rules, there was an intimidating atmosphere about Paddington Green which Ashton hoped would have a demoralising effect on Park.

'You can have first crack at him, Inspector.'

'You're forgetting Chief Superintendent Orwell.'

Ashton shook his head. 'Orwell is going down a different road; he thinks what happened at Lansdowne Mews was drug-related. He can have Park after we've finished with him.'

'Well, all right, but I doubt we can get Park into Paddington Green.'

'I know a man who can,' Ashton told him. 'While you talk to your superiors, I'll have a word with him.'

Following the last reorganisation Ashton was now answerable to the Deputy DG but Peachey was in Washington liaising with the CIA, which gave Ashton the perfect excuse to ring Hazelwood. Victor had been locked in conference at the Foreign and Commonwealth Office with Bill Orchard when Ashton had left Vauxhall Cross to meet up with O'Meara. Although the meeting must have ended some time ago, he decided to try the office first on the off chance that the FCO had raised certain matters which Victor had felt he must attend to before going home. The supposition proved incorrect and he immediately rang the house in Willow Walk. Forced to use veiled speech because his Cellnet phone was not crypto protected, he briefed Hazelwood and asked him to pull a few strings with the Assistant Commissioner (Crime). When he switched off the phone, Ashton knew he had Victor's wholehearted support. Not so the Inspector; he was too far down the chain of command to gauge what sort of response his request would meet with.

Time crawled by. Park got more and more heated and finally did call his solicitor only to find he was not at home. While he waited for an answer from the Met, Ashton took O'Meara aside and discussed how they should conduct Park's interrogation. With no solid evidence to prove that the BT engineer was the hacker, there was, he argued, a lot to be said for letting the officers of the Q District have first crack at him. If Park got the impression the police reckoned he had murdered Wilks, he would be a lot more pliable when they got to interview him.

O'Meara wasn't too happy with the unspoken implication that they would dangle a carrot in front of him to ensure he co-operated with them. She still wasn't entirely sold on Ashton's tactics when Victor Hazelwood rang back to inform him there was a cell waiting for Park at Paddington Green.

There were only a handful of onlookers when they walked out of the house and the Rastafarian wasn't among them. Either few of the neighbours knew Park and therefore didn't care where he was being taken or else the sight of police cars in Westbourne Terrace was not a novelty. Ashton walked up the street and got into the Ford Granada next to Daniels, leaving the back seat to to Terry Hicks.

'Any luck, Mr Ashton?' Daniels asked.

'Not a lot, Eric. We've got the right man but we couldn't find the stuff we were looking for.'

'So where are the police taking him?'

'Paddington Green; we'll follow on behind.'

'Do you want me there when you question him?' Hicks asked in a plaintive voice.

'No, we'll drop you at the nearest Underground station and you can go on home to Alperton.'

'I've been thinking,' Daniels said. 'Maybe Park left the stuff with his girlfriend.'

'What girlfriend?'

'A woman in her thirties, about five seven, fairly slim, light brown hair, leather bomber jacket, T-shirt, short skirt, calf-high boots. I got a pretty good look at her when she passed the streetlight up ahead.'

'I should think you did,' Ashton said. 'Why do you reckon she knows Park?'

'By the way she acted when she saw one of the uniforms standing outside the front door. Turned smartly about and walked off.'

'That's worth knowing,' Ashton told him. 'It's one more fast ball I can throw at Park.'

Orchard could not remember the last time he had stayed on at the office long after everybody else had departed but this evening was one of those rare exceptions. He had returned from the Foreign and Commonwealth Office with a list of points to check which covered two pages of A4 and although the Queen's visit to India was still two years away, experience had taught him there would be a considerable number of changes made to the schedule before the tour programme was finalised. Since there would be God knows how many conferences to effect the various amendments, it was only prudent to stay ahead of the game.

He had earmarked the likely trouble spots, grading them as high, medium, and low security risks. Top of the list was Amritsar in the Punjab, which he had underlined three times. Indian nationalists had long memories and the city held a special significance in the struggle for Independence.

In 1919, extremists in the movement for Indian self-government had caused major disturbances in many parts of the country and nowhere had the rioting been more prevalent than in the Punjab. On 10 April 1919, the garrison commander of Amritsar, Brigadier General Dyer, had called out the Gurkha and Sikh troops under his command, after learning that a huge crowd of demonstrators were gathering in the Jallianwala Bagh. The Jallianwala Bagh was a walled garden with few exits, and without giving the mob adequate warning to disperse, Dyer had ordered his soldiers to open fire on the crowd. When the ceasefire was sounded, 379 Indians were dead and a further 1,200 were wounded.

In his defence at the subsequent Commission of Inquiry, Dyer had stated that he had believed the unrest throughout the country was on a scale similar to that which had preceded the Indian Mutiny of 1857–8, and had been determined to nip it in the bud. The Inquiry hadn't agreed with Dyer; instead the committee had severely censured the Brigadier General and required his resignation. As for Anglo-Indian relations, the incident had left a bitter legacy and history had been revised to some extent in later years with the number of fatalities being increased to over a thousand. Orchard had heard rumours that some of the exits in the Jallianwala Bagh were being walled off in advance of the fiftieth anniversary of Independence celebrations to make the massacre appear even more horrendous.

Amritsar was a trouble spot all right, and the walled garden was the sort of target to attract the Ananda Marg, a religious Hindu sect which had been linked to terrorist attacks around the world. Good Intelligence was the prime requirement; obtaining it was the problem. Head of Station, Delhi, was a hugely popular figure among the diplomatic fraternity but he didn't have any quality foot soldiers working for him. His input to Vauxhall Cross was entirely dependent on the goodwill of the Indian Intelligence Bureau and the Indian Central Bureau of Investigation. What was needed was a totally independent source of information and he could think of no one better qualified to fill the role than Logan Bannerman, Reuter's senior correspondent in Delhi. The trick was how, when, and where to arrange a meeting with him. It was a problem that Orchard eventually took home with him.

Ashton was in the police canteen drinking coffee with Sergeant O'Meara when the Inspector from Harrow sent word that Mungo Park was all theirs and awaited them in the interview room number six. He neglected to mention that the duty solicitor, a Mr Derek Meakin, was representing him. Before Meakin even opened his mouth, Ashton had him pegged as supercilious, arrogant and self-righteous.

'Your name please, officer,' he said.

'My name?'

'Yes. For the record.'

'For the record this is not an interview,' Ashton said, and switched off the video.

'That does it. I'm advising my client to keep silent and decline to answer any questions you may put to him. I'm also going to report you to the Police Complaints Authority.' Meakin glanced in O'Meara's direction as he pushed his chair back and stood up. 'Your colleague is being very stupid,' he said, 'don't make the same mistake.'

'Sit down please,' Ashton said. 'I'm Keith Messenger, write that down on your legal pad.'

Messenger was a standard alias used to preserve anonymity. Every defector who had ever walked into the British Embassy had been given the name. Ashton himself had travelled as Messenger with a passport to prove it.

'And this officer,' he continued, pointing to O'Meara, 'is G. D. Noone. That's spelled no one but pronounced Noone.'

'No one pronounced Noone,' Meakin snorted. 'Are you trying to be funny, Mr Messenger?'

'I never joke about national security. Your client stole a classified document when he was employed by British Telecom.'

'Rubbish,' Park snapped.

'He was cleared for occasional access to Top Secret and was required to sign a declaration when he left BT to the effect that he understood the provisions of the Official Secrets Acts still applied to him even though he was no longer in their employ. Despite this, your client used his technical skills to raid the data base of a government department, part of which he then sold for monetary gain.'

Park waved his hands dismissively. 'You already know what this is about, Mr Meakin. The police took my place apart and couldn't find a bloody thing.'

'You're forgetting the twelve hundred pounds that were hidden under the floorboards in your bedroom.'

'My client denies all knowledge of the money,' Meakin said. 'He maintains the cash must have belonged to one of the previous tenants.'

'And we've got forensic scientists who don't agree,' O'Meara told him calmly. 'They can prove the cache is a very recent innovation.'

'She's bluffing, Mr Meakin.'

'You gave the document and the decoder to your girlfriend for safekeeping,' Ashton said.

'What girlfriend?'

'Now you're being stupid, isn't he, Mr Meakin? We've got dozens of witnesses who saw her tonight. She turned back when she saw the police on your doorstep.'

'Yeah? What's her name, where does she live?'

'I don't know but you're going to tell us.'

Park turned to his solicitor. 'What did I tell you? The police are trying to frame me.'

'One person has already been murdered because of your client and I'm not referring to the unfortunate Mr Wilks.'

'Who?'

'Lorraine Cheeseman.'

Meakin blinked, which told Ashton he'd recognised the name and had been taken completely aback.

'Park fixed her up with a false identity from a file he stole from a government department. That's why she was killed.'

Ashton had no reason to suppose anything of the kind but the whole idea was to rattle Park and it was working because he didn't look quite so cocksure as he had a few minutes ago.

Now all Ashton had to do was give the screw a few more turns. 'But that's small beer,' he continued. 'Your client is sitting on a whole list of government officials which shows what they do, where they live. And Mungo knows precisely how much the IRA would pay him for that information. He's already a prime suspect in one murder case and a probable accessory in another. If he sells the printouts in his possession to the Provos, he would be well advised to plead guilty to whatever charges are laid against him. He'd be a lot safer inside.'

'Are you threatening my client?'

'If we don't get these printouts back we'll have to take remedial action. This means warning every individual that he or she is at risk and we're talking about several hundred people.'

They would have to be told why they were at risk and because of the numbers involved, they would know there must have been a major breach of security.

'To many it would be obvious that the information must have been stored on a database which had been illegally accessed. Sooner or later somebody will find out the names of the engineers who installed the system. Who can say what will happen then?'

'I take that as a veiled threat to my client,' Meakin said.

Ashton shook his head. 'I'm just trying to point out a few home truths. Not all of those who are in jeopardy are grey suits warming a chair behind a desk. Some of them, especially the ones on the ground in Ulster, have been living on the edge for years. I can name you half a dozen who are alive today because they shot first.'

Most of what Ashton had told him was a fabrication but it had sounded convincing and there had been enough rubbish written about the SAS for people like Meakin and Park to swallow it. The solicitor looked pensive and his client was definitely subdued. O'Meara was also unhappy but for very different reasons. She didn't approve of Ashton's methods and had said so loud and clear over coffee in the police canteen when they had been discussing tactics.

'Now I know why you wanted me,' she had told him angrily. 'It's because I'm black and therefore expendable.'

But she had declined to withdraw from the interrogation when given the opportunity to do so.

'What's in it for me?' Park suddenly blurted out.

Meakin cleared his throat noisily. 'I'd like to confer with my client in private. We seem to be breaking fresh ground and I need to take further instructions.'

'I think I can help you,' Ashton said. 'Your client was playing the World Wide Web and quite by chance, broke into an unguarded system. It was graded Confidential but this didn't convey an awful lot to him and he let it run on out of curiosity. It was only after he'd obtained a printout that he appreciated its real significance. By then he was too scared to know what to do with it. Am I right, Mungo?'

Meakin reached out, grabbed his client by the arm. 'Don't answer that before I know what is on offer.'

Ashton smiled. 'Well now,' he said, 'towards the end of your conference when you were taking instructions from Mr Park, he asked you what he should do about the document. You advised him to make a statement to the appropriate officer. Isn't that what happened, Mr Meakin?'

'Yes. Now tell me what my client can expect to receive.'

'At a guess I should think he will be charged under Section 1 (2) (b) of the Official Secret Act of 1920, neglecting to restore a classified document to a police officer. That's a misdemeanour and he'll get no more than a slap on the wrist.'

'I think we can live with that,' Meakin said.

'Good. So what have you done with the document, Mungo?'

'Like you suggested, I gave it to the girlfriend for safe-keeping.'

'Her name and address?'

'Samantha Yule, 88 Silverthorpe Avenue; it's off the Edgware Road.'

'Did you run the whole programme from A to Z?'

'There was nobody whose name began with a Z.'

'OK. Now think very carefully before you answer the next question. Apart from the identity you provided for Lorraine Cheeseman, have you provided the same service for anybody else?'

'No.'

'You'd better not be lying to me.'

'I'm not looking for more trouble than I've already got on my plate.'

'You were hired by Basil Wilks?'

'Yes.'

'Who was he acting for?'

'I haven't the faintest idea. Ask Mrs Scarsdale, she might know.'

Ashton mulled it over. It was of course a matter of judgement but he fancied that if Park had known who Wilks had been acting for, he wouldn't have hesitated to shop him. How Wilks had found the BT engineer was only of marginal interest to him and he didn't propose to waste any time questioning Park about it.

'All right, Sergeant,' Ashton said, turning to O'Meara, 'Park is all yours. Get a statement on tape for the record. I'll wait for you in the canteen.'

'You're not staying?' Meakin said incredulously.

'I'm not a police officer,' Ashton told him, 'but don't worry, I'll send in the genuine article.'

It took O'Meara a little over half an hour to record a statement from Park which satisfied all three parties. After that they drove round to 88 Silverthorpe Avenue, Ashton and Daniels in the Granada, O'Meara and two DCs in the unmarked Ford Sierra. Ashton remained outside the house while the three Special Branch officers had a quiet word with Samantha Yule. When they emerged a short time later with Park's girlfriend, O'Meara was carrying a fairly large brown paper parcel.

'That's the woman I saw in Westbourne Terrace,' Daniels said, angling the rear-view mirror to see her better. 'Head down, shoulders hunched; she doesn't look a happy soul.'

'Well, it just hasn't been her day.'

Ashton opened the door and got out of the Granada to meet O'Meara as she walked towards the car. The package she gave him consisted of 476 A4 sheets numbered in sequence.

'They're in alphabetical order,' O'Meara said, 'You'll find page 4 is missing.'

Abbot Roland, Ambrose Michael Gifford, Anning Jonathan Neil, Ashton Peter, Beale Juliette: Page 4 would have been Ashton Harriet née Egan.

'Frank Warren will sleep a lot easier in his bed tonight thanks to you.'

'I'm happy for him,' she said tartly.

'You've arrested Samantha Yule?'

'Yes. I want a statement from her incriminating the boyfriend in case Park and his solicitor allege coercion.'

'Right. I think we should interview Mrs Scarsdale when Q District have finished with her.

'*We?*' O'Meara repeated with emphasis.

'Yes. Does that bother you?'

'Only if you try to pull the same stunt as you did this evening. I am not your stooge, Mr Ashton. Next time I'll conduct the interview and you can play second fiddle. That way I've only got myself to blame if I have to face a disciplinary hearing.'

Chapter Ten

━━━━━━◆━━━━━━

The gates had been locked hours ago, closing off the short cut to Rylett Close through the park and on down the side of the Royal Masonic Hospital, which was the usual way home for Ashton. Harriet of course would take issue with the word 'usual'; due to the unsocial hours he worked there was no set routine. Dinner in the Ashton household was any time between 7 and 10 p.m., except for the not-so-very-occasional blip when he returned home even later. Tonight was one of those blips. Alighting from the Richmond-bound train at Ravenscourt Park, Ashton walked down the staircase to the booking hall below and out on to the street. Although it was a little late in the day to make amends, he set off at a cracking pace and kept it up all the way to Rylett Close via King Street and Goldhawk Road.

There was a light on in the hall but nowhere else as far as he could see. Thinking Harriet had gone to bed shortly after his last phone call, he entered the house with all the stealth of a burglar. He was less successful with the security chain which rattled as he tried to engage the lug in the slot.

'I hope that's you out there,' Harriet called from the living room at the back.

'If it isn't you're in trouble, girl.'

Harriet appeared in the hall wearing a quilted dressing gown designed more for warmth than glamour. 'Have you eaten?' she asked.

'I had a mystery sandwich in the police canteen. I think the filling had died of natural causes.'

'Will scrambled eggs do you?'

'There's no need,' Ashton said, and kissed her.

'I think there is.' Harriet went into the kitchen, took an already opened packet of smoked salmon out of the fridge and fetched a carton of farm laid eggs from the larder. 'You can make the toast,' she told him.

'I think I can handle that.'

'Is Frank safe now?'

'For the time being.'

'What does that mean? You got the file back, didn't you?'

'Yes, but I had to persuade Victor to adopt a softly-softly approach against his better judgement. Frank Warren is safe while the IRA observes the truce; the minute they revert to the bullet and the bomb he's on a knife edge. All it needs is for one of our people to be killed by the Provos and he's out on his ear. No question.'

Harriet broke four eggs into a mixing bowl, added a dash of milk and whisked them furiously. 'I don't think that's right.'

Ashton knew Harriet had always had a soft spot for Frank ever since the days when the Admin Wing had been located at Benbow House in Southwark. It had been Harriet who had sent a card congratulating Mary and Frank on becoming grandparents when Barbara, their daughter, had given birth to a son. And although they had only been colleagues for approximately fourteen months, she had learned more about Frank's personal life than Ashton ever had. But for Harriet he would never have known about Phil, the son who was perpetually out of work, living rough and hooked on a cocktail of crack and amphetamines.

'Frank wouldn't agree with you,' Ashton told her in the sure knowledge that Harriet wouldn't leave it alone. 'He realised he had put hundreds of lives at risk as a result of his stupidity. That's why he wanted to resign.'

'And you talked him out of it.'

'Yes, and dropped Victor in it at the same time.'

Harriet took a pair of scissors to a slice of smoked salmon and cut it up into small pieces. 'What is it with you and Victor?' she demanded. 'You're so damned loyal to him, you're blind to his faults.'

'Listen, if the IRA does break the ceasefire there's not much

Victor can do except remind everybody to be vigilant. He can't warn them that the Provos may know the home address of every SIS officer because he would be admitting he was aware there had been a major breach of security and had done nothing about it. And why? Because yours truly has persuaded him to let sleeping dogs lie so that good old Frank Warren could eventually retire on a full pension.'

'I'm proud of you,' Harriet said.

'If you're dishing out accolades you might like to remember Victor. Of the two of us, he's the one who has most to lose and he has a legion of detractors in the Foreign and Commonwealth Office who are just longing for an opportunity to bring him down.'

The two slices of bread popped up from the toaster looking more burned than brown. With his back to Harriet, Ashton disguised their charcoal appearance with a large dollop of butter on each slice.

'You've retrieved the file, haven't you, Peter?'

'Yes, it's in my combination safe at the office.'

Harriet turned the gas off, brought the saucepan over to the worktop and dished up the scrambled eggs.

'Looks delicious,' Ashton told her.

'Don't try to change the subject.'

'I'm not.' Ashton sat down at the kitchen table and started to eat. 'Ask any question you like,' he said between mouthfuls.

'All right, I will. You're not out of the woods yet, are you?'

'Not by a long chalk. The hacker is a man called Mungo Park; he was hired to steal the profile of any woman in the SIS. Yours was the first name up on the screen but he didn't stop there; he ran through the entire file, copied all 476 entries. Yours was the only one he sold but the other 475 were in his possession for damned near three months before they were recovered. Park won't admit it of course but he was looking for a buyer. Why else would he have stolen the whole file? And we've only his word that he made just one copy.'

'Do you think he was lying?'

'I'd like to believe he wasn't.'

'Well, you have got a problem.' Harriet left the kitchen and went into the living room. A few minutes later she returned with a bottle of Bell's and a siphon. 'Neat, soda or with water?' she asked.

'Just a little soda, please.'

He watched Harriet pour two somewhat large doubles. It was on the tip of his tongue to ask her how long she had been drinking whisky but wisely thought better of it.

'Did Park say anything you could actually take on trust?'

'There were a couple of things. He told me the man who'd hired him had been very specific about the information he was to retrieve from Frank's system, but he'd never met the client, didn't know his name or why he wanted the information.'

'What about this go-between who dealt with both men?'

'He's dead,' Ashton said bluntly. 'Put his head on a railway line last night and waited for a train to run over it.'

'Oh my God,' Harriet said in a horrified voice, 'what a terrible way to die.'

'The police suspect he didn't do it voluntarily.' Ashton finished the scrambled eggs, put the plate to one side and reached for the whisky. 'The question which really floors me is why did the client want to steal the identity of an SIS officer? I mean, Park has the necessary equipment and technical know-how to raid any system which isn't crypto protected. He could have lifted an identity from the Department of Health and Social Security records at Newcastle-upon-Tyne.'

'How many times did this Lorraine Cheeseman see Dr Ramash posing as me?'

'Once a fortnight over a period of eight weeks.'

'Then I think whoever killed those women wanted to implicate the SIS in some way. But don't ask me why.'

Ashton didn't; he hadn't really heard what Harriet had just said. His whole attention had been focused on the nightdress she was wearing. The shapeless quilted dressing gown so tightly belted around her waist had somehow come undone to reveal what lay underneath. Oyster-coloured, all satin and lace, the nightdress was the most exciting thing he had seen on Harriet in months.

'When did you get that?' he asked.

'This morning.' Harriet removed his plate, knife and fork and put them in the dishwasher. 'I was tired of looking antiseptic.'

'You've never looked that way to me,' Ashton said, enfolding her in his arms as she straightened up.

'You could have fooled me,' Harriet told him softly.

'I didn't know how to reach you. So many bad things have happened to us in the last few weeks.'

'I hope you do now.'

Ashton ran his hands up and down her flanks as if moulding the satin to her skin. She backed into him, her head bent forward and he kissed her neck, nibbling it gently, then ran a hand across her firm belly before cupping her breasts. Harriet raised the quilted dressing gown above her hips and sashayed from side to side, arousing him even further.

'Let's go to bed,' he said in a voice that was lost somewhere in the back of his throat.

Harriet turned about and threw both arms around his neck. 'Jesus, Peter,' she said through gritted teeth, 'what makes you think I can wait that long?'

The phone call was made over an unguarded radio link by a Russian speaker in Delhi. It was received by a man who answered to the name of Feliks at Headquarters, St Petersburg Military District. Because this establishment had been targeted by GCHQ the conversation was intercepted and recorded by a special telegraphist of 242 Signal Squadron based at Gallowgate Camp near Levisham in North Yorkshire.

The message was intended for a F. A. Marchukov, President of MIC Airlines, advising him that the contract had been agreed and a down payment of $250,000 received. A flight plan with refuelling stops at Larnaca and Delhi should be submitted to the appropriate authorities as soon as possible. The conversation was intercepted at 05.00 Greenwich Mean Time. In Delhi it was 10.30 a.m.; in St Petersburg the clocks were showing 09.00. A copy of the English text was sent to the Defence Intelligence Staff at the Ministry of Defence where it was routinely passed to DI3 (Air) without comment.

★   ★   ★

Ashton sorted through the incoming mail which the assistant chief archivist from Central Registry had delivered to his filing clerk while he had been conferring with Hazelwood. Nothing from the BND, no word either from Canberra yet but that was perhaps expecting rather a lot because the time difference meant the signal he'd dispatched yesterday morning would have reached the British High Commission during silent hours. There was, however, a note from Frank Warren reiterating much of what he had already told him verbally before Hazelwood's PA had rung to say his presence was required upstairs.

None of the BT engineers Frank and Brian Thomas had interviewed had had a good word to say for Mungo Park. Cocky – too bloody clever for his own good – a conniving little git with a nasty temper were just some of the character references they'd given him. But you couldn't hang a man up by his thumbs simply because he was unpopular.

'Can you spare a minute, Peter?'

Ashton looked round to see Frank standing in the doorway, a nervous smile on his lips.

'Of course I can,' he said, 'come on in.'

'I just wanted to thank you for everything.'

Ashton knew what was coming and cut him short before he became too effusive.

'It was nothing, Frank.'

And he wasn't being modest. He had spent an uncomfortable twenty-five minutes with Hazelwood before morning prayers, going over the same ground they had covered last night when he'd phoned Victor at home to inform him the printout had been recovered. After sleeping on it, Victor had come to the conclusion that no matter what he might have said last night, Frank Warren had to go, not in two years' time but right now. Sacking Frank was only part of the action Hazelwood had in mind. He wanted a list drawn up of those officers most likely to be targeted by the IRA. They would then be informed why they were considered to be in a high-risk category and urged to relocate. Victor also had in mind the contingency fund to compensate those who suffered financially as a result of moving house. Whether this was strictly legal was beside the point. It was Kelso who had offered computer access to the

Commandant of the Training School and thereby made the stand-alone system vulnerable to penetration. Consequently, it was in his interest to ensure the finance branch toed the line.

'I'm not going to forget what you have done for me, Peter.'

'A word of advice,' Ashton said tersely, 'don't open that bottle of champagne just yet. The Director could easily change his mind.'

What the hell was he saying? The decision had already been taken and he was simply ducking and weaving because he didn't have the guts to tell Frank.

'It's all right,' Warren told him, 'I know the score. I'm hoping for the best but preparing for the worst.'

'I'm sure it won't come to that.'

Nothing could be more hypocritical than to make such a claim without doing something to justify it. Maybe he would be tilting his lance at a windmill but he could tackle Hazelwood again and make him see that sacking Frank wouldn't solve anything. It might even prove counter-productive. Better to leave the accusing finger pointing at Mungo Park than to alert Whitehall to the fact that a really serious breach of security had occurred within Vauxhall Cross.

The phone rang, interrupting the argument he was preparing mentally for Hazelwood's benefit. With a murmured 'Excuse me' to Frank Warren, he lifted the receiver to find he had Sergeant O'Meara on the line.

'Do you still want to question Mildred Scarsdale?' she asked without any kind of preamble.

'Yes. I'd like to see what's inside the Chubb safe too.'

'You can do both at the same time if you meet me at the Steadfast Agency in Shooter Place.'

'Where's that?'

'Off Long Acre. Leicester Square is the nearest Underground station.'

'What time?'

'In half an hour?'

'Make it forty minutes,' Ashton told her. Vauxhall Cross was not well served by public transport and he wanted to get off a memo to Hazelwood urging him not to give Frank his marching orders until they'd spoken.

'Right, nine thirty it is.' O'Meara paused, then said, 'And this time, Mr Ashton, I'll do the talking. OK?'

'Yes. What did you get from Samantha Yule last night?'

'Very little. She did however give her boyfriend a watertight alibi, which delighted Mungo Park and his solicitor, Derek Meakin. Didn't make us too popular with Q District.'

Ashton said he could understand why they should feel a bit miffed at losing their prime suspect and then hung up. At some stage during their brief conversation Frank Warren had slipped away, which meant he could get a note off to Victor without wasting precious time getting rid of Frank. The memo he wrote, though short and very much to the point, was not entirely truthful. To stay Victor's hand, Ashton claimed it was vital the head of the Security Vetting and Technical Services Division remained in post at least until the assessment of those officers most at risk had been completed. Before leaving for Shooter Place he delivered the note to Hazelwood's PA. Morning prayers was still in session when he hopped on a 77 bus to Charing Cross.

Sergeant O'Meara was waiting for him outside the entrance to the Steadfast Enquiry and Research Agency with a locksmith from Chubb and a plump, worried-looking woman in her fifties, whom he correctly assumed was Mildred Scarsdale.

'I've already told the police all I know,' she informed him after O'Meara had introduced her.

'Well, we don't think you have,' Ashton said. 'Do we, Sergeant?'

'We want to satisfy ourselves you haven't overlooked any-thing – unintentionally, of course. Now let's go inside.'

Mildred Scarsdale opened her handbag, took out a key ring and unlocked the front door, then picked up the pint of milk which had been left on the step. The aroma of cheap scent in the hallway was overpowering.

'It wasn't always like this,' Mildred Scarsdale told them. 'When I first came to work here, a printer rented the ground floor. He used to turn out wedding invitations, menu cards, personalised stationery – that sort of thing. Went bust four years ago. Since then we've had a succession of tarts. Landlord makes a fine thing out of it.'

The outer office where Mildred Scarsdale held sway was furnished with a desk, three-drawer filing cabinet, stationery cupboard and two upright ladder back chairs only one of which had a padded seat. Although in good condition, none of the items matched and were obviously second-hand. A large old-fashioned typewriter protected by a dust cover took up a disproportionate amount of space on the desk.

'Where's the safe?' O'Meara asked.

'In here,' Mildred said, and opened the communicating door.

The safe was in the far corner of the room beyond the lavatory. Free-standing and slightly over five feet high, it weighed, Ashton calculated, close on two hundredweight and he marvelled that it hadn't gone through the floor. The man from Chubb checked to see what particular model he was required to open, selected the appropriate key from the collection in his metal work box and unlocked the safe.

'Anything else I can do?'

'The desk drawers are locked?' Ashton said.

'I have a key,' Mildred told him.

'What about the filing cabinet?'

'That too.'

'It would seem we have everything,' O'Meara said. 'Thank you for your help.'

'How do you propose to lock the safe when you've done with it?'

'I'm not bothered; we're going to remove the contents and take them away for examination.'

O'Meara waited until the locksmith had departed before asking Mildred if anything was missing from the safe. It took only a cursory inspection for her to assert that nothing had been taken.

O'Meara looked at the answer machine on the desk, rummaged around inside the safe and produced a small box containing a number of brand-new cassettes.

'Where are the others?' she demanded.

'What others?'

'Don't play games with me, lady. You know damned well I'm talking about the used tapes. Your Mr Wilks was the kind of enquiry agent who would record every telephone conversation he had with his less reputable clients.'

'If you say so,' Mildred said, and tossed her head, which Ashton thought was a curious gesture for a woman of her age.

'I took a statement from Mungo Park,' O'Meara said, switching to a different line. 'In it he claimed he had received two cheques from you; one for £750 as a down payment, and a second for £250 in settlement of his account. Correct?'

'That sounds about right,' Mildred said cautiously.

'Park subsequently returned the cheque for £250 and took £1,200 from the petty cash instead.'

In the unlikely event that Mildred Scarsdale had no idea what was coming next, she found out soon enough. O'Meara wanted to see the current main account, petty cash book, cheque book and bank statements. It didn't take long to discover that Mildred had been keeping two sets of books, one for the benefit of the Inland Revenue, the other for the personal information of the late Mr Wilks. There was nothing small about the amount of money that had flowed into and out of the petty cash account.

'I didn't want to know where the money came from or what it was for,' Mildred declared before O'Meara could ask her for an explanation.

'How very trusting of you, Mrs Scarsdale.'

'Listen, Mr Wilks was very good to me when I was desperate and I don't forget a kindness. I didn't ask any questions, I kept the books the way he wanted and prepared the accounts for audit.'

'The Inspector of Taxes will be asking you some very awkward questions.'

'You're wrong. When the balance sheet was returned by the accountants, it was Mr Wilks who signed the income and expenditure certificate. I'm in the clear.'

'Because you only dealt with the legitimate side of the business?' O'Meara suggested.

'Yes.'

'Prove it.'

'Certainly.' Mildred returned to her office, produced the same bunch of keys and unlocked the three-drawer filing cabinet. 'Everything's in here,' she said, 'correspondence, reports, itemised expenses, invoices.'

'You can unlock the desk drawers while you're at it,' Ashton said, intervening for the first time.

'There are only personal things in the drawer.'

'Then you've got nothing to hide, have you?'

'You might not understand this, Mr whatever your name is, but I value my privacy.'

'Just do as the man says,' O'Meara told her sharply.

Mildred's reluctance to unlock the drawers was understandable. Nestling inside was a steel-loaded rubber cosh and a can of Mace.

'I bet you didn't get this from Max Factor.' Ashton picked up the can. 'Half empty,' he said. 'Don't tell me it evaporated.'

'Possession of Mace is an offence in this country,' O'Meara said, 'but I'm sure you know this already.'

'Mr Wilks gave it to me for protection.'

'Whose? Yours or his?'

'Both of us, I suppose. I only used it the once.'

'And when was that?'

'The day before yesterday.'

'On Mungo Park?'

'I tried to, but he took the can away from me and sprayed Mr Wilks and myself.'

O'Meara gazed at the telephone on Mildred's desk. 'There's only one number for the Steadfast Agency in Yellow Pages, which means you answer every incoming call. Yes?'

'Except when I'm away, then the phone is permanently switched through to Mr Wilks.'

'So all the clients who wanted the agency to do something illegal and were naturally reluctant to put it in writing would telephone and make an appointment to see him?'

'I can't say. Whenever anybody wanted to speak to Mr Wilks and wouldn't tell me what it was about, I'd ask for their name and put them on hold while I briefed him. If Mr Wilks agreed to accept the call, I would patch them through; if he declined, I would make some excuse and hang up. I never eavesdropped on any conversation.'

'But afterwards he told you what had transpired?'

'I can only recall a couple of times when he did.'

'You mean Mr Wilks usually refused to answer your questions?'

'I never asked any.'

'You didn't?' O'Meara sounded incredulous. 'My God, you are a paragon of virtue.'

'You liked Mr Wilks very much, didn't you?' Ashton didn't wait for a reply. 'When you learned he had died in suspicious circumstances, you told the police you suspected he had been murdered and named Park as the killer. We know he didn't murder him but I believe the person who did was the man who indirectly hired Park to hack into a government file. Now anything you can tell us about that particular client will be immeasurably helpful.'

'I would like to help you but I can't. Mr Wilks never met the client, never talked to him either; everything was done through a middleman.'

'He must have known how to get in touch with the middleman. Otherwise, how could he have delivered the printout to him?'

'Mr Wilks was given a phone number.'

Mildred thought he might have committed the number to memory but even so he would have jotted it down in his notebook which was always kept under lock and key.

'In the safe?' O'Meara said.

'Yes.'

'Well, it's not there now, is it? Or the used tapes?'

'No,' Mildred avoided looking at either of them. 'After murdering him, the killer must have used his keys to get into the office and open the safe.'

'Didn't he ever say anything to you about this middleman?' Ashton asked.

'Only that he spoke English with an Indian or Pakistani accent.'

'The middleman could be the client?' O'Meara suggested tentatively.

Mildred begged to differ. Mr Wilks had told her the middle-man represented a Mr V. J. She didn't know whether these were simply his initials or whether his name was actually Veejay. She had no idea how he knew the agency could provide the kind of service he wanted.

O'Meara turned about to look at the three-drawer cabinet. 'Perhaps he started out as a legitimate client?'

'It's possible,' Ashton said. 'How do you propose to find out?'

'I plan to have the cabinet removed and Mrs Scarsdale and I will go through every file together.'

'That could take days.'

'Then you had better square it with the Deputy Assistant Commissioner, Special Branch,' O'Meara told him.

Chapter Eleven

Hugo Calthorpe could name half a dozen high-fliers in the SIS who would see a posting from the Head of Station, Moscow to the same appointment with the British High Commission in Delhi as a disastrous move, career wise. Had he aspired to head one of the major departments, Calthorpe would have shared their opinion but he was not an ambitious man. Furthermore, the thought of spending the rest of his service within the confines of Century House and subsequently Vauxhall Cross had appalled him. It was the kind of face-saving explanation voiced by those who had been passed over for promotion but in his case it happened to be true. Calthorpe had spent over six years in Moscow and had been highly regarded by both Sir Stuart Dunglass and his predecessor. On Calthorpe's return to London following an extended tour of duty in the USSR, Dunglass had made it known that he intended to employ him as the chief instructor at the Training School before making him Deputy DG to Victor Hazelwood when the latter eventually moved to the Director's chair.

Although flattered that he should be considered for the appointment, it was not a job he'd wanted. He'd had some experience of Hazelwood's methods when Victor had been the Assistant Director in charge of the Eastern Bloc but the knowledge that they would be working hand in glove was not the reason why he had turned the appointment down. The fact was he and his wife, Mary, both hated London and had no desire even to live within commuting distance of the capital. With the exception of eighteen months on the Soviet Armed Forces desk as a Grade III Intelligence officer back in 1971, Calthorpe had spent his entire service abroad. He had done two stints with the British Embassy in Washington and had had a lively time in Rome with the anarchist *Brigate Rosse*, who specialised in kidnapping and murdering members of the judiciary. When he left the SIS at the compulsory retirement age, he planned to live in the Algarve and had already bought a villa at Albufeira. However, in requesting to be considered for an appointment in Asia, the only relevant point Calthorpe could make was the fact that he had never been employed East of Suez.

Nevertheless it had been enough to persuade Sir Stuart Dunglass to look favourably upon his application. He had been assigned to Delhi because it so happened the resident physician to the British High Commission had insisted the then Head of Station should be sent home on medical grounds. As had been said many times around Whitehall, successful administration was often the result of the wise manipulation of coincidence.

Calthorpe had been blessed with a retentive memory and an ear for languages. Consequently he had mastered Hindi in a few months and had learned to write it in the Devanagari script. There had been no need for him to learn Hindi. Although Article 349 of the Constitution Act of 1950 provided that Hindi should be the official language, English was still used for official purposes and for the transaction of business in Parliament. The fact that Calthorpe had taken the trouble to learn the official Indian language had done his stock a power of good with officers of the Intelligence Bureau and the Central Bureau of Investigation. Foremost among his many acquaintances was Brigadier Ghani Kumar Choudhury, Deputy Chief of the Intelligence Bureau.

Whenever they met, it was always at some hotel or restaurant frequented by Westerners and Japanese businessmen. On this particular occasion Choudhury had suggested they dine at the Taj Palace Hotel on Sardar Patel Marg close to the Diplomatic Enclave in the Chanakyapuri District. Leaving his bungalow in the grounds of the British High Commission, Calthorpe drove off in the opposite direction to pick up Willingdon Crescent which skirted the North and South Blocks of the Secretariat, a permanent reminder of the British Raj. Still heading in a northerly direction, he continued on to Connaught Place, the Piccadilly Circus of Delhi but on a much larger scale. He went round Central Park looking for somewhere to leave his Volkswagen and eventually came across a vacant space near the Odean Cinema on Radial Road Number 5. After locking the vehicle, he retraced his steps to Central Park where he hailed a taxi and told the driver to take him to the Taj Palace Hotel.

It was customary for Calthorpe to arrive at a rendezvous some ten minutes ahead of Choudhury. On entering the hotel, he took a copy of *Time* magazine from the display rack in the lobby, paid the concierge and sat down in an armchair. The magazine told Choudhury that nobody had followed Calthorpe to the Taj Palace Hotel. Had he been empty-handed, the Indian would have ignored him and left the hotel after making a bogus enquiry at the reception desk for the sake of appearances.

Choudhury was over six feet, which made him the taller man by approximately five inches. He was also several pounds lighter but since Calthorpe tipped the scales at a mere ten stone one, the Indian looked positively emaciated in comparison. The long and short of it, Calthorpe thought as he stood up to greet the Deputy Chief of the Intelligence Bureau.

'I thought we'd talk over dinner,' Choudhury told him.

'Good idea.' Six o'clock was a little early for Calthorpe's liking but he put a brave face on it.

The Taj Palace had four restaurants – the Isfahan, which specialised in tandoori platters; the Hindi, famed for its Northern and Western Indian dishes; the Tea House of the August Moon, where you could eat Chinese, and The Orient Express. One of the most imaginative restaurants Calthorpe had ever seen, The Orient Express was a replica of a railway carriage. Boarding the observation platform, the two men followed the head waiter into the dining car and were shown to a table for two.

'Whisky?' Choudhury asked.

'With water please,' Calthorpe said.

'Good. Make that two large whiskies with a small carafe of water.'

After passing out of the Indian Military Academy at Dehra Dun, Choudhury had been commissioned into the 5th (Frontier

Force) Gurkhas and had virtually ceased to be an orthodox Hindu from that moment on. As a young officer he had drunk rum with his Gurkha soldiers and had seen active service, taking part in the overwhelming defeat of the Pakistani Army in the East which had led to the recognition of Bangladesh in December 1971. He spoke excellent English and had been an exchange student at the Staff College, Camberley. It was not a period of his life he cared to talk about. So far as the virulent anti-British members of the Congress Party and the Hindu nationalists of the Bharatiya Janatā Party were concerned, Choudhury had been tainted by the twelve months he had spent in England.

'Was anybody watching the British High Commission when you left?' he asked while they were waiting for their drinks to appear.

By anybody Choudhury was referring to reporters from the more scurrilous English language newspapers whose editors were always sniping at the erstwhile Raj and whipping up anti-British feeling. For the Deputy Chief of the Intelligence Bureau to be seen in the company of the SIS Head of Station would spell the end for Choudhury.

'Not a soul,' Calthorpe assured him.

'Good.'

'So when do I learn why you asked to see me?'

'It has everything to do with the Central Bureau of Investigation. They are anxious to interview various relatives of Mr V. J. Desai.'

'Desai.' Calthorpe frowned. 'Should we know this man?'

'I doubt it.'

'What's he done?'

'The CBI believe he was the brains behind the murder of Lieutenant General Rao Narain Singh, the former C-in-C of Eastern Command.'

Calthorpe gave a low whistle. Although the assassination had occurred before he had joined the British High Commission, he'd heard of the General and knew him to be the leading exponent of armoured warfare in the Indian Army. A dozen questions sprang instantly to mind but he was unable to voice them while the *maître d'hôtel* was waiting to take their orders for dinner. To speed things along, he had the same as Choudhury – seafood pancake followed by coq au vin.

'Who actually killed the General?' he asked after the head waiter had left their table.

'Three gunmen from the Ananda Marg. A man claiming to represent the military arm of the movement phoned the *Times of India* shortly after news of the General's death had been announced on All India Radio. He accused Rao Narain Singh of favouring the Muslim element of the population, which was ridiculous. He also stated the General had been executed because he had been treacherously lenient in his dealings with the Communist Government of West Bengal. However, the Chief of the CBI is convinced the real motive for the killing was to publicise the Ananda Marg and to demonstrate they are a force to be reckoned with.'

'And V. J. Desai? How was he linked to the crime?'

'The Delhi police received an anonymous tip-off. The writer alleged that V. J. Desai was the Director of Military Operations.'

'How do you know it wasn't a poison-pen letter?' Calthorpe groped for another way of putting it. Good as Choudhury's English was, he wasn't sure the Indian would understand the expression. It was, as he admitted to himself moments later, an insulting assumption.

'It could have been purely libellous, written out in spite but the fact is V. J. Desai is a prominent member of the Ananda Marg sect and he is well qualified to be the Director of Military Operations.'

Desai had been a captain in the Bombay Sappers and Miners; in training to be a bomb disposal expert, he had acquired the skill to construct an explosive device as well as the ability to neutralise one. On active service in Kashmir, he had demonstrated great tactical awareness and a cool head under fire. In Choudhury's opinion, had Desai stayed in the army he would probably have made one-, possibly two-star rank.

'He's clever all right, the CBI can't place him within three hundred miles of Ranchi when the General was shot.'

'Ranchi is where it happened?'

'Yes, three miles outside the city limits.'

'And these relatives you mentioned in passing?'

133

'The Central Bureau would like to question his sister-in-law, Mrs Z. K. Desai; they have reason to believe she has been living in London for the past two years. Unfortunately they do not have an address for her.'

'Finding her should not be too difficult,' Calthorpe told him. 'She will have been subjected to the usual immigration procedures on arrival. They'll have her on record.'

'I wonder. She is said to be travelling on a British passport these days.'

'You'd better give me her date and place of birth.'

'She was born in Agra on the sixteenth of April 1959. Her maiden name was Ramash.'

Calthorpe froze in the act of reaching for his whisky. The name immediately rang a bell with him and he knew in exactly what context: the overseas airmail edition of the *Daily Telegraph*, a triple murder in London. Choudhury wouldn't have seen it because it hadn't been reported in the *Times of India*. And if the biggest English language newspaper which published simultaneously in Bombay, Delhi and Ahmadabad hadn't carried the story, none of the Hindi papers like the *Hindustan* would have bothered with it.

'Was she a doctor?' he asked.

'Yes, as a matter of fact she studied medicine at the University of Delhi and later qualified as a clinical psychiatrist. Do you know of her?'

'Well, I think the odds against there being two female psychiatrists in London with the same name, initials, medical qualifications and ethnic background would be extremely high.'

'I wouldn't know, Hugo.'

'If I'm right, the lady is dead.'

'What?'

'She was murdered about three weeks ago, tied up and strangled.'

'Has anyone been arrested?'

'I haven't seen anything in the newspapers.'

Calthorpe stole a glance at his wristwatch: 6.20 p.m. and London was five and a half hours behind Delhi. Dinner with Choudhury shouldn't take more than an hour, so with any luck Calthorpe would be back at the High Commission before eight.

Allow half an hour to draft the signal to Vauxhall Cross and about as long again to encode it. If he gave it an Op Immediate precedence, the clear text should land on Bill Orchard's desk before he called it a day and went home. But first things first; he needed a lot more information from Brigadier Choudhury, otherwise the signal to Vauxhall Cross was likely to receive the file-and-forget treatment.

'Tell me something, Ghani Kumar,' he said, leaning a little closer to the Indian, 'what makes the CBI believe Dr Ramash was residing in London?'

If you were on shaky ground there was a good and a bad time to see Victor Hazelwood. The DG was at his most amenable when he'd had to attend some conference across the river and had managed to fit in lunch at the Atheneum before returning to Vauxhall Cross. He was at his most irascible when he had dined in the staff restaurant on the mezzanine floor and hadn't found anything on the menu to his liking. Ashton was on shaky ground because of the note he'd left with Victor's PA before leaving to meet O'Meara. He was not aware that there had been a rush on the steak and kidney pudding with the result that Hazelwood had been faced with a choice between steamed fish and shepherd's pie, neither of which had appealed to him in the slightest. It did, however, become obvious that all was not sweetness and light with his old guide and mentor the moment he opened the communicating door and walked into the DG's office.

'Who the hell do you think is in charge here?' Hazelwood demanded, and waved the memo at him. 'You or me?'

Ashton didn't respond. It was one of those occasions when it was best to say nothing and let Hazelwood blow off a head of steam.

'What's the matter, the cat got your tongue? You urged me not to do anything about Warren before we've talked. So why don't you tell me why he is so vital?'

'He'll be invaluable in assessing those of us who are most at risk.'

'We don't need Frank for that. I can tell you the prestige

targets for the IRA – myself, Clifford Peachey, the five assistant directors and the Commandant of the Training School.'

'I don't think it's that simple,' Ashton told him. 'I'm not saying they wouldn't give their eyeteeth to put any one of you in the ground but I've a hunch they will go for a softer target. They know that we raise our warning state at the first hint of trouble. It only takes a rumour for us to go from Bikini Black to Bikini Orange and suddenly you've got three armed officers living with you night and day. Maybe the assistant directors don't fare quite so well but each one will have a couple of bodyguards. The Provos are very publicity-minded; their aim is to bring off some headline-grabbing spectacular; taking casualties is the last thing they want. I believe they will go for the senior desk officers—'

'Like you,' Hazelwood said, interrupting him. 'That's what this is all about, isn't it? We know Park sold your wife's profile sheet and you want special protection for Harriet.'

'You don't hear me asking for it.'

'Of course I don't, you're much too clever for that. You prefer the subtle approach.' Hazelwood opened a cigar box and took out a Burma cheroot. 'It's not Frank Warren you're trying to save.'

Ashton clenched both hands, digging the nails into the palms, trying to hold his anger in check. Some things he couldn't control, the way his eyes narrowed, the harsh grating sound of his voice.

'Listen to me. Harriet is not a prestige target; killing her would bring them no kudos, only outright condemnation – young London housewife, mother of a two-year-old boy, recently suffered a miscarriage, mother just died of cancer. That wouldn't go down well in Boston, wouldn't do Noraid a power of good either. No, they'd want to hit somebody with an Irish connection even if it's only the surname.'

'The lowliest clerical assistant could compile a list of people with Irish-sounding names.'

'But the clerical assistant can't tell us which officers have served in Northern Ireland since the present troubles began back in '69. That's where Frank comes in.'

Hazelwood found a box of Swan Vestas, struck one and lit the cheroot. 'It would seem we're in accord,' he said.

'What?' Ashton said incredulously.

'Frank stays. Without him it would take twice as long to draw up a list of vulnerable personnel and put them in ascending order of risk. In fact you can tell him to start on the donkey work now.'

'What about Roy Kelso?'

'I'll inform him. You won't be involved.'

'That's what I hoped. Roy Kelso wouldn't take it well coming from me.'

'You've misunderstood me. The security review will be conducted by Jill Sheridan who will submit her recommendations to Clifford Peachey. The experience will add another string to her bow, which will be all to the good, career wise.'

Career planning wasn't something Victor had been noted for. As a subordinate you could expect an honest appraisal from him, highlighting your performance and ability in the annual confidential report he was obliged to write. It most certainly wouldn't occur to him that if you were given such and such a job it would raise your profile and improve your prospects of promotion. No, one of Jill's admirers had been lobbying on her behalf, probably Robin Urquhart.

'Is there something else you wanted to see me about?' Hazelwood asked.

'Yes, I need to retain Sergeant O'Meara,' Ashton said, and then told him what they had learned from Mildred Scarsdale and how they hoped to identify the man known as V. J.

'And you're worried the Deputy Assistant Commissioner in charge of Special Branch might take your sergeant away?'

'I'd hate to lose her before she'd examined all the files we took from the agency.'

'And Wilks thought this V. J. was either an Indian or a Pakistani?'

'Yes.'

'All right, brief Bill and tell him to have a word with Special Branch.'

When you were two rungs down the ladder from an assistant director, you didn't order people of Bill Orchard's seniority to do this or that without giving offence. This was certainly true of Kelso, Garfield, Benton and Jill Sheridan but good old Bill was the least rank-conscious officer in The Firm. Had he repeated Victor's instructions word for word, Bill wouldn't have turned a hair. Ashton, however, chose to put it more diplomatically.

'Naturally I'll talk to the Deputy Assistant Commissioner at Special Branch,' Orchard said, when he'd finished. 'The only thing I don't understand is why the Director should think the Asian Department would need to know about this Mr V. J. I mean, where is our interest apart from his supposed nationality? Granted he probably murdered those three women but that's a police matter. We're an Intelligence-gathering organisation, why should it concern us?'

'Because he stole my wife's identity to set up one of the victims.'

'Yes, that is a bit of a puzzle.'

It was all of that, Ashton thought.

On day one, Clifford Peachey had flown British Airways Concorde to New York, arriving there in theory an hour and ten minutes before he had taken off from London. He had then switched to American Airlines to make a dog leg down to Washington National where he had been met by the SIS Head of Station and conveyed to his house in Georgetown for lunch. From there he had been delivered to the CIA at Langley, Virginia. He had done the grand tour for VIPs – a ten-minute chat with the Director and then on to meet the Deputy Directors for Operations, Intelligence, Science and Technology and Administration. The guide dog who had been assigned to look after him and make sure he didn't get lost in the complex was a middle-ranking officer in the CIA's East Asia Division called Warren Treptow.

In the course of making small talk as they walked round the complex, Peachey had learned that Treptow knew Ashton and wished to be remembered to him. The last time the American had seen him was up at Lake Arrowhead, California, when Ashton had taken a bullet in the shoulder and was trapped inside a Ford Thunderbird that had landed on its roof after rolling over and over down a steep embankment. Peachey had come away from Langley with the impression that Treptow had a sneaking admiration for Ashton, which was more than could be said for Head of Station and his deputy. Their recollection of Ashton was more recent than Treptow's and dated back a mere six months. There had been a shoot-out involving Ashton on Nine Mile Road near Richmond, Virginia which had left three people dead, angered Richmond Police Department and won him no friends at all in the US Treasury's Secret Service. Head of Station and his deputy claimed Ashton had damaged the special relationship they had enjoyed with the CIA and had let it be known they never wanted to see him on their patch again. It was a point Head of Station had returned to over dinner last night and would have gone on and on about it if Peachey hadn't told him that nobody he'd met at Langley had seemed the least bit offended.

If yesterday had been frantic, today had been éven more so. The morning had been taken up by an extended visit to the Defence Intelligence Agency, following which Peachey had been whisked to Fort Mead to meet the top brass of the National Security Agency which, on a bigger scale, was in the same line of business as Government Communications Headquarters, Cheltenham. Now, less than three hours before he was due to catch British Airways Flight 218 which departed at 18.25 hours, he was in the FBI building on Pennsylvania Avenue. Although Peachey hardly knew Director Louis Freeh, he'd had a lot to do with Dean Rennert, Head of the Identification Division when he'd been with MI5. At the height of the Cold War they had kept each other informed of the KGB and GRU officers they had identified in the Soviet Embassies in London and Washington and had met twice a year to exchange information. Following the demise of the Warsaw pact, the liaison visits had gradually fallen by the wayside. In fact it was more than twenty-one months since they had last met and they had a lot of catching up to do. Peachey was on the point of leaving for Dulles International when Rennert dropped his bombshell.

'This truce you have with the Provos,' he said without any kind of preamble, 'do you think it will hold?'

'I hope so.'

'Are you still living at the Belmont Court in Cheyne Walk?'

'How do you know my address?' Peachey asked, his heart

suddenly skipping a beat. 'I only moved in there five months ago.'

'I got it from our Boston field office the day before yesterday. We keep an eye on Noraid and those who actively support the IRA. Anyway, one of our agents picked up this whisper that some fringe group of the Provos had got wind of your address in London. Seems they also knew you had left MI5 for the SIS.'

Chapter Twelve

Morning prayers were still half an hour away when Ashton walked into his office and found Bill Orchard waiting for him. The Head of the Asian Department was not noted for being an early bird; usually he arrived on the dot of eight twenty which, considering he lived in Kent and was entirely dependent on the notoriously unreliable south-east line, was a truly remarkable achievement. The fact that he had also pared his travelling time to the bone and had never been known to be late was indicative of a lucky streak that could only be attributed to St Christopher.

'Morning, Peter,' he said. 'I hope you don't mind me camping in your office but I thought you would like to see this signal from Delhi before I show it to Victor.'

The signal from Head of Station ran to the equivalent of two and a half sheets of A4. When the Cold War was on, Calthorpe wouldn't have sent a signal like this one which took up so much air time. He would also know that even in today's more relaxed climate there was a strong possibility that the lengthy transmission would be captured by the Russian Intercept Service.

After reading the text, Ashton could see that it just about rated a security classification of Confidential but on the face of it, the Op Immediate precedence was hard to justify. There was nothing so urgent that it couldn't have been sent to London in the diplomatic bag but Calthorpe was no fool and he wouldn't have sent it via the radio link unless he had good reason.

'Is there something going on in your part of the world that I don't know about, Bill?'

'No, things are pretty quiet even in Kashmir.'

Ashton wasn't taken in; the denial was too pat and it was obvious to him that Orchard was observing the need-to-know principle. He returned to the signal and read it a second time.

'What do you think?' Orchard asked when he'd finished.

'Calthorpe's right, there can't be two psychiatrists practising in London with the same name and initials. The British passport would explain why Immigration couldn't find any record of Ramash when she entered this country, especially if she didn't fly direct to the UK from India. She probably didn't use British Airways either.'

'The Indian authorities believe she spent a few days in Rome in June last year. She might have flown BA then. I mean there was no need for any subterfuge; as far as Immigration was concerned, she was a British citizen going on holiday.'

'Maybe. The trouble is we don't know if she did have a British passport; Calthorpe merely reports that Ramash is said to be travelling on one. In other words, it's a rumour. If the police found a passport in her name, they haven't said anything to us.' Ashton shrugged. 'Mind you, there's no reason why they should have.'

'When I show this signal to Victor, I'd like to inform him that we're already moving on it.'

'Fine. Don't take this the wrong way but what have you done so far?'

'Well, nothing,' Orchard said, colouring. 'You're the one who's had any dealings with the police. They don't know me from Adam.'

'And I know somebody who has more to do with them than me.' Ashton lifted the receiver, punched out extension 0127 and got Brian Thomas.

'A question for you,' he said. 'Do you know if Orwell found a UK passport for Ramash?'

'If he did, he hasn't told me.'

'OK. Do me a favour; ring the divisional station in Ladbroke Road and ask him. You can tell Orwell she was the sister-in-law of V. J. Desai.'

'Who?'

'Desai – that's spelled Delta, Echo, Sierra, Alpha, India. He's a prominent member of the Ananda Marg.'

'Is that the Hindu terrorist organisation?' Thomas asked.

'The same. You can also say our source of information is the Indian Central Bureau of Investigation in Delhi.'

'I'm sure that will impress him no end,' Thomas said in a voice as dry as dust.

'Just ring me back as soon as you can,' Ashton told him, and put the phone down.

'What else can you do for me?' Orchard asked.

'You want a lot for your money, Bill.'

'Well, I come from Leeds and like most Yorkshire folk, I know a bargain when I see one.'

'I'm going to try V. J. Desai on Sergeant O'Meara and ask her if he or anybody with the initials V. J. features in the agency files. And at present, that's about as far as we can go.'

'It's not much,' Orchard said in a mournful voice.

Ashton knew what he meant. Morning prayers were now just over ten minutes away and they were unlikely to hear from Brian Thomas before Orchard had to wend his way upstairs.

'You'll just have to pad it out a bit,' Ashton said cheerfully.

'Then again maybe I won't have to,' Orchard said as the phone rang.

It was, however, not Brian Thomas on the line. On the other hand, Orchard did get a brief respite. In her rather prim voice, Hazelwood's PA informed Ashton that morning prayers were to start fifteen minutes later than usual and his presence was urgently required by the Director.

It rapidly became evident to Ashton that he wasn't the only one Victor had summoned. On the way to the PA's office he passed Jill Sheridan and Roy Kelso heading purposefully towards the lifts. Jill seemed inordinately pleased with herself and wished him a cheerful good morning with a bright smile that flashed like a neon sign – on one moment, off the next. Kelso looked worried and was so preoccupied with his own problems that he walked right past Ashton without saying a word. Ashton presumed Jill had just been informed that she was to carry out the security review, which would certainly annoy Kelso and worry him more than a little. Some things you couldn't second guess; it never entered Ashton's head that he would be told to draw a 9mm Browning semi-automatic pistol from the General Stores Section.

'What's going on?' he asked.

'Clifford Peachey is on the hit list,' Hazelwood said tersely. 'While he was in Washington, a friend of his in the FBI warned him the Provos knew he was living in Cheyne Walk and had left MI5 to join us.'

'Where is he now?'

'At home. His flight from Washington arrived Heathrow at 06.45 this morning. By the time you've drawn a pistol and ammunition, Roy Kelso will have a car waiting for you in the basement garage.'

His instructions from Hazelwood were simple: he was to get himself round to Belmont Court in Cheyne Walk and stay there until two officers from Special Branch arrived to look after Ann Peachey. As soon as they had taken over from him, he was to bring Clifford into Vauxhall Cross.

When he reported to the General Stores Section, the armourer had already picked out a 9mm High-Power semiautomatic pistol for him. Ashton signed for the weapon and thirteen rounds of Parabellum ammunition in the arms register, then removed the box magazine from the butt and loaded it with all thirteen bullets.

He pushed the loaded magazine into the butt and slapped it home; turning away from the armourer, he pulled the slide back to chamber a round, then squeezed the trigger and, at the same time, eased the hammer forward with his thumb. With one up the spout, he had only to cock the hammer, which was a hell of a sight quicker than feeding a 9mm into the breach.

'How are you going to carry it?' the armourer enquired. 'Hip or shoulder?'

'Hip.'

There was nothing discreet about the 9mm Browning; it was powerful and bulky. The jacket Ashton had on hadn't been tailored to accommodate such a cannon, which meant the weapon was going to show no matter what sort of holster he wore. He chose a hip merely because it was easier to put on.

'When do you expect to return this gear, Mr Ashton?'

'Three, possibly four hours from now, depending how lucky I am.'

Ashton went down to the basement garage, asked the

transport clerk who had been detailed for the job in Cheyne Walk and was relieved to learn that Eric Daniels had been stood up for it. He walked over to the Ford Granada where the former RMP sergeant was waiting for him.

'I hope you've been told what this is all about,' he said.

'We're doing a bit of minding?'

'That's right.' Ashton opened the front near-side door and got into the car. 'Are you armed, Eric?' he asked before Daniels fastened the seat belt.

Daniels reached under the facia to the right of the steering column and produced a .357 Ruger Speed Six with a four-inch barrel.

'Neat,' Ashton said laconically.

'Has Scotland Yard authorised us to carry firearms?'

'I didn't ask.'

'Let's hope we don't get stopped by a police car then,' Daniels said, and pressed the revolver into the spring clips which held it fast under the dashboard with the pistol grip within easy reach of the driver.

Leaving Vauxhall Cross, they picked up the Albert Embankment, went on down Nine Elms Lane and used Chelsea Bridge to cross the river. Chelsea Embankment took them past the grounds of the Royal Hospital and into Cheyne Walk. Nobody had said speed was essential, which was just as well because it was stop-go all the way to Belmont Court.

Calthorpe left the British High Commission at four thirty in the afternoon, drove past the Norwegian Embassy and then headed west on Kautilya Marg. At the junction with Sardar Patel, he turned left, continued on past the Taj Palace Hotel and thence over the railway bridge into the cantonment, another reminder of the Raj. Sardar Patel merged into Parade Road and suddenly the clock turned back fifty years. Logan Bannerman, chief correspondent for Reuters in Delhi, lived just outside the old military and civil area with his Indian wife, Sumitra, on the road to Janakpuri. But Calthorpe didn't go straight to their bungalow; instead he crisscrossed the cantonment, one eye continually darting to the rear-view mirror to see if he was being followed.

Kyber Lines, Asmara Lines, up The Mall into Church Road then down Maude Road and west on Tigris. On past Kabul Lines into Sadar Bazar, a right turn to head northeast to Kotwali Road and thence into Church Road again. He drove past large, sprawling bungalows with wide verandas fronted by lawns and rampant bougainvillaea while doubling back to Parade Road. Some four hundred yards from the Taj Palace Hotel, Calthorpe turned left and followed the railway as it curved round the northern periphery of the cantonment. Finally satisfied that nobody was tailing him, he made his way to Bannerman's place on the Janakpuri Road.

The letter from Bill Orchard instructing him to liaise with the Reuters man had arrived in the diplomatic bag that morning. From the content it was clear that Orchard had written it before he'd received his signal concerning Dr Ramash, the late sister-in-law of V. J. Desai. In his capacity as Head of the Asian Department, Orchard had decided that his letter merited a Top Secret classification, which had made life difficult for Calthorpe.

Wary of using the public telephone in case there was a third party listening in, Calthorpe had no idea whether he would find Bannerman at home until he turned into the bungalow's grounds. Parked down the side of the building was the relic of British Colonial rule, the Hindustan Ambassador, a 1950s Morris Oxford manufactured under licence.

Calthorpe got out of the Volkswagen and climbed the short flight of steps leading to the veranda. Before he could ring the bell, Sumitra opened the door and made a traditional obeisance to him, hands pressed together, fingertips in line with the mouth, her head bowed.

'Who is it, Sumitra?' Bannerman asked in a harsh voice from somewhere inside the bungalow.

'It's Hugo Calthorpe.'

'Well, you'd better invite him in then.'

Logan Bannerman was in the sitting room at the back of the bungalow, sprawled in a teak and cane planter's chair with leg rests extending from the arms, and a shelf for drinks. He was wearing a short-sleeved white shirt and a pair of faded khakis with brown shoes. He was a thin wiry man not much above five feet six. Too many summers had dried out his skin, giving him a leathery appearance which made it difficult to judge his age. He looked well into his retirement years but in fact he had celebrated his fifty-first birthday just four months ago on 17 June.

'So what brings you here, Hugo?' he asked, and motioned Calthorpe to take a chair.

'I want to pick your brains about the celebrations for the fiftieth anniversary of Independence in two years' time.'

'Got a royal visit coming up, have we? HM and Phil the Greek?'

'You didn't hear me say that,' Calthorpe told him sharply.

'Course you didn't,' Bannerman agreed cheerfully.

The two officers from Special Branch arrived at eleven twenty, much to Eric Daniels' disappointment, though he did his best to hide it. The apartment the Peacheys rented in Belmont Court was the last word in comfort and he would have been happy to look after them indefinitely. For him the good life had been confirmed when Ann Peachey had served real French coffee and chocolate biscuits at ten o'clock. It had ended eighty minutes later when the Special Branch officers relieved them.

They made better time on the return journey. Ashton rode in the back with Clifford Peachey, both of them making only spasmodic attempts at conversation. They could not discuss the background to the current threat from the IRA in front of Eric Daniels because very few people were aware that there had been a major breach of security at Vauxhall Cross and it was essential to keep it that way. If that hadn't been inhibiting enough, there was also a mutual antipathy between the two men which involved Harriet and dated back to the day Ashton had begun to take an interest in her. Long before they had met, Peachey had cast himself in the role of her surrogate father when she had been employed in K2, the MI5 section that dealt with subversives. Right from the outset Peachey had made it clear that he didn't think Ashton was good enough for her. Not surprisingly his attitude had not endeared him to the younger man.

Back at Vauxhall Cross, Ashton went straight to the General Stores Section where he unloaded the Browning and returned the thirteen rounds of ammunition and the hip holster to the armourer before seeking out Frank Warren. Sooner rather than later there would be an inquest on this latest development in the saga of the stand-alone system. Victor had every right to ask how the Provos had learned where his deputy was living so soon after he had moved into Belmont Court. The trouble was the Head of the Security Vetting and Technical Stores Division made such a convenient scapegoat that it wasn't necessary to look elsewhere for a culprit. If that was the preferred solution, it followed that Mungo Park had made more than one copy of the file.

A very down-in-the-mouth Frank Warren was going through the vetting papers of the latest SIS intake under training at Amberley Lodge when Ashton walked into his office. There was no need to ask the reason for his hangdog expression.

'I take it you've heard the news about our Deputy DG,' Ashton began.

'From Roy Kelso. He and Jill Sheridan are sitting in judgement on me right now.'

'Come on, Frank, Jill has simply been charged with conducting a review on our security arrangements. She's not sitting in judgement on anybody; she has to submit her report and recommendations to Clifford Peachey.'

'I can't see him being neutral,' Warren said with a bitter laugh.

'Have you been interviewed yet?'

Warren shook his head. 'They are taking evidence from Ken Maynard.'

'Maynard? From the finance branch?'

'Why not? After all, he wrote the programme. Of course by now he probably wishes he hadn't.'

'Why's that?'

'Terry Hicks is a member of the Inquiry, he's the technical adviser to Jill Sheridan.'

Frank seemed to think she would find herself playing second fiddle to Hicks once the technological whiz-kid got on his hobby horse. But he didn't know Jill; she would squash Hicks like a bug if he tried to come the old soldier with her.

'Tell me something, Frank; was the profile card for Peachey as detailed as, say, yours or mine?'

'So far as I know it was. I can guess what you're thinking, Peter, but the task of preparing the input cards was shared between the whole vetting section. I knew what the total number should be but I haven't called every one up on the Visual Display Unit.'

'I'd like to take a look at Peachey's sheet.'

'I can't help you there, Peter. I wiped the whole programme. Remember?'

'I was thinking of the printout we retrieved from Mungo Park.'

'It's no longer in your safe, Peter.'

'What!'

'Jill Sheridan needed it for her security review so Roy Kelso got permission from the Director to look up the number sequence of your combination.'

Like everyone else who had been issued with a safe, Ashton had set up his own combination which, in accordance with standing orders, was routinely changed every three months. When he was off sick, away on holiday, or out of the country on detached duty there might be occasions when his colleagues needed a sight of certain documents lodged in his safe and couldn't afford to wait until he returned. To meet this contingency, he was obliged to put the combination to his safe in a sealed envelope which was then held by the chief archivist in central registry. Jill Sheridan had gone to Hazelwood, convinced him she needed to see the printout and he had given her written authorisation to open the sealed envelope containing the combination to his safe.

'Victor could have waited,' Ashton said, voicing his thoughts.

'Waited for what?' Warren asked.

'It's not important. How did you share the task of preparing the input cards?'

'I split up the alphabet; I won't say it worked out evenly.'

'So who did the P?'

'Brian Thomas, he's next door.'

'Good, let's go and see him.'

Even before he asked Brian Thomas to produce the input card for the Deputy DG, Ashton had a strong premonition that the actual format would be totally different from the run-of-the-mill. Peachey was a stopgap replacement who had been within eighteen months of retirement when he had joined the SIS back in March. The input card showed that his current PV status was not due for renewal until May 1998, by which time he would be a fully fledged civilian. There was a chance that he might be extended in post to complete three years in the appointment but that was irrelevant.

'According to the input card we don't have his security file?'

Warren nodded. 'That's held by MI5. Naturally we had a sight of the edited version before he came to us.'

The edited version meant that the operational contents had been temporarily removed. In Peachey's case this would have included extracts of the many interrogations he had conducted before going to K1, the Kremlin watchers. In pruning the file, MI5 had simply been observing the need-to-know principle and they had retained custody of the complete document in case any of the characters Peachey had interviewed in the past resurfaced in some other security context.

'There's no home address for Mr Peachey on this input card,' Ashton observed.

'That's easily explained,' Thomas said. 'He hadn't exchanged contracts on the flat in Belmont Court when I made out the input card.'

'The rest is also easy to explain,' Warren said, chipping in. 'When the Deputy DG finally did move in, Roy Kelso sent for me and said we didn't need to show his address on the profile sheet. He made the point that where he lived was only of interest to assistant directors and since they already knew his address, I could leave it out.'

'Does that ruling apply to Jill Sheridan and the others?'

'No, we've recorded where they live but then we have custody of their security files.'

'I think the Director should see this input card,' Ashton said. 'Mind if I walk it upstairs, Brian?'

'Be my guest. Incidentally, Orwell confirmed that Dr Ramash did have a British passport. It was found amongst her personal effects.'

'Does Bill Orchard know this?'

'Yes, he answered the phone in your office when I rang back. I caught him just before he left to attend morning prayers.'

'Good.'

'The passport wasn't kosher; it was stolen from a house in Ealing three years ago in the June of 1992. According to Orwell, the old-fashioned blue-coloured passports with hard covers were very popular with the criminal fraternity. Don't get me wrong, they weren't stolen to order but if a housebreaker came across one, he would take it because it was worth fifty-odd quid to him. There was a ready market for them amongst illegal immigrants.'

'Well, now we definitely know how Dr Ramash bypassed Immigration when she entered the country.'

'Yeah. I'm afraid I didn't have any luck with V. J. Desai. Orwell has never heard of him.'

'Never mind, Brian. I guess we can't win them all.'

Win them all? Ashton grimaced. That was rich considering he was running around busily getting nowhere. The input card he was holding proved the IRA hadn't obtained Peachey's home address from the Security Vetting and Technical Services Division. However, convincing Hazelwood that this was the case was another matter altogether.

The PA who looked after Hazelwood saw it as part of her duty to ensure he wasn't badgered by difficult subordinates. As Ashton knew to his cost, he occupied pride of place in her list of troublesome officers. Consequently she had taken great pleasure in informing him that the Director had told her he was not to be disturbed under any circumstances while he was conferring with the Deputy Assistant Commissioner in charge of Special Branch. She did, however, promise to let him know the moment Hazelwood was free. The phone started ringing as Ashton walked into his office But it wasn't the PA who was calling.

'Are you still interested in Fyodor Aleksandrovich March-ukov?' the squadron leader in DI3 (Air) asked.

'Yes. What's he been up to now?'

'A GCHQ signals unit in North Yorkshire picked up a radio

telephone conversation over an unguarded link between an unidentified male in Delhi and a man known as Feliks at Headquarters, St Petersburg Military District. The message was for Marchukov, who apparently is the president of MIC airlines. The guy in Delhi indicated that some kind of deal had been struck and he had received a down payment of 250,000 US dollars. On the strength of this, Marchukov was requested to submit a flight plan with refuelling stops at Larnara and Delhi.'

DI3 (Air) had alerted the Air Attaché at the British High Commission in Delhi and the station commander at RAF Akrotiri in Cyprus. Where, when and just what the airline was required to deliver had not been mentioned. However, the squadron leader recalled that when last reported on, Marchukov was said to be an arms dealer.

'When was his conversation intercepted?' Ashton asked.

'Thirty-two hours ago at 05.00 Greenwich Mean Time.'

'I take it Marchukov hasn't submitted a flight plan yet?'

'Correct.'

'And all this conversation was conducted in plain language over an unguarded link?'

'It's almost as if they wanted us to intercept it.'

'My thoughts exactly.' Ashton thanked the squadron leader for calling, asked to be kept informed of any developments and put the phone down.

Lorraine Cheeseman had had some sort of relationship with Major General Marchukov and had adopted his name. She had then assumed Harriet's identity and had been murdered along with Dr Ramash who was the sister-in-law of V. J. Desai, the man whom the Indian Central Bureau of Investigation believed was the director of military operations for Ananda Marg. And then there was Clifford Peachey who had been targeted by the Provos which some people believed was due to the information they had obtained from Mungo Park. In short it was the typical jigsaw the SIS was required to solve and, as usual, there was a good chance that not all the individual pieces belonged to the same puzzle. You would never see the complete picture because some of the pieces were bound to be missing, but in the end there would be enough of the whole to make a valid assessment. And nobody could reasonably expect more than that.

Ashton lifted the receiver and phoned Sergeant O'Meara. She had no news for him, they were still going through the legitimate files looking for a client named Veejay or somebody whose initials were V. J. She wasn't exactly thrilled when Ashton told her that the man in question could be a Mr Desai.

Hazelwood's PA eventually buzzed Ashton shortly after 3 p.m. with the news that the Director was now free if he still wanted to see him. Victor listened to what he had to say without once interrupting him, then examined the input card for himself before ringing Jill Sheridan.

'I'd like you to find the entry for Clifford Peachey in the printout,' he said, and hooked the handset into the amplifier on his desk so that Ashton could hear both sides of their subsequent conversation.

'OK, I've got it,' Jill said presently. 'What is it you want to know, Victor?'

'Just give me the details which appear on his profile sheet.'

'Well, there's his surname, Christian name, date and place of birth, marital status and the date when his PV status is due for review. Then, under remarks, it says "For further details refer to security file held by MI5." '

'It doesn't give his present home address?'

'No, that box is blank.'

'Thank you, Jill, that will be all.' Hazelwood disconnected the handset from the amplifier and set it down on the cradle. 'Frank Warren owes you a debt of gratitude,' he said. 'This is the second time you've saved his bacon. Now go and do the same for Clifford.'

'I thought Special Branch were looking out for him?'

'So they are,' Hazelwood told him. 'Your job is to find out how the Provos discovered his home address.'

Chapter Thirteen

One moment Ashton was fast asleep the next he was wide awake. Turning his head to look at the alarm clock on the bedside table, he saw the luminous hands were showing ten minutes past five on a dark, wet and windy morning. Beside him Harriet lay very still on her back, breathing deeply. He envied her, wished he could nod off but that was out of the question now because, much against his will, Clifford Peachey occupied his thoughts.

Then suddenly his bowels turned to water and he started to hyperventilate. Clifford Peachey at risk? Jesus Christ, what about Harriet? Between them, Basil Wilks and Mungo Park had sold her identity to a third party and maybe, for good measure, one of them had supplied a copy to the IRA. He should have phoned Harriet from the office and warned her not to go anywhere near the Ford Mondeo in case it had been booby-trapped. What could he have been thinking of? She could so easily be killed and Edward too.

'Are you awake, Peter?'

'Yes.'

'What's the matter?' Harriet asked softly.

'Nothing.'

'Don't be silly, I know you better than you think I do. So tell me what's bothering you.'

'It's not important.'

'Not important?' Harriet echoed. 'Now you're being ridiculous. One moment we are both sleeping peacefully and the next your body jerks as if you'd had an electric shock and suddenly we're both wide awake.'

'Let's try counting sheep, maybe we'll drop off.'

'Counting sheep never did anything for me,' Harriet said in a low voice. 'And I want to hear what's on your mind.' She gave him a playful dig in the stomach with a finger. 'Come on, I won't give you a minute's peace until you do.'

'It has to do with The Firm,' Ashton said, and then told her everything that had happened yesterday after Hazelwood had called him into his office.

'Frank Warren is off the hook,' he continued, 'and as a reward Victor has given me the job of discovering how the Provos learned that Clifford Peachey had moved house to Belmont Court.'

'I'm glad Frank has been cleared.'

'Yes, I thought that would please you, knowing how you've been rooting for him.'

'You're wrong, Peter, this time it's personal. If the IRA didn't get Clifford's address from the stand-alone system, then perhaps Park wasn't lying when he told you he'd made only one copy of the file and hadn't sold anything to the IRA. Or am I guilty of wishful thinking?'

'No, no, I believe your profile sheet was only seen by this man V. J.'

'Have you spoken to Clifford?'

'No, he'd left the office before Victor even briefed me. Told his PA he was suffering from jet lag. I suspect he didn't want to admit he was worried about Ann.'

'Well, he would be. Still, you can see him first thing this morning.'

'Maybe so, but I don't expect to get much help from Clifford.'

'Aren't you carrying your natural antipathy a bit far?'

'That isn't a factor.'

Ashton hesitated. Harriet's PV status had been suspended for three months which in practice meant she had no security clearance whatever. By rights he shouldn't tell her anything but that was plain ridiculous. In withdrawing her clearance, Victor had overreacted and had placed Ashton in an impossible position. Besides, Harriet knew the former MI5 man better than most.

'According to Clifford's friend, the FBI only learned that the Provos were on to him approximately four days ago. It's five months since he joined us and signed the lease on his flat in Belmont Court. It seems to me there are three possibilities: first, there is a Republican sympathiser inside MI5; secondly, we've got a mole in the SIS who is well disposed towards the Provos; or thirdly, Clifford blew his own cover through carelessness.'

'I would discount that possibility,' Harriet told him. 'You won't find anybody more security-conscious than Clifford.'

'We all make mistakes, love, nobody is infallible.'

If he was inclined to discount anything it would be the mole in the SIS. It had nothing to do with a touching faith in the integrity of the organisation he belonged to but rather the fact that any such mole would have had ample opportunity to garner information on more important targets. Why bother with the Deputy DG when you could finger the Director?'

'Did you ever meet anyone in MI5 who you thought identified with the IRA?'

'No.'

'OK. Do you know if Clifford ever served in Northern Ireland?'

'Clifford was in charge of K1, the Kremlin watchers, the day I joined the Security Service.'

'He must have cut his teeth on something. Why not Northern Ireland? This latest IRA campaign has been with us for over twenty-five years. Didn't he ever tell you what he did before K1?'

'No.' Harriet yawned. 'I've already said Clifford is very security-conscious.'

'Yeah, he's a paragon of virtue.'

'Look, instead of asking all these questions, why don't you read his personal file?'

Ashton wished he could but nobody at Vauxhall Cross had ever seen the complete file. All the operational stuff had been removed before it was sent across for Hazelwood's information. Even he wouldn't know if Peachey had done a stint with the army's 10th Int. Company. If the Deputy DG refused to talk about his past or gave Ashton reason to suspect he was being economical with the facts, Ashton would just have to refer the whole business to Hazelwood.

'You will sort it out,' Harriet murmured, and snuggled up to him.

'Thanks for the vote of confidence.'

'Oh, I have absolute faith in you.'

Very gently, he slipped his left arm under her neck, his other around her waist. She lay very still, her breathing gradually becoming more and more shallow until he could no longer hear her above the sound of the rain beating at the window.

The old-fashioned clockwork alarm which Ashton had carted around with him ever since his student days at Nottingham University failed to wake him and he would have slept on far longer but for the pins and needles in his left arm. He washed, shaved, dressed hurriedly, ate breakfast on the run and left the house. He walked swiftly through the drizzling rain towards the Underground and got as far as the gates to Ravenscourt Park when he suddenly remembered he hadn't done anything about the car. Retracing his steps, Ashton let himself into the house and collected the 'Peeper' from the umbrella stand in the hall.

The peeper was a stave some four feet in length with a mirror slotted into the tip at an angle of five degrees. Ashton pushed the mirror under the Ford Mondeo and walked round the car, checking the underside to make sure nothing had been attached to the chassis. A sixth sense warned Ashton that he was being watched and he looked up quickly to see Harriet looking at him with some amusement from the front bedroom. He gave her a cheerful wave, then carried on with the inspection. He carefully examined the interior of the Ford but could see nothing to indicate that anybody had tried to break into the vehicle. He aimed the sensor at the car and pressed it to deactivate the alarm and unlock the doors. He crawled inside the Mondeo and looked under the dashboard, then tripped the bonnet release and checked out the engine compartment.

The days when the IRA hot-wired a few sticks of gelignite and an electric detonator to the ignition were long since gone. In twenty-five years the bomb-making business had moved with the times into the high-tech era. Tremblers were now all the rage and they could mould Semtex to resemble a fuse box, even stamping it with a part number. There were, however, no extraneous attachments on the Ford Mondeo and the fuse box contained no foreign matter.

'Won't she start?'

Ashton stepped back a pace before he straightened up. He recognised the face and knew the man lived in Rylett Close but couldn't put a name to him.

'My wife said the engine was acting up yesterday,' he said, lying effortlessly. 'I found a loose connection.'

'Fair enough. I just wondered if you needed a helping hand.'

'Well, thank you.'

'Don't mention it,' the man said, and walked on.

Ashton closed the bonnet, walked round to the back and, waiting until the neighbour was out of sight, opened the boot and looked inside. Satisfied that the vehicle hadn't been booby-trapped, he slammed the lid down and activated the alarm and central-locking system before returning to the house where he found Harriet waiting for him in the hall.

'What brought all that on?' she asked.

'An innate sense of caution. If you're going to use the car today don't assume it's clean because I've been over it. Check the underside with the peeper before you get in.'

'Yes, sir.' Harriet saluted him, an amused smile on her lips. 'Have you any other instruction for me?'

'Yes, give me a kiss.'

'You're going to be late into the office.'

'Who cares?' he said. 'I'll probably be late home anyway.'

Morning prayers had been going for some twenty minutes when Ashton finally arrived at Vauxhall Cross. The clerical officer who filed everything Central Registry directed to General Duties for action barely gave him time to hang up his raincoat before she walked into the office with a phone message from Defence Intelligence and two priority signals, one from Canberra, the other from the BND, the *Bundesnachrichtendienst*, in Berlin. Ashton picked up the phone, rang the squadron leader in

DI3 (Air) and learned that Marchukov had submitted a flight plan.

'He's refuelling at Bahrain as well as Larnara and Delhi,' the squadron leader informed him.

'What's his final destination?'

'Kuala Lumpur.'

'He's going the long way round, isn't he?' Ashton said.

'Well, I suppose you could liken his Tupolev 154C to a tramp steamer going from port to port offloading cargo from St Petersburg in Cyprus, then picking up another load for delivery in Bahrain. On the second leg to Bahrain he will be overflying the Lebanon, Syria, Jordan and Saudi Arabia.'

'What's the date and time of departure from St Petersburg?'

'Today 12.00 hours GMT, his ETA at Larnaka airport is 15.10 hours.'

The Tu-154C would be cruising at 500 knots or 575 miles an hour at a height of 35,000 feet. The plane would spend two hours on the ground at Larnara before departing for Bahrain. Cruising at the same height and speed, the 1,125 mile flight would take approximately one hour and fifty-five minutes, which put the estimated time of arrival at Bahrain International airport at 19.05 hours GMT.

'What about the rest of the flight?' Ashton asked.

'We're still waiting to hear from Delhi. I know what you're thinking and I agree it's not unusual for a pilot to set off knowing that only half the flight plan has been confirmed. He appears to have a slip crew on board so it could be he will stop over in Bahrain until clearance is given for the rest of the flight.'

'What's the payload?'

'It's 39,680 pounds, the maximum permissible for this type of aircraft.'

'Do we know what the plane is carrying?'

'There's a fairly detailed manifest listing the firms and agents involved with a general description of the cargo. I can send you a photocopy of what we have so far or would you prefer to wait until we hear from Delhi?'

Ashton decided not to wait. Before sending the photocopy on to Bill Orchard for information, he thought it would be interesting to hear what, if anything, the Department of Trade and Industry had to say about the agents and firms listed in the manifest.

The signal from Canberra was in response to one he had sent to the British High Commission and was in the nature of a holding reply. Roger Cheeseman was in Tokyo attending a seminar on international law and thereafter would be engaged on a lecture tour of South East Asia sponsored by La Trobe University. Arrangements would therefore be made to interview him about the late Mrs Cheeseman's involvement with Major General Marchukov on his return in late November.

The signal from the BND in Berlin was much more informative. Detective Chief Superintendent Orwell had told him that after 6 July 1994, when Lorraine Cheeseman had sent her husband a letter from a fictitious address in North London, nothing had been heard of her until 9 August this year when she had resurfaced in Kensington. Now, those thirteen intervening months were no longer unaccounted for. According to the *Bundesnachrichtendienst*, Lorraine Cheeseman had been the Berlin representative of MIC Airlines with an office on Waltersdorfer Chaussee in the Rudow District within easy walking distance of the U-Bahn station.

Marchukov International Carriers transported freight not passengers, and operated out of Schönefeld Central airport sixteen miles southeast of the city. There was no scheduled service as such and flights were fairly infrequent, which did not augur well for the profitability of MIC, especially as most inbound flights were three-parts empty on arrival. In practically every case the short-haul Antonov An-26 were fully laden with consumer durables on the return journey. With a maximum payload amounting to 12,125 pounds the range of the Antonov was reduced to 683 miles which meant the planes could not reach St Petersburg without a refuelling stop. Both Customs and the *Kriminalpolizei* believed the refuelling stop was a former military airfield near Gorzów Wielkopolski approximately forty miles inside Poland. Although unable to prove it, the agencies were also convinced that the consumer durables, having been off-loaded here to wait onward movement at a later date, were replaced by top-of-the-range BMWs, Mercedes and Porsches which had been stolen to order and driven across the border.

The *Kripo* had kept an eye on Lorraine Cheeseman, pre-
viously known as Larissa Marchukova, because the luxury
apartment in the Charlottenburg District and her lifestyle did
not accord with the salary she might reasonably be expected to
receive as the Berlin rep of a rundown airline. The BND had
taken an interest in Mrs Cheeseman because of her connection
with a former major general in the Soviet Air Force. Both the
Kripo and the BND had come to the conclusion that, if not
actually engaged in prostitution, she was certainly liberal with
her favours. However, she had been very selective in that all her
companions had been wealthy businessmen or affluent politicians. A few days before her departure from Berlin on August,
she had been seen dining at the Bristol Hotel Kempinski with an
Indian gentleman registered as V. J. Ramash.

Ashton marked it up for Bill Orchard to see with the query
'Could this be Desai travelling under an assumed name?' He
then rang Victor's PA to ascertain whether morning prayers
were over yet. Specifically, he wanted to know if he had
authority to interview Clifford Peachey and should this be
the case, had the Deputy DG been warned to expect him? A
few minutes later he got a yes to both questions.

Clifford Peachey was quietly working his way down the clutch
of files that awaited his attention in the pending tray when
Ashton was shown into the Deputy DG's office by the PA.

'No peace for the wicked,' Peachey said with a faint smile,
and waved him to a chair. 'Mind if I smoke, Peter?'

Ashton shook his head. He could hardly object; furthermore
Peachey had no intention of waiting for his permission. Opening the bottom drawer in his desk, he produced a tin of his
favourite Dunhill mixture and proceeded to fill the briar pipe
which rested permanently against the old-fashioned pen and ink
stand.

'Fire away,' he said cheerfully, and struck a match.

'This friend of yours in the FBI,' Ashton began.

'Dean Rennert. What about him?'

'How close a friend is he? I mean, do you write to one
another at all?'

'We exchange birthday cards.'

'So Rennert would certainly have your previous home address in London?'

'That's true enough but I haven't got around to sending him a change of address card yet. Very remiss of me I know.' Peachey examined his pipe. 'You were perhaps wondering if Dean has a misplaced sense of humour and was twitting me about the Provos?'

'Something like that. Have you ever served in Northern Ireland, sir? I know you were in K1 when I first met you but I was thinking of way back in the mid-seventies or early eighties?'

'Like a good many officers from MI5 I did a spell over there from June '72 to March '74. Before your time, I imagine?'

'Very much so.'

Ashton had been a member of the University Officer Training Corps while reading German and Russian at Nottingham. He had joined 23 Special Air Service Regiment of the Territorial Army when he was taken on by British Aerospace as a technical author and translator after graduating with a good upper second. Bored to tears by his job, he had volunteered for a nine-month tour of duty in Northern Ireland with the regular army's Special Patrol Unit.

'Who were you with – 10 Company of the Intelligence Corps or the Force Research Unit?' Ashton enquired.

'The FRU.' Peachey drew on his pipe and made the spittal bubble in the stem. 'Strictly as a back-room boy,' he added. 'I was never on the street.'

'But you ran some of those who were?'

'From a distance,' Peachey agreed.

'Did you lose any?'

'Is that relevant?'

'It could be; if the Provos took out one of yours, some grieving relative might have shopped you out of revenge.'

'After more than twenty years?'

'They have long memories in Ireland,' Ashton said. 'They haven't forgotten Cromwell yet.'

'Well, let me set your mind at rest. I didn't lose anybody. At least not to my knowledge. We were very careful.'

Not every handler had been careful. Ashton had witnessed

the brutal execution of two informers on the night of Sunday, 10 February 1980. It had happened in Waverley Crescent, part of a large council estate on the periphery of Catholic West Belfast. He and Corporal Sally Drew, WRAC, had been sitting in the dark observing the street from the front bedroom of a semi-detached when a black taxi had drawn up opposite the alleyway between their house and the neighbouring one on the left. Three men and a woman had got out; two of the men had been wearing knitted masks that had completely enveloped the head and neck, leaving tiny holes for the eyes, nose and mouth. The third man had his wrists tied behind him and had had to be supported because his legs had kept buckling under him.

The woman's hands had also been lashed together behind her back but she had made a break for it and had fled down the road screaming for help. But she hadn't been able to run very fast in high heels and the taxi driver had caught up with her in no time. He had dragged the woman back to the alleyway kicking and screaming and the whole bloody neighbourhood had ignored her terrified cries. And so had Ashton because he had listened to Corporal Sally Drew and had been persuaded their cover would be blown if he intervened and seven months of hard and dangerous undercover work would go down the drain. So he had radioed for help instead while the Provos gunmen hooded and shot their victims in the head. And in the fifteen years since then, Ashton had lost count of the number of times he'd asked himself whether he'd been grateful for any excuse to chicken out.

'What's on your mind, Peter?' Peachey asked.

'I was trying to work out how the IRA tagged you as MI5. Are you sure your cover wasn't blown in Northern Ireland?'

'Positive. I rarely met my stoolies after the initial briefing. We communicated through drops, by pay phone and sometimes I would use a cutout. On the few occasions when a meet was essential, it always took place in a Protestant area.'

'All right, let's consider your friends and neighbours. Before you moved to Cheyne Walk, you were living in St John's Wood?'

Peachey nodded. 'Scott Ellis Gardens just behind Lord's Cricket Ground.'

'How many of your neighbours knew you were in the Security Service?'

'None. They were all under the impression I was a senior civil servant in the Home Office.'

'Did you give your new address to any of them?'

'I think Ann may have told some of her bridge friends.' Peachey frowned. 'And some of the ladies at the gold club,' he added.

'And presumably your new phone number?'

'Possibly.'

'Perhaps you could get their names and addresses from Ann.'

'You're not seriously suggesting that one of her closest friends could be an IRA sympathiser, are you?'

Ashton chose not to answer the question. 'Frank Warren didn't have your new address on his stand–alone system. I've checked the input card myself. As a matter of fact we don't have your security file but I expect you're aware of that?'

'Quite so. Gower Street wanted to hang on to the file because there's a lot of operational stuff on it.'

'When we had a sight of it, your new address wasn't recorded on the file.'

'It is now,' Peachey told him. 'And you're on the wrong track. We have an ongoing commitment with 10 Int. Company and the Force Research Unit. Because of this, every man and woman in the Security Service is subject to Irish screening in addition to the usual positive vetting. They are required to list every friend, acquaintance, and relative with an Irish connection, no matter how remote it might be.'

And by remote, Peachey meant English friends whose only connection was the fact they had gone on holiday to Ireland. The names were then run past the Special Branch of the Royal Ulster Constabulary and anyone in MI5 with the slightest connection with Sein Fein, the Provisional IRA, or the Protestant Ulster Defence Association was precluded from serving in Northern Ireland. Furthermore, an individual's employment could be terminated altogether should Special Branch turn up an Irish connection which had not been listed either deliberately or unintentionally.

'Well, that would seem to be it for the time being,' Ashton said after Peachey had finished his dissertation.

'For the time being?' Peachey repeated, and raised his eyebrows.

'We'll need to talk again after you've got those names from Ann. I'm hoping that you may think of some names too. It's not your friends I worry about,' Ashton told him, 'it's who their friends are.'

Chapter Fourteen

———⟫⟫·◦·⟪⟪———

When the white van pulled up outside the house the Ashtons' daily was upstairs cleaning the bathroom while Harriet was in the utility room transferring a load from the washing machine to the tumble dryer. The radio in the kitchen was competing with Edward who was banging his drum and winning the noise level hands down so that Harriet didn't hear the doorbell. She didn't hear Mrs Davies calling to her either, a state of affairs which persisted until the older woman walked into the utility room to inform Harriet that the man from Fairway Aerials had arrived to install the satellite dish.

'I don't know anything about a satellite dish,' Harriet said, 'and I don't want one either.'

'Will you tell him then?'

'Yes, right now.'

Harriet went out into the hall, unhooked the security chain and opened the door to find the man from Fairway Aerials was Terry Hicks. It was on the tip of her tongue to ask him what he was doing in Rylett Close but she bit it back, conscious that Mrs Davies was just behind her.

'No, don't tell me,' Harriet said in a resigned voice, 'after all I've said to my husband he has gone out and bought a satellite dish, hasn't he?'

Hicks was quick on the uptake. 'Afraid so,' he said. 'Paid for it with his gold card.'

Harriet looked back over her shoulder at Mrs Davies, told her that it looked as though the Ashtons were about to help keep Rupert Murdoch in the style he had become accustomed to and said she would see to the engineer.

'What did you say your name was?' she asked.

'Terry,' Hicks said, poker-faced.

'You'd better come in Mr Terry and I'll show you where the television is.'

'That would be a help.'

'I hope this aerial isn't going to look too unsightly,' Harriet said for her daily's benefit, as she showed Hicks into the sitting room. 'What's the idea?' she asked him when they were alone. 'Are you putting everything back again?'

Not so very long ago 84 Rylett Close had been a safe house. While no building was ever impregnable, the SIS had come very close to converting the property into a veritable fortress. The sentries had been the TV cameras mounted under the eaves which had covered the front, back and east side of the house, while the shared wall with the other semi-detached had been protected by audio sensors. The external line of defence had been an infrared intruder system which triggered a flashing light on the monitor screen in the cellar whenever the invisible fence was broken. Finally there had been a sophisticated burglar alarm connected to Hammersmith police station.

With Perestroika came the so-called peace dividend, the Treasury's favourite love child. Among many cuts, the SIS had been ordered to sell off fifty per cent of their housing stock at a time when the bottom had fallen out of the property market. Number 84 Rylett Close had been one of the houses put up for sale but thanks to Victor Hazelwood, the Ashtons had been able to buy it at a knockdown price before it was advertised by the Property Services Agency. Before they moved in, the house had been decommissioned, as Kelso had put it. The TV cameras, the infrared intruder system, and the audio sensors had all been removed. The burglar alarm had been left *in situ* but it was no longer connected to the police station. Should anyone break into the house while they were out, the alarm would emit a plaintive warble which in all probability the neighbours would ignore on the grounds that, like so many others, it was apt to go off for no good reason.

'What are we getting then?' Harriet asked.

'Well, the neighbours will think it's a satellite dish. However, from under the eaves it will throw an infrared fence around your

Ford Mondeo, always provided the car is parked right outside the house.'

The system not only sounded an audio alarm, it also presented an image on the monitor screen and automatically photographed the intruder. The only thing it couldn't do was alert the police.

'I thought we could put the monitor screen down in the basement like we did before.'

'It's a cellar, Terry. The estate agents who sold the property to the SIS called it a basement because it sounded bigger and they could push up the asking price.'

'Yeah, well, whatever; that's where I'll put the monitor.'

'Who's going to watch the screen?'

'I guess either you or Mr Ashton. So far as I know there are no plans to draft in Special Branch. I was planning to run a line up from the cellar and connect it to a buzzer in the sitting room. The idea is that when the buzzer starts whirring, you nip down to the cellar and see what's going on outside. Of course I could put it out in the hall so that you could hear it wherever you happened to be downstairs – in the kitchen, utility or dining room.'

'And when we are asleep upstairs, Terry?'

There was, Harriet learned, a simple answer to that question. The monitor screen was linked to a video cassette recorder loaded with a four-hour tape. Whenever the infrared fence was broken, the VCR was activated and would continue to record for however long the infra-red system was capturing an image. The moment the fence was restored, the VCR switched itself off. Anybody who intended to steal the car or rig it with a bomb would aim to do so as quickly as possible. There was therefore no possibility that the camera would run out of film.

'First thing you do in the morning is check the VCR digital display,' Hicks continued. 'That will tell you whether the camera recorded anything overnight.'

A double zero in the frame indicated that nothing untoward occurred. Numerals showed how many feet had been shot, in which case the tape had to be rewound and played back.

'If you see anything suspicious, you should phone the duty officer of the European Department and an army bomb squad will be round here in no time.'

Earlier that morning, Harriet had been mildly amused by Peter's antics as he had inspected the car inside and out. Although familiar, from her days in MI5, with the passive defence measures which he had taken, she had never seen him put theory into practice before and had thought he was taking the possible IRA threat to Clifford Peachey a bit far. Now she didn't know what to think.

'Who arranged all this?' she asked. 'My husband?'

'No, according to Frank Warren it was the DG himself who ordered it. I'm not sure anybody has informed your husband yet.'

Things had to be getting serious if Victor Hazelwood was concerned for their safety. To Harriet it was a clear indication that Clifford Peachey was not the only one at risk. Her mouth suddenly dried up and there was this fluttering sensation in her stomach that she remembered from Berlin when the Turkish *Gastarbeiters* from the Kreuzberg District had rioted on Katzbach Strasse and she had ended up in hospital with a fractured skull.

'This dish is to protect our car, correct?'

'Right.'

'Well then, isn't there a risk the camera and the warning buzzer will be triggered every time somebody goes past the car?'

'It shouldn't happen too often,' Hicks told her. 'There's a built-in ten-second delay after the fence has been broken before the rest of the system is activated. Even a person half crippled with arthritis could walk past the Ford Mondeo in that time.'

'Let's hope you're right. How long will it take you to install the dish?'

'The rest of the day. Hopefully I'll be finished before your husband arrives home from the office.'

'I'll leave you to it then,' Harriet said, and turned away.

'Any chance of a cup of coffee?' Hicks asked before she could escape.

'Black, white, with or without?'

'Oh, I like it with all the trimmings. Wouldn't mind a chocolate biscuit either.'

Harriet just knew it was going to be one of those days.

*   *   *

Hazelwood was enjoying his third Burma cheroot of the day and a cup of the local supermarket's French coffee when Clifford Peachey poked his head round the door and asked if he could spare him a few minutes.

'Take all the time you need,' Hazelwood told him and waved a large hand at the nearest chair. 'Coffee?'

'No thank you.'

'I assume Ashton has been to see you.'

'He left my office only a few minutes ago.'

'And?'

'He appears to think the IRA could have got their information from one of Ann's friends. She gave our new address to a number of them and Peter would like to know their names.'

Hazelwood sensed his deputy was not best pleased with Ashton and was reluctant to involve Ann in something which could jeopardise some of her friendships.

'Peter had to start somewhere,' he said quietly.

'Oh, I don't dispute that but I don't believe the line he's taking will lead us anywhere.'

'Maybe you should phone Dean Rennert this afternoon and apply a little pressure. Persuade him to find out how the Boston office learned the Provos had got hold of your new address. We want to know who said what to whom so that we can take effective action.'

'What do you mean by effective action, Victor?'

'Not what you're thinking,' Hazelwood assured him. 'I do realise that no Irish American is going to set up one of the heroes from the old country so that Brits can put him in the ground. What we've got to do is educate them about the real world.'

The current truce was being observed by the two largest paramilitary organisations, the Ulster Defence Association and the Provisional IRA. But the fringe groups, the Loyalist Ulster Volunteer Force, the Ulster Freedom Fighters on the one hand, and the Irish National Liberation Army and the Continuity IRA on the other, were still engaged in tit-for-tat sectarian killings.

The first step therefore was to convince Dean Rennert that it was the INLA faction which had singled out the Deputy DG.

'And then what?' Peachey asked. 'Even if I win Dean

Rennert over, which shouldn't be difficult, the IRA sympathisers up in Boston will still see it as a setup.'

'Who has inflicted the most casualties on the Irish National Liberation Army? The Security Forces or the Provisionals?'

'Factions within INLA itself; the whole organisation is riven with personal feuds.'

'All right, let's forget the internal divisions. Where does that leave us?'

'The Provisionals have been known to discipline them when they've disapproved of their actions,' Peachey conceded.

'And they won't like it if the INLA were planning to do something which was guaranteed to end the peace process.'

'Like killing me?' Peachey smiled. 'You can't be serious, Victor?'

'You are the deputy head of the SIS. Take it as gospel, even the lot we've now got in Parliament would be a bit miffed if you were shot down on the streets of London. That's what Rennert has to convince the people of Boston.'

'Before they give us a name they will want to know what we intend to do with it.'

'We'll have a heart-to-heart talk with the Provisionals and tell them what's going on and the possible consequences if they sit back and do nothing about it.'

'Just how do you propose to contact the IRA?'

'Oh, that's a job for MI5,' Hazelwood said airily. 'They've had plenty of practice at it.'

It had happened in '73 when the Heath Government had been in power and there had been a repeat performance with the next administration. On one occasion contact had been initially established by a highly respected civil servant in the Northern Ireland Office. Another time, the Security Service had used the managing director of a brewery across the border in Dundalk. Hazelwood had absolutely no doubt that MI5 still had the ability to get in touch with the IRA High Command any time they liked. The fact that Clifford Peachey did not deny it was for him proof that his assumption was justified.

'What exactly are we going to say in our message to the Provos?'

Hazelwood stubbed out his cheroot in the brass shell case.

'That's easy,' he growled. 'To whet their appetites we'll give them most of what we get from the FBI. We'll also make it clear that we want to meet one, possibly two of their representatives face to face. The time and place is to be of their own choosing provided it is on neutral ground.'

Peachey thought his former colleagues in MI5 might be willing to contact the Provisionals on behalf of the SIS but beyond that they would draw the line. There was no way the Security Service was going to do their dirty work for them.

'I wouldn't expect them to do so,' Hazelwood said. 'We'll find our own representative.'

'Have you got someone in mind?'

'Oh, I think that will be a job for General Duties.'

'Meaning Ashton?'

'Well, there is only one man in that particular branch,' Hazelwood said amiably.

The flight plan submitted by Marchukov, which DI3 (A) had photocopied for his information, landed on Ashton's desk just before lunchtime, courtesy of the Whitehall Special Dispatch Service. The first thing he did after reading it was to make two additional photocopies of the document. One copy went to the chief security officer at the Department of Trade and Industry with a covering letter asking what, if anything, was known about the agents named in the flight plan. In addition Ashton wondered if the DTI could shed any light on the sort of freight which was awaiting onward movement at Larnaka and Bahrain. He sent the second copy to the Mid East Department, marking it up for the attention of the Assistant Director on the grounds that Bahrain had been Jill Sheridan's old stamping ground and there was a chance she might have heard of Bryce and Bryce, Import and Export.

Some people had an uncanny knack of popping up at the least convenient moment. Ashton had just taken a bite out of the ham sandwich he'd bought from a delicatessen on the way into the office when Bill Orchard descended on him.

'This signal from the BND,' Orchard said, waving the flimsy at him, 'other than a name, do you have any reason to believe that V. J. Ramash and V. J. Desai are one and the same person?'

'No, but it would be a hell of a coincidence if they weren't.' Ashton shoved the half-eaten sandwich back into the bag and deposited it in the top drawer of his desk. 'I mean, think about it, Bill, a man calling himself V. J. hires Mungo Park to hack into Frank Warren's stand-alone system and then bestows my wife's identity on Lorraine Cheeseman a.k.a. Larissa Marchukova. Look at the dates on that signal again; Lorraine Cheeseman leaves Berlin on the fourth of August and a few days later she starts seeing Dr Ramash, sister-in-law of V. J. Desai. Now, who else could have recruited her in so short a time?'

'I haven't the faintest idea.'

'Do we know where Desai's brother is now?'

'He died approximately three years ago, had a bad heart.'

'And when did the Indian Central Bureau of Investigation last see V. J. himself?'

'I've asked Hugo Calthorpe to find out.'

'I'm guessing Marchukov put Desai in touch with Lorraine Cheeseman.'

'I won't ask you why,' Orchard told him.

'That's a relief, I'd only have to admit I was guessing again.' Ashton picked up the flight plan in the pending tray and showed it to Orchard.

'You might like to see this,' he said.

'Marchukov International Carriers,' Orchard intoned, 'St Petersburg to Kuala Lumpur, stopping at Larnaka and Bahrain—'

'Marchukov is also refuelling at Delhi,' Ashton said, interrupting him, 'but he's still awaiting clearance for that leg.'

'Interesting.'

'Does that mean you want to be kept informed?'

'Yes. I'd like to know Marchukov's estimated time of arrival at Delhi, then I can tell old Hugo to do a bit of snooping and find out what is on board the Tu–154.'

'If we get sufficient advance warning,' Ashton said.

'Quite so.' Orchard waved the signal at him again. 'May I keep this?' he asked.

'I'd sooner you took a photocopy. I need it for the file we've opened on Marchukov.'

Orchard said he quite understood and would leave him in

peace to get on with his lunch. Ashton opened the drawer, took out the ham sandwich and managed a couple more bites before Sergeant O'Meara rang. After examining the legitimate business records of the Steadfast Agency with Mildred Scarsdale, she believed they had found a Desai who could fit the bill.

'He appears to have a partner. At any rate the company is registered as Desai Hakkison Lal, Wholesale Electrical Goods. The business address is Goldfield Way, The Industrial Estate, Greenford.'

'Whereabouts is that?' Ashton asked.

'Near Northolt and South Harrow. The firm wrote to Mr Wilks on the twenty-eighth of June this year saying the agency had been highly recommended and Desai Hakkison Lal therefore wished to employ his firm to examine the credit worthiness of K. P. Roy of Hood Road, Southall and four other retail businesses, all Indian owned. The clients settled their account with Mr Wilks the day after he had presented his bill. The bill was paid with a company cheque.'

The more Ashton heard, the more he was sure O'Meara had found the right man. A fortnight after receiving the credit ratings from the agency, Mungo Park had been hired to break into the stand-alone system. On Thursday, 17 August, thirteen days after leaving Berlin, Lorraine Cheeseman had assumed Harriet's identity and attended the first of eight sessions with Dr Ramash.

'Don't get too cock-a-hoop,' O'Meara warned him as if reading his thoughts. 'There's a downside to all this. I tried to ring Desai Hakkison Lal and got an unobtainable signal, same thing with the fax number. The firm has gone out of business.'

'So what's our next move in your opinion?'

'Well, I don't know about you, Mr Ashton, but I'm going to look around that industrial estate and ask a few questions.'

'Fine. I'll pick you up from your place in half an hour.'

'You won't hear me objecting,' O'Meara said, and hung up.

Since, in theory, he was answerable to the Deputy DG, Ashton rang Peachey to let him know where he was going and why; then called the transport section and told the supervisor to make Daniels available. The last thing he did before leaving was to call on Frank Warren and sign for two false warrant cards which were good enough to deceive the Commissioner of the

Metropolitan Police. As Head of Security Vetting and Technical Services, Frank delivered the obligatory warning that playing the law game or, more accurately, masquerading as a police officer was a very serious offence. He also reminded Ashton that the SIS accepted no responsibility for what he was proposing to do. It was, of course, another way of saying 'don't get caught'.

The Industrial Estate on Goldfield Way was down by the Grand Union Canal and was home to a car body repair shop, a furniture store, DIY centre, a printer specialising in graphic designs, a builder's merchant and a derelict shoe factory, which had gone out of business in the recession of '92. In addition there were half a dozen low-level buildings which the developers had claimed were ideal for offices or stores. However, five of the properties had remained empty even in the boom years. The sixth had been taken by Desai Hakkison Lal, Wholesale Electrical Goods, but it too was now back on the market. Since it was located at the bottom of the industrial estate near the canal, Ashton reckoned Desai could not have found a more isolated position for the business if he'd tried. The DIY centre and furniture store were the closest work units and they were a good four hundred yards away round a slight bend in the road.

'Let's take a look at the place,' O'Meara said, and got out of the car.

There wasn't a lot to see. The office furniture consisted of two steel desks, a three-drawer filing cabinet and a pair of tubular steel chairs. There was also a telephone balanced precariously on the windowledge and a fax machine that had been left on the floor.

'Ex MoD,' Ashton said.

'What is?'

'The furniture. The Property Services Agency disposes of those items which are considered surplus to requirement. Go to any of the big office suppliers and you can get all the furniture you need for a song. You simply pay cash and cart it away.'

O'Meara moved to another window and peered inside.

'There's nothing in the stockroom,' she observed, 'just the racking. I suppose you'll tell me that's ex MoD too?'

Ashton joined her. 'You're right,' he said, 'I will. The stuff has probably come from an ordnance depot that's been closed down.'

'Knowing that doesn't get us very far. I'll talk to the other firms on the site and see if they can tell me anything about Desai Hakkison Lal.'

'Why don't we split up the estate between the three of us?' Ashton suggested. 'You take the DIY centre, I'll have a word with the manager of the furniture store and Daniels can try his luck with the car body repair shop further up the road.'

'And what are you going to tell those people if they want to know who you are?'

'We'll say we've reason to believe Desai Hakkison Lal had fraudulently obtained goods to the value of X thousand pounds.'

O'Meara raised both hands. 'I don't think I want to hear any more. Whatever you do don't arouse the manager's suspicion.'

'You worry too much.'

'Only since I met you, Mr Ashton. We'll meet back at the car soon as we've finished.'

Their enquiries produced a mixed bag of success and failure. Daniels had no luck at all with the foreman and panel beaters at the car body repair shop, all of whom claimed they'd never laid eyes on anybody from Desai Hakkison Lal. O'Meara was told the firm had moved into the premises at the beginning of April but nobody was quite sure when they had moved out. The manager of the furniture shop was a goldmine of information. He had actually met the two Indians at the beginning of March when they had visited the estate looking for a suitable property to rent. They had introduced themselves and asked if he knew how long the units down by the canal had been standing empty. Hakkison Lal, a jovial, rather plump man in his mid-forties, had done most of the talking. The manager also told Ashton that Desai was roughly his height and build but was a surly-looking bugger, the sort of man he wouldn't like to cross. When asked to describe his features, all the manager could remember clearly was the fact that the left side of his face was pockmarked as if Desai had had smallpox earlier in his life.

He had been known as 'Busty' even when a young man before he had become flabby and his chest had begun to look as though some cosmetic surgeon had given him a couple of silicon implants. He was an old Gulf hand and had spent thirty-seven years in Bahrain, which made him the senior European inhabitant of the island. He remembered how Bahrain had been when he had first seen the place in 1958 as a nineteen-year-old National Serviceman in the RAF.

Bahrain International Airport had simply been Muharraq Airfield in those days, a refuelling stop for the long-haul turbo props of British Overseas Airways Corporation, the hub for Middle East Airlines and home to Gulf Aviation flying piston-engine Doves and Herons to Kuwait and the Trucial States. There had also been a couple of RAF Hastings flying doggedly back and forth to Aden. And then there was Saudi Airlines which used to bring in the oilmen from Dammam for five days' rest and recuperation.

Back in the fifties, Bahrain itself had had few attractions. There had been the Souk and BOAC's Speedbird Hotel in Manama and a cinema in Awali, the headquarters of the Bahrain Petroleum Company in the centre of the island, but that had been the lot. Consequently many of the oilmen on rest and recuperation from Saudi Arabia where alcohol was prohibited, had made straight for the officers' and sergeants' messes at RAF Muharraq where they had spent the next five days propping up the bar.

According to the erks Busty had served with, Aden was the arsehole of the world and Bahrain was a thousand miles up it. For seven months of the year the temperature nudged 105° Fahrenheit in the shade with 98 per cent humidity so that for much of the time you were reduced to a greasespot, breathing air through a wet blanket. Every airman had counted the days to go before boarding the charter plane from Airwork to begin the long journey home. Busty had been the only man to stay on and take his discharge locally.

He had done so because he had been in love with one of the Foreign Office girls who was employed as a shorthand typist at the British Consulate in Manama whom he'd met at the Combined Services Yacht Club. It was also a fact that he had been a Dr Barnardo's boy and had had no kith and kin waiting for him back in England. The offer of a job as stock controller with Mackenzie McGovern had come later.

However, nothing in life was ever permanent. The Foreign Office girl hadn't given him even so much as a backward glance when her eighteen-month tour in post was up and it had been time for her to leave Bahrain, and he had parted company with Mackenzie and McGovern in 1988. These days he was in charge of the air freight division of Bryce and Bryce, another Import/Export giant. These days he had an Italian wife and two teenage children. These days he owned a villa in the South of France, kept a Ferrari 456GT as well as a Daimler Jaguar in the double garage in his house on the Jufair Road, and was worth approximately £2.5 million.

For someone of his standing to be checking the freight awaiting collection in the transit shed rented by Bryce and Bryce at the international airport was a little odd. But so was the cargo: eight pallets each weighing 400 pounds, the individual loads wrapped in canvas secured by broad webbing straps and cushioned by rubberised shock absorbers. The goods were described as aluminium household cooking utensils, the carrier was MIC Flight 101 and the destination shown on the bill of loading was Kuala Lumpur. Busty didn't believe a word of it; so far as he was concerned, he would breathe a lot easier when the Tu-154C lifted off on its way to Delhi.

Chapter Fifteen

———⟫•◦•⟪———

Shortly after Clifford Peachey telephoned him from London, Dean Rennert walked into Louis Freeh's office somewhat embarrassed by the knowledge that he was about to unload the mother and father of all problems on to the FBI Director. In a few brief sentences Rennert reminded the Director of the information he'd given the Deputy DG of British Intelligence regarding his own personal security and then went on to relate the conversation he had just had with the Englishman. From the expression on his face, he could see that Freeh didn't like the implications one bit.

'Let me get this straight, Dean, the SIS wants us to name the IRA man who told one of our field agents in Boston that they knew Peachey's home address?'

'That's broadly correct,' Rennert agreed, 'but the implied threat to Deputy Director Peachey was actually made by one of the fringe groups. The Brits say the man almost certainly belongs to the Irish National Liberation Army.'

'Why so?'

'I guess because they aren't observing the truce. The INLA are a murderous lot; one of their more notable feats was to burst into a Presbyterian church during evening service and open fire on the congregation with submachine guns. When they departed they left six dead and God knows how many wounded behind them.'

'Well, I don't want to shield those kind of people any more than you do, Dean, but it's not that simple. We will have to go to the White House for a decision and there's the Irish vote to consider.' Freeh paused, then said, 'If we did give them the information they've asked for, what will the Brits do with it?'

'They will pass it on to the Provisional IRA at a time and place of their choosing. In other words the IRA gets to choose the location.'

'And then what?'

'British Intelligence is confident the Provos will deal with the problem.'

The point which Rennert wished to impress upon the Director was the fact that for the first time in years the British Government was talking to Sinn Fein, the political wing of the IRA. Although it was still too early to say where the talks would lead, Peachey had told him the Government was bound to make some concessions to the Republican movement, which could only be at the expense of the Ulster Unionists. One terrorist outrage was all it would take to wreck the talks and the IRA knew it. Confronted with the probability that a Republican fringe group was prepared to do just that, they would not hesitate to initiate remedial action.

'In other words, the IRA would kill them.'

'They might kneecap them as a warning,' Rennert suggested.

'Who put that thought in your mind? Clifford Peachey?'

'He did raise the possibility.'

'Sounds like a snow job to me.'

'I don't believe Cliff would do that to me, Director. We go back a long way.'

'Well, I'm not going to con the President. The bottom line is the guy will be found in a ditch with several bullet wounds in the head. And the fact is, whether the British do it or the IRA, we will still be a party to murder.'

Freeh shook his head. 'Why can't they move Peachey to a secret location and keep him there until the talks are concluded?'

'The talks could drag on for months, leaving British Intelligence without a Deputy Director.'

'That would be a small price to pay if it leads to a settlement.' Freeh smiled. 'I hope you realise I am playing the devil's advocate here?'

'I figured you were,' Rennert told him.

'OK, I'm the President, now convince me why I should do something for the Brits which could make me highly unpopular at home?'

There were, Rennert argued, grounds for thinking the INLA was determined to wreck the negotiations and would stop at nothing to do so. They were opposed to any sort of compromise and were determined to keep the war going in the naïve belief they would eventually be victorious. It was no use urging the British Government to keep on talking no matter what happened. Public opinion wouldn't stand for it. Furthermore, the Government had to carry the majority of the population of Northern Ireland with them and they happened to include the Protestant Ulster Unionists who wanted no truck with Dublin. It was also a fact that the present government would fall without the support of the Ulster Unionists.

'We're not in business to save the Tory Government,' Freeh told him.

'I was trying to point out how little room for manoeuvre they have,' Rennert said in an injured tone.

'I know you were, Dean. Like I said, I'm playing the devil's advocate.'

'Sure.'

'Who will represent the Brits if the IRA agrees to a meet? The President is bound to ask me.'

'Peter Ashton. You met him roughly a year ago, Director.'

'I remember him well,' Freeh said drily. 'So does the Treasury's Secret Service, the Richmond Police Department and several other agencies when he made a return visit to this country six months ago. He's not what you would call a smooth-tongued diplomat.'

'Peachey reckons the IRA would know exactly where they stood by the time he had finished explaining the facts of life to them.'

Freeh didn't say anything. Instead he buzzed his PA and asked her to get him the White House Chief of Staff. The subsequent telephone conversation was cryptic and largely one-sided. Rennert gathered the President had a very busy schedule and would be unable to see the FBI Director before the upcoming weekend. Freeh told the Chief of Staff the problem couldn't wait; that what he wanted was ten minutes of the President's time and a quick decision. By the time he put the phone down, Freeh had got what he wanted.

'You're off to Boston, Dean, soon as I get the President's OK.' Freeh got to his feet and moved towards the door, gently steering Rennert in the same direction. 'Let's be clear about one thing,' he added, 'British Intelligence and the IRA are not going to meet face to face anywhere in this country.'

O'Meara was not the sort of police officer who was easily satisfied. In her opinion what they had learned from the manager of the furniture store and the DIY centre was all well and good. However, before leaving the industrial estate, she insisted they ought to call on the printer and the builders' merchant in case either of them could shed even more light on Desai Hakkison Lal, Wholesale Electrical Goods.

The rush hour was already in progress when they picked up the Uxbridge Road but most of the traffic was heading out of London and they had a reasonably clear run into town. After dropping O'Meara at Scotland Yard, Ashton continued on to Vauxhall Cross with Daniels. His clerical officer had left a note on his desk asking him to call Jill Sheridan when he returned. He looked at the phone and hesitated. 'Always clear your desk before you go home'; that had been the first thing Hazelwood had said to him when he had joined Victor on the Russian Desk more years ago than he cared to remember. Ashton picked up the phone and tapped out the number of Jill's extension, which was his third mistake. Allowing himself to be influenced by a hoary old maxim was his second mistake; his failure to get Daniels to drop him off at the nearest tube station so that he arrived home early for once, was his first major error. There was a fourth; he should have hung up before Jill answered.

'Hi, it's me, Peter,' he said. 'My clerk left a message . . .'

'Yes. Come on up,' Jill said, and cut him off.

Ashton put the phone down. Sometimes he wondered how or why the two of them had ever got together. Their engagement hadn't lasted all that long; six months at the most before Jill had broken it off in the October of '89 when she had been selected to run the Intelligence network in the United Arab Emirates from Bahrain. They had parted amicably enough but the flat they had been buying in Surbiton on a joint mortgage had rapidly become a bone of contention. They had purchased it at the height of the property boom and had had to put it on the market when the bubble had burst. Despite slashing the asking price to the bone, nobody had shown any interest in the flat and things had reached the point when Jill had announced that she was no longer prepared to pay her share of the standing order to the building society. The threat had eventually come to nothing because Jill had returned prematurely to London and had decided that she and the new man in her life would buy Ashton out.

The one thing Jill had never lost was her capacity to surprise him. Instead of one of her elegant, expensive-looking suits, she was wearing trainers, white ankle socks with matching shorts and a loose-fitting sweat shirt. She also sported pristine sweatbands on both wrists.

'Badminton,' Jill told him cryptically. 'I'm due on court in ten minutes' time. You should take it up, the exercise would be good for you.'

'I don't belong to a badminton club; I'm not even sure there is one in my neighbourhood.'

'Good heavens, you don't have to belong to a club. There's a court down in the basement next door to the Motor Transport Section.'

'I didn't know that.'

'There was an office circular about it which went the rounds roughly a month ago. Of course the two shower cubicles were already there for some reason but the court itself was one of Roy Kelso's projects. It's about the only innovation of his which hasn't turned out to be a disaster.'

The coffee machine on the fourth floor which dispensed a liquid that bore a strong resemblance to brown Windsor soup at the exorbitant price of 50 pence a cup had also been the brainchild of the Admin King. So too was the stand-alone system dedicated to the Security Vetting and Technical Services Division. The obvious contempt in Jill's voice told Ashton that Kelso was not going to emerge unscathed from the inquiry if she had anything to do with it.

'About this flight plan you sent me,' Jill said, abruptly getting to the point. 'There is not an awful lot I can tell you about Bryce and Bryce. I never had anything to do with them when I was in Bahrain. All I know is tittle-tattle picked up at various dinner parties. You'd be better off asking the Department of Trade and Industry.'

'I already have,' Ashton told her, 'but I'd still like to hear your tittle-tattle.'

'Well, for what it's worth, the Bryce brothers are East Enders who have been described as a couple of cockney barrow boys on the make by some of the expats I met out there.'

'Are you saying they sailed pretty close to the wind?'

Jill thought about it for a few moments, then nodded. 'I suppose I am. Naturally they don't foul their own doorstep but if they were playing away from home as it were, they would bend the rules.'

'Can you give me an example?'

'They have been known to circumvent the sanctions the UN has imposed on the Iraqis. Saddam Hussein has been told he can sell a limited amount of oil to buy food and medical supplies for his people provided he co-operates with the UN inspection teams. However, he won't let the teams into the presidential palaces so no oil sales, no food and no medical supplies. Bryce and Bryce help the Iraqis get round that problem – for a consideration, of course.'

Both the Jordanian and Syrian Governments were unhappy about the effect sanctions were having on the Iraqi people and were anxious to do what they could to ease the plight of their neighbours. Learning of their desire, Bryce and Bryce had contacted the appropriate authorities and offered their services. They had purchased medical supplies on behalf of both countries and had then shuffled the paperwork in such a way that it was impossible for the UN to discover who had purchased what from whom and where it was going.

'This is what you've learned about them since leaving Bahrain in '91. Right?'

'Yes.'

'So what were they up to when you were out there running the Intelligence network?'

'They were busy cutting the throats of their competitors. Mackenzie McGovern was the biggest import agency when I arrived in Bahrain; they weren't by the time I left. Their warehouse in Manama burned to the ground and they lost all their stock. Bryce and Bryce stepped in and supplied Mackenzie McGovern's customers with the goods they had ordered. It was to be a purely temporary arrangement, you understand, until Mackenzie McGovern acquired another warehouse and replenished their stock, which they did very quickly. But somehow most of their former customers decided to stay with Bryce and Bryce.'

'Was it arson?'

'A lot of people thought so but it was never proved.' Jill got to her feet, picked up the badminton racket and a large zipper grip containing her street clothes and a bath towel. 'And that's really all I can tell you, Peter,' she said, and moved round the desk towards the door. 'Fact is, I wasn't sent out to the Gulf to keep an eye on the business ethics of the local tradesmen. As I said earlier, your best bet is the Department of Trade and Industry. Better still, why don't you have a word with Dougal Flaxman? He was the Third Secretary, Commerce when I was in Bahrain.'

'Thanks for the tip.'

'Any time.' Jill fell in step with him as they went down the corridor. 'How is Harriet bearing up?' she asked.

'Some days are better than others but she's doing OK.'

'It can't be good for her to be stuck all day in the house.'

'Harriet is not chained to the kitchen sink,' Ashton said, and gave the call button for the lift a vicious jab.

'I'm sure she isn't but having some interest outside home and family might be good for her.'

Ashton followed her into the lift and pressed the buttons for the ground floor and basement. 'You sound like an agony aunt, Jill.'

'You're wrong, I just don't like seeing a good brain going to waste. Has she given any thought to going back to work?'

'She resigned from MI5.'

'I was thinking of our own firm. She would be a natural to run the Security Vetting and Technical Services Division.'

'That's Frank's job.'

'It won't be for much longer.'

'Look, even if the appointment did become available, I don't think she would be interested. Harriet is not a career woman.'

The lift jerked to a halt on the ground floor and the doors opened.

'A nest builder, is she?' Jill said contemptuously.

'It's better than being a cuckoo,' Ashton said, and left her speechless.

Busty glanced at his wristwatch and was convinced it must have stopped quite some time ago. He could not believe that only a couple of minutes had passed since the last time he had looked at it, then he saw that the second hand was still moving and swore under his breath. Bahrain International Airport was the last place he wanted to be at two fifteen in the morning but at the same time he knew there would be no sleep for him until that damned Tu-154C of Marchukov International Carriers trundled down the runway and lifted off.

Everything about MIC Flight 101 stank to high heaven. A Tu-154 normally had two pilots, a flight engineer and a navigator; with a slip crew there should have been eight men on board the plane but there were only seven. With a payload of 44,000 pounds, the maximum cruising range was down to 1,800 miles which meant the plane would have precious little fuel in hand. In fact, the tanks would be practically bone dry when the Tu-154 reached Delhi. On the other hand, with a payload of only 12,000 pounds the range went up to 41,000 miles which was enough to make Kuala Lumpur in one hop with fuel to spare. It was of course no way to run an airline; transporting goods at a fraction of the capacity over the maximum distance was the short cut to bankruptcy.

He didn't really know what payload Flight 101 was carrying on the leg to Delhi. Although it was a full 44,000 pounds on paper, seeing was believing and he hadn't been allowed on board the plane. The freight door was on the port side of the cabin forward of the wing with a ball mat inside and roller tracks going all the way back to the tail. The fact that the last of the eight pallets was in full view of the door when the fork lift truck had finished loading them on to the Tu-154 suggested the paper figure was probably correct. However, there was no physical reason why the pallets could not have been positioned four abreast across the width of the cabin whereas even from the ground, Busty could see they had been lined up one behind the other. That hadn't been the only thing he had noticed. Just before Marchukov had closed the door in his face, he had seen one of the aircrew clip on two parachutes to the foremost pallet and hook up the static lines.

He wasn't likely to forget the venomous look Marchukov had shot him as he closed the door. A nasty piece of work, the Russian – rude, bad-tempered, aggressive, overbearing, arrogant; a dozen adjectives came readily to mind. He was built like an ox too: broad shoulders, barrel chest, large hands that had nearly broken Busty's fingers when he had introduced himself to Marchukov. Right now, he wouldn't like to be in that air crewman's shoes because as sure as there would be a tomorrow, Marchukov was going to make life hell for him. The President of Marchukov International Carriers hadn't wanted any witnesses around when the pallets were rigged for a para drop and the man had been plain careless.

Busty couldn't think why he should be concerned for the Russian when he too wasn't exactly fireproof. The pallets loaded on to the Tupolev 154 had arrived by ship from Larnara and had been offloaded at Manama where they had been put on a truck and driven across the causeway linking Bahrain Island with Muharraq to await onward movement in the transit shed belonging to Bryce and Bryce. It was only after the consignment had been in his charge for close on a month that he had decided to check the movements of the container ship after sailing from Manama. To his alarm he had discovered the ship had gone to Karachi and thence to Bombay. If Delhi was the ultimate destination for the aluminium household cooking utensils, the goods would have got there a lot sooner if they had stayed on the container ship.

Busty lit a cigar. He ought to protect himself otherwise he would be left holding the baby if anything did go wrong. No good tipping off the local authorities. The Bahrainis would take a hard line with him and like as not he would end up in prison wearing leg irons. He couldn't go to Bryce and Bryce either; his bosses were in the scam up to their eyeballs which was why they had set him up as the sacrificial goat. The only safe course for him was to confide in British Intelligence.

Four years ago, he would have known who to approach; in 1991 he would have gone straight to Jill Sheridan. On the Bahrain Embassy staff list she was down as the personal assistant to the Second Secretary Consul but according to Henry Clayburn who had been doing a number with her, she was in fact running the Intelligence setup in the United Arab Emirates.

The Tupolev was on the runway now and Marchukov was giving the three Soloviev turbo fan engines full throttle. 'Not much longer,' he muttered to himself, and even as he spoke the plane started to roll forward. From a slow-moving start, the Tupolev rapidly gathered speed until it was thundering down the runway. The nose came up and seconds later the freighter lifted off and climbed away. When he could no longer see the navigational lights, Busty left the terminal building, got into the Daimler Jag and drove off down the causeway towards Manama.

He would write to Ms Sheridan in London but would leave her name off the outer envelope when he addressed it to the Foreign and Commonwealth Office. No, he wouldn't. Clayburn had returned to London with her and they had married a few months later.

Ordinarily that wouldn't have bothered him but from what he'd heard, Henry Clayburn still had a twenty-five per cent stake in Bryce and Bryce. The only thing he could do was to contact the Second Secretary Consul at the embassy but he would need to be damned careful how he went about it.

Chapter Sixteen

<hr />

The infrared passive defence system installed by Terry Hicks at 84 Rylett Close had two distinct advantages over burglar and car alarms. It did not go off by accident and the warning buzzer couldn't be heard by the neighbours. It couldn't be heard by the Ashtons either after they had retired for the night. Consequently Ashton's first task every morning was to check the video cassette recorder in the cellar to see if it had been activated during the night. The routine had been established when the system had come on line five days ago. This morning for the first time ever, the digital display indicated that six minutes of the four-hour tape had been used up.

Ashton rewound the tape and played it back. The clock in the top left-hand corner of the frame showed that the camera had started tracking at 00.37 hours. The infrared image of the Ford Mondeo appeared on the screen but there was no sign of an intruder; then a small blob at kerb level caught his eye and he put the cassette on hold. Ashton moved closer to the screen and found himself looking at a cat which was sitting bolt upright facing the car, its head swivelled round to the left. He backed away from the screen and set the film running again. The cat suddenly reared up, tail bushing out before it had second thoughts and dived for cover under the car as a large tomcat appeared from the left moving at speed.

For the next four and a half minutes the tom attempted to get at the cat under the Ford Mondeo. Each time he poked his head under the chassis he reared back twice as fast as the one in hiding lashed out. Finally the smaller cat made a break for it with the tom in hot pursuit. When both felines broke the infrared fence on the far side of the vehicle, the screen automatically went blank. After rewinding the tape yet again, Ashton left the cellar and went upstairs into the kitchen.

'You were a long time,' Harriet observed.

'Yes. There was some footage I had to view.'

'Had somebody been tampering with the car?'

Ashton shook his head. 'No, it was just two cats having a dust-up — a randy tom and the object of his affection who wouldn't come out from under the car.'

'It was probably a neutered cat,' Harriet told him. 'The tom would have attacked it out of sheer frustration.'

'You learn something every day.' Ashton poured some muesli into a bowl, peeled a banana and sliced it up, then added the milk. 'Can't think why we didn't hear them, they must have been yowling their heads off. Still, at least we know the system works.'

'Who else has had one installed?'

Ashton stopped eating, a spoonful of muesli with a slice of banana on top halfway to his mouth. 'I don't know. I shouldn't think Clifford Peachey needed one; he's had a couple of baby-sitters looking after him for the past week.'

'So we're rather privileged?'

'I suppose you could put it like that,' Ashton said, and carried on eating.

'Terry Hicks told me his instructions had come from Victor himself.'

'So?'

'So what does Victor want from you?'

'You've a nasty suspicious mind, love.'

'With good reason,' Harriet said.

'Look, when I was standing up for Frank Warren we got into a heated argument, and Victor accused me of wanting him to authorise special protective measures for you. I told him he was talking nonsense and I heard no more about it. Then the FBI warned Clifford Peachey that the IRA were on to him in a big way and my guess is Victor decided he wasn't going to take any chances. Nobody could guarantee that your profile sheet hadn't been seen by the Provos.'

'Fine. I just hope there is no hidden agenda.'

Ashton let it ride. So far as he was concerned there was no hidden agenda. Victor might have told him to find out how the Provos had discovered Clifford Peachey's home address but that instruction had been rescinded forty-eight hours later. Although no explanation had been offered, he suspected the Deputy Director had complained about the grilling he had received from him. The inference that one of his former colleagues had either been guilty of careless talk or had deliberately disclosed his new address to a known IRA sympathiser had probably angered him beyond measure. The fact he'd as good as said that Ann Peachey could have been responsible for the leak because she had given their new address to her golfing and bridge friends must have been the final straw.

Whatever the reason, Victor had told him to forget the Provos and concentrate on what he had dubbed the Marchukov connection, which had more loose threads than a moth-eaten sweater. And five working days later there were still just as many loose ends that wouldn't unravel. The Department of Trade and Industry had been unable to shed any light on the sort of freight which had been awaiting onward movement at Larnara and Bahrain. The DTI hadn't known too much about the various agents listed in the flight plan for MIC Flight 101 either. In fact he had learned more about Bryce and Bryce from Jill Sheridan than he had from them.

As for Flight 101, it was to the best of Ashton's knowledge still sitting on the ground at Lahore. While en route to Delhi the captain had reported that the inertial navigation system on the Tu-154C was malfunctioning shortly after the plane had entered Indian air space. Although Marchukov International Carriers had rectified the fault within twenty-four hours, the aircraft had been impounded by the Pakistan authorities following allegations by the Indian Government that the Tu-154 had deliberately ventured into the prohibited air space of Kashmir.

That left V. J. Desai, the senior partner in Desai Hakkison Lal. He had entertained Lorraine Cheeseman to dinner at the Bristol Hotel Kempinski in Berlin where he had registered as V. J. Ramash. A few days later, on 4 August, she had left Berlin and turned up in London and, in the light of what had subsequently happened, it was reasonable to assume he had followed her to England. However, Immigration had no record of a Mr V. J. Desai or V. J. Ramash entering the country before 8 June when his company had contacted Basil Wilks, or thereafter up to the date of O'Meara's enquiry.

Faced with this impasse, O'Meara had gone after Hakkison Lal. If the firm had simply been a front, it followed that unless Hakkison Lal was extremely stupid and naïve, he must be an accomplice. Unfortunately, Desai's partner was proving equally difficult to find. Mildred Scarsdale only knew his business address. She had, of course, paid in the cheque the agency had received from the firm but she couldn't recall which high street bank it had been drawn on, let alone the particular branch. Currently, O'Meara was trying to have the bank traced through the Steadfast Agency's account with the NatWest.

'Peter!'

Ashton looked up guiltily. 'What did you say?' he asked.

'Do you think you could look after yourself for a few days?'

'I don't see why not. Where are you off to?'

'I thought I would drive up to Lincoln and see how my father is coping.'

'Good idea,' Ashton said with a conspicuous lack of enthusiasm. 'When are you planning to leave?'

'Tomorrow morning if that's OK with you?'

'Sure.'

'I won't stay more than a week.'

Ashton hadn't supposed Harriet would drive up there and back in a day but it had never occurred to him that she would be away quite so long.

'I also need a break,' Harriet added. 'To be honest, this place is beginning to get on top of me.'

He did not have to ask her why.

Hugo Calthorpe turned into the grounds of the government rest house on the trunk road to Agra and parked his Volkswagen well away from the ubiquitous Hindustan, the only other vehicle on the lot. Meeting Brigadier Choudhury somewhere out of town was all very well but he couldn't help thinking that the Deputy Chief of the Intelligence Bureau should have picked a later time for their meeting. If he had just put it back by an hour the first of the tourist buses would have pulled into the rest stop before going on to Akbar's Tomb and the Taj Mahal. As it was, Calthorpe felt, horribly conspicuous.

Choudhury was waiting for him at a table in the open. There was no welcoming smile from him, no cheery wave; the Brigadier looked implacable, even hostile, rather like the note he had sent Calthorpe last night – 'Government Rest House Milestone 71 to Agra at 09.30 hours. Be there.'

All Calthorpe got in return when he greeted Choudhury was a brief grunt. When a bearer came forward to ask what they would like to drink, Choudhury waved him away.

'I'd like you to look at these snapshots,' he said, and produced a glossy envelope. 'Then perhaps you will give me an explanation.'

The envelope contained twenty-four coloured snapshots, all of them featuring the same village from different viewpoints. In some of the pictures the village was littered with parachutes, four of which had apparently failed to open properly with the result that two of the eight pallets had burst open on impact. In the final group of photographs, the contents of all eight pallets had been neatly laid out on the ground.

'It's probably unnecessary for me to tell you this,' Choudhury said. 'However, for the record, the air drop comprised sixty 7.62mm Enfield L1A1 rifles, thirty Enfield general-purpose machine guns and a further fifteen GPMGs with kits for the sustained fire role. Finally there were 60,000 rounds of ammunition including 10,000 in boxes of 50 round belt feed for the machine guns.'

'Should this mean something to me?' Calthorpe asked.

'Look in the other pocket of the envelope,' Choudhury told him curtly.

Calthorpe did so and extracted a sheet of A4 not much thicker than rice paper. On it was typed a list of random eight-figure serial numbers, some incorporating a letter of the alphabet. Calthorpe knew without counting that there were a hundred and five registered numbers in all, one for each weapon.

'I won't insult your intelligence by pointing out the obvious.

However it might surprise you to hear that until very recently, the self-loading rifles and general-purpose machine guns were stored at the Royal Logistical Corps depot in the Dhekélia Sovereign Base Area. The items were disposed of some months ago on the grounds that they were surplus to requirement. Rumour has it the weapons and ammunition were originally purchased by Inter-Continental Arms based in Hong Kong. Undoubtedly the items were sold over and over again on paper before they were dispatched from Larnaca.'

'Why are you telling me all that?' Calthorpe asked.

'The village is called Udhampur; it's in Kashmir ninety miles southwest of Srinagar. The population is a hundred per cent Hindu. Do I need to say any more?'

Calthorpe shook his head. Kashmir was a war zone, had been ever since Independence Day when the Hindu ruler of a predominantly Muslim population had declared for India instead of Pakistan. At the request of the Maharajah, the Indian Army had moved in to maintain law and order. So too had the Pakistan Army, although they hadn't been invited.

'It is our contention that the arms were destined for the Kashmir Liberation Front, a guerrilla organisation more interested in robbing banks than they are in attacking the Indian Army and Regional Police Force. Due to a navigational error, the weapons were delivered to the wrong village.'

'When did this air drop take place?'

'You mean you don't know?' Choudhury contrived to sound astonished. 'I find that very strange considering the interest the Defence Attaché at the British High Commission showed in the flight plan for MIC 101. He was constantly on to Air Traffic Control, Delhi, wanting to know if Marchukov International Carriers had filed one yet.'

Short of actually saying so, Choudhury could not have made it plainer that he believed the British had organised the air drop. Calthorpe's first instinct was to deny any involvement but the the fact that the SIS had been interested in Marchukov and not what the plane was carrying sounded unconvincing even to his ears.

'The captain adhered to the flight plan as far as Bahawalpur,' Choudhury said when he realised the SIS Head of Station was not going to be drawn. 'He then veered off course and descended to six hundred feet to come in under our radar screen, making it difficult for us to intercept him. Naturally the captain could not maintain that low altitude in the mountains but thereafter he gave the finest exhibition of contour flying our Air Defence Command has ever seen. He flew up the valleys and skimmed the crests with the result that the Tu-154 only appeared now and then on our radar screens.'

Marchukov had allowed himself no margin of error and had obviously handled the transport like a fighter plane with no thought for the possible consequences. Radio silence had not been broken until after the paradrop on Udhampur had been completed. When he had come up on the air, Marchukov had informed Air Traffic Control that his inertial navigation system was defective and it was his intention to make an emergency landing at the nearest airfield.

'I imagine you were not too surprised when you learned the nearest one happened to be in Pakistan. To be precise, the Pakistan Air Force base at Lahore, which could hardly have been more convenient.'

'Now just a minute,' Calthorpe said heatedly. 'As a representative of Her Majesty's Government, I resent these insinuations. Let me remind you the Pakistan authorities impounded the plane, and the crew are under arrest. They have even offered to make the crew available for questioning by officers from your Central Bureau of Investigation.'

'Yes indeed, they have been most co-operative. In fact they handed the crew over to us. Unfortunately, Marchukov, the man we really want to interrogate, was not with them. Within six hours of being arrested, he was released following representations by a member of your diplomatic staff in Islamabad.'

'Are you sure of these facts?' Calthorpe asked.

'We definitely know the man who engineered his release was an Englishman. We assumed he was acting for the British High Commission. Anyway, all we were left with were six Latvians.'

'Latvians!' Calthorpe repeated incredulously.

'Yes. The only member of the crew was ex-Major General Marchukov. The Latvians can't tell us who hired the plane; we believe that was why the people behind the operation did everything they could to shield Marchukov from interrogation.'

'A question: where did you hear these rumours concerning Inter-Continental Arms?'

'From people in the trade; we asked four of the leading arms dealers who they thought had purchased the weapons. Three out of the four were certain Inter-Continental Arms had fronted the deal. They have a bad reputation.'

Calthorpe wasn't impressed. No one who was organising a clandestine operation would use a broker whose bad habits were known to the world and his wife. London, of course, would have to be advised of the allegations Choudhury had made against The Firm, which would undoubtedly spur Hazelwood into action. One didn't have to be clairvoyant to know that he would start the ball rolling by taking a good hard look at Inter-Continental Arms, Hong Kong. Or to be more accurate, Roger Benton, Head of the Pacific Basin and Rest of the World Department would be told to get on with it.

'Can I keep the photographs?'

'I've no objection,' Choudhury told him, 'though why London should want to be reminded of a bungled operation is beyond my comprehension.'

'And I can't understand why anybody halfway intelligent should think we've nothing better to do than stir up trouble in Kashmir.'

Calthorpe knew it was not the happiest note on which to end what had been a difficult meeting but he had taken all the stick he was going to from the Deputy Chief of the Intelligence Bureau.

Since her elevation to Assistant Director, Ashton could not recall a previous occasion when Jill Sheridan had come down from the eyrie to see him. Usually when they had something to discuss it was the other way round. Since he was tucked away in a corner behind the door for security reasons to do with the VDU, he heard only the clack of heels, assumed it was his clerical officer and asked her if she would mind getting him a cup of coffee.

'Let's have fifty pence then,' Jill said.

Ashton turned about. 'Sorry about that,' he said, 'I thought you were somebody else. Can I get you a cup?'

'Not if it's that brown Windsor sludge from the machine.' Jill came further into the room and perched her rump on the edge of his desk. 'A week ago you asked me what I knew about Bryce and Bryce . . .'

'And you told me more than I learned from the DTI.'

'Well, now we can go one better; it seems we've acquired a whistle-blower who is very unhappy with Bryce and Bryce.'

The informer had contacted the Second Secretary Consul at the embassy by telephone and had used some kind of synthesiser to disguise his voice. He had declined to identify himself even by a codename and had purported to be representing a third party. Information of interest to the British Government would be left in various dead letter boxes chosen by the source and the embassy notified of the location after the material had been deposited. The information was on no account to be transmitted via the satellite link; instead it was to be sent to London in the diplomatic bag or by hand of Queen's Messenger.

'Ordinarily we would have ignored the approach,' Jill continued. 'We didn't because he told the Second Secretary that I had been in charge of the Intelligence network in the United Arab Emirates from '89 to '91 while masquerading as a personal assistant. His first communication was tucked inside an empty packet of cigarettes, which he left on the Awali Road behind Milestone 6. It was collected late yesterday afternoon and reached us this morning in the diplomatic bag.'

The note had been composed on a word processor, which meant there were none of the individual characteristics associated with a conventional typewriter. It was also a fact that the purpose-built computer system helped to protect the identity of the source.

'According to the whistle-blower there were eight rather special pallets awaiting collection at Bahrain by MIC Flight 101. The pallets were special because in his opinion they were going to be delivered by parachute. On the bill of loading, the cargo was described as aluminium household cooking utensils. Although the source hadn't inspected the pallets he's pretty sure they contained small arms and ammunition.'

'It would explain why the aircraft has been impounded at Lahore,' Ashton said.

'Yes, well, chummy has got to come across with a lot more information before we can consider granting him immunity from prosecution.' Jill paused, then added, 'Or it could be asylum if the Bahrain authorities learn what he has been up to and decide to make an example of him.'

'The down payment to Marchukov was $250,000.' Ashton pursed his lips. 'It doesn't seem enough to me.'

'Frankly, I'm more interested in the cooking utensils. That's a job for chummy because you can bet they are no longer on board the Tu-154.' Jill stood up and made towards the door, then stopped and turned about. 'Incidentally, did you ask Harriet if she wanted to take over the Security Vetting and Technical Services Division?'

'We've been over this ground before. She wouldn't be interested.'

'That means you haven't told her it's on offer. Why can't you let Harriet make up her own mind for once? Frightened she will say yes?'

'I know how she feels about Frank Warren, you don't.'

'Frank will be gone by the end of the year. That's one of the recommendations I've made in the inquiry and believe me, it will be accepted. So will my sponsorship, if Harriet decides to break out of her shell.'

'She will never want Frank's job, she likes him too much. Illogical as it may seem to you, Harriet would feel she had made it that much easier for The Firm to get rid of Frank.'

'Well, you should know your wife but I still don't know why you can't allow Harriet to make up her own mind about the job.' Jill shook her head as if perplexed. 'After all, what's your problem?' she asked, and walked out before he could think of a suitable answer.

Life had always been one long surprise with Jill but this latest example of her capacity to astonish him was something else. He had learned from experience that there was always a hidden motive when Jill went out of her way to help somebody. Ms Sheridan was hellbent on becoming the first woman to be appointed Director General of the SIS. Try as he might, Ashton couldn't see how Harriet could possibly help her to climb those last two steps to the top of the ladder.

He switched off the terminal and was about to get a cup of coffee from the vending machine near the lifts when O'Meara rang him with the news that she had traced Hakkison Lal. It had taken a full working week for the high street banks to check their records before the Midland pinpointed the branch which had dealt with the current account of Desai Hakkison Lal. 'It was opened by Hakkison Lal with a certified cheque for three thousand pounds,' O'Meara continued. 'The cheque was drawn on his own personal account at the Stanmore Branch of Lloyds Bank. He also furnished letters of credit.'

'So you've got his home address.'

'Only with some difficulty; Hakkison Lal believes in spreading his money around. He has more than one account with all the high street banks. The statements are sent to a Post Office box number. All the managers I spoke to are under the impression that Hakkison Lal spends most of his time abroad, at any rate that was his explanation for using a box number.'

'Sounds like a tax fiddle to me,' Ashton said.

'No doubt the Inland Revenue will agree with you when they examine his business records. The fact is the banks couldn't furnish his current home address but the Post Office could. Perhaps you won't be surprised to hear that he lives in a better part of Hampstead on Upper Heath Row.'

'When are you going to question him?'

'This evening,' O'Meara said, 'around six o'clock. We will have Lal under visual and audio surveillance by then. You're welcome to be present when I call at the house.'

'Thanks.'

'That's the good news, now for the bad.'

O'Meara could find no trace of Desai. The manager of the Midland Bank in Greenford, who had met him when he and Hakkison Lal had arrived to open their trading account at the branch, could tell her nothing about his background. Desai had had little to say and was so retiring the manager wondered if he understood more than a few words of English.

'I think he was boxing clever,' Ashton said.

'You may be right. However, my other piece of news is even

199

worse. Mungo Park's solicitor rang the Chief Superintendent at Paddington Green to inform him that his client had decided to plead not guilty to the offence he had been charged with under Section 1 (b) of the Official Secrets Act of 1920.'

'The little shit.'

'His solicitor, Derek Meakin, couldn't have been more pleased.'

'He's an even bigger shit,' Ashton growled.

'I think so too. The fact is everybody from the Crown Prosecution Service to my Assistant Commissioner wants to know if you people are prepared to give evidence in court?'

There was no way Victor Hazelwood could allow any of his officers to give evidence in court unless the magistrates agreed the trial should be held in camera. Even then it would be a risky business; the press would learn that Park was being tried under the Official Secrets Act and the Opposition in the House of Commons would take the matter up. All hell would break loose and somebody's head was bound to roll.

'We won't give any evidence,' Ashton said.

'Is that official?' O'Meara asked.

'No. I'll brief the DG and call you back.'

Bad news travels fast. Hazelwood had already heard from the Permanent Under Secretary at the Home Office that Park had changed his mind about pleading guilty. Consequently, he had agreed the Crown Prosecution Service should drop the charge.

Chapter Seventeen

Hazelwood knew that among his many friends and acquaintances, there were a considerable number for whom autumn was the best time of the year. He hated the season; for him the turning of the leaves was the harbinger of the long winter to come, the nights drawing in earlier and earlier until it was dark by four o'clock in the afternoon. The days were tolerable up to Christmas; beyond that, January and February and even March were an unremitting grey. He had often promised himself that in their retirement years, he and Alice would winter in the sun. Gazing across the murky Thames at the Houses of Parliament, Hazelwood thought they might well be looking at the winter holiday brochures a lot sooner than either of them had anticipated.

He had lost his grip and was no longer on top of the job, that was the bottom line. A year ago he would have asked a few pertinent questions when Roy Kelso had first mooted the idea of a stand-alone system for the Security Vetting and Technical Services Division. He should have asked for a detailed justification showing what advantages the stand-alone system would have over existing procedures. Then he would have seen the project for what it was, a potentially dangerous piece of window-dressing. But he had allowed Kelso to go ahead because the necessary equipment had been offered up as surplus to requirements by the Department of Energy and the project wasn't going to cost the SIS a bean.

The damned system had brought them nothing but trouble. It had become basically insecure when the facility had been extended to the Training School at Amberley Lodge. If the system had been confined to Vauxhall Cross, Park would never have been able to steal the whole damned file. And as Jill Sheridan had pointed out in her report, the fact that it had been recovered intact with the exception of Harriet Ashton's profile sheet didn't mean they were out of the wood. A man like Mungo Park could have committed half a dozen names and addresses to memory.

The communicating door to the adjoining room hadn't been closed properly and Hazelwood became aware of voices in the PA's office. Recognising them, he turned away from the window, went over to the door and, opening it, almost bumped into Clifford Peachey.

'Come on in,' he said.

'I was about to,' Peachey told him.

'So how did it go?' Hazelwood returned to his desk and sat down. 'Is Five prepared to assist us?'

'Within limits. They will use their channel of communication to pass on anything we have for the Provisionals. They will also broker a meeting between the two sides but that's it.'

'I'm not complaining. What did they think of our information?'

Three days ago the FBI had sent them the name of the man who'd boasted of targeting the Deputy Director. Within minutes of receiving it, the name had been passed to MI5 for evaluation by the Royal Ulster Constabulary and the army's 10th Intelligence Company operating in Northern Ireland. Unless the name meant something to the Provisional IRA nothing would come of meeting them face to face.

'Barry Nolan is not unknown to the Security Forces,' Peachey told him.

Barry Nolan came from a family of hard-line Republicans. His grandfather, Liam, had taken part in a series of bomb attacks launched by the IRA against targets in London, Coventry and Manchester in the spring of 1939. Betrayed by a police informer, he had been charged with conspiring to cause explosions and had been sentenced to ten years' imprisonment with hard labour. He had therefore spent the entire war behind bars sewing mailbags. His habit of crowing at every defeat inflicted on the British had resulted in him spending long periods in solitary confinement for his own protection. This regime had been instituted following a particularly severe beating by other inmates of Strangeways which had left Liam Nolan blind in one eye.

The father, Patrick Nolan, had carried on the family tradition but had been a somewhat incompetent terrorist. On Tuesday, 18 January 1955, while on his way to bomb an unmanned sub-power station outside Dundrum, he had run into a police roadblock. The explosive device was being transported in a small Singer van which he had stolen the previous afternoon from outside a pub where the Falls Road merged with Divis Street. Spotting the roadblock at the last minute, he had attempted to execute a three-point turn at speed on an icy road and had ended up unconscious in a ditch. He had been luckier than his companion, who had gone headfirst through the windscreen, severing his jugular in the process.

Patrick Nolan had subsequently spent five years in Crumlin Road Gaol; his companion had died in the ambulance on the way to hospital. The incident had eventually become part of IRA mythology with the allegation that the 'B' Specials manning the roadblock had waited until the wounded man was past saving before they summoned the ambulance.

'Barry Nolan was only fourteen years old when the troubles started all over again in 1969,' Peachey continued. 'Thanks to his father and grandfather's influence, Barry Nolan took to the streets when things went pear-shaped. This happened after the IRA decided to drive a wedge between the army and the people on the Lower Falls who had initially welcomed them.'

Nolan had started by throwing stones at foot patrols and military vehicles; within a matter of weeks, he had graduated to petrol bombs. During this phase of his career he had never been arrested because he could outrun the 'snatch squads' and there had been plenty of Republican sympathisers who had been prepared to give him a cast-iron alibi. A few weeks after his fifteenth birthday, he'd helped to kidnap a nineteen-year-old girl who had been denounced for dating a British soldier. She had been taken to a house on the Derrybeg Estate in West Belfast where three women auxiliaries had given her a savage beating with broomsticks. Rumour had it that Nolan had been accorded the privilege of cropping her hair and shaving her head with a cut-throat razor until she was practically bald. As a final punishment, the girl had been tarred and feathered before being tied to a lamppost.

'It's thought Nolan killed his first man in 1975. The victim was a fifty-six-year-old Catholic informer, or "tout" in IRA parlance. There have been another eight since then, only one of whom was a soldier and he was a part-timer in the Ulster Defence Regiment.'

Hazelwood opened the cigar box on his desk, took out a Burma cheroot and lit it with a match. 'If we know all this about him, why isn't he doing nine life sentences in the Maze?'

'Nolan lives south of the border in County Monaghan.'

'So why haven't we tried to get him extradited?'

'Based on previous experience, it was felt the evidence against him wouldn't be strong enough for Dublin.'

'All right, Clifford, what caused him to break with the Provos?'

'The Provisional IRA made him the Commander of the South Down Brigade in 1989. Two years later the Army Council removed him, ostensibly for lack of aggression. Nolan claims he had argued that the political wing should forget about the ballot and stick to the bullet and had left the Provos for the Irish National Liberation Army because they had disagreed with his policy. The fact is, like all the other IRA leaders, Nolan demanded protection money from businessmen of every description and participated in armed robbery. He had been found wanting by the Army Council because he had held on to a greater percentage of the money than had the other brigade commanders.'

'Are you sure the FBI hasn't given us a rabbit?' Hazelwood asked. 'Here is a man who is in hiding south of the border, who is only prepared to take on the softest of soft targets. Do we really believe that he has the guts to go after you?'

'Both the RUC and the army reckon Nolan has two or three gunmen under his command who are capable of doing a quick in-and-out hit. Intelligence also believes he has recruited a really top-notch bomb maker. So, yes, I think Nolan does represent a definite threat.'

There was, Hazelwood decided, nothing more to be said on the subject. However, he did have two questions for his deputy. Specifically, he wanted to know how long it would take MI5 to establish contact with the IRA and when they might expect to hear from them.

'The Security Service can get in touch with the Army Council in a matter of hours,' Peachey told him. 'How long it will take them to respond is anybody's guess. There could be a lot of toing and froing before a neutral rendezvous is agreed. If you press me, I can't see the meeting being arranged in less than seventy-two hours.'

'Then you'd better tell MI5 to get started.'

'Are you still planning to use Ashton as our envoy?'

'He did nine months undercover in Belfast,' Hazelwood said. 'I can't think of anybody who is better qualified for the job. Can you?'

Calthorpe left the British High Commission, picked up the Sardar Patel Marg and followed it into the cantonment as far as the junction of Parade Road with Station Road where he made a right turn. On the previous occasion when he had called on Logan Bannerman at his bungalow on the Janakpuri Road, he had taken elaborate precautions to make sure nobody was following him. This time he didn't bother. The hot weather season was over, the rains had come and gone and the winter climate was more than tolerable but even so, few people were about at three o'clock in the afternoon. Consequently he practically had the roads to himself and was confident he would spot in the rear-view mirror any vehicle attempting to shadow his Volkswagen.

Besides, what he wanted to discuss with Logan Bannerman was urgent and he couldn't afford to waste time on boy scout tomfoolery. The Air Attaché at the British High Commission had denied any involvement in the paradrop on Udhampur; he had been tasked by DI3 (Air) in the Ministry of Defence to check on the flight plan Marchukov was about to submit for MIC Flight 101. The diplomatic staff had also denied any knowledge of a covert operation and were requesting guidance from the Foreign Secretary. Nevertheless it was possible the operation could have been sanctioned in London. It wouldn't be the first time some private security firm had been given the nod on the basis of 'Don't get caught because we will only disown you'. And it was to do with this possibility that Calthorpe wanted to see Bannerman in case he had heard something on the grapevine. The trouble was Bannerman's home phone number was out of order and the press office had told him that he'd called in sick two days ago.

The first thing Calthorpe saw when he turned into the drive was the faithful Hindustan parked down the side of the bungalow. As was usually the case when he rang the bell, it was Sumitra who came to the door. On this occasion however, Logan was not at home, sick in bed.

'He's up in the hills,' Sumitra told him.

'The hills?' Calthorpe repeated blankly.

'Ranikhet.'

'But his car is still here.'

'He went up by train as far as the railhead at Kathgodam. After that, I imagine he either hired a taxi or caught a bus.'

'But what's he doing in Ranikhet?'

'Getting information for you, Mr Calthorpe. He'd heard that the leaders of the Ananda Marg were holding some kind of secret meeting in the village. I told him he was risking his neck for nothing, but of course he never listens to me.'

Measured in a straight line, Upper Heath Row was less than half a mile from Willow Walk, which meant Hakkison Lal and Victor Hazelwood were practically neighbours. Knowing how Victor disliked eating out when he was at home, Ashton doubted if they knew one another by sight. In many ways, 15 Upper Heath Row bore a striking resemblance to Willow Dene, the somewhat unoriginal name Hazelwood had given to his house when he'd bought it.

Like Willow Dene, the property owned by Hakkison Lal had been built in 1900 when things were done on a grand scale. Beneath the slate roof, Ashton guessed there would be at least six large bedrooms, two bathrooms and various other rooms. The walls were Mendip stone and in common with the properties on Willow Walk were eighteen inches thick. The respective properties differed in two respects: Hakkison Lal had had the Virginia creeper stripped from his walls and he owned the entire house whereas Hazelwood's Willow Dene was still covered in ivy and was the result of a conversion which had seen the original building divided into three maisonettes.

Hakkison Lal was a small, rather plump and jovial-looking man in his early forties. Nature had given him a round face with muted cheekbones, a broad nose and dark flashing eyes. His jet-black hair was combed straight back and glistened with oil. He was a bundle of nervous energy, excitable and not lacking in self-esteem. He clearly liked to impress people with his wealth and wasted no time in relating the battle he was having with the planning officer who had refused him permission to build on a garage for his Rolls-Royce. The longer he went on about it the more impatient O'Meara became; finally she butted in to remind Hakkison Lal why she had arranged to see him.

'Yes, of course, you want to talk about V. J. Desai, my former business partner.' Lal shook his head. 'A terrible man, very surly and so untrustworthy. I should never have gone into business with him.'

'Then why did you?' O'Meara asked.

'Because he is family, he is my wife's second cousin.'

'Was he born in this country, Mr Hakkison Lal?'

'No. But he came from the same village as my wife, a place called Jalangardh in Uttar Pradesh. It's midway between Kanpur and Lucknow. My father and his family also lived there. As for me, I was born in England.'

Ashton wondered what were the chances of verifying the family history Hakkison Lal had so willingly provided. About zero, he decided. India was made up of hundreds upon thousands of villages and it was unlikely the registration of marriages, births and deaths was as comprehensive as that maintained at St Catherine's House. Hakkison Lal undoubtedly knew this, which was why he was so damned cheerful.

'When did Mr V. J. Desai arrive in this country?' O'Meara asked in a voice as smooth as silk.

'The seventh of March, it was a Tuesday.'

'And less than three weeks later you formed a partnership trading as Desai Hakkison Lal, Wholesale Electrical Goods?'

'Yes indeed; that was my big mistake, Sergeant. He drew all the money out of the bank account which I had opened for the partnership. He also sold all the stock we had obtained on credit from the manufacturers.'

'We are anxious to find him, Mr Lal.'

'And so am I. My goodness, yes.' Lal raised both hands and turned them inwards as if he was about to strangle somebody. 'What I wouldn't like to do to that man. He cost me thousands of pounds.'

'Why didn't you report him to the police?'

'How could I, Sergeant? He was part of my wife's family.'

'Where is he now?'

'I wish I knew; he is certainly not in London.'

'Where did Mr Desai stay when he arrived?'

'With us to begin with. As I have already said, he is family and it is our duty to look—'

'Why didn't he stay with his sister-in-law?' O'Meara asked, bringing Lal up with a jolt.

'His sister-in-law?'

'Yes, Dr Z. K. Ramash.'

Lal stared at her, mouth open, eyes blank like a boxer who has just taken a good body shot that has left him winded and hanging on the ropes.

'The lady in Lansdowne Mews,' O'Meara continued relentlessly. 'You must have heard of her. She was murdered; it was in all the newspapers.'

Lal visibly groped for an explanation, then seizing the first thing to come into his head, he told her that his wife's second cousin was an only child.

'When did Mr Desai leave this house?' O'Meara asked.

'Let me see now; he stayed ten days with us, then I let him have the flat above one of my shops.'

'At what address?'

'I think you are being a very rude young lady,' Lal said, and wagged an admonishing finger at her. 'You won't let me finish what I was going to say. I think you are deliberately trying to confuse me.'

'The address?' O'Meara said calmly, unimpressed by Lal's histrionics.

'It's 761B Kingsbury Road.'

'That's not far from where the late Mr Basil Wilks lived.' Ashton said.

'Is it?' Lal shrugged. 'I have mini markets all over North London.'

'But we won't find V. J. Desai in the flat above that particular mini market, will we, Mr Lal?'

'No, Sergeant, as I have already told you, he has gone and taken my money with him.'

'When did you discover this?'

'Over a fortnight ago. I telephoned him at the warehouse in Greenford and at the flat but couldn't get an answer. So I went round to see him that same evening. The next morning I rang the Midland Bank and learned he had drawn every penny out of the business account.' Lal's voice rose a full octave and quivered with anger. 'The blighter had actually forged my signature on the cheque.'

It didn't matter whether his story was true or false; in the end his rage was genuine. After observing him closely, Ashton had come to the conclusion that Lal could work himself up to such an extent he really believed he had been wronged.

'Where do you think Mr V. J. Desai is now?'

'I don't know, Sergeant. I imagine he has gone home.'

'Home being Jalangardh in the Uttar Pradesh?'

'How clever of you to remember.'

If ever there was a time to reveal the iron hand in the velvet glove Ashton thought it was now while Lal was full of over-weening confidence. He glanced at O'Meara, caught a faint nod and moved in.

'Immigration has no record of your wife's second cousin either entering or leaving this country,' he said curtly.

'It is scarcely my fault if they are so inefficient,' Lal told him.

'Don't give me that shit. Desai never filled out a landing card; he didn't have to, he was travelling on a British passport under a false name, as you know damn well.'

'That is slander,' Lal spluttered. 'If you don't withdraw that allegation and apologise to me, I shall instruct my solicitor to sue you.'

'I doubt it. I think you will be much too busy fighting extradition. The Central Bureau of Investigation in Delhi would like to have a word with you.'

There wasn't a grain of truth in the assertion. In fact, Ashton had no reason to suppose the Central Bureau was even aware of Lal's existence but the man with mini markets all over North London couldn't know that.

'Of course they are primarily interested in V. J. Desai, one-time captain in the Bombay Sappers and Miners who is currently the Director of Military Operations for the Ananda Marg. He's the man who planned the assassination of Lieutenant General Narain Singh, the former Commander-in-Chief of Eastern Command. He's very good at that sort of thing.'

'I do not know what you are talking about. I have never heard of this General.' Lal wagged his finger again, this time at Ashton. 'I think you are making this up to frighten me.'

Hakkison Lal was right, he was trying to make the Asian sweat. Ashton told him it was no use pretending he hadn't covered for V. J. Desai while the latter was in Berlin wining and dining Lorraine Cheeseman at the Bristol Hotel Kempinski because the German Intelligence Service had been keeping the lady under surveillance. Then there was the Steadfast Agency whose services had been engaged by Desai Hakkison Lal.

'Dr Ramash, Lorraine Cheeseman and Basil Wilks; people have a habit of dying round your wife's second cousin.'

'I have had enough of your insinuations,' Lal told them. 'I am going to make an official complaint to the Commissioner of the Metropolitan Police. You will find I am not without influence.'

'That's your privilege, sir,' O'Meara said politely. 'But since you have been consorting with a known terrorist, I recommend you seek the advice of your solicitor first.'

After that exchange, Lal got a little shrill and ordered them out of the house. He wasn't prepared to put up with police harassment and was going to bring their conduct to the notice of the Home Secretary. To emphasise the point, he slammed the door behind them with enough force to rattle the letter box.

'It would seem we are not too popular with Mr Hakkison Lal,' Ashton observed.

'I just wish we could prove half the things we've accused him of,' O'Meara said in a flat voice.

'There's a lot of circumstantial evidence against Lal and beneath all the bluster he's worried.'

'I hope you're right, Mr Ashton.'

'Believe me, sooner or later he will make a mistake and you've got him under surveillance. Right?'

'It's not a hundred per cent.'

She had a couple of night watchmen parked down the street who would follow Hakkison Lal if he left the house, and the only public call box in the neighbourhood had been bugged, quite illegally. But O'Meara hadn't been able to persuade her superiors that she had sufficient evidence for the Home Office to authorise a phone tap on the house.

'I jumped in too soon and I'm going to end up with egg on my face.'

'You're wrong,' Ashton told her, 'that's not going to happen. We'll get the address of every mini market he has in North London and the names of the people who live above the shops.'

Armed with that information, British Telecom would be requested to furnish duplicate copies of the relevant phone bills together with an update on each subscriber. The same applied to the Steadfast Agency and Wilks's private number at his flat in Gayton Court.

'According to Mildred Scarsdale, Wilks conducted the shady side of his business over the phone.'

'That's right,' O'Meara agreed, 'but he was crafty enough to use the public call box.'

'Maybe he did, but it doesn't follow that everybody was as cautious as Wilks. Somebody who worked for Lal might have phoned Wilks at the office or his flat. If they had, one of his numbers would show up on their phone bill. It's a stone-cold certainty Wilks was given a contact number to put him in touch with Desai. I'm banking Lal has got a mobile and was the go-between.'

There would have been at least three exchanges. The first when Wilks had learned what the client wanted from him. The second when he had obtained the material and wanted to know what to do with it. And the third a matter of an hour or so after Mungo Park had turned nasty.

'How do you know Lal didn't use a pay phone whenever he had to consult Wilks?'

Ashton didn't but the way he saw it, everybody was capable of making a mistake somewhere along the line. Lal must have thought he'd finished with Wilks after they had taken delivery of Harriet's profile sheet, then weeks later he had received a totally unexpected call from him.

'Don't you see, he panicked and used his mobile to relay instructions from Desai. If I'm right, the night Wilks met his death, the number of a pay phone will show up on Lal's phone bill.'

Ranikhet was about 8,000 feet up in the foothills of the Himalayas, roughly forty miles from the narrow gauge railhead at Kathgodam. Like the more famous hill stations of Simla and Naini Tal, it had been a place of respite in the hot weather season for officials of the Indian Civil Service and the military from the garrison towns on the plains. Detachments from the South Staffordshire Regiment and the King's Own had been the last British troops to occupy the barracks above the village and they had departed in June 1947, or so Bannerman had learned from a faded plaque in what had once been the Gymkhana Club. Nowadays, the population of Ranikhet was temporarily swollen by the more adventurous backpackers who aimed to climb the Pindari glacier.

However, the tourist season had ended six weeks ago and only the permanent residents were left, which was just as well since Bannerman hadn't arranged hotel accommodation in advance. As it happened, he was the only guest staying at the Hotel Excelsior, formerly the Gymkhana Club. He had felt conspicuous from the moment he had walked out of the station at Kathgodam and boarded the single-decker bus to Ranikhet, the one European face among all the passengers. Six or seven weeks ago there would still have been the odd backpacker to keep him company and provide an additional object of curiosity.

Sumitra had sensed trouble when she had learned why he was going to Ranikhet and had begged him not to go. At the time he had pooh-poohed her fears but now he was beginning to feel exposed and wished he had stayed at home. In conversations with various Indian politicians, he had argued that the political aims of the Ananda Marg were drawn from the Hindu Magasabha and its military-terrorist arm, the Rashtriya Swayam Sewak Sangh or RSSS, which had been active in the 1920s. They had preached that India was one and indivisible and anyone who did not accept this was a traitor.

The Ananda Marg preached the same philosophy and intended to unite India and Pakistan by force of arms. A major conflict between the two nations would undoubtedly suit their purpose. At least that had been the proposition Bannerman had put forward to anybody who would listen to him.

And somebody had, because a hand-written note had been delivered to the press agency inviting him to meet V. J. Desai, who wished to correct some of his misconceptions about the Ananda Marg. It was the word 'correct' which now sent a shiver down his spine. Bannerman promised himself that this would be the last night he spent in the Hotel Excelsior; first thing tomorrow morning he would catch the bus to Kathgodam.

Hearing a faint rattle, he closed his diary, left it on the bedside table and went to see who had just tried the door to his room.

There was no more reassuring sight than the stately figure of the senior and very old bearer who could remember the days when the hotel had been a club frequented by the burra sahibs and their memsahibs. The only thing which disturbed Bannerman was the note the bearer gave him. V. J. Desai had left him to cool his heels for over twenty-four hours and now he calmly expected Bannerman to drop everything and make his way to the old District Commissioner's bungalow. It was, however, a summons he couldn't ignore and still call himself a newspaper-man.

Bannnerman tipped the bearer, closed the door after him and then retrieved the .32 Webley revolver he had left under the pillow. As a matter of routine, he swung out the cylinder, checked that all six chambers were loaded, then locked the cylinder home and slipped the revolver into his jacket pocket.

He left the hotel and started up the hillside towards the District Commissioner's bungalow. It was a cold night made brilliant by a full moon in a cloudless sky that picked out the sandy-looking path which meandered through fir trees. He had been told it would take ten minutes to reach the bungalow and he was roughly halfway there when he had this prickly feeling that somebody was following him. He turned about and found it hadn't been his imagination working overtime. Worse still, when he looked back over his shoulder, he saw there was now a second man ahead, blocking his path. Bannerman didn't hesitate, drawing the revolver he faced one potential assailant and then the other.

'Get out of my way,' he shouted. 'I'm armed and I will shoot if I have to.'

He said it in English and repeated the warning in Hindi but they still came on and he could see that each man possessed a knife with a curved blade. He went for the nearest man, aimed at his legs and fired. The revolver made a feeble noise not unlike a Christmas cracker and the same thing happened when he squeezed the trigger the second time. Suddenly it dawned on Bannerman that sometime last night when he was asleep in bed, an intruder had broken into his hotel room and deftly removed the Webley from under his pillow and taken it away to doctor the ammunition. The bullets had been separated from the cartridge cases and the cordite removed. The rounds had then been reassembled leaving only the percussion cap in the base of the cartridge, and the revolver returned without him knowing a damned thing about it. That last drink he'd had before going to bed? The barman must have put a sleeping draught in it to ensure he didn't wake up. Idiotic really – they could have smothered him in bed but maybe the hotel proprietor had objected.

The man behind Bannerman slid the knife into the left lung, the one in front stabbed him in the chest and stomach.

'Oh you bastards,' he gasped, and coughed up blood which ran down his chin to join the rivers flowing from his chest and stomach.

Chapter Eighteen

━━━━━━━━━◆━━━━━━━━━

Inevitably at morning prayers, there were always certain matters which fell within the need-to-know category and were therefore not disclosed to all and sundry at the daily meeting. One such example was the IRA's response to a proposed meeting with a representative of the SIS.

Clifford Peachey had thought it unlikely that a meeting could be set up in less than seventy-two hours and had envisaged a period of negotiation before a neutral rendezvous was agreed. In fact the Provisionals had come back in half the time. Although the SIS had given them the right to choose the time and place, Hazelwood didn't like the way they had gone about it. He had been informed of their terms and conditions by Clifford Peachey a few minutes before morning prayers and had been seething ever since.

'Munich,' he said tersely, and waved Peachey to take a chair. 'Any thoughts why the IRA should have chosen that particular city?'

'They could have an active service unit lying doggo in the area which they can call on as a backup.' Peachey took out his pipe and proceeded to fill it from the tin of Dunhill Standard Mixture. 'They undoubtedly believe we will do the same by drawing on one of our specialist units deployed in Germany.'

'But we haven't got any SAS detachments based in Germany.'

'They would regard that as our problem, not theirs. The fact is, Victor, they won't send any of their top men to meet us face to face unless they are well covered. They don't trust us.'

'You can be damned sure I don't trust them. I don't like the way they are calling the tune. The meeting either takes place between 10.00 and 19.00 hours tomorrow or not at all. We're being hustled.'

'I think we should forget the idea.'

'What are you saying, Clifford?'

Peachey struck a match and lit the pipe, then puffed away until he was satisfied it wouldn't die on him. One of the attractions of being a pipe smoker was that the ritual of lighting up bought you time to work things out.

'I'm saying we are asking too much of Ashton. The opposition know the area, you can see that by the contact numbers they've given us. They will also be armed. Ashton will be going in blind with no armed response team to watch his back, and politically our hands are tied.'

Peachey was right. Although Rowan Garfield had a couple of useful contacts in *Grenzschutzgruppe 9*, the antiterrorist force, they could hardly ask for their assistance without involving Berlin. And the German Government would have a fit when they learned British Intelligence had arranged a meeting with the IRA on their territory without consulting them. In view of the time limit which the Provisionals had imposed, getting an SAS team out on the ground would be a chancy business. Furthermore, the Foreign and Commonwealth Office wouldn't allow them to put their firearms in the diplomatic bag.

'As I see it,' Peachey continued, 'we have two options. Either I personally meet the Provisionals or no one goes to Munich. In that event, I can leave the service earlier than was originally planned. I'm pretty sure the Irish National Liberation Army has no idea that Ann and I have bought a cottage up in Yorkshire.'

'I'm afraid neither solution is acceptable and Ashton is still the best man for the job. We'll just have to do the best we can do for him utilising our own limited resources. That's if he agrees to go.'

'I'm glad you're leaving it up to him,' Peachey said quietly.

'Well, if Ashton doesn't fancy Munich, I'd say you and Ann could be feeding two hairy-chested policemen well into your retirement years.'

Hazelwood eyed the number of cheroot stubs that were already in the cut–down shell case and vowed he wouldn't yield to temptation. 'It could be that you will be doing that anyway,' he added lugubriously.

Calthorpe worked in the restricted area of the British High Commission which was out of bounds to visitors and members of the staff who lacked the requisite security clearance. This was not a problem for him; as Head of Station, Delhi, nearly all his business was conducted outside normal office hours and far away from the High Commission itself. Indeed, since assuming the appointment, Calthorpe had not received a single member of the public at his office. However, this ceased to be the case at five minutes past eleven that morning when the duty messenger informed Calthorpe an Indian lady who refused to give her name wished to see him forthwith.

When he went downstairs, Calthorpe wasn't altogether surprised to find Sumitra Bannerman waiting for him in one of the rooms on the ground floor set aside for visitors. Her eyes were puffy and bloodshot from weeping and it was obvious that something pretty terrible had happened to Logan.

'My husband has been murdered,' Sumitra told him before he could ask. 'His body was found yesterday morning. He had been stabbed to death.'

Sumitra had known her husband was staying at the Excelsior in Ranikhet because Bannerman had telephoned to let her know he had arrived safely. What Bannerman hadn't told her was the phone number of the hotel. When there had been no further word from him, she had called the Reuters office in Delhi and reported his absence to the bureau chief. It had then taken Reuters less than two hours to ascertain that the body of their erstwhile senior correspondent was lying in the mortuary at Almora forty miles east of Ranikhet where it awaited formal identification prior to burial.

'I'm terribly sorry.' The words sounded trite and he desperately wanted Sumitra to know he genuinely meant it. 'Is there anything I can do to help?' he added lamely. 'Anything at all?'

'I think you have done more than enough already, Mr

Calthorpe. My husband would be alive today if it weren't for you.'

Calthorpe couldn't bring himself to refute the allegation even though he hadn't asked Logan Bannerman to do anything which would have put him in harm's way. Above all he hadn't asked him to get close to the leaders of the Ananda Marg. That had been the newspaperman in Logan but he couldn't point that out to Sumitra.

'Would it be too painful to talk about it?' he asked tactfully.

'I don't know anyone else who would be interested to hear what had happened to my husband.'

'You have no family?'

'They did not approve of Logan.'

It was as if a damn had burst under pressure. She spoke rapidly to give a disjointed and rambling account of what she had learned from Reuters. Bannerman had been found on a narrow footpath leading uphill towards the old District Commissioner's bungalow which was no longer occupied. None of the staff at the Excelsior had seen him leave the hotel and the manager hadn't been aware Sumitra's husband was missing until the police had arrived to enquire if a Mr Logan Bannerman was staying at the Excelsior.

'They had found his wallet lying in the scrub nearby. His murderers had taken every rupee he had but had left his credit cards . . .'

'Murderers?' Calthorpe repeated.

'There were signs that he had been attacked by at least two men.'

'And he was unarmed.'

It was more of an observation than a question but Sumitra took it as such and told him that Logan had kept a small revolver at home. She hadn't actually seen him take the .32 pistol but the weapon hadn't been in the centre drawer of his writing desk when she had looked for it after learning that her husband had been murdered. The small cardboard box containing the revolver ammunition had been opened and six of the twenty-four rounds it had contained had been taken.

'My husband also took his journal with him but it was not found among his effects by the hotel staff.'

'Perhaps Logan had it on him when he was attacked?' Calthorpe suggested.

'No, the journal was like so,' Sumitra told him and used both hands to illustrate its size. 'It was bound in leather and quite thick, too big to fit in his jacket pockets.'

Calthorpe made a mental note of several questions which he couldn't put to Sumitra without causing her unnecessary distress. Specifically he wanted to know whether any leaders of the Ananda Marg were known to be in Ranikhet when Bannerman was killed. He also wondered if the police had reason to suspect that Bannerman's room at the hotel had been broken into. Finally, he couldn't understand why the appropriate authorities had apparently made no attempt to get in touch with the next of kin. For some of the answers he would have to go cap in hand to Choudhury while others fell within the province of the British Consul, Delhi.

'My husband died for you,' Sumitra said, repeating the accusation. 'What will you do for him, Mr Calthorpe?'

'His death won't go unpunished; the police will find the men who killed him and they will stand trial.'

'You have more faith in the authorities than I do.'

'We will offer a reward for information leading to his arrest,' Calthorpe promised her rashly.

'Good, that's what I wanted to hear.' Sumitra stood up. 'Thank you for your time,' she added with a quiet dignity that left him feeling humble.

Roger Benton, the Assistant Director in charge of the Pacific Basin and the Rest of the World Department, had celebrated his forty-seventh birthday on Monday, 9 October. He was not an ambitious man and had no desire to be considered for the appointment of Deputy Director General when Clifford Peachey retired, something he might reasonably expect as the longest serving head of an operational department. However, for someone who professed that all he wanted to do was soldier quietly on to compulsory retirement at aged sixty, he prided himself on running a tight, highly efficient organisation. Minutes after receiving a copy of the signal which Hugo Calthorpe had sent to London, the Hong Kong desk had produced the file relating to Inter-Continental Arms.

All he had been able to give Bill Orchard at that stage was a general briefing on the company, who owned the firm, what services Inter-Continental Arms provided, and a list of known clients. The company was owned by a South African living in Pietermaritzburg who had served in the army for six years, rising to the rank of sergeant. However, he was said really to have learned his trade in the Security Police and was believed to be still active in the Citizen Force Reserve. Since he only visited Hong Kong once a quarter, the day-to-day running of the business was left to the office manager. He was an Australian who had fought in Vietnam. Needless to say Inter-Continental Arms was not quoted on the stock exchange. The company offered expert advice on internal security matters including personal protection, and could provide experienced instructors to assist in the training of local forces in counter insurgency operations. The firm could also provide appropriate weapons systems and riot control munitions. Recent client states had been Fiji, Bangladesh, Nepal, Burundi and Liberia.

There was, however, nothing on the file concerning the 7.62mm Enfield L1A1 Rifles, general-purpose machine guns and small arms ammunition which Inter-Continental was alleged to have purchased in Cyprus. Benton had therefore immediately fired off a signal to Head of Station, Hong Kong, requesting he investigate the allegation as a matter of some urgency. He had also made enquiries of the Ministry of Defence and the Department of Trade and Industry. He had anticipated the replies would be spread over several days but unusually all three addresses had responded that afternoon. After summarising the latest information, he walked the end result along to the Asian Department.

Until recently Roger Benton had regarded the Asian Department as an absolute doddle. Bill Orchard rarely had anything to disclose at morning prayers and while a nasty civil war was being waged in Sri Lanka by the Tamil Tigers, the SIS involvement was limited to maintaining a watching brief. The same applied to the two British hostages who had been kidnapped almost eight months ago by Kashmiri separatists. Like a volcano which had remained dormant for a considerable number of years, Bill Orchard's department had now suddenly erupted. It had started in a small way with the preliminary planning of the official visit of HM the Queen and HRH the Duke of Edinburgh to Pakistan and India in 1997 to mark the fiftieth anniversary of Independence. The lava had really begun to flow with the discovery that the late Dr Z. K. Ramash had been related by marriage to V. J. Desai, the Director of Military Operations conducted by the Ananda Marg. The paradrop of small arms and ammunition of British origin on Udhampur which the Indian Government alleged had been intended for the Kashmir Liberation Front had caused a second eruption. Judging by the worried expression on Orchard's face, it seemed there had been yet another development.

'Don't tell me,' Benton said cheerfully, 'more trouble, Bill?'

'I'll say there is,' Orchard said heatedly. 'Logan Bannerman has been murdered in Ranikhet. I've just received an emergency cable from Hugo Calthorpe. Apparently the local police are convinced he was attacked by thieves and would be alive today if he hadn't tried to fight them off.'

'But you're not satisfied they're right?' Benton suggested.

'His widow insists he'd heard the Ananda Marg was holding some kind of secret meeting in the village. Calthorpe has a number of questions he intends to put to Brigadier Choudhury, the Deputy Chief of the Intelligence Bureau.'

'Was Bannerman a useful source of information?'

'Very.'

'You're going to miss him then.'

'Yes, he would have been invaluable in running down this nuclear business.'

'What nuclear business?' Benton asked.

It transpired there had been one other new development. The MoD had reported that their Defence Liaison Officer in Delhi had been told on good authority that India would have both a strategic and tactical nuclear capability within three years. The Atomic Weapons Research Establishment at Aldermaston thought it would be at least six years before Delhi possessed the dual capability and the Foreign and Commonwealth Office had placed an embargo on any similar Intelligence-gathering in

Islamabad for fear it would encourage the Pakistan Government to engage in a nuclear arms race with their immediate neighbours.

'And guess who will get the blame if it all goes pear-shaped,' Orchard grumbled.

'Well, I'd like to say something to cheer you up,' Benton said, 'but I can't. Choudhury was right about two things: the MoD confirmed that the rifles, machine guns and ammunition dropped on Udhampur had been declared surplus to requirements by the Ordnance Depot, Dhekélia. And they were purchased by Inter-Continental Arms.'

'I'm overjoyed,' Orchard remarked sourly.

'The Department of Trade and Industry granted an export licence because they understood the weapons and munitions had been acquired on behalf of the Government of Nepal, a friendly country. Mind you, how they could have granted a licence when it was known the firm had provided various services for the regimes in Burundi and Liberia is beyond me. Anyway, Inter-Continental Arms subsequently informed the DTI that Nepal no longer wanted the arms. The firm's office manager in Hong Kong showed the actual correspondence to our Head of Station. This included further letters informing the Department of Trade and Industry that Inter-Continental Arms had sold the weapons and ammunition on to the RAO Corporation, Karachi, agents for the Government of Pakistan and were therefore returning the export licence. The DTI emphatically deny this.'

'I don't imagine Hugo Calthorpe will have much joy if he tries to sell that to Choudhury.'

'How right you are, Bill. We've been framed: question is who by and why?'

Ashton supposed he might have guessed something was in the wind when he walked into the DG's office and found Clifford Peachey occupying one of the spare armchairs. Had he really been on his toes he should have realised that in asking him how well he knew Munich, Victor had some hidden agenda in mind. The fact that he hadn't even been within fifty miles of the city had merely drawn the jocular comment that now was his chance to see the place. Then Hazelwood had suddenly presented him with some notes on the life and times of Barry Nolan, one of the most ruthless killers in the Irish National Liberation Army and he'd had an inkling of what was coming next.

'Is this the man who knows your current address?' he asked Peachey.

'So the FBI has told us.'

After waiting for the Deputy Director to say how this information might affect him, Ashton finally turned to Hazelwood for enlightenment.

'I don't see the connection with Munich,' he said quietly.

He soon learned that and a lot more besides, particularly his role in the scheme of things. In view of what he was being asked to do, the lack of human and material resources appalled Ashton, but at least Hazelwood was brutally frank with him.

'You don't have to do it, Peter,' Peachey said from the sidelines. 'I certainly wouldn't in your shoes.'

'I'm not ready to make any kind of decision yet,' Ashton told him. 'I want to know why the Provisionals should be impressed by the information we have on Barry Nolan and his family. There is nothing to distinguish it from any other potted biography 10 Intelligence Company can produce at the drop of a hat.'

'What would make them sit up and take notice in your opinion?' Hazelwood asked.

'We might grab their attention if we could tell them how Nolan had obtained his information.'

'According to the FBI office in Boston, Nolan's source was one of the men who helped Clifford to move house. It seems he was over here on a long-term scouting mission for the INLA and had been working for the Brent Brothers Removal Service for approximately twenty-one months when he returned to Ireland. The firm told us they were sorry to lose him, said he was a good worker.'

'Does he have a name?' Ashton asked.

'Hopkinson, Daniel Hopkinson, known as "Hoppy".'

'Very original.'

'Actually it's quite apposite: his right leg is half an inch shorter than the left.'

'And when was Nolan in Boston?'

'From Wednesday, the twenty-seventh of September to Thursday, the twelfth of October,' Hazelwood told him.

'What was he doing over there? Fund-raising?'

'He was passing the hat around.' Hazelwood reached for one of the Burma cheroots in the cigar box and added to the fug Peachey was busy creating with his pipe. 'Are you now ready to make up your mind?' he enquired between puffs.

'Almost.' There were so many adverse factors that Ashton wondered why he'd hesitated. The Provisionals were in the driving seat, which didn't augur well, and he would be on his ownsome. 'What about the Training School?' he asked. 'Can't they provide me with a backup from the permanent staff?'

Ashton had in mind the warrant officer on loan from Special Forces who taught close-quarter combat to the new intake and ran refresher courses for the old hands. Until recently the post had been manned by the SAS, currently it was filled by an acting warrant officer from the Special Boat Squadron of the Royal Marines.

'I'm afraid our tame bootneck is not available,' Hazelwood told him.

'I thought the induction course had completed the basic training phase?'

'They have and he's gone to the Seychelles on fourteen days' leave. We'd never get him back on time.'

'You really know how to encourage a man.'

'Is that a no, no?' Hazelwood asked.

'It will be if I can't persuade Eric Daniels to watch my back.'

'You are referring to the Daniels in the Motor Transport Section?' Hazelwood said in an incredulous voice.

'Why not? The Military Police trained him in close-protection duties and he has had some practical experience at it. And in a hostile situation too which is more than can be said for some of the specialists who have been seconded to us in the past. Of course we'll need protective clothing.'

'You know where to get it, Peter.'

'And a concealed weapon.'

'I don't want to know about that,' Hazelwood growled.

'Have you considered what Daniels' wife might have to say about all this?' Peachey asked.

'No reason why I should. They were divorced six years ago and he's not involved with anybody.'

Daniels was, however, showing every sign of being interested in Sergeant O'Meara but as far as Ashton could tell, she wasn't even aware of his existence.

'What about Harriet then?' Peachey again, the self-appointed surrogate father. His almost obsessional concern for Harriet grated on Ashton.

'She's up in Lincoln with her real father,' he said cuttingly.

Peachey turned a delicate shade of pink but he wasn't going to be put off.

'I don't think Harriet would be very happy if she knew—'

'Listen, if I do go to Munich, it'll be for Harriet, not you. She's at risk just as much as you are, perhaps more so. Park stole her profile sheet and it ended up in the hands of a terrorist organisation.' Ashton pointed an accusing finger at the Deputy DG. 'You told me this "Hoppy" character discovered your new address; what I want to know is how he fingered you in the first place. My guess is he got your number while you were working at Gower Street. He could have latched on to Harriet at the same time.'

'That's ridiculous,' Peachey said angrily. 'You're simply trying to justify yourself. A whiff of danger works on you like an aphrodisiac.'

'The day after you returned from Washington, an infrared passive defence system was installed at 84 Rylett Close. It wasn't something I asked for; the Director ordered the work to be carried out because Harriet was considered to be at risk.'

That was one way of looking at it. Alternatively, a cynic might conclude that Victor had put the security measures in hand to wind him up to the point where he would willingly volunteer to meet the IRA delegation face to face.

'Has Harriet been targeted by the INLA?' Peachey asked.

'Let's say I believe in taking adequate precautions,' Hazelwood told him, then turned to Ashton. 'You'd better sound out Daniels,' he said. 'Time is running on.'

It took Ashton longer to call for a lift and make his way down to the basement garage than it did to get a positive response from Daniels. The former MP sergeant looked bored out of his skull and was more than willing to go anywhere and do anything.

Roy Kelso managed to get them two seats on British Airways Flight BA956 to Munich which departed Heathrow at 20.15 hours, and the Pay Branch rustled up £500 worth of Deutschmarks. From the General Stores Section they each drew a RBR 1000 Concealed Undervest which was designed to be inconspicuous even when worn beneath only a shirt. The garment was guaranteed not to ride up and in addition it helped to mould the armour to the body. The undervest was meant to be worn with a plate to reduce the blunt trauma effect caused by energy transfer when a projectile is stopped by the armoured jacket. Without it, the wearer could suffer serious injury to the neck from whiplash. Unfortunately, they had to forgo the plate because it would be picked up by the metal detectors when they went through security at Heathrow.

But it was the armourer who provided the real surprise packet with a couple of 5.45mm PSM pistols which had been specially made for the old KGB and Spetsnaz forces, the Russian equivalent of the SAS and Royal Marine Commandos. Small and weighing a fraction under a pound, this particular version of the 5.45mm semiautomatic was made of specially hardened plastic which meant the weapon produced no reaction from a metal detector. The ammunition was just as remarkable; it too was made of plastic with a flechette-type nose shaped like an arrowhead that shattered after penetration to inflict maximum collateral damage.

Chapter Nineteen

Ashton checked his appearance in the full-length mirror on the back of the wardrobe door. Front, back left side and right; there were no telltale rucks and bulges. He thought RBR Armour Limited, manufacturers of the 1000 Concealed Undervest, were right to claim their garment clung to the body like an extra skin. Reaching behind his back, he tucked the plastic version of the 5.45mm pistol into the waistband of the dark blue pinstripe trousers, then slipped on the matching jacket. Visually there was nothing to show that he was wearing a bulletproof vest and was carrying a semiautomatic. He picked up the packed overnight bag he had left on the bed and went downstairs into the kitchen, switching off the lights behind him.

The minicab had been ordered for 5.45 p.m. which meant he had less than ten minutes in hand. Lifting the receiver off the hook, he tapped out the Egans' number in Lincoln. The phone rang out at least a dozen times before it was answered by a man with a quavery voice who didn't sound a bit like his father-in-law.

'Is that you, Frederick?' he asked.

'Yes, who's this?'

'It's me, Peter.'

'You'll be wanting Harriet. I'll go and fetch her,' Egan said, and put the phone down with a clatter before Ashton could ask how he was keeping. Silence ensued for a full minute, then he heard a faint unintelligible mumble followed presently by light footsteps which gradually became louder as Harriet drew near the phone.

'You've caught me at a bad time,' she told him. 'I was getting Edward ready for his bath. Can you call me back in half an hour, darling?'

'Of course I can. I'll ring you from the airport.'

'Airport?' she echoed sharply. 'Where are you going at this time of night?'

'Munich. I'm attending a conference, standing in for Clifford Peachey at the last minute.'

'Oh.'

He could almost see Harriet frowning and moved swiftly to pre-empt any further questions. 'You know what the Germans are like, the conference starts promptly at eight thirty tomorrow morning, so I didn't have any choice.'

'How long does it last, this conference?'

'I'm booked on the ten p.m. flight tomorrow night. There's an earlier one at five p.m. but I doubt the meeting will be over in time.'

The time of the return flight from Munich was the only thing he had told Harriet which was remotely true. The fact that he could tell her such a pack of lies and get away with it made Ashton despise himself.

'I'm a little surprised they didn't send you in the first place.'

'Why's that?' he asked.

'Because Clifford hardly understands a word of German,' Harriet told him.

'I didn't know that.'

'Well, you do now. Look, I've got to go – Edward's shouting for me.'

'I love you,' he said.

'And I love you too, Peter. Ring me when you can. Bye.'

Ashton hung up a fraction after Harriet. Lifting the phone again, he called Mrs Davies to let her know that he proposed to leave the light on in the hall during the hours of darkness and would she please remember to switch it on again before leaving the house. A few minutes later the minicab arrived to pick him up.

Ravenscourt Park to Heathrow via the Chiswick High Road and M4 motorway was not an uplifting experience at the best of times. On a wet and windy evening such as this it was downright depressing. The journey was, however, mercifully short.

Ashton paid the minicab off outside Terminal 1 and walked inside. Everything had been done in one hell of a rush and the plane tickets hadn't arrived from the tame travel agency Kelso dealt with before Ashton had gone home to throw a few things into an overnight bag. He had asked the Admin King to have them delivered to the British Airways information desk where he would pick them up but somehow, somewhere along the line, the wires had got crossed. Loitering near the desk and doing his utmost to appear inconspicuous was Ken Maynard, the former warrant officer of the Royal Army Pay Corps who had joined the SIS straight from the Ministry of Defence. He was a short man with dark hair that was receding towards the monk's patch on the crown. He also wore glasses with tortoise-shell frames which continually slipped down his nose so that half the time he seemed to be peering over the top of them. This made him look somewhat owlish and ensured he did not go unnoticed in a crowd.

When he spotted Ashton, he immediately turned his back on him and drifted away from the information desk as if to take a closer look at one of the overhead screens. Ashton moved up to his shoulder and stood there next to him.

'Plane ticket,' Maynard said out of the corner of his mouth, and passed the voucher to him. 'Daniels has already got his. You'll find him in the departure lounge.'

'Right.'

'You are both staying at the Eden Hotel Wolff near the Hauptbahnhof.' Maynard tucked a slip of paper into the pocket of Ashton's raincoat. 'Confirmation fax,' he added, still talking out of the corner of his mouth.

'Thanks.'

Ashton parted company with him and walked off towards the bureau de change. Halfway there he glanced at his wrist-watch, looked up at one of the airport clocks, and then, as if suddenly there was no time to change his money, he turned swiftly about. He didn't catch anybody on the hop, which really didn't prove anything one way or the other. Making his way to the nearest check-in counter, Ashton collected his boarding pass and went through Immigration. There was a moment of farce at Security when his overnight bag was put on one side for further examination after it had been screened by the X-ray machine, whereas he had no trouble at all with the metal detector and body sweep.

He made no attempt to look for Daniels amongst the crowd in the departure lounge. Maynard had told him that he had gone ahead and the ex-RMP sergeant was quite capable of watching the monitor screen to see when flight BA956 was boarding and from which gate. More importantly, Ashton didn't want to make himself even more conspicuous by going in search of Daniels when Ken might have already compromised him. Instead he located the nearest pay phone and called Harriet again. By the time they finished saying goodbye, the monitor screens were showing Flight BA956 boarding at Gate 47.

After working late at the office, Orchard had not been best pleased when the duty officer of the Asian Department had phoned him at home in Wrotham just as he was about to have dinner. His wife, Mary, had scarcely been tickled pink either when he'd told her his presence was urgently required at Vauxhall Cross. In fact, they'd had a blazing row and tempers had become even more frayed when he managed to scrape the paintwork on the Audi while reversing out of the garage. The tale of woe hadn't ended there either. Outside the peak period, there was only one train an hour to London Victoria from Wrotham and Borough Green and he'd only caught the 19.46 by the skin of his teeth. The train had just gone through Bromley when Orchard suddenly realised that in his haste, he had failed to lock the Audi after leaving it in the station yard.

He phoned Mary as soon as he arrived at the office, explained what the problem was and asked her if she would please go to the station and lock the car with the spare set of keys. The request earned him a brief lecture on carelessness but that was a small price to pay for peace of mind. No longer distracted by the vision of what some joyrider might do to his beloved Audi, he was able to concentrate on the Op Immediate signals which had arrived almost simultaneously from Islamabad and Delhi.

Orchard had asked Head of Station, Islamabad to find out what he could about the European who had secured the release of ex-Major General Marchukov after he and his crew of MIC Flight 101 had been arrested by the authorities when their Tu-154 had landed at the Pakistan Air Force Base, Lahore. Following extensive enquiries, Head of Station had learned that a Mr P. J. Ingram, sales representative for the communications division of Inter-Continental Arms had checked into the Ambassadors Hotel, Lahore, two days before the paradrop of arms and ammunition on the village of Udhampur. The following afternoon, Ingram had had a long meeting with the Deputy Commandant of the Regional Paramilitary Constabulary whom he had subsequently entertained to dinner that night at the Holiday Inn on Egerton Road.

Rumour had it that the Deputy Commandant was thinking of re-equipping the Force with the Clansman range of combat radios and Inter-Continental was anxious to secure the contract. In furtherance of this aim it was said that palms had been greased in Islamabad before Ingram had arrived in Lahore. However, as far as Head of Station had been able to ascertain no order for Clansman radios had been placed with Inter-Continental Arms. On the other hand, somebody with the necessary political clout had arranged for Major General Marchukov to be rushed by air ambulance from the Pakistan Air Force Base at Lahore to Islamabad less than six hours after his Tu-154 had been impounded and the crew arrested. That same day the Russian had been put on a Pakistan International Airlines 737 to Kuala Lumpur. Among the other passengers on the plane was Mr P. J. Ingram. At KL both men had caught the same internal flight to Singapore where they had parted company, Ingram flying on to Hong Kong by Cathay Pacific, Marchukov to lose himself in Indonesia, courtesy of Singapore Airlines.

In his summation, Head of Station, Islamabad had stated there was sufficient circumstantial evidence to conclude that Marchukov had been employed by Inter-Continental Arms. Furthermore, Marchukov hadn't been compelled to make a forced landing at Lahore; that had been part of the overall plan and it had been Ingram's job to ensure the Russian was not put in the bag.

Orchard had no quarrel with the conclusions Head of Station had drawn. Unfortunately, these latest revelations only provided more ammunition for Brigadier Choudhury, who had already accused the SIS of masterminding the paradrop of arms and ammunition supposedly intended for the Kashmir Liberation Front. He noted that Head of Station had realised this and had not copied his signal to Hugo Calthorpe, which was just as well.

Orchard initialed the signal to indicate that he had seen it. The way forward was to discover who Inter-Continental Arms were working for, which would entail interviewing the general manager and Mr P. J. Ingram at length. That was something he would have to raise at morning prayers because Hong Kong fell within Roger Benton's remit as Head of Pacific Basin and Rest of the World Department.

The signal from Delhi was more straightforward. Brief and to the point, it answered some of the questions he had raised with Hugo Calthorpe. Much to their chagrin, the Indian Central Bureau of Investigation had been forced to admit that they had lost track of V. J. Desai after he had delivered a lecture on Hindu Nationalism to students at the University of Mysore on Wednesday, 15 February 1995. At various times between then and the beginning of May when he was now known to have been in London, he had allegedly been sighted in Singapore, New York and Rome. However, the Central Bureau was quite adamant that the leaders of the Ananda Marg had not forgathered in Ranikhet and were of the opinion that Logan Bannerman had been murdered by dacoits who had been reported in the area. They could not say why the appropriate authorities had made no attempt to contact the next of kin but promised this matter would be investigated rigorously.

In what amounted to a postscript, Calthorpe casually let it be known that he had promised Bannerman's widow that the SIS would offer a reward for information leading to the arrest of the killers. He thought the sum of fifty thousand pounds should do the trick and would London kindly authorise this and arrange the necessary transfer of funds?

'Damned cheek,' Orchard said aloud.

'Sir?' the duty officer enquired politely.

The telephone spared him an explanation. Answering it, Orchard was not surprised to hear Mary's voice on the line. He was, however, a little perturbed when she asked him if he was sure he had left the Audi in the station yard.

'What are you trying to tell me?' he asked with a sinking feeling.

'The Audi wasn't there. I can only assume some joyrider has borrowed it.'

His name was Patrick Lenihan. Born in Newcastle, County Down, on 21 September 1954, he was a Dublin man by adoption. To say Lenihan was a leading Republican was an understatement. Gerry Adams and Martin McGuinness might be spokesmen for Sinn Fein but he was the political brain of the movement, the one who had formulated the policy of the bomb and the ballot box. At this particular moment in time, his stock with the IRA High Command had never been higher because it had been his philosophy which had brought the British Government to the negotiating table.

Of necessity he had to earn his credibility on the streets of Derry. If he hadn't placed the car bomb which had killed a corporal in the Royal Anglian Regiment and maimed another soldier for life, nobody would have listened to him. In fact it had taken more than one successful operation to make him a force to be reckoned with in the Republican movement. So while Lenihan had not been actively engaged at the sharp end again, he had planned a series of bomb attacks that had resulted in heavy loss of life among the security forces. That the British had lacked sufficient evidence to charge him with anything other than membership of an illegal organisation had further enhanced his reputation. Released from prison after serving a mere twenty-one months, he had moved south and continued the good work.

A man like Patrick Lenihan did not get where he was without making a number of enemies along the way, some of whom had left the Provisionals and joined the Irish National

Liberation Army because they had fundamentally disagreed with his policy. To these former comrades he was a traitor who should be taken out, put up against a wall and shot. To ensure this did not happen, Lenihan never went anywhere without a bodyguard.

The man who accompanied Lenihan to Munich was Frank Kennedy, one of the best snipers to have operated in the bandit country around Crossmaglen. A crack shot with a .50 calibre RAI model 500 long-range rifle, he was also equally proficient with a handgun. But it was the basic instincts of the hunter which he had honed when a sniper that had made him such an effective bodyguard.

There was usually a second bodyguard to spell Frank Kennedy but he had been left behind on this trip. His services had been dispensed with because an active service unit tucked away in the Munich area had been put at the disposal of Patrick Lenihan.

The active service unit numbered four and consisted of three men and a woman whose ages ranged from early to late twenties. To preserve what they naïvely believed was their anonymity they used only their first names in front of the visitors from Dublin. For their part, neither Lenihan nor Kennedy gave the slightest indication that they knew everything there was to know about them. This charade particularly applied to Cathal and Mairin at whose flat in the suburb of Mitter Sendling they had been staying since arriving in Munich yesterday.

Mairin was currently employed as a hospital cleaner at the Rechts der Isar Clinic. Before this she had been a waitress at one of the city's many *Biergartens*. Following a spell as a petrol pump attendant at an all-night garage, Cathal had recently become a dishwasher at the *Ratskeller* in Marienplatz. Both were overqualified for the work they were doing. Mairin was a trained nurse while Cathal had read chemistry at Trinity, a discipline that had stood him in good stead when it came to making a delayed-action bomb. However, menial jobs which were beneath the dignity of the indigenous population were easy to come by and suited their purpose. Being casually employed allowed them to come and go pretty much as they pleased.

Mairin had worked from eight to four that day. Subsequently, she had relieved Cathal at the airport, who earlier on had phoned the manager of the *Ratskeller* to inform him he had a bad case of diarrhoea and wouldn't be coming in. At 23.50 Mairin returned to the flat in Konrad Celtis Strasse to report that she thought there might have been three, possibly four, British Secret Servicemen on British Airways Flight BA956. Under questioning by Kennedy, who wanted to know how she had identified the SIS officers, Mairin had to admit intuition had had a lot to do with it.

'Intuition,' Kennedy growled, 'I might have known it.'

'If you had seen them you would have come to the same conclusion,' Mairin told him heatedly. 'There was this tall, dark-haired man. Although he seemed very laid back you could tell just by looking at him that he was alive to everything that was going on around him.'

'He wasn't laid back,' Kennedy sneered, 'he was pissed out of his mind. He'd probably travelled first class and hadn't stopped drinking from the moment the plane took off.'

'I know a drunk when I see one,' Mairin said, glaring at Kennedy.

'You stupid little bitch, just what the hell are you inferring?'

'Hey, you don't talk to Mairin like that.'

For all Cathal was only five feet six and weighed less than nine stone, he feared no man, no matter how big. He knew a dozen ways to kill or maim somebody for life using his bare hands and had put theory into practice when he'd interrogated a captured British Army captain before strangling him.

'That will be enough, all of you.' Lenihan didn't need to raise his voice. His authority was such that nobody cared to disobey him. 'It doesn't matter whether or not Mairin has correctly identified the SIS men,' he continued in the same reasonable voice. 'By early tomorrow morning we will know who we are dealing with.'

Kennedy signalled his unhappiness with a worried frown. 'I don't see how that will help us if we walk into a trap. Personally I don't trust the Brits.'

'Neither do I, Frank, but Prime Minister Major wants to go

down in history as a good European and they won't do anything to antagonise the Germans.'

'What do you think their game is?' Cathal asked.

'They may be hoping to cause further blood-letting between ourselves and the Irish National Liberation Army and other wings of the Republican movement.'

'And how will we react?'

Lenihan smiled. 'Well, Cathal, if there is any funny business we'll just have to make an example of their chief spokesman.'

Ashton hung his raincoat up in the wardrobe, then unzipped the overnight bag and unpacked it, a task that took him all of two minutes. Although they had made their way independently of one another from the airport to Eden Hotel Wolff on Arnulf-strasse, Daniels didn't keep him waiting for long before he came tapping on his door.

'What do you reckon?' he asked after Ashton had let him into the room. 'Were they waiting at the airport?'

'Maybe. Of course they would need to watch the Haupt-bahnhof as well in case we arrived by train. And that would still leave one very big barn door wide open because we could have put a car on the shuttle and driven the rest of the way.' Ashton shrugged his shoulders. 'Seems a waste of time and effort to me. I mean, unless they already know our faces how did they expect to identify us?'

Although they'd had to sit next to one another on the 757 they'd acted like strangers exchanging no more than a few words of conversation. In accordance with the instructions he had given him, Daniels had made sure he was among the last to leave the plane at Munich. By the time the former RMP sergeant was waved through Immigration and Customs, Ashton had been in a taxi heading towards the city.

'I think I may have seen a Provo in the Arrivals Hall. A small Irish-looking girl in her early twenties, had hair blacker than a raven and glossy.'

'Was she attractive, Eric?'

'She had a good figure,' Daniels admitted.

Ashton smiled. Ever since he had known him, Daniels

had had an eye for a pretty girl. 'Were you followed to the hotel?'

'No. If a car had been tailing us I would have spotted it.'

To have latched on to them Ashton figured the opposition would have had to have witnessed the charade he had acted out in the lobby of the Eden Hotel Wolff. In order to let Daniels know how to find him he had returned to the desk as Daniels was about to register, to ask the receptionist if she hadn't perhaps given him the wrong key? 'I do not think so,' the girl had told him, 'you are in 496.' Ashton had apologised, said he had obviously misheard her the first time and, turning away, had walked over to the lifts.

'Guess they will know our faces soon enough tomorrow,' Daniels said.

'Well, you can bet the Provos will give us the runaround until they do. They will also take a few candid camera shots for future reference.' Ashton crouched in front of the mini bar and unlocked it. 'What do you fancy?' he asked.

'A whisky if there is one.'

'You've got a choice of three – Johnnie Walker Red Label, VAT 69 or Bell's Extra Special.'

'I'll have the VAT 69.'

'Anything with it?'

'No thanks.'

Ashton passed the miniature back over his shoulder and told Daniels there was a spare glass in the bathroom, then poured himself a beer into a plastic tumbler.

'How are you going to play it tomorrow?' Daniels asked him from the bathroom.

'All I've got is a list of phone numbers which I'm supposed to call tomorrow morning starting at nine thirty. However, I plan to keep them waiting for a good ten minutes which should give you enough time to rent a car.'

'And then what?'

'You come back here and stay put in your bedroom until I learn where the rendezvous is.'

'My job is to watch your back, Mr Ashton. How can I do that if you are in one part of the town and I'm cooling my heels in another?'

'You don't have to live in my shadow all the time, Eric. Soon as I learn anything you will be the first to know. That's why I need you at the other end of the phone.'

'I don't like it.'

'Neither do I but what choice do we have?'

Ashton didn't have to dot every i and cross every t for him. Before he'd volunteered for the job, Daniels had been told they could expect no material assistance from the SIS Head of Station because officially they weren't in Munich or anywhere else in Germany. In practical terms this meant no two-way radios, no mobile telephones or any other piece of equipment which might have led the German authorities to suspect the British were conducting some sort of covert operation without their knowledge and consent.

'These clandestine jobs are all very well,' Daniels observed, 'but I'll be of no use to you unless I'm in the right place at the right time.'

'You think I don't know that? Believe me, I've no intention of arriving at the RV before you've had time to get into position.'

'OK, but what do we do if somehow they manage to change the rv after I have left the hotel?'

'That's the jackpot question,' Ashton told him, and made no attempt to answer it.

Chapter Twenty

———————⟶⟫⟩◦⟨⟪⟵———————

To his colleagues Orchard had always been a liberal with a capital L which meant he was a staunch opponent of the death penalty, against all blood sports and was in favour of legalising cannabis. He became a fully fledged member of the flog 'em, hang 'em and shoot 'em brigade ten minutes before morning prayers when Mary telephoned to let him know the police had found the Audi in a field three miles outside Maidstone. The car had been totally trashed. All four wheels had been stolen, the main beams, side and tail light assemblies smashed, the seats slashed with a knife and the paintwork burned with sulphuric acid. There had been enough evidence inside the car for the police to conclude that all four joyriders had been smoking pot. In Orchard's opinion summary execution was too good for their likes; he wanted them to suffer before they were strung up. He was still seething with anger when morning prayers began. On those hitherto infrequent occasions when he'd had something to impart, he had been diffident; today he was positively aggressive. Roger Benton, Head of Pacific Basin and the Rest of the World Department, was particularly taken aback to be told he should arrange for P. J. Ingram and the Australian general manager of Inter-Continental Arms to be interrogated forthwith. Before Hazelwood could remind him there was only one DG so far as he knew, Orchard was up and running again, this time with matters arising from the murder of Logan Bannerman. There were no interruptions until he touched the reward of fifty thousand pounds which Calthorpe wished to offer for information leading to the arrest of the killers.

'I hadn't realised we had given Hugo such a generous allocation from the SIS vote,' Kelso observed acidly.

'We haven't,' Orchard told him. 'He's asked us to transfer the necessary funds.'

'Then he is going to be very disappointed.'

'It's a question of honouring a promise made to the widow. Hugo gave his word that we would offer a substantial reward.'

'I have news for you,' Kelso said. 'The contingency fund was cut by fifty per cent in this year's budget and there's a good chance it will be overspent before the end of January next year. So I'm afraid Hugo will have to renege on his promise.'

'That's out of the question,' Orchard said angrily. 'We can't go back on our word.'

'It's not our word, it's Hugo's and he should have consulted us before opening his mouth.'

'I have a question for Bill,' Hazelwood said in a tone of voice that brought everybody to heel. 'Suppose we did find the money, how does Hugo plan to disburse it? After all, we don't want to broadcast that we used Bannerman to do the odd bit of snooping from time to time.'

It transpired that Calthorpe had already taken that consideration into account. Without seeking agreement from London, he had taken it upon himself to approach the bureau chief of Reuters in Delhi. Logan Bannerman had been the agency's senior correspondent and Calthorpe had wanted to know if Reuters would accept fifty thousand from the British High Commission towards whatever reward they were planning to offer.

'And were they planning to offer one?' Hazelwood asked.

'They weren't slow to accept our donation,' Orchard told him, avoiding the question.

'Was the bureau chief aware of Bannerman's occasional involvement with the SIS?'

'He knew Logan received the occasional confidential briefing from the Press Attaché at the British High Commission and that it wasn't entirely a one-way street.'

'That's a somewhat coy answer, Bill.'

'Well, I'm sorry, Director, but it's the best one I can give you. No bureau chief is going to admit he is happy about his agency staff working for an Intelligence service. The most you can hope for is that he'll turn a blind eye to what is going on and keep his mouth shut.'

'And is that the situation in Delhi?'

'Yes. The present bureau chief has always known the score; he was in place before Hugo Calthorpe became Head of Station.'

'Fifty thousand pounds,' Hazelwood mused in a voice which suggested to Orchard that he was not convinced it would be money well spent.

'Naturally, the money won't be handed over unless the killers are apprehended and indicted for murder.'

'That isn't quite what you said earlier, Bill. I don't recall anything about an indictment before the reward was paid.'

'It was an oversight on my part,' Orchard said hastily.

'I trust Hugo is not going to be similarly afflicted?'

'I guarantee he won't.'

'Good. Now tell me what we hope to get for our money?'

'First and foremost the reason why Logan was killed.'

'If these men were hired assassins, they won't know why their paymaster wanted him dead. It's more than likely they weren't sufficiently interested to ask.' Hazelwood picked up a pencil and began to drum it on the table top. 'No, the first task for Hugo is to question the widow. When did Bannerman tell Sumitra he was going up to Ranikhet? Was it after he came home from the office? Or did somebody phone him at the bungalow?'

He had other questions for Orchard to pass on to Delhi. What time did Bannerman return from the agency the night before he left for the hills? Was it later than usual? Was it his practice to stop off somewhere on the way through the cantonment? And if so, where? Finally, what else did Bannerman tell his wife about the people he was going to meet in Ranikhet?

'If I remember correctly, Sumitra told Hugo Calthorpe that her husband had learned the leaders of the Ananda Marg were holding a secret meeting up there.'

'Yes. Apparently, Bannerman said he was doing a bit of snooping for Hugo Calthorpe.'

'Good, then you can tell Head of Station, Delhi I want

answers to my questions soonest.' Hazelwood turned to Roger Benton. 'Same goes for your man in Hong Kong,' he added.

Orchard could see the fifty thousand slipping through his fingers like water as Hazelwood went round the table the way he always did when he was bringing morning prayers to a close. Rowan Garfield of the European Department had nothing of interest to impart and what Jill Sheridan had to offer from her source, who worked for Bryce and Bryce in Bahrain, had been overtaken by the more detailed information coming from Delhi which had identified the true nature of the domestic cooking utensils lifted from Larnaka by Marchukov International Carriers. Kelso looked as if he was about to reopen the question of the reward money but an impatient wave by Hazelwood deprived him of the power of speech. As was his custom at morning prayers, Peachey gave a lifelike impression of a sphinx. It was, Orchard decided, a case of now or never.

'What can I tell Hugo Calthorpe about the reward money?' he asked in a voice loud enough to arrest the exodus from the conference room.

Hazelwood turned about, his eyes glinting. 'For God's sake, Bill,' he snapped, 'what do you think we are running here? Some sort of charitable organisation? No, Hugo had better roll up his sleeves and get me some answers first.'

Ashton turned into the Hauptbahnhof and made his way towards the nearest bank of pay phones in the concourse. There was no need to keep the man from Dublin waiting beyond the appointed time of nine thirty. Daniels had left the hotel at ten minutes to eight and had returned three-quarters of an hour later with a VW Passat he'd rented from Hertz. Selecting the end phone to his right, Ashton lifted the receiver, dug out some loose change and then fed the meter before punching out the first contact number on his list. It burred at least a dozen times before anyone deigned to pick up the phone.

'Well, don't be shy,' Ashton said after a lengthy silence. 'Speak to me, we haven't got all day.'

'Neither have we,' the contact told him.

The man was softly spoken which made it difficult to catch

his accent. Ashton thought he could make out a faint Irish brogue but wondered if that was simply wishful thinking on his part.

'So where do we meet?' he asked.

'Not so fast. Give me the next contact number on your list.'

'It's 55-77-81.'

'And the one after that?'

'It's 56-24-43.'

'All right, you're from London. Now tell me where you are calling from?'

'What's that got to do with it?' Ashton demanded.

'We didn't ask for this meet, you people in London did. Now you either answer my question or I hang up and we go our separate ways.'

'I'm at the Hauptbahnhof,' Ashton said.

'How well do you know Munich?'

'This is my first visit.'

'Better get yourself a map then.'

'I already have.'

'Good. I'll be waiting for you in the Café Weisburg on Lillian Board Weg.'

'Where's that?'

'You take the U-Bahn to Olympiazentrum and then try reading your map. These are the ground rules: you will come on foot, you will be alone and you will come unarmed. I will allow you exactly fifty minutes to get to the RV, starting now. If you fail to comply with any of these conditions, there will be no face-to-face meeting. Do I make myself clear?'

'Perfectly. How will I recognise you?'

'You won't have to,' the Irishman told him, and terminated their conversation.

Ashton hung up, then lifted the receiver again and tapped out the number of the Eden Hotel Wolff. When the switchboard operator answered, he asked for room 477 and quickly briefed Daniels. After finding Lillian Board Weg on the city map, Daniels reckoned it would take him roughly thirty minutes to get to the Café Weisburg.

'I think not,' Ashton told him. 'You're staying put. The RV I've been given has got to be a ruse.'

'How come?'

'Take a good look at your map, Eric. If the café exists, it's on the fringe of the Olympic Park. Our friends in Dublin intend to take a good look at me before proceeding any further. If they spot you in the area, we can forget our heart-to-heart talk and the whole business will have been a complete waste of time. I'll be in touch again soon as I'm satisfied they've stopped playing games. However, if you've heard nothing from me by 10.30 hours, make your way to the ice stadium and try to pick up my tracks from there.'

'I hope you know what you're doing.'

'So do I,' Ashton said, and hung up.

'You will come unarmed.' That was what the man had said and for a moment he thought about leaving the PSM 5.45mm semiautomatic pistol in a rented locker at the Hauptbahnhof but on reflection decided it was not a good idea. For one thing he was pushed for time; for another, he didn't see why the Provos should have it all their own way.

The diagrammatic layout of the Municipal Train System in the bottom left-hand corner of the map showed that Olympia-zentrum was on Line 3 of the U-Bahn. He also noted that the nearest station for that particular line happened to be in Marienplatz, which was well served by the MTS. Obtaining a ticket from the vending machine, Ashton went on to the platform and caught a train going to Berg am Laim. Two stops down the line he alighted and switched to the U-Bahn.

Hazelwood was busy preparing some notes for the next meeting of the Joint Intelligence Committee when Clifford Peachey announced his presence with a discreet cough.

'I can see this isn't a good time,' he said, 'but something has come up which could affect Ashton.'

'Sounds ominous.'

'That depends on how you look at it. The fact is Frank Kennedy hasn't been seen in any of his usual haunts for the past two days.'

Hazelwood frowned. 'Should the name mean something to me?' he asked.

'He's one of Lenihan's bodyguards.'

'Well, I've certainly heard of him. Who hasn't? Lenihan is the political brain of Sinn Fein and an ex officio of the Provisional's High Command. Am I right in thinking he also dropped out of sight?'

'Lenihan isn't at his Dublin address; the same applies to the cottage he owns in Roscrea.'

'What's the source of this information?'

'It came from the Garda's Special Branch; they regularly exchange information on terrorist activity with the RUC. My former colleagues in Five are ninety per cent certain that Lenihan is in Munich.'

'Can he fly to Munich without passing through the UK?' Hazelwood asked.

It transpired Peachey had anticipated the question and had got Roy Kelso to make enquiries. According to the friendly travel agency which looked after the SIS, Lufthansa operated a direct flight once a week from Dublin to Munich. However, between them Aer Lingus and Lufthansa offered five scheduled flights every day to Frankfurt.

'He could then have caught an internal flight to Munich,' Peachey continued. 'Alternatively, there is a perfectly good train service from Frankfurt.'

'What about this bodyguard, Frank Kennedy? Could he have taken the same route?'

'I'm only guessing, Victor, but I don't believe the Irish authorities would put any obstacles in his way. Not at a time like this when the ceasefire is at stake. They want to see a settlement in Northern Ireland as much as we do.'

'I'm sure you're right. What I want to know is whether Sinn Fein and the Provisionals are of the same mind?'

'I'm afraid that's a judgement we have to leave to the politicians. All I would say is that the Provisional IRA would never have sent Patrick Lenihan and his bodyguard to Munich if they weren't anxious to maintain a ceasefire.'

'Then you'd better pass the good news on to Ashton.'

'What?' Peachey stared at him, completely taken aback. As if in a trance he looked at his wristwatch. 'It's almost five past ten,' he said in a voice that sounded curiously high-pitched. 'How am I going to contact him?'

'Try phoning the Eden Hotel Wolff.'

'But Ashton will already have left for the RV.'

'You won't know that until the operator on the hotel switchboard has tried his room. And if he isn't available, ask for Eric Daniels and give him the names.'

'Is that wise, Victor? I mean the information came from the Garda and we don't want to queer the pitch for the RUC, do we?'

It didn't take long to discover that Hazelwood didn't mind how many pitches he queered. He had no idea what good it would do Ashton if he knew the names of the men he was dealing with but that was no excuse for withholding information from the man in the field. In the relatively short time that he had been Hazelwood's deputy, Peachey had learned there were occasions when there was no arguing with Victor and this was one of them.

Mairin looked up at the threatening sky and wondered how much longer it would be before the heavens opened and the rain came down in stair rods instead of this persistent drizzle. The prospect of a thorough soaking didn't worry her. What bothered her was the fact that she and Cathal were going to look pretty conspicuous. Anybody observing them tinkering with the Yamaha motorbike would question why they didn't take shelter in the nearby Olympic Hall and fix the machine after the rain eased off. But taking risks was all part of the job when you were on active service, fighting the Brits. Fighting was, however, the operative word and it angered her that they were putting themselves on the line for nothing. There would have been some point to what they had been ordered to do this morning if it resulted in the death of the British official but the aim of this shenanigan was to facilitate peace talks with the enemy.

Mairin wasn't in favour of the truce and she knew Cathal was also dead against it. This wasn't the time to kiss and make up, not when victory lay within their grasp. She and Cathal had spent months planning two operations – a four-hundred-pound car bomb in Celle which would demolish half the married quarters in Montgomery Road and a fail-safe ambush in Osnabrück that couldn't go wrong. Now all that painstaking and meticulous work had gone for nothing because even if the ceasefire ended tomorrow, they would still have to start again from scratch. Months had gone by without a shot being fired in anger, and since their unit had been prohibited from even reconnoitring the intended targets, there was no telling what additional defensive measures the Brits had put in place during this phoney peace. Maybe Barry Nolan and the INLA had got it right, that it was the bullet and not the ballot box which was going to unite Ireland. Maybe the time had come for her and Cathal to throw in their lot with the INLA?

The bleeper intruded upon her thoughts; unzipping the top pocket of the leather jacket, Mairin took out the short-range radio, extended the aerial and turned up the volume. A voice she had come to hate then gave her a roasting for failing to stay on listening watch. Frank the drunk from Dublin on his high horse and treating every member of the active service unit as he would a shit-scared bunch of rookies. Her bottom lip curled in disgust; if ever a man was living on his past reputation and needed a shot of Bushmills to steady the nerves, it was him.

'Our friend will be arriving any minute,' he said, winding up, 'so stay on your toes.'

Mairin waited for the other two to answer up, then gave him the standard response of 'Wilco'. 'Bloody fool,' she said, cupping a hand over the mike.

'Let me guess,' Cathal said, looking up at her as he crouched beside the Yamaha, 'the bodyguard – right?'

'Who else? He's got the wind up in case something goes wrong.'

'Nothing will, Richard and Eamonn won't let us down.'

'I know that.'

Richard was covering the entrance to the Olympiazentrum station on Line 3 of the U–Bahn, leaving Eamonn to watch the junction of Walter Bathe Weg with Lillian Board Weg from Brundage Plaza. The Brit had been told to make his way to the Café Weisburg on the Lillian Board Weg and since nobody knew what he looked like, it was their job to identify him.

'It's a pity Frank can't believe it,' she added.

'Well, like you said, he's a little bit nervous.'

Mairin smiled. Frank wasn't going to be the only one. There were a number of ways of delivering a message and Cathal thought up a beauty for the Brit which would make him shit his pants.

Daniels put the phone down and reached for the town map of Munich on the bedside table. Ashton had instructed him to stay put until he was satisfied the opposition had stopped playing games but to his way of thinking, the phone call from London put things in a different context. He left the bedroom, rode one of the lifts down to the lobby and went out into the street. At a swift walking pace, he made his way to the hotel car park, got into the VW Passat and started up. Knowing where Ashton had been told to RV with the Provos, he had taken the precaution of working out what he thought was the quickest way to the Café Weisburg on Lillian Board Weg and committing it to memory.

He shifted into gear, drove out of the car park, made a right on Arnulfstrasse, then turned on to the Landshuter Allee and put his foot down. Ashton had a good thirty-minute start on him, which meant that right now he couldn't be too far from the RV. And if Ashton was no longer at the Café Weisburg by the time he arrived there, Daniels hadn't the faintest idea how he could reestablish contact with him. What they needed, what they hadn't got, were a couple of ultra-high-frequency hand-held radios with an operating range of 4 kilometres, like the PVS 5400 manufactured by Mr Plessey. Tyres swishing on the wet surface, the wipers going full speed to keep the windscreen clear of spray, he weaved in and out of the traffic, one eye constantly darting to the rear-view mirror on the lookout for a police car. To be stopped for speeding would kill off any chance of intercepting Ashton before he reached the RV.

Daniels continued on Landshuter Allee towards the Georg Brauchie Ring Road, the Olympic Park and the 950 foot high TV Tower on his right. He tripped the indicator to show he was moving across to the slip road, then headed east on Georg Brauchie. Leaving the ring road after three-quarters of a mile, he turned into the Olympic Park and stopped by the ice stadium to get his bearings and pinpoint Lillian Board Weg on the map.

Ashton walked out of the Olympiazentrum and went on down the road towards Brundage Plaza. Instead of the persistent drizzle which had greeted him when he'd left the hotel for the Hauptbahnof, the rain was now falling steadily. It was not the kind of day for hanging about on street corners and he automatically made a note of the weather-beaten Opel Kadett parked by the kerb on the opposite side of the road. The vehicle was facing the U–Bahn station and the driver was staring fixedly ahead as if determined not to look in his direction. If he was right about the driver, there would be at least one other member of the surveillance team in the vicinity. That was the usual procedure but although Ashton kept his eyes peeled, he didn't spot the backup. There were, he concluded, two possibilities: either the second man was too good for him or the Provos were short of manpower in this neck of the woods.

Skirting Brundage Plaza, he picked up Lillian Board Weg and started up the incline towards the bridge over the ring road. With nobody else in the immediate vicinity, he felt naked and vulnerable. The time was 10.19, and if Daniels was following his instructions to the letter, he would still be in his room at the Eden Hotel Wolff waiting to hear from him.

Mairin heard a low whistle on the transceiver and turned up the volume in time to hear Eamonn say that he had a message for her. Pressing the transmit button, she told him to send it.

'Subject has just passed my position,' he informed her. 'He's roughly six feet tall, give half an inch either way, has dark hair cut fairly short, powerful-looking body – hard to judge his weight but it has to be in excess of thirteen stone, say one hundred and eighty-five pounds. He's wearing a fawn–coloured military-style trench coat with the belt buckled loosely behind his back.'

'Are you sure he's the Brit we're waiting for?'

'Trust me, we've checked him over and he fits.'

'Roger and out,' Mairin said, and switched off the transceiver.

'Time to go?' Cathal asked.

He did not wait for confirmation; straddling the motorbike, he started the engine, engaged first gear and barely gave Mairin time to mount the pillion before he let the clutch out and took off.

Ashton saw the motorcyclist and pillion rider when they appeared from behind the Olympic Hall and turned on Lillian Board Weg. They were dressed in black from head to toe – crash helmets, bomber jackets and skin-tight leather jeans. He estimated their speed to be in the region of twenty to twenty-five miles an hour which the way he read the situation had sinister implications. A motorbike could beat a car hands down when it came to making a quick getaway after a shooting and was one of the reasons why the Provisionals set such great store by them. Ashton had lost count of the number of police officers who had been shot in their own cars by a gunman riding on the pillion seat.

Suddenly, Ashton had a horrible feeling that he was about to become one more statistic. He tried reminding himself that the IRA had agreed to this meeting but a stronger voice suggested that maybe the Provisionals were planning to resume hostilities and he was destined to be the first fatal casualty. If so, they couldn't have picked a better location for an assassination. There were no onlookers in the area, and the sound of pistol shots would be lost in the wide open space of the Olympic Park or drowned by the noise of the passing traffic on nearby Georg Brauchie. Mouth dry as dust, his heart pumping overtime, Ashton watched them cross the bridge over the ring road and draw even nearer, still doing under thirty miles an hour. At twenty-five yards, the rider's face was completely obscured by the black visor attached to his crash helmet.

This is it, Ashton thought, and remained transfixed to the spot, then at the very last moment, he recovered his wits and moved back on to the grass verge. Neither rider looked at him as they went by and he wondered if their job was to create some sort of diversion for the killer. He glanced up the lane in the direction of the bridge; as he did so, the motorcyclist opened the throttle and out of the corner of his eye, Ashton saw the pillion rider lob something high into the air over his shoulder. A voice inside his head told him it was a grenade and he didn't stop to question the assumption. Chances were it was primed with a four-second fuse and you can cover a pretty fair distance in four seconds if you put your mind to it.

He started running, legs pumping like pistons, while he counted slowly – 'one thousand, two thousand, three thousand' – before throwing himself flat on the ground.

Chapter Twenty One

Instead of the usual crump, the grenade made a hollow popping sound. The base plug was known to carry as much as two hundred yards from the point of impact yet, although Ashton was still inside the danger zone, no metal fragments cleaved the air above his head. A home-made bomb then, which had lacked sufficient explosive to shatter the casing into lethal fragments? Or maybe there had been a partial misfire and the rest of the high-explosive filling was quietly fizzing away? Ashton gave it another minute, then got to his feet and slowly retraced his steps.

The bomb consisted of a miniature parachute attached to which were a small lead weight and the remains of an electric light bulb, the cause of the hollow popping noise when it struck the asphalt surface. There was also a small sheet of notepaper that had been tied on to the chute directly above the lead weight. Somebody with a mathematical bent had gone to a lot of trouble to put the fear of God into him. The lead weight had been the critical factor; too heavy in relation to the parachute and the contraption would have plummeted straight back to earth. The object of the parachute was to check the rate of descent so that the bikers could make a clean getaway.

He had run away from an electric light bulb. The knowledge that he had been frightened and humiliated made Ashton burn with anger. No doubt those two pint-size pisspots in black leathers thought it had been one hell of a joke and were laughing their socks off right now. He reached under his trenchcoat and felt for the PSM 5.45 semiautomatic nestling in the small of his back. He wished he had stood his ground instead of running away, wished he'd pulled the handgun and let fly. That would have given them something to think about, except that in reacting immediately he wouldn't have fired over their heads and there would have been two very dead Provisionals lying on Lillian Board Weg and hostilities would inevitably be resumed. Ashton crouched beside the parachute, untied the sheet of notepaper and smoothed it out. Although the rain had made the ink run, the message was still faintly legible. It read: '56–18–29, Chinese Temple, English Garden.' The six digits tallied with the fourth contact number on the list Hazelwood had provided, which he supposed was the Irishman's droll way of ensuring he realised the note was intended for him. He slipped the soggy piece of paper into his raincoat pocket and straightened up just as a car crossed the bridge and headed towards him. A dark green VW Passat bearing a registration number Ashton had seen once before. He moved forward, mentally willing Daniels not to flash the headlights or sound the damned horn to attract his attention as they passed one another going in opposite directions. The bikers might have gone but the man in the Opel Kadett or A. N. Other could still be watching him, possibly from the vicinity of Brundage Plaza. Keeping the right arm close to the ribs, he pointed the index finger at Daniels, then used it as a pointer-staff to describe a small square.

The bewildered expression on his face told him that Daniels didn't know what the hell to make of the hand signal. There would have been no confusion had he made a circular motion with the index finger but the very last thing he wanted was Daniel executing a three-point turn on Lillian Board Weg. Anybody observing the manoeuvre would soon put two and two together and come up with the right answer.

He ignored the VW Passat as it came abreast of him, didn't even so much as glance at Daniels. 'Keep on going, keep on going; don't slow down, don't look at me': if there was such a thing as mental telepathy, he hoped Daniels would get the message. The constant note from the VW engine which gradually faded into the distance persuaded him that he had.

Ashton walked across the bridge and made his way to the ice rink. Provided Daniels had understood his message in its entirety, he would drive through Brundage Plaza and exit on the main road just below the U-Bahn station. He would then turn right, head due south, cross the ring road and make another right into the Olympic complex to arrive back at the ice rink.

Ashton took shelter from the rain in the entrance to the ice rink while he consulted the street map. The English Garden had been laid out in the shallow valley of the Isar and was roughly four to five miles from his present location. No arbitrary time limit had been imposed for the journey, which meant he could afford to wait a few minutes. So far he had done everything the Provisionals had asked of him, at least that was the impression Ashton hoped he had managed to convey. Furthermore, they would surely have expected him to make for the nearest cab rank, which happened to be by the ice rink.

A dark green VW Passat turned into the Olympic complex, drove past the solitary BMW in the taxi rank and then parked in a vacant slot facing the ice rink. Leaving his temporary shelter, Ashton walked over to the VW and got in beside Daniels.

'That was brilliant, Eric.'

'Nice of you to say so, Mr Ashton, but you don't know how close I was to sounding the horn.'

'Well, you didn't; that's what counts.' Ashton opened the map yet again. 'I've been given another rv, this time it's the Chinese Temple in the English Garden.'

'And I've had a message from London,' Daniels told him.

'They haven't called it off, have they?'

'Nothing like that. Mr Peachey gave me some information on the people you'll be meeting today. He thinks you might find it very useful.'

'So let's hear it.'

For the next ten minutes, Daniels repeated everything he had been told about Patrick Lenihan and Frank Kennedy. He also described their physical characteristics in some detail.

'Of course Mr Peachey has nothing on the active service unit which is providing the backup.'

'No matter, I've already made their acquaintance. I think you may have seen them as well – two bikers in black leather? A little on the puny side?'

'I can't say I did.'

'How about a ten-year-old Opel Kadett? Used to be white but is now looking weatherbeaten – big patches of bare metal on the offside front wing. Could have initially been caused by a sideswipe at some time but rust has done most of the damage. Registration number is something like M ZX 4 . . . I didn't get the last two digits.'

'I saw what looked like a white Opel further up the road from the U-Bahn station.'

'Facing in which direction?' Ashton asked.

'The vehicle is pointing towards the ring road.'

In order to follow him the moment he left the Oympic complex, the driver had gone a little way up the road and made what amounted to a U-turn. The surveillance team were obviously in radio contact with one another and the Opel driver had been told the location of the next RV had been delivered. Somebody would have to alert him when he left the complex because the driver couldn't see the exit from his present position above the U-Bahn.

'One of the Provos must be watching this damned car park,' Ashton said, voicing his thoughts.

'Then they know you're not alone.'

'Not necessarily; they could have the exit in sight from a vantage point across the road.'

'Let's hope you're right,' Daniels said in a voice which suggested he thought this was plain wishful thinking.

'I'd better go,' Ashton said. 'Give me a good ten minutes before you follow. When you arrive at the English Garden, find a spot where you can watch the Chinese Temple without being obvious. Your best bet is the bottom end of Königinstrasse where there are no buildings to obstruct your view.'

'Right.'

'And keep an eye out for the bikers and the Opel Kadett.' Ashton paused, one hand on the door lever. 'I haven't the faintest idea what is going to happen at the Chinese Temple. Maybe I'll meet this Patrick Lenihan, then again it could be just another checkpoint. You'll just have to play it by ear. OK?'

'I still don't like it,' Daniels said.

'I already know that.' Ashton leaned forward in the seat,

reached under the trench coat and pulled the 5.45mm semi-automatic from the waistband of his slacks. 'You'd better hold on to this,' he said. 'I might be tempted to use it if those two jokers on the Yamaha pull another stunt like they did a few minutes ago.'

Ashton got out of the car, slammed the door behind him and walked over to the solitary BMW on the cab rank.

Lenihan allowed the phone to ring a full minute, then satisfied the call was meant for him, he answered it and gave the subscriber's number of the flat in Mitter Sendling. The girl who liked to be known simply as Mairin told him that she was ringing from a pay phone outside the Scheidplatz U-Bahn station roughly halfway between the Olympic complex and the English Garden.

'The Brit has not complied with your instructions,' she told him with a certain amount of satisfaction. 'He did not come alone.'

'Can you describe the man who is with him?'

There was a significant pause and he knew Mairin hadn't actually seen anyone even before she admitted it. Soon after meeting her for the first time, he had come to the conclusion that she didn't approve of the ceasefire and wouldn't shed too many tears if hostilities were resumed. Although it was usually unsafe to make snap judgements on the strength of a brief acquaintance, Lenihan saw no reason to change his original opinion.

'So what exactly did you see?' he demanded harshly.

'A dark green VW Passat, licence number M ZX 699,' she retorted angrily. 'There's a sticker in the rear window which proclaims the car has been rented from Hertz.'

'What else?'

'The vehicle was first spotted when it crossed the ring road from the direction of the Olympic complex. It then continued on Lillian Board Weg and exited on to the main road below the U-Bahn station where the driver turned right. Subsequently he made another right turn to bring himself back to the ice rink which we think was his original starting point.'

'That's a presumption, surely?'

'No, a deduction,' Mairin said firmly. 'Cathal and I were in the vicinity of the Olympiahalle. We'd have seen him if he had been lurking anywhere else. And he timed it just right; the other Brit was walking towards the bridge when he appeared heading in the opposite direction. The driver couldn't have been doing more than twenty miles an hour when they passed each other.'

'What's the speed limit on Lillian Board Weg?'

'Forty kilometres.'

'So we're talking about a difference of five miles an hour, Mairin.'

'Yes but—'

'Did you observe anything which suggested they actually knew one another?' Lenihan said, interrupting her.

'No, but they were acting suspiciously.'

It was the clearest indication yet that Mairin was determined to wreck the talks before they had even began. To this end she was ready to bend the facts in order to prove that the Brit was not adhering to the ground rules. In his eye, this made her unreliable and he was unwilling to take anything she told him on trust. For all Mairin knew, the driver of the VW Passat could be a tourist, but of course, he wasn't about to point this out to her.

'Circulate the licence number,' Lenihan told her, 'and warn the other two to look out for the vehicle.'

'I already have.'

'Good. If it's seen in the vicinity of the English Garden you may take appropriate action.'

'I understand.'

'I also want you to understand that the driver is not to be harmed. That's a direct order.'

Lenihan put the phone down confident that Mairin knew what would happen to her if she disobeyed him.

When seen from a distance the Chinese Temple resembled five parasols mounted one on top of the other in diminishing order of size. From the list of places to visit which appeared on the reverse side of the city map, Ashton discovered that the English Garden had been the brainchild of Sir Benjamin Thompson, Earl of Romford, who had been busily reforming the Bavarian Army at the time. The actual landscaping had been laid out between 1804 to 1832 by a man called Sckell, which left Ashton none the wiser. Renowned for its trees, artificial lake, temple and brooks, the garden was, according to the author of the notes, a wonderful place to visit in every season. On a wet autumn day, not too many people appeared to agree with the writer's opinion.

Ashton paid off the taxi and walked across the grass to the Chinese Temple. Since leaving the Olympic complex, he hadn't seen any sign of the bikers nor of the white Opel Kadett, but of course they'd had prior knowledge of the second RV and could afford to hang back or race ahead. There was nobody waiting for him who resembled the description of either Patrick Lenihan or Frank Kennedy. He took out the torn piece of sodden note-paper and looked at it again to satisfy himself that the phone number really did tally with the fourth one on the list. Not four hundred yards away there was a pay phone near the cab rank on Tivolistrasse; if the Provos failed to contact him within the next ten minutes, he proposed to call 56–18–29 and see what happened then.

As Ashton had suggested to him, Königinstrasse was the best viewpoint Daniels could hope to find which would enable him to keep the Chinese Temple under observation. And he had also been right in thinking his best bet had to be the bottom end of the street where there were no buildings on one side of the road to obstruct his view. The only drawback was the fact that he was approximately seven hundred yards from the RV. At that distance a man looked no bigger than a thumbnail and he could have done with a pair of binoculars.

There was no sign of the white Opel Kadett which had appeared in his rear-view mirror shortly after he had pulled out on to the main road. He had taken evasive action, leaving the main road to circle Luitpold Park, then Bayern Plaza and on around the post office in Angererstrasse. He had kept to the back streets twisting this way and that until it had become evident he'd not only shaken off the Opel Kadett but had managed to get himself lost in the process. By the time Daniels had got his bearings, he was approaching the Hauptbahnhof.

Daniels opened the glove compartment and took out the packet of Benson and Hedges. He had lost count of the number of times he had tried to give up smoking but the fact was he enjoyed it too much. His latest attempt had lasted all of three months and he had begun to think he had cured himself of the habit but in the end the temptation to have a quick drag had proved too strong for him. He switched on the ignition, pushed the cigar lighter home and waited for it to pop out. He was about to light up when a green and white BMW cruised slowly past and pulled up in front of him. He sat there mesmerised by the illuminated sign on the car roof, the cigar lighter halfway to the cigarette between his lips. Daniels couldn't think why the police should be interested in his vehicle but it seemed they were. Suddenly galvanised into action, he reached into the glove compartment, grabbed the 5.45mm semi-automatic which Ashton had left behind and quickly hid it under the passenger's seat.

Two police officers approached the VW Passat, one on either side of the car. Doing his best to ignore them, Daniels recharged the cigar lighter and lit his cigarette, only deigning to acknowledge their presence when the nearest officer tapped on the window.

During his time in the Military Police, Daniels had served in the British Army of the Rhine and had acquired more than a smattering of German. However, he pretended otherwise when the officer spoke to him.

'I'm sorry.' He smiled and tapped his chest. '*Ich Englander, verstehen?*'

'Please to get out of the car,' the officer told him in broken English.

'Why?'

'You have to blow in this bag.'

'What for?' Daniels asked.

'Because you drive like so,' the officer said, and described a wavy line with his free hand.

Somebody had made a note of the VW's licence number and had then phoned the *Polizei* alleging that the driver of the said vehicle was under the influence of alcohol. There were no prizes for guessing the identity of the police informant, Daniels thought grimly. 'Anything to oblige,' he said, and blew into the bag.

He'd had a VAT 69 from the minibar in Ashton's room last night and two miniatures from his own bar before turning in but surely to God that had passed through his system by now.

'Your name, please?'

'Daniels, Eric Daniels.'

'You have a driving permit?'

'Not on me.'

'Passport?'

'It's in my room at the hotel.'

'Hotel?'

'The Eden Hotel Wolff.' Daniels dropped his cigarette and stepped on it.

'Please not to make a mess,' the officer told him.

'Sorry.' Daniels bent down, picked up the stub and pocketed it. 'OK now?' he asked.

The officer looked at the bag he was holding, then showed it to his colleague and asked his opinion. Daniels wondered what the hell was going on. The bag was still the same colour as it had been before he'd blown into it, but for some reason the officers weren't happy about the result and insisted on taking him back to the hotel. He didn't like that one bit because there was no way of letting Ashton know he wouldn't be around to watch his back. What really made him sick was the fact that he was locked in the back of the BMW, leaving the second officer to drive his VW Passat. He hoped to God the German didn't take it into his head to look under the passenger's seat because then the fat really would be in the fire.

Scratch one ex-military policeman. It was, Ashton thought, highly unlikely that the driver of the VW Passat parked by the kerbside on Königinstrasse could be anyone other than Eric Daniels. Just what he had done to merit the unwelcome attention of the *Polizei* was not entirely clear but it looked as if they had breathalysed him. That being the case, Lenihan's people must have marked his card and reported him for drink driving. Naturally they had assumed he was armed and were banking on the police discovering that for themselves.

Daniels must have done something which had confirmed the opposition's suspicion. There had been no need for the men in the Opel Kadett to follow him all the way to the English Garden; they had known the location of the next rv and they had only to look at the map to see Königinstrasse was the best vantage point to keep the Chinese Temple under observation. Clever, too damned clever for him. Ashton shook his head; the inescapable truth was the fact that he had been outsmarted and outmanoeuvred at every turn.

The phone rang for the second time that morning. Answering it, Lenihan wasn't surprised to hear Frank Kennedy's voice on the line. Nor was he surprised to learn that the Brit had had somebody watching his back.

'He's on his own now,' Kennedy said, and chuckled. 'His friend has been picked up by the police for drink driving.'

'Clever,' Lenihan said. 'Who thought of that?'

'Mairin.'

Mairin. He wished it had been anybody but her; she was too clever by half and exerted a dangerous influence over the other members of the active service unit. Mairin had her own ideas on how to unite Ireland and was a potential recruit for the INLA if ever he saw one.

'I think we should run one more check to make sure the Brit is clean.'

'That's already in hand, Pat.'

'Good. I'll wait to hear from you again,' Lenihan said and hung up.

The boy was between ten and twelve years old and why he wasn't in school was a mystery to Ashton. He was thin and had a pinched look about him as if he wasn't getting enough to eat. He was wearing hand-me-downs which were roughly a size too big for him but the sodden raincoat was of good quality as were the long trousers. The mountain bike he was straddling looked brand new.

'I was told to give you this,' the boy said, handing him a sealed envelope which was just large enough to accommodate a 'thank you' note.

'Who told you?'

'That man over there,' the boy said, and jerked a thumb in the direction of the cab rank. 'He pointed you out and gave me ten Deutschmarks.'

The way his voice rose told Ashton that ten Marks was a fortune to him. He also suspected the mountain bike had been stolen. 'What man?' he asked, looking round.

But the boy had already slipped away and was pedalling furiously along the circuitous path which eventually connected with Königinstrasse. Ashton ripped open the envelope and took out a notelet which was wrapped around a Polaroid photograph of himself in profile. It had been taken shortly after he had picked up the message and had started walking towards the bridge over the ring road. The photographer had also managed to get the VW Passat in the frame. The definition was very poor and he was virtually unrecognisable but that wasn't the point. There was no contact phone number on the notelet and the print was clearly intended to authenticate the message, which instructed him to make his way to the Gasthof Adler in the Hirschgarten. On a more subtle level, the Polaroid was telling him that the Provos had a much better image that had been captured by a camera fitted with a telephoto lens.

Well, he too had a message, one that was anything but subtle and was intended for the ears of Mr Patrick Lenihan. Leaving the Chinese Temple, Ashton walked across to the pay phone by the cab rank. The Provos had supplied a list of four contact numbers and while three of them could refer to various pay phones in and around Munich, it stood to reason that the fourth would be permanently manned. His confident assumption was not misplaced. Acting on a hunch, he rang 56–18–29, the fourth number on the list and got the same voice he'd heard at the Hauptbahnhof.

'You can forget the Gasthof Adler,' Ashton said.

'In that case we go our separate ways.'

'You've got it wrong; I'm simply changing the venue, Mr Lenihan.'

The sharp intake of breath which followed told Ashton that he'd scored a direct hit.

'You've obviously got the wrong number,' Lenihan said in a voice full of bluster.

'Rubbish. We've spoken before; you are the man who sent me on a wild-goose chase to the Olympic complex. And I'll tell you something else; Frank Kennedy should get a grip on those clowns in the active service unit, especially those two morons in black leather. Their idea of delivering a message was to throw a fake bomb at me. If I'd been armed, they would be dead.'

Ashton mixed truth with lies. He led Lenihan to believe that he knew a great deal more about his personal life than he had disclosed and stated that Dublin had kept the British Government informed of Frank Kennedy's movements as well as his own. He also implied that Lenihan could find himself in serious jeopardy if he called off their meeting and the ceasefire broke down as a result of his action.

'Are you threatening me?' Lenihan demanded.

'Of course not, but we both know what happened to Michael Collins in August 1922 and it wasn't we Brits who ambushed and killed him.'

'That sounds like a threat to me.'

'The new venue is Harras station on Line 6 of the U-Bahn,' Ashton said, talking him down.

'Impossible.'

'Where's the difficulty? It's only two and a half miles from the Gasthof Adler.'

'Go to hell.'

'The time is now 12.15; be there at 13.00 hours.'

'Did you hear what I said? Go to hell.'

'You can bring Frank Kennedy with you but nobody else. Understand?'

'Are you deaf or just plain stupid?'

'Oh, by the way,' Ashton said unperturbed, 'this conversation has been recorded. I think Dublin would be interested to hear it, don't you?'

If you were going to lie, Ashton believed there was no point in settling for a little one.

Chapter Twenty Two

From Königinstrasse to the Eden Hotel Wolff on Arnulfstrasse was less than four miles but to Daniels it seemed ten times as far. Somehow he managed to resist the urge to look round and see if the other police officer was still following them in the VW Passat. If he was no longer there, it could mean he'd taken the car to Police Headquarters for a detailed inspection. There were no grounds for doing so but all over the world there was a breed of policeman who, on discovering the person he had apprehended had not committed an offence, continued to harass the individual in the hope of finding an alternative charge which might stick. Daniels had met the type in the army and in civilian life; he just hoped the two Germans had not been cast in a like mould.

To his relief, the second policeman was still directly behind them when they stopped outside the hotel. There was, however, no room for him to park the VW Passat and he continued slowly up the road looking for a vacant space. Alighting from the BMW, Daniels saw he had found a slot thirty yards on.

'We go inside now,' the first officer said.

'What about my car?'

'It will be quite safe, Herr Daniels.'

'The hotel has its own car park.'

'No need, my comrade will stay with the car.'

Things were going from bad to worse. While they were inside the hotel, the other police officer could virtually take the VW apart. Looking for what? Daniels mentally asked himself, and felt sick in the stomach when it suddenly occurred to him that maybe they suspected he was a drug dealer.

'Which room you in?'

'Room 477 but we can do with some help.' Daniels smiled. 'To understand each other better,' he added.

Among other facilities the hotel ran a business centre. Aware of this, Daniels went over to the reception and asked one of the assistant managers to send one of the bilingual secretaries up to his room. With the assistance of an interpreter there was a chance he might learn why the police were so interested in him.

A chambermaid was changing the bed linen in the adjoining room when they stepped out of the lift on the fourth floor.

'Pound to a penny my room hasn't been done yet,' Daniels said.

'Excuse please?'

'Nothing – forget it.'

Daniels slipped the plastic card into the lock, got a green light and opened the door. As he had anticipated, his room was just how he'd left it, the bedclothes in an untidy heap, yesterday's *Evening Standard* still filling the wastepaper bin. Daniels opened the hanging cupboard to get at the safe, spun the twin combination dials to the setting he had chosen, then opened it up and reached inside for his passport.

'Here you are,' he said, and handed the document to the police officer.

'You have driving permit?'

'It's in the passport at the back.'

The rental agency had wanted to see it when he had hired the car. After signing the agreement and paying the deposit with his credit card, he'd slipped the driver's licence inside the passport and had inadvertently put both documents in the safe when he'd returned to the hotel. He didn't attempt to explain this to the German, just stood there listening to a lecture delivered in halting English on the duty of every citizen to carry some means of identification at all times.

The bilingual secretary arrived in the middle of the homily and, without waiting to be asked, took it upon herself to interpret the patrolman's lecture. When he'd finished, Daniel asked her to find out if the police officer was now satisfied. It was the start of an idiotic three-way conversation. The girl would translate what he had told her into German only for the police officer to respond in his version of English.

There was no limit to his curiosity. He wanted to know why Herr Daniels had come to Munich, when he had arrived, how long he would be staying, and the nature of his business. Of all the questions put to him, the hardest to answer was the one relating to the purpose of his visit. With no cover story to fall back on, Daniels was forced to improvise. The only safe thing he could do was to pass himself off as a representative of the travel agency which Kelso used on behalf of the SIS. He was even prepared to give the German the phone number of Vauxhall Cross in the knowledge that any incoming call from an outsider was automatically diverted to the Assistant Director in charge of Admin Wing. It didn't come to that because the German changed tack and began to ask him about his private life.

'This has gone on long enough,' Daniels told the girl. 'Why does he want to know where I was born?'

At the back of his mind was the nagging worry that the longer the interrogation continued, the greater the likelihood that Ashton's pistol would be discovered. There was another, equally pertinent factor: his chances of linking up with Ashton again were already minimal; they would become nonexistent if he didn't get away in the next few minutes.

'He says he needs the information for investigative purposes,' the girl informed him after a lengthy and heated exchange with the officer.

'OK, tell him I want his name.'

'His name?'

'Yes, and his badge number if he has one.' Daniels moved to the bedside table and picked up the phone. 'He's detaining me unlawfully and I'm not going to stand for it any longer. I'm going to call the British Consul General here in Munich and ask him to lodge an official complaint with the appropriate authorities. Tell him that.'

The girl did as he asked, making the point forcefully to leave no room for doubt. Although there was no immediate climbdown, Daniels recognised the repeat homily on identity cards as a face-saving expedient on the part of the police officer. To show that he had taken the lecture to heart, Daniels tucked the passport and driver's licence into the breast pocket of his jacket, then patted his chest as if to reassure himself that the documents were safe and sound. After that it was apologies, handshakes and smiles all around.

Daniels was even more relieved when he walked out of the hotel and was presented with the keys to the VW Passat by the other patrolman. More smiles and handshakes followed but he didn't once look back as he made his way to the car some thirty yards further up the road.

Twelve thirty came and went, then it was 13.00 hours and there was still no sign of Lenihan and Kennedy. Even in the off-peak times a train departed from Harras for Kieferngarten every eight minutes and Ashton was beginning to feel a bit conspicuous. At half-past one Ashton promised himself that he would give them another ten minutes after which he would simply walk away. Whether he would have actually carried out his threat was never put to the test; a bare three minutes before the self-imposed deadline expired, with a train waiting to depart from the platform, Lenihan and his bodyguard finally put in an appearance.

Kennedy was the first man on to the platform. He might have been one of the best snipers to have operated in the bandit country around Crossmaglen but that was light years ago and he was now running to fat. It showed in the thickness of his thighs, in the beginning of a pot belly and the plump round face, by-products of too many pints of Guinness washed down with too many shots of Bushmills Irish, or so Ashton thought.

Lenihan followed his bodyguard onto the platform a few moments later. If Kennedy had given him an all-clear, Ashton hadn't seen the signal. As the only passenger still waiting to board the train, he'd had the IRA's top sniper in sight from the instant Kennedy had first shown himself and was satisfied the man was not equipped with a two-way radio or a mobile phone. However Lenihan was noted for being a cautious man and it wasn't his style to take anything on trust. Somebody had checked the station out to make sure Lenihan was not going to walk into an ambush and that somebody had to be on the train. Ashton wished Daniels was there to watch his back and redress the odds.

Ashton crooked a finger at Kennedy, then boarded the second coach of the six-unit train. There were seven other passengers in the car; an elderly couple, a young mother with a girl under school age, a conscript soldier and two men in their early thirties who were holding hands while looking adoringly into each other's eyes. Ashton waited until Lenihan and Kennedy boarded the train before he turned right and went to the far end of the coach well away from the gays. Like meat in a sandwich, he found himself sitting between the two Irishmen.

'This is cosy,' he observed, looking straight to his front.

'Let's get on with it,' Lenihan growled. 'Who the hell are you?'

'Messenger. Ralph Messenger.'

'That's a cover,' Kennedy said. 'British Intelligence is full of Messengers.'

He was right. Messenger was a blanket codename given to defectors and all SIS personnel on detached duty. It had been in use for far too long and, instead of concealing the identity of an individual had quite the reverse effect. Ashton made a mental note to take the matter up with Hazelwood and suggest it was time for a change.

Lenihan said, 'All right, Mr SIS man, what's the word from London?'

The doors closed with a pneumatic hiss and the train began to pull out of the station a lot more smoothly and much quieter than Ashton usually experienced on the District Line.

'London strongly recommends you do something about Barry Nolan; he's becoming a problem.'

'Not for us,' Kennedy said out of the corner of his mouth before Lenihan had a chance to answer.

'He's going to break the ceasefire.'

'We're not responsible for what the INLA does,' Lenihan told him curtly.

'Nolan intends to assassinate Mr Clifford Peachey, the Deputy Director of the SIS.'

Ashton hesitated, wondered just how much information he should impart to this so-called political brain of Sinn Fein. He could not forget that this gaunt-faced, scholarly-looking individual who seemed typecast for an academic was the same man who had blown a twenty-three-year-old corporal in the Royal Anglian Regiment to pieces and had planned many other operations which had resulted in the deaths of a number of bystanders as well as members of the security forces. As far as he was concerned, it was a case of once an IRA man always an IRA man. But what the hell, he could hardly be giving anything away when Peachey had already been targeted.

'The Intelligence-gathering was done by a man called Daniel Hopkinson. He worked for the removal firm our Deputy Director used when he moved house. You could say the information was handed to him on a plate. It was pure luck but these things happen.'

'I don't know why you are telling me all this when I've already made it clear that we have nothing to do with the INLA.'

'Save the crap for the politicians. INLA, Continuity IRA, the Real IRA; you tolerate these breakaway factions because there are times when you find them useful.'

The train drew into Implerstrasse and stopped. A second or two later, the doors opened.

'This is where we get off,' Lenihan announced. 'I've had enough of your blather.'

'I don't think so,' Ashton said. 'I don't believe you're the kind of man who'd willingly put himself in jeopardy.'

A priest, a young woman in a short dark grey PVC raincoat, two middle-aged housewives, and a plump man carrying a briefcase got into the coach. Kennedy was already on his feet but when Lenihan made no effort to join him, he sank back into his seat. Presently the doors closed and the train pulled away, rapidly gathering speed.

'Nolan has been fund-raising in Boston,' Ashton continued as if nothing had happened. 'But I expect you already know that.'

'We'd heard.'

'He was telling everybody that the INLA was the only organisation which was really carrying the fight to England. He also told your number-one financial contributor that SIS would be burying their Deputy Director before the year was much older.'

'Where did you get all this information?' Lenihan asked.

'From the FBI and your chief fund-raiser. They expect you to do something about Nolan.'

'I knew it,' Kennedy said, 'he's trying to set us at each other's throats. Don't listen to him.'

'I didn't ask for your advice,' Lenihan told him.

'There's been a change of policy,' Ashton said, unfazed. 'London, Dublin, Washington: they're all agreed that the Provisionals, Continuity IRA, the Real IRA and INLA are all cast in the same mould. In other words, if any faction perpetrates a terrorist attack on any individual property, it will be assumed the outrage had the tacit approval of the Provisional IRA.'

'Meaning what?' Kennedy snapped.

'I'm in Munich to confer with the political strategist of Sinn Fein,' Ashton said icily, 'not some second-rate, over-the-hill bodyguard.'

'You're really asking for it, Mr Secret Serviceman.'

'Leave it,' Lenihan said, then half turned to face Ashton. 'But it's still a question I'd like you to answer.'

'It means you will have broken the ceasefire.'

'And then some politician will roundly condemn us and express his horror and revulsion.' Kennedy smiled. 'I'm trembling in my boots.'

'You'll find it will be more than a slap on the wrist this time.'

'What are you telling me?' Lenihan asked.

Ashton remained silent. The train had pulled into Poccistrasse and the coach was rapidly filling up. A tall, overweight man sat down next to Lenihan and began reading his copy of the *Suddeutsche Zeitung*. Although the coach three-parts emptied at Marienplatz, the fat man stayed for a further two stops beyond the town centre, finally alighting at Universität.

'So let's be hearing you,' Lenihan said when he judged it safe to resume their conversation.

'There will be no safe haven south of the border for anybody. You will be harried night and day by the Garda. Your phone will be tapped, your letters intercepted; in fact everything that can be done will be done to ensure you are unable to function.'

The Garda would of course stay within the law but there were others who wouldn't hesitate to go outside it. Lenihan's cottage in Roscrea would be burned to the ground, the car he was travelling in could be forced off the road or shunted from behind. And there were other, more extreme measures which could be taken should he prove obdurate.

'What sort of measures?'

'You could simply disappear without a trace like so many victims of the IRA have. It could be that some people might consider it more advantageous to leave you alone for the time being and go for a softer target instead, like your bodyguard.'

The threat had no substance. No matter what the INLA did there was no plan to eliminate the political brain of Sinn Fein but Lenihan was not to know that. What he had been told was a mirror image of his own executive actions in the not-so-distant past. Furthermore, Ashton had been chillingly believable because he had meant every word. Should anything happen to Harriet, he would not hesitate to kill Lenihan and anybody else who stood in his way.

'I don't like being threatened.'

'The remedy is in your hands,' Ashton told him. 'Look, all we want is for you to make sure Nolan doesn't break the ceasefire. That's not so very much to ask, is it?'

'I don't suppose it is,' Lenihan said quietly.

'Good, I'm glad we're in agreement.'

'What about the tape recording you made?' Kennedy demanded.

'It's not for sale.'

The train had pulled into Giselastrasse and had been standing at the platform for approximately half a minute. From observation, Ashton had calculated the average waiting time was fifty seconds. Judging it to perfection, he got to his feet and made it through the doors even as they were closing. Turning about, he caught a final glimpse of Kennedy shaking a first at him as the train began to move out of the station.

The elation Ashton felt vanished when he discovered that he had not been the last passenger to alight from the Line 6 train to

273

Kieferngarten. There was, he thought, something vaguely familiar about the ginger-haired man who was wearing a donkey jacket over a check shirt and Levis.

As far as Daniels could tell from Königinstrasse, Ashton was no longer in the vicinity of the Chinese Temple. Undeterred, he continued on down the road, turned right into Tivoli and made his way to the taxi rank where there was a pay phone. He thought there was a faint chance that Ashton might have left a message for him tucked inside the telephone directory. He rippled through the pages, held the directory upside down and gave it a good shaking but nothing fell out. As a final check, he went through all the listings under the letter D to see if anything had been written in one of the margins. After drawing another blank, he reluctantly conceded defeat. The population of Munich numbered 1,300,000, according to the *Michelin Guide* and he reckoned the city had to cover approximately 150 square miles. Trying to find Ashton in an urban sprawl of that size would be ten times worse than looking for a needle in the proverbial haystack. There was nothing he could do for Ashton, nothing at all. The operation had been a preordained disaster before they had even left Heathrow. No means of communication other than by landline, no physical backup, playing away from home on ground that was well known to the opposition, outnumbered by at least three to one and no idea who they would be negotiating with until far too late in the day: the list was endless.

Daniels left the pay phone, walked back to the car and got in. The time was two forty-six and in the absence of any information on Ashton's whereabouts, he proposed to return to the hotel and await developments. If there was still no sign of him by six o'clock, he would phone London and seek their advice. A cock-up, a complete, monumental bloody cockup, but sometimes you got away with it. He hoped this was one occasion.

Ashton moved to the communicating door and looked through the window into the next coach. The ginger-haired man was

274

still with him and was making no effort to disguise the fact. He had alighted at Odeonsplatz when Ashton had got off the train and had promptly followed his example and boarded the next one to Harras. There was not the slightest doubt the Provo gunman was following him and didn't care if he knew it.

If Lenihan had decided to have him killed, the man entrusted to do the job would never have shown himself beforehand. The ginger man could therefore be a decoy whose task was to distract him while his partner got close enough to make sure he didn't miss. But that meant Lenihan was prepared to break the ceasefire and destroy everything he had worked for. In any case, there were easier ways of resuming hostilities and it certainly wasn't necessary to go all the way to Munich when there were softer targets at home. No, Lenihan was after something much more tangible; he wanted to know whether or not their conversation had been recorded. If a tape existed, he was determined nobody in Dublin, London or Washington should hear it. That had been his intention before he and Kennedy had arrived at Harras. And after they had boarded the waiting train, at least two members of the active service unit must have slipped in the end coach before the doors closed. However many there had been in this backup team, Ashton was sure only Ginger had been quick enough to stay with him when he had ditched Lenihan and Kennedy at Giselastrasse.

Ginger couldn't afford to lose sight of him. He needed help to deal with the situation but there was no way he could communicate with the other members of the active service unit with a mobile phone or a hand-held radio while they were below ground. The answer was to take him out of the game before his friends arrived on the scene.

Ashton unfolded the street map for the umpteenth time. One of the pluses for Herr Max Sussmann's map was that apart from all the usual information, it also showed the location of every cab rank in the city. Goetheplatz: next stop down the line, a cab rank within spitting distance of the U-Bahn station – that was the place for him. Ashton put the map away and moved up to the doors a few minutes before the train emerged from the tunnel. The doors were still opening when he alighted from the coach and started walking at a fast pace towards the exit. There was no need for him to look round; he had developed a sixth sense on the streets of Belfast during a nine-month tour of duty with the regular army's Special Patrol Unit and knew Ginger was shadowing him. Once up at street level, he started running and threaded his way through the traffic to the accompaniment of angry blasts on the horn from irate drivers. Regardless of the fact that there wasn't a pedestrian crossing in the immediate vicinity, the Irishman followed him across the road, provoking another cacophony.

Ashton turned the corner of Haber Strasse with Walther, ducked into an alley and pressed himself into the service entrance of the delicatessen. He had been about twenty yards ahead of the Irishman when he had ducked into the alley and he could hear him coming like a steam train.

Most street fights are settled by whoever gets in the first blow, especially when the victim is caught off guard and unprepared for the assault. It was no different in this instance. The Irishman was level with Ashton when he realised the alley was going nowhere. At the same time he also sensed Ashton's presence in the doorway and walked into a vicious left hook as he turned to face him. His eyes were already glazing when Ashton hammered him with the right and there really was no need to kick the legs from under him because he was going down anyway but this was a situation where the Queensberry rules didn't apply. The back of his skull hit the cobblestones with a sickening crunch which made Ashton think he might have killed him. He did not, however, stop to find out; bending down, he grabbed hold of both ankles and dragged the Irishman into the service entrance, then quickly went through his pockets. The mobile phone and a switchblade told Ashton he hadn't assaulted some innocent German. An added bonus was the fact that nobody had witnessed the one-sided fight.

Leaving the alley, he walked round to the taxi rank at the top of Walther Strasse and told the lead cab driver to take him to the Eden Hotel Wolff on Arnulfstrasse. They were booked on to British Airways Flight 955 departing 21.10 hours but there was no telling what kind of reception might be waiting for them at Munich airport. Stuttgart wasn't too far away, two hours on the autobahn, and either BA or Lufthansa was bound to have an evening flight to London. No problem then; in fact it was going to be plain sailing from now on. For the first time that day it so happened his optimism was justified.

O'Meara put the phone down. Tracing the local calls Hakkison Lal had made on his mobile had not been the relatively simple task Ashton had imagined. None had lasted long enough to be shown individually on his quarterly bill and it had taken British Telecom several days to establish that Hakkison Lal had never phoned Basil Wilks at the Steadfast Agency or at his flat in Harrow. At her request, they had then checked the calls made by Wilks from both the office and his home address. As a result, they had subsequently furnished proof that he had rung Hakkison Lal from the office the night he had been killed. The information would obviously be of interest to the investigating officer at Northolt Road Police Station and O'Meara was conscious that there was a limit to how long she could withhold it from him.

Chapter Twenty Three

It had been the best homecoming Ashton had ever known. He had phoned Harriet from Stuttgart to ask how much longer she was thinking of staying in Lincoln and had been told that she and Edward could be packed and on their way in half an hour. British Airways Flight BA961 had arrived Heathrow at 20.15 hours; seventy minutes later, and shortly after he had let himself into the house Harriet had turned into Rylett Close and parked the Ford Mondeo outside number 84.

As a matter of routine, Ashton had informed the duty officer of the European Department that he and Daniels were back. Although his immediate superior was Clifford Peachey, he had in fact been tasked by Victor and he'd thought it was more appropriate to submit a brief report to him. He had therefore tried to raise the DG on the Mozart cipher-protected telephone but had got an engaged tone. While there was nothing so urgent that it couldn't wait until the morning, he resolved to try again later, a decision that had been temporarily erased the moment Harriet crossed the threshold. It was only when he was drifting off to sleep that Ashton remembered he hadn't called Hazelwood. By then, it had gone midnight and he'd persuaded himself that Victor wouldn't take kindly to being hauled out of bed in the wee small hours. Ashton learned how big a mistake that had been when Hazelwood sent for him prior to morning prayers.

'Tell me something, Peter,' he said in an injured tone of voice, 'why is it I have to get my information second-hand from a junior Intelligence officer instead of you? I'd really like to know.'

'I tried to reach you but your number was engaged.'

'When was this?'

'About 21.10 hours. I meant to phone again.'

'So why didn't you?'

'Harriet came home,' Ashton told him and left it at that, something Hazelwood wasn't prepared to do.

'I rang your house not once but several times and never got an answer. All I can think is that you two obviously made a night of it.'

There was no mistaking the inference. In a none-too-subtle way Hazelwood was implying that Ashton and Harriet must have been going at it hammer and tongs. It shocked Ashton because it revealed a coarseness in Hazelwood which he'd never suspected; it angered him because there was some truth in the allegation. He coloured, recalling what Harriet had urged him to do to her in the privacy of their bedroom and how eagerly she had responded to his touch. But the fact was, it was she who had been in control, turning the volume down on the Mozart and the BT phone in the kitchen until the bell was no longer audible. Without him knowing it, she had also disconnected the extension on the bedside table, something he'd only discovered this morning.

'I'm waiting,' Hazelwood said impatiently.

'What?'

'For God's sake, I want to know what you made of Lenihan. Will he take action to ensure people like Barry Nolan maintain the ceasefire?'

'I think he might but I'm not sure he will enjoy the wholehearted support of the Army Council. If the active service unit in Munich is anything to go by, a significant percentage of the Provisionals would be happy to resume hostilities.'

'I presume you are speaking from personal experience?'

'Yes. They tried to make life difficult for us.'

In a few brief sentences he told Hazelwood what had happened at the Olympic complex, about the encounter Daniels had with the German police and his own run-in with the ginger-haired man.

'He went down pretty hard,' Ashton said in conclusion.

'What exactly are you telling me? Is he dead?'

'He could be in a coma with a fractured skull.'

'That's all we need. Have you got any more good news for me?'

'Daniels could be at risk; he had to rent a car.'

Hazelwood paused in the act of reaching for a Burma cheroot. 'I must be getting dense in my old age,' he said, 'but I fail to see the connection.'

'The operation was set up in a hurry and there was no time to provide us with cover identities. Daniels paid the initial deposit in cash but the agency still wanted to see his passport and driving licence.'

'You should never have taken Daniels.'

'We did the best we could and Eric isn't to blame for what happened.'

'Nobody under your control ever is.' Hazelwood recovered sufficiently to open the cigar box and help himself to a cheroot. 'This reluctance to apportion blame is one of the reasons why you will always be a Grade 1 Intelligence officer.'

'Well, my name is Ashton, not Sheridan, or Kelso, or Garfield, or Benton.'

Hazelwood finally got around to lighting the cheroot with a match. 'The best thing you can do,' he said between puffs, 'is shuffle some of the files lying in your pending trays to the out tray.'

It wasn't easy to put a smile on your face when you were burning up with anger but lately Ashton had had a lot of practice at it. Leaving Victor's office, he told the PA next door she could send in the next Christian, then went down to the fourth floor and fed a 50 pence coin into the vending machines near the lifts. At the best of times, the coffee bore more than a passing resemblance to gravy browning. This morning, the machine excelled itself and dispensed a liquid that looked as if it belonged in an oil sump. The telephone intervened before Ashton could sample the coffee; answering it, he had to suffer a triumphant Rowan Garfield instead.

'You're a hundred per cent wrong,' Garfield told him.

'About what?'

'About your old enigma Pavel Trilisser. He's about to become the Russian Ambassador to the UN.' Garfield laughed.

'I wouldn't say he was in the right place to succeed Boris Yeltsin, would you?'

Ashton scowled. Peachey had asked him to write a paper on who might succeed the Russian President should his heart condition deteriorate even further. He'd thought it likely the Head of the European Department had been given the same task and there was no reason why the Deputy Director shouldn't have sent Garfield a copy of the paper for comment, but it was hardly a tactful thing to do. It certainly hadn't made Garfield any the less defensive.

'Do we know why the present incumbent is being relieved?' Ashton enquired.

'Apparently he's not enjoying the best of health.' Garfield snorted. 'And if you believe that, you will believe anything.'

'What's your source, Rowan?'

'The Foreign and Commonwealth Office. The news was released yesterday while you were in Munich engaged on heaven knows what.'

'I don't suppose the CIA are too happy about it.'

'I don't imagine they are, but they can't veto his appointment. Neither can the State Department. The Russians can send who they like to represent their country at the United Nations. Besides, the Cold War is over and Pavel Trilisser is no longer the bogeyman he used to be. In fact he is something of a hero. If you remember he sided with Yeltsin when the Communist hardliners moved against Gorbachev in August 1991.'

Ashton raised his eyebrows. He didn't need Garfield to remind him how the former Deputy Head of the old KGB's First Chief Directorate had emerged from every constitutional crisis smelling like a rose.

'Well?'

The hectoring tone of voice told Ashton that Garfield was waiting for him to admit that the paper he'd written on Yeltsin's possible successor was flawed.

'It seems I was wrong about Trilisser. As long as he's in New York he's got to be out of the running.'

'That's a first.'

'What is?'

'You eating humble pie,' Garfield said, and quickly hung up in his determination to have the last word.

Ashton put the phone down, opened the safe and transferred the in, pending and out trays to the desk. Before dealing with the files awaiting his attention, Ashton produced a balance sheet accounting for what little he and Daniels had spent of the five hundred pounds worth of Deutschmarks provided by the pay section. He then filled out a claim form for their hotel bills which he had settled with his own credit card. He was about to make a start on the files when O'Meara telephoned with the news that BT could prove Basil Wilks had talked to Hakkison Lal the night he had been killed.

'We have to decide how we are going to use this evidence,' O'Meara said. 'I've been sitting on it for twenty-four hours now and I'm getting itchy. I can think of two senior police officers who would hang me out to dry if they ever discovered I'd deliberately withheld this information from them.'

'We'd better meet.'

'Fine. Whereabouts?'

It was a good question. At eight thirty in the morning they weren't exactly spoiled for choice. The pubs were closed, so were the museums and they would look a mite conspicuous taking a walk through Green Park, ankle deep in fallen leaves.

'I'll meet you outside 18 Matthew Parker Street,' he said, coming to a decision. 'It's off Storey's Gate and is no more than a ten-minute walk from where you are.'

'What time?'

Ashton looked at his wristwatch. He would have to phone the Foreign and Commonwealth Office and seek their permission but he didn't expect them to object to what he had in mind. It was, however, advisable to allow himself some time in hand in case the appropriate official was not readily available.

'How does nine thirty suit you?' he asked.

O'Meara told him nine thirty was fine by her.

Every government ministry from the Department of Trade and Industry to the Treasury had its own security organisation. The department which looked after the Foreign and Commonwealth Office was located in a four-storey Edwardian house on Matthew Parker Street. Fronted by an impressive wrought-iron gate and railings, it had always struck Ashton that the property surely deserved a more dignified name than number 4 Central Buildings.

O'Meara was waiting for him outside the entrance. She was wearing calf-length boots with a brown leather skirt and matching jacket over a white silk blouse. Although the forecast was for fine weather with light variable winds, O'Meara didn't believe in chancing it and was carrying a plastic mac that had been repeatedly folded in two until it was roughly the size of an A4 jiffy bag.

Ashton shepherded her through the gates and on into the narrow hallway where he showed his ID card to the security guard on duty at the reception desk and asked which interview room he had been allocated. In the entrance hall itself, there was a large round, mahogany table liberally covered with ancient back numbers of *Field*, *Punch*, *Country Life* and the *Reader's Digest* which always reminded Ashton of a dentist's waiting room. The spiral staircase served as an internal fire escape and as a necessary back-up for the solitary lift which was sometimes out of order. As luck would have it, this morning was one of those occasions.

The interview room was on the second floor at the back of the building. Thick net curtains in the sash window were meant to frustrate any would-be Peeping Toms across the road. By the same token, it restricted the view from inside the room, not that that was much to write home about.

'So what have we got exactly?' Ashton asked, waving O'Meara to one of the two fireside chairs.

'One phone call made from the offices of the Steadfast Enquiry and Research Agency at 18.25 hours the night Basil Wilks was killed. The area code of the number dialled is for Cricklewood and the subscriber's address is 263 The Broadway, which happens to be the Head Office of Hakkison Lal Mini Markets.'

'With outlets all over North London,' Ashton intoned drily.

'Something else you should know. The number is not a mobile; Mr Lal does have one but there is no record of him ever ringing Wilks at the office, or his flat. For that matter BT can't find any record of Wilks using either of his phones to contact Lal except for that one instance. As you might guess, a large number of calls were made by Lal from the head office but the printout shows that all of them were to his various mini markets and the home numbers of the managerial staff.'

'Including the phone at 761B Kingsbury Road where V. J. Desai was staying?'

'Yes, but they were all made during or shortly after normal business hours, which means Lal will have little difficulty in accounting for them.'

'It's like we thought,' Ashton said, 'Wilks and Lal used pay phones to contact one another.'

'They were clever all right.'

'But what did they do in an emergency? Maybe Hakkison Lal invariably works late and happened to be in the office when Wilks rang at 18.25 hours. But what if Mr Mini Market wasn't at the Cricklewood address?'

'The phone there is on an answer machine, a Rapport 20,' O'Meara told him. 'With a compatible BT Remote Interrogator, Lal can call in from wherever he is and retrieve any messages on the answer machine.'

'They had a drill,' Ashton said, taking it a stage further. 'If Wilks left a message on the machine, he had to allow a specific period of time to elapse before he tried the same number again.'

'Or rang Lal at home?' O'Meara suggested.

Ashton didn't think so. The Indian was simply a go-between for V. J. Desai and would have withheld his number from Wilks. And knowing that he had been employed to do something that wasn't kosher, Wilks would have had no desire to find out who he was dealing with.

'It was a pretty good system,' Ashton continued, 'but the night he died, Wilks broke the rules. He rang the contact number from the office which meant it was traceable. I don't believe he did it with malicious intent; Mungo Park had turned nasty and he panicked.'

'I can name two others who will turn nasty if I don't show them this printout from BT before the day's over. Three if you include the Assistant Commissioner, Crime, who is now taking an active interest in both the Wilks and Ramash investigations.'

There had been a number of significant developments while Ashton had been in Munich. In the absence of a suicide note, the investigating officers at Harrow had suspected that Wilks had not willingly put his head on a railway line and waited for a train to come down the track. Now they could prove it; a post mortem had revealed that Wilks had been injected with morphine.

'Enough to kill him?' Ashton asked.

O'Meara shook her head. 'No, Wilks was still alive when they carried him down into the cutting; however, he was unconscious. Although his head had been completely shattered, the pathologist found traces of chloroform in the mouth and the remains of the nasal passages.'

In attempting to trace his movements, officers from 'Q' District had interviewed the so-called maid who looked after 'Miss Birch' and had learned that Wilks had left the office between six thirty and six forty-five. His body had been found at five thirty the following morning.

'We've got a time gap of roughly eleven hours,' O'Meara said. 'After phoning his contact from the office, I believe Wilks was told to call back later, which means he may have wandered around London, killing time for as much as an hour. When he rang from a pay phone, he was told where and when to meet V. J. Desai. I've a hunch the RV was somewhere in the Northwick Park area.'

'Because his body was found roughly a mile from South Kenton station?' Ashton suggested.

'Yes. I don't see the killers driving any distance with an unconscious man in the boot of their car or whatever.'

Killers? Ashton frowned: well, yes, one man couldn't have overpowered Wilks while he was driving, assuming he'd picked up the investigator in a vehicle of some sort.

'We know V. J. Desai was living in the Kingsbury area,' Ashton mused. 'That's not far from Northwick Park and he could have acquired the necessary local knowledge.'

'What local knowledge?'

'One of the killers was a walking timetable; he knew all the train movements and when it was safe to go down into the cutting. V. J. Desai and his accomplice would have held the unconscious Wilks in the flat above the mini market on the Kingsbury Road until it was time to move him on.'

'Well, now you know why I have to send a photocopy of the BT statement to 'Q' District. There's also Detective Chief Superintendent Orwell.'

'What about him?'

'Somebody at Vauxhall Cross produced a photograph of V. J. Desai and faxed two copies to my boss. I think your Mr Peachey had something to do with it. Anyway, it was suggested Orwell might like to see a copy.'

'And?'

'Well, as you know, he already had a witness who saw Lorraine Cheeseman with a black man when she arrived at the house in Lansdowne Mews to see Dr Ramash. When the Chief Superintendent showed her the fax, she immediately identified the black man as V. J. Desai.'

Orwell had come full circle. Because of a remote connection, he'd originally surmised that the triple slaying had been committed by some, as yet unidentified, terrorist organisation. The discovery of cannabis and 40 grams of crack on the property and Lorraine Cheeseman's previous criminal history had led him to assume it had been a drugs-related crime. Following the identification of Ananda Marg's Director of Military Operations, he now had the satisfaction of knowing he had been right the first time around.

'The ball is in your court, Mr Ashton,' O'Meara told him quietly.

'OK. When you get back to Scotland Yard, give me a couple of hours and then you can tell the world and his wife what you have learned form British Telecom.'

'And what are you going to be doing in those two hours?' she asked.

'Having a quiet word with Mr Mini Markets.'

'You'd better make sure you're long gone before Orwell turns up on the doorstep. I'm going to be skating on thin ice as it is; if you are caught with Lal, I really will go under.'

'Not if I have anything to do with it,' he said.

Ashton saw O'Meara off the premises, then borrowed the phone at the reception desk to ring the MT section at Vauxhall

Cross. After telling the transport supervisor to send Daniels round to 4 Central Buildings, he got back to the switchboard and asked the operator to transfer him to Peachey's extension. As was not unusual, morning prayers was overrunning but he managed to raise the PA to the Deputy DG and left a message with her.

Daniels was the finest driver the SIS had but even the best couldn't always anticipate what the other road users might do. Crossing the river by Vauxhall Bridge, he had turned right on Millbank and continued on up to the Houses of Parliament. As he went round Parliament Square to get into Great George Street, a white van emerging from Broad Sanctuary on his left had cut in front of him and clipped the offside wing of the Ford Grenada. By the time Daniels had sorted that little problem out and delivered Ashton to Cricklewood Broadway, the two hours' grace he'd asked for had been cut in half.

The head office of Hakkison Lal Mini Markets was on the top floor of a narrow three-storey building that had been jerry-built in the very early 1920s and had been accumulating grime ever since. There was a newsagents at street level run by a youngish-looking Indian whose family name also happened to be Lal. He was, Ashton learned, a distant relative of Hakkison and lived in the flat above the shop with his wife, their two children, his mother-in-law and her unmarried daughter. Flashing his ID card, Ashton told the newsagent he was a senior officer with the Home Office Immigration Service and wished to see Mr Hakkison Lal regarding one of his employees. To reach his office, Ashton had to go through the narrow passageway into the lane behind the building and use the external staircase inside the coutyard. The man who owned the mini markets all over North London was not overjoyed to see him.

'I am very busy,' he snapped. 'Go away, I have nothing to say to you.'

'Well, that's a shame,' Ashton told him, 'because you're in deep trouble and I'm here to help you.'

'What nonsense. I am not listening to you. In fact if you do not leave my office at once I will send for the police.'

'I wouldn't bother, they will be here shortly with a bundle of printouts from British Telecom.'

Lal caught his breath. 'What printouts?' he asked hoarsely.

'Phone bills relating to the Steadfast Agency, your head office and every mini market you own. The police know that Wilks spoke to you the night he was killed. They can prove you were the go-between for V. J. Desai because they've got a record of every call made from your Cricklewood number. You could be looking at a life sentence as an accessory to murder.'

'Murder,' Lal repeated in a hollow voice.

'It's not suicide any more. The pathologist who performed the autopsy will testify that Wilks was pumped full of morphine shortly before he was left on the railway line.'

'I know nothing of this.'

'I doubt the jury will believe you. I mean, you have already admitted that V. J. Desai is related to you by marriage.'

'He is not really my wife's second cousin.'

'Unless you want to end up in Parkhurst, you will have to do better than that.'

'How?'

'You can start by telling me where we can find V. J. Desai.'

'And if I do this I will not go to prison?'

'It's your best hope,' Ashton said carefully.

It wasn't much of a guarantee and he hadn't committed the SIS in any way but Lal seemed to think the Intelligence service was on his side and drew comfort from that misapprehension. Once he started talking there was no stopping him.

Mairin walked into the Hertz Agency in the centre of town armed with the licence number of the VW Passat, a plausible cover story and an implacable determination to make at least one of the Brits pay for what they had done to Eamonn. He was lying in hospital with a fractured skull and a broken jaw, the victim of a vicious attack. What angered her even more was the attitude of the big man from Dublin; to maintain the ceasefire, he had prohibited any form of retaliation. Well, that was something she and Cathal would have to think about.

'I've had an accident, Jutta,' she said, focusing on the Dymo name tag the receptionist was wearing. 'Or to be more accurate, one of your cars reversed into mine.'

'When was this?' Jutta asked.

'Yesterday afternoon.' Mairin opened her handbag and took out a slip of paper. 'It was a green-coloured Volkswagen Passat, licence number M ZX 699. The driver was an Englishman.'

'Yes?'

'The Passat was not damaged but I have a big dent in the rear bumper and my insurance company won't pay for that. I'm not covered, you understand?'

'What is it you want from us? We will not pay for the repair.'

'I don't expect you to. The Englishman gave me his name and address in London.'

'Then you must write and send the bill for repair.'

'Oh, I intend to but I think he gave me a false name and address.' Mairin looked at the slip of paper in her hand. 'He told me his name was Mr Ralph Messenger and that he lived at 61 Tiptree Road, Lewisham.' She smiled hesitantly at Jutta. 'I know it's asking a lot, but I wondered if you could possibly compare it with the details on the rental agreement?'

The German girl frowned and Mairin thought she was going to refuse on the grounds that it was not company policy to disclose such information. But Jutta merely asked her to wait while she consulted the office manager. A few minutes later Jutta returned with the information that the Englishman in question was Mr Eric Daniels of 147 Inkerman Road, Camberwell.

Chapter Twenty Four

———————⟫•⟫•◦•⟪•⟪———————

Within minutes of returning to Vauxhall Cross, Ashton found himself in the conference room on the top floor about to undergo the kind of grilling normally associated with the Star Chamber of yesteryear. Seated across the long table from him were Hazelwood, Peachey, Bill Orchard and Jill Sheridan. The inquisition had originally started in the DG's office with just the Deputy DG in attendance; it had rapidly adjourned to the conference room after Victor had decided the presence of Bill Orchard and Jill Sheridan was required. While Ashton could appreciate that what he had to report would be of interest to the Head of the Asian Department, he failed to see that the same necessarily applied to Jill. He could only assume Victor believed there was some connection with the Board of Inquiry, which she had chaired.

'Now that we are all here, you'd better start at the beginning again.' Hazelwood paused, then told him not to spend too long on the background, a sign that he wanted to spend as little time as possible in the smokeless zone of the conference room.

Ashton did his best. Largely for Jill's benefit, he outlined the sequence of events which had culminated in the murder of Basil Wilks.

'Do we know why he was killed?' Jill asked.

'All Hakkison Lal will admit to is that he acted as a go-between. It's his best defence and I don't believe anybody is going to shake him. I can only guess at the motive.'

'Then share it with us, Peter.'

'Wilks wanted to meet V. J. Desai face to face, a man he'd

never seen, never spoken to before. That made Wilks dangerous in Desai's eyes and he had him killed to preserve his own anonymity.'

'And where is Desai now?' Orchard asked.

'According to Lal he's in America. He went up to Manchester and caught a United Airlines flight to New York. Desai holds an American passport under an assumed name. One other point: he didn't travel alone; there was a man called R. S. Joshi with him. Lal couldn't say whether he also held an American Passport.'

'Couldn't or wouldn't?' Hazelwood snorted. 'Ten to one he was lying in his teeth.'

'No, I believe he was telling the truth. V. J. Desai is the Ananda Marg's Director of Military Operations; he knows a thing or two about personal security and wouldn't tell anybody anything they didn't need to know.'

'I thought you told me Lal is related to the man by marriage?'

'That was his original story; he changed it once we had proof that Wilks had phoned him shortly before he was murdered.'

'So how does he now account for his involvement with Ananda Marg?'

'He's a sympathiser and contributes to their fighting fund. It's a personal thing with him.'

The seed had been planted in 1947 with the partition of India and certain events which had happened a good twelve years before Lal had been born. Prior to Independence, his grandparents had lived in Kasur, a small town approximately fifty miles south of Lahore which was destined to fall within Pakistan. His grandparents with their three sons and two daughters had set out for Firozpur over the border in India on the twelfth of August, three days before Independence. Elements among the Muslim population of Kasur had in fact begun to attack the Hindu minority the night before and the family had seen their old house burning as they waited at the station for the first train to Firozpur. When it had departed early the following morning, something in excess of a thousand people had crammed into or on top of the four coaches.

'They were everywhere,' Ashton continued, 'standing in the aisles, lying under the seats, in the luggage racks, riding the couplings, precariously balanced on the running boards and hanging on to the door handles for dear life.'

'Can we get to the point?' Hazelwood growled.

'The point is the train was stopped five miles short of the border. The mob had torn up a section of the track and it seems the driver and fireman were hacked to death before they could put the engine into reverse. A bloody massacre followed in which Lal's grandparents and three of their five children had their throats cut. One of the two survivors of the family was twelve-year-old Pandit, the boy who eventually fathered Hakkison Lal.'

Although Lal had been born in England, his heart, as he had told Ashton, had always belonged to India. When he was sixteen his father had sent him to Firozpur to meet the uncle he had never seen and members of his mother's family. Three years later, he had returned to India to marry the bride who'd been chosen for him.

His father had always maintained that the massacre would never have happened if India hadn't been partitioned. 'One of the principal aims of the Ananda Marg is to unite the Indian subcontinent which is why Lal had become one of their supporters,' Ashton finished

'Do you believe this story, Bill?' Hazelwood asked, turning to Orchard.

'It has a ring of truth,' Orchard said cautiously. 'Of course I should want to hear how he became involved with V. J. Desai and this R. S. Joshi before committing myself.'

Hazelwood nodded. 'So would I. How about it, Peter?'

'Ananda Marg had him on their subscription list.'

'Are you trying to be funny?'

'Absolutely not. You join a political party in this country and it isn't only your yearly subscription they're after. They want you to do all kinds of things from selling raffle tickets to organising fund-raising social events. Hakkison Lal paid his subs to a right-wing extremist of the Hindu National Party—'

'The Bharatiya Janatã Party or BJP for short,' Orchard said, interrupting him.

'Whatever. Anyway, this extremist is a front man for Ananda Marg. Consequently both Lal's business and private life are known to the movement. He claims that back in early March he had a phone call from a sympathiser on the staff of the Indian High Commission in London. This man told Lal that he was required to provide accommodation for two very important guests. It was an order not a request. A few days later the two men walked into his head office in Cricklewood. Although he had never seen either of them before they identified themselves to his satisfaction.'

'Did Lal tell you why they had come to this country?' Orchard asked.

'He couldn't. The fact is Lal didn't want to know and closed his eyes to what was going on around him. It's one thing to give money to a terrorist group, quite another matter to be caught up in the action.'

'You sound as if you actually believe him,' Peachey observed.

Ashton frowned. The Deputy DG clearly didn't and it was true that Lal had told him a pack of lies about his family when he and O'Meara had gone to his house in Hampstead. But not today; even the most consummate actor could not have conveyed fear like Lal had. The man had been frightened of his own shadow and had been eager to tell Ashton everything he knew.

'We're all waiting for an answer,' Hazelwood said.

'Well, all right, I believe him.'

'In other words, we don't know why V. J. Desai came to this country and are never likely to unless—'

'The penny's just dropped,' Ashton said, interrupting him. 'He was here to find out whether it was necessary to kill his sister-in-law, Z. K. Ramash.'

Everybody stared at him as if he had taken leave of his senses.

'Would you care to expand that statement?' Hazelwood said.

'The evidence to support it is a little thin.'

'I'm surprised it's not threadbare.'

Undeterred, Ashton told him that since they had been related by marriage it was reasonable to assume they knew a great deal about one another. It was also his contention their paths had crossed somewhere in Europe earlier in the year in circumstances when his sister-in-law was the last person Desai would have wanted to see. Without Ramash being aware of it, he had followed her back to England, discovered where she was living and then looked round for somebody to interrogate his sister-in-law.

'I can't explain at the moment how he got hold of Lorraine Cheeseman.'

'Don't let that put you off,' Hazelwood told him, and drew a faint smile from Peachey.

But nobody smiled when Ashton pulled his next rabbit out of the hat. Worried that the good doctor might take her information to MI5 or the SIS, Desai had arranged for Ramash to meet a member of the Intelligence Service.

'They didn't hack into Frank Warren's stand-alone system and steal Harriet's identity in order to discredit us. The profile sheet was needed to provide Lorraine Cheeseman with the right background because it was her job to assess how much of a threat Ramash was to V. J. Desai.'

'And in giving Ramash the thumbs down, she signed her own death warrant,' Jill said quietly.

'Well, I think Desai would have killed her anyway; she knew too much about him.'

At the end of the day it was still conjecture, as Hazelwood was quick to point out. Afforded the opportunity to interrogate V. J. Desai over a period of months rather than days he thought it probable they would be able to fill in the blank spaces. But the police had to find him first and then apply for extradition, assuming they had sufficient evidence.

'I don't understand why we'd never heard of this man before Hugo Calthorpe cabled you about Dr Ramash,' he said, looking straight at Orchard.

'V. J. Desai had been carded ever since we learned he was Ananda Marg's Director of Military Operations.' Orchard cleared his throat, a nervous mannerism which came to the fore when his department was being criticised. 'The information came from Hugo's predecessor who gave the source a very low grading.'

'We should have asked for an update,' Hazelwood told him.

'Wouldn't have made any difference if we had,' Ashton said tersely.

'Why is that?'

'Because we're still organised for the Cold War. There's nothing wrong with having geographic departments like the European, Mid East, Asian and Pacific Basin as long as we don't operate as though we are dealing with power blocs like the Warsaw Pact. I mean, what is morning prayers but a report on the lines of "look what's happened in my bailiwick"?'

'I think it's a little more than that,' Hazelwood said acidly, 'but don't let me inhibit you.'

Ashton took him at his word and ploughed doggedly on. The way he saw it, they weren't geared up to deal with international terrorist groups, which enjoyed a safe haven in the host country and struck at a soft target a continent away. Ashton believed a separate department should be established, with responsibility for tracking any terrorist group from the moment its personnel left the country. Naturally, the initial warning would come from the Mid East, Asian, or whatever department happened to be appropriate.

'And then what?' Hazelwood demanded.

'We hit them first for a change.'

A snort told Ashton that Victor didn't think much of his idea. Peachey's reaction was impossible to read because as usual he was giving his impression of a sphinx. Orchard looked as if he didn't quite know what to make of the proposal while Jill Sheridan appeared to be either in deep thought or else had her mind elsewhere.

'Very interesting,' Hazelwood said. 'Now suppose you put theory into practice and start tracking V. J. Desai.'

Calthorpe headed into the cantonment on Sardar Patel Marg and made the usual right turn at the junction of Station Road with Parade Road. He was becoming something of a regular visitor to the bungalow on the Janakpuri Road even though he was not always made to feel welcome. And in view of the questions Bill Orchard expected him to put to Sumitra he certainly was not going to be greeted with open arms on this occasion. She was bound to ask about the reward he had rashly promised the SIS would offer for information leading to the arrest of Logan's killers and he didn't know how he was going to tell Sumitra the fifty thousand was entirely dependent on what he learned from her.

The signal from Bill Orchard had arrived yesterday evening. Anxious to get the business over and done with, Calthorpe had got the Volkswagen out and driven straight to the bungalow only to find that Sumitra was not at home. He had tried to ring her before setting off but her phone appeared to be dead and an operator-assisted call had elicited the information that the line was out of order. The phone had then given an unobtainable signal when he had tried to ring Sumitra again this evening, but this time when he swung into the drive there was a noticeable difference. Yesterday evening the car had been missing, this afternoon the faithful Hindustan Ambassador was parked down the side of the bungalow.

Calthorpe stopped the Volkswagen, switched off the engine and got out. As he climbed the short flight of steps leading to the veranda, he could see the front door had been forced and was hanging askew. The hall looked as if it had been wrecked in an earthquake. The drawers in the hall table had been pulled out and the contents emptied on to the floor, a large photograph of Indira Gandhi with Logan Bannerman in the background, had been taken down off the wall, laid flat and then jumped on until the glass had been shattered into hundreds of fragments. A number of floorboards had been ripped up and tossed aside, presumably to see if anything had been stashed beneath.

He called out to Sumitra and kept on calling her name until he heard a faint whimper coming from one of the rooms at the rear of the bungalow. After trying two bedrooms, both of which had been ransacked, he found her lying on the floor in the third. The curtains were still drawn and in the prevailing gloom, he literally stumbled over Sumitra. A low pitiful moan of agony ended as a chilling rattle in the throat which alarmed Calthorpe.

'Oh my God,' he said breathlessly, 'I'm sorry. I'm so sorry.'

Calthorpe backed off, carefully edged his way towards the windows and opened the curtains, then returned to Sumitra. Her face had been battered almost beyond recognition, the eyes closed to narrow slits, a mask of congealed blood on her mouth and chin from a broken nose. But it was the soles of her feet which horrified him most; somebody had beaten them with a bamboo cane until the skin on each foot had burst like an overripe tomato. If that wasn't enough, she was nursing her ribs with both arms.

'Don't move me,' she croaked.

'I'm not going to,' Calthorpe assured her.

Sumitra needed medical treatment, not the rough and ready first aid he was capable of. The way she was holding herself suggested several ribs had been cracked and he was frightened her lungs might be punctured if he attempted to pick her up. Furthermore, the Volkswagen would hardly make an ideal ambulance.

Assuring Sumitra he wouldn't be long, Calthorpe left the bedroom to look for the telephone. Yesterday evening, the operator had told him the line was out of order, which he discovered was more or less correct when he walked into the sitting room. The line had actually been cut and the phone had then been smashed with a heavy blunt instrument. He returned to Sumitra, told her he was going to fetch an ambulance and would be back in no time.

Calthorpe ran out of the bungalow, got into the Volkswagen and started up. Fifty was usually his top speed; that afternoon he overtook everything on the road, weaving in and out of the bullock carts heading into town, the speedometer rarely indicating less than seventy.

It was only the second time Urquhart had been to Jill Sheridan's house in Bisham Gardens, which overlooked Waterlow Park. On that first occasion a little over a fortnight ago he had arrived by taxi; this evening instead of a black cab he was riding in a Porsche 911 driven by the most attractive chauffeuse in London. Jill had telephoned to invite him to have a drink with her after work at the National Liberal Club in Whitehall Place. Knowing her as he did, the Liberals were the last political party he would have expected Jill to support but of course one did not have to be a fully paid up member to join the club and the yearly subscription was a good deal more reasonable than White's,

Boodle's or Brooks's, not that Jill would have been allowed to join any of them.

He had assumed her invitation had everything to do with the Board of Inquiry she had chaired, copies of which had yet to reach the Foreign and Commonwealth Office and Cabinet Secretary. Jill deservedly enjoyed a reputation for being forthright and it would be typical of Hazelwood to sit on the proceedings while he did his best to make her tone it down. However, to his surprise, Jill hadn't mentioned the report and when he had raised the subject, she had defended Hazelwood, maintaining that he and Clifford Peachey needed to consider all the recommendations. Jill, he learned, had invited him to the Liberal Club because she valued his opinion and there were a number of ideas she wished to air before putting them forward officially.

The club however was not a suitable venue to discuss matters relating to national security and she'd wondered if he would care to have supper at her place, assuming he didn't have a prior engagement. Urquhart had news for Ms Sheridan; if he had been invited to dine with the Head of the Civil Service, he would have invented some excuse for absenting himself at the last moment in order to be with her.

'I'm afraid it won't be anything fancy,' she had told him apologetically, 'just smoked salmon with the usual trimming. And wine,' she added, 'there's always a bottle chilling in the fridge.'

He wouldn't have complained if bread and cheese was all she had to offer.

The house was in darkness as Jill turned into the driveway until a sensor triggered the powerful security light under the eaves of the house. Another sensor automatically raised the up-and-over door of the double garage enabling her to drive straight inside. The place was a veritable fortress; alighting from the Porsche, Jill went over to the side door where there was a control panel on the wall and tapped out a code which instantly switched on every light in the house.

'All I've got to do now, Robin, is switch off the alarm and then we can think about supper.'

She left him standing there in the garage while she disappeared inside the house. In no time at all, or so it seemed to Urquhart, she was back again. It transpired that once Jill crossed the threshold she had exactly twenty seconds to knock the alarm off, otherwise all hell would break loose.

'The Royalty and Diplomatic Protection Department could learn a trick or two from you,' Urquhart told her admiringly.

'I don't believe in doing things by half, Robin. The alarm is linked to Highgate police station on Archway Road. There is an infrared fence front, back and on both sides of the house. If anybody should try to sneak up on me in the middle of the night, the alarm goes off as soon as the fence is broken and hopefully the boys in blue arrive on the double.'

Urquhart followed her through the utility room and on into the kitchen. The only thing he was permitted to do towards their supper was to draw the cork from a bottle of Chablis and find a couple of wine glasses in the sideboard. He also listened attentively to Jill as she sliced and buttered a small brown loaf. And what she had to say was pretty startling. In her view, ever since the Berlin Wall had come down, the Western Powers had been unfocused. For many, the last visible enemy had vanished with the demise of the Soviet Union, but that was to ignore the facts of life.

'World War III has already started, Robin, and it's being waged by Islamic fundamentalists. We're just not organised to deal with the threat. This especially applies to the SIS.'

As well as being the youngest head of department, Urquhart had always regarded Jill as easily the best and the brightest. He knew his opinion was not shared by Hazelwood who'd given her a well above average grading in his annual assessment instead of the outstanding she deserved. However, Victor's predecessor had thought sufficiently highly of Jill to promote her to Assistant Director. This evening she was demonstrating an ability to look outside her own department and come up with some innovative ideas.

'I don't have to tell you how well-equipped terrorists are these days,' Jill said as she wheeled their supper into the drawing room on a dinner wagon. 'Especially the Islamic groups. They have a sophisticated arsenal of Stinger antiaircraft missiles, heavy and light mortars, Kalashnikov assault rifles and all the Semtex explosive they want. They're not short of a bob or two and there are any number of countries in the Middle, Near, and Far East willing to provide them with a safe haven.'

This meant that in addition to her own fiefdom, the Asian, Pacific Basin and the Rest of the World Departments were engaged in combating the threat posed by Islamic fundamentalists. And if you took the Muslims of Bosnia-Herzogovina into account, so was Rowan Garfield's European Department.

'That's the weakness of our present organisation,' Jill continued. 'Oh, we all get together to exchange information every day at morning prayers but essentially we operate in watertight compartments.'

Urquhart wiped his lips on his napkin. 'So what are you suggesting?' he asked.

'We need to form a new department with sole responsibility for conducting worldwide antiterrorist operations.'

'The Treasury will never hear of it on financial grounds.'

Jill turned to face him. 'Most of the manpower can be found from within existing resources.'

The new organisation would consist of the Intelligence-gathering section whose task was to plot the movements of known terrorists in conjunction with existing departments and an operational branch charged with taking executive action.

'What exactly does that mean, Jill?'

'It means we don't wait to be attacked; instead we take them out at the first opportunity.'

'The politicians will never agree to that.'

'Never is too definite a word. They will change their minds as soon as a terrorist group has the ability to wage nuclear, chemical or germ warfare. We have to be ready for such an eventuality.'

She had obviously given a lot of thought to her proposals. Amongst other things, she considered command and control of the new organisation should be vested in Clifford Peachey or whoever succeeded him as Deputy Director General of the SIS. She talked of a new concept of operations, that the new department would be essentially aggressive, that its mission was to seek, find and then strike.

There was a moment when Urquhart wondered if the concept was entirely her own idea, only to reject the thought as unworthy.

'Have you written a paper on this?' he asked.

'No, I wanted to use you as a sounding board first.'

'Well, I recommend you get cracking on the first draft.'

'I doubt whether my views on future strategy would carry much weight with Victor or Clifford Peachey.'

'Don't belittle yourself, Jill.' Urquhart rested a hand on her left knee and gave it an affectionate pat. 'There are people outside the SIS who think very highly of you.'

'Meaning you, Robin.'

'Well, that goes without saying.' Jill didn't seem to object that his right hand was still resting lightly on her knee and, plucking up courage, he moved it a little higher until the tips of his fingers were just underneath the hem of her skirt. 'But there are others.'

'Who for instance?'

'Sir Ranulph Jordan, the Permanent Under Secretary of State and Head of the Diplomatic Service,' he added in a strained voice.

'Tell me you aren't joking.'

'You know I'm not, I couldn't be so cruel.'

'No, of course you couldn't. Forgive me?'

Jill half turned sideways and leaning forward, kissed him lightly on the lips and not the cheek as he had anticipated. In doing so, she made it easier for his hand to slip even higher up her leg. Any moment now he knew she would take hold of his wrist and move the offending hand away. Rosalind would also be dragged into the conversation to remind him he had a wife at home who was paralysed from the waist down, as if he was likely to forget. That was what had happened the last time he'd been here. The seconds ticked by, a full minute passed, then another and still she didn't do anything. He could feel himself erecting and knew it showed, which was very embarrassing. Then Jill placed a hand on his wrist and he wished the earth would open up and swallow him.

'I think we would find it more comfortable upstairs, don't you, Robin?'

'Comfortable,' Urquhart repeated, unable to believe what he'd heard.

'More civilised then,' Jill said, and took him by the hand.

A little unsteady on his feet, Nolan left the crowded bar and made his way to the Gents. As the commanding officer of the South Armagh battalion of the Irish National Liberation Army, he enjoyed a great deal of prestige in his adopted village of Castlegreenore across the border in County Monaghan. The respect he was accorded manifested itself in a number of ways. People were always buying him drinks in the pub and once a week, regular as clockwork, the local flesher would give Caitlin, his common-law wife, a choice cut of meat at no charge.

Nolan unzipped his fly, stepped up to the urinal and experienced that great sense of relief that comes when an overfull bladder is emptied. He heard the door open and a muffled sound of footsteps as if the man was trying not to make a noise. As he started to look over his shoulder, something round and hard pressed against the bone behind his left ear.

A quiet voice said, 'That's right, Barry, it's a .38 revolver you're feeling.'

'Are you the polis?' Nolan asked.

'Better for you we were.'

We! This meant there was a second man. He was probably the other side of the door to prevent anybody entering the urinals while they were talking.

'I've got a message for you from Dublin, Barry.'

'Yeah?' Nolan shook himself, then zipped up the fly. 'What about?'

'You've got forty-eight hours to turn in your weapons and explosives.'

'Who says?'

'Lenihan.'

'Tell him to go fuck himself.'

Still pressing the revolver against his head, the stranger grabbed him by the testicles and crushed them in a grip of iron. Nolan groaned in agony. There were black spots in front of his eyes, the world started to revolve, and the bile rose in his throat. He sank down on his knees, his head tipping forward in the urinal bowl.

'Get Caitlin to kiss them better,' the stranger told him, and left as quietly as he had arrived.

Chapter Twenty Five

———⟫▸•◦•◂⟪———

It wasn't the happiest of morning prayers for Orchard. It had got off to a bad start when Mary had telephoned him fifteen minutes before the meeting with the news that the insurance company had at last written to them about the Audi. Apart from the more obvious signs of vandalism, the garage which had recovered the vehicle had also discovered that the joy riders had drained the radiator and kept the engine running until it had seized up. The estimate from the garage had been such that the insurance company had decided the Audi was beyond economical repair. They therefore proposed to give him a cheque for the residual value of the car which, since it was almost four years old, meant that he was several thousand pounds out of pocket. It was a practice common to all insurance companies but Orchard felt particularly aggrieved because the insurers would not take the hitherto immaculate appearance of the Audi into account.

Five minutes into the meeting he also knew Hazelwood would give him a roasting before the morning was much older. Roger Benton had received a detailed report from Head of Station, Hong Kong, concerning the activities of Mr P. J. Ingram, sales representative for the communications Division of Inter-Continental Arms whereas he'd heard nothing from Hugo Calthorpe. The apparent tardiness didn't reflect well on his department and Victor was bound to take him up on it. When it came to his turn to speak, he would just have to ad lib as best he could. Right now, however, the spotlight was still on Roger Benton, and Ingram, it appeared, had been very co-operative.

'Of course he had every reason to be.' Benton smiled. 'The South African owner of Inter-Continental Arms lives in Pietermaritzburg and leaves the day-to-day running of the business to his Australian office manager. He took himself off to Manilla a week ago since when he hasn't been heard of. Ingram has therefore been left to hold the baby and is understandably nervous. Ingram is thirty-six years old and looks incredibly young for his age. Head of Station says he's immature, naïve, and goes on to describe him as a Walter Mitty character.'

Ingram claimed he had gone to Uppingham but in fact had been educated at Walton Abbey College, a fee-paying educational establishment but was not listed amongst the Headmasters' Conference schools. Despite leaving Walton Abbey College with just three O levels, he had told prospective employers that he had been offered a place at Brunel University to read computer sciences but had turned it down because he'd wanted to join the army. He had enlisted in the Royal Signals, which was true, and had been selected for officer training at Sandhurst, which was untrue. According to Ingram, he had damaged his right knee so badly on the assault course at the Royal Military Academy that he had subsequently been medically downgraded and discharged, whereas he had actually bought himself out of the army.

'Where did Head of Station get this information?' Hazelwood asked.

'From Ingram himself. It was confession time. He was led to believe that both India and Pakistan were applying for his extradition. By the time Head of Station had finished laying it on with a trowel he was worried sick what his inmates would do to him while he was in prison awaiting trial.'

Ingram had got the job of sales representative for the Communications Division on the strength of his eight months' service in the Royal Signals. The appointment had been advertised in the *Daily Telegraph* and successful applicants had subsequently been interviewed at Burleigh House in The Strand.

'Burleigh House is a very narrow building with two rooms on each floor. It's the sort of anonymous place you'd walk past without noticing it was there. Anyway, Inter-Continental Arms had rented two rooms on the top floor for one day only. With hindsight, Ingram now reckons he was the only applicant.'

'And how long has he been working for the firm, Roger?'

'Twenty-seven months.'

'Not exactly quick on the uptake,' Hazelwood observed.

The office manager arranged the sales trips. Ingram was merely an errand boy whose expertise owed everything to the 1985 edition of *Jane's Military Communications*.

'The business trip to Lahore was no exception. Ingram's job was to keep the client happy,' Benton continued. 'The contract was virtually in the bag, or so the officer manager told him. All he had to do was wine and dine the Deputy Commandant of the Regional Paramilitary Constabulary for a couple of days. Apparently he had some reservations about re-equipping the force with the Clansman range of combat radios and was making life difficult for the regional commander who was in favour of the deal. Then the day Ingram was due to fly to Lahore, he was given last-minute instructions.'

Ingram was informed that Major General Fyodor Aleksandrovich Marchukov, the President of Marchukov International Carriers, would be visiting the Pakistan Air Force base in Lahore while he was staying at the Ambassador Hotel. The owner of Inter-Continental Arms was convinced the Russian was a man he could do business with and Ingram was therefore required to make Marchukov's acquaintance and then persuade the General to accompany him to Kuala Lumpur. To this end two reservations had been made in his name on the Pakistan International Airline departing Islamabad at 16.00 hours on 22 October, the day after Marchukov was scheduled to arrive in Lahore. The fares had been pre-paid and the tickets would be awaiting collection at the Pakistan Airlines information desk. It was, however, necessary for him to confirm the reservations twenty-four hours before departure.

'You won't be surprised to hear that the air fares were charged to Ingram's Mastercard without his knowledge.'

'And he seriously expects us to believe this?' Hazelwood said incredulously.

'Well, Head of Station did say he was extraordinarily naïve

and the fact is the Mastercard was chargeable to Inter-Continental Arms.'

'Correct me if I'm wrong,' Hazelwood said, looking round the table, 'but didn't Marchukov inform Air Traffic Control, Delhi that his inertial navigation system was defective and he proposed to make an emergency landing at the nearest airfield?'

'That's correct, Director,' Orchard said, conscious that Hazelwood was now gazing at him expectantly.

'Which just happened to be the Pakistan Air Force base, Lahore?'

'Yes.'

'And Lahore had never featured in the flight plan he had submitted for clearance?'

'So I understand from Ashton.'

'Yet Inter-Continental Arms knew precisely when he was going to be in Lahore. What does that suggest to you, Bill?'

'I'd say there were grounds for thinking Inter-Continental organised the arms drop on Udhampur. I'm also inclined to agree that Ingram was easily duped and had no idea what was going on.'

'Any other thoughts?' Hazelwood asked, looking round the table again.

'I'm not entirely with Bill on this,' Jill said.

Orchard thought it almost inevitable that Ms Sheridan would feel compelled to make a contribution. As the youngest and most junior assistant director, she was determined to make a name for herself within the SIS and outside it too by all accounts. Much as Jill irritated him, he had to admit that what she had to say was invariably worth listening to and this morning was no exception. She could not forget that Inter-Continental had sold the surplus arms and ammunition they had purchased in Cyprus on to the Rao corporation, Karachi. She also recalled the phone call made by a Russian speaker in Delhi to Headquarters, St Petersburg Military District which had been intercepted by 242 Signal Squadron. The message was intended for Marchukov advising him that the contract had been agreed and a down payment of 250,000 US dollars had been received.

'The weapons which were dropped on Udhampur were owned by a Pakistan corporation, yet the money for chartering the TU 154 appears to have been raised in India.' Jill shook her head. 'It just doesn't make sense to me, Victor.'

'What about it, Bill?'

'It doesn't make sense to me either, Director. On the other hand, it wouldn't be quite such a mystery if the sales invoice to the Rao Corporation was a forgery.'

'Better for us if it's genuine,' Jill said quietly.

'Let's move on.' Hazelwood smiled. 'Except the ball is still in your court, Bill. I am of course assuming that Hugo has talked to Sumitra Bannerman.'

Here we go, Orchard told himself. This is where the roof falls in.

When it was a question of getting something done in a hurry, it wasn't a question of what you knew but who you knew in Whitehall with the necessary clout. A year ago Ashton could have gone straight to the CIA chief in London and asked for his assistance in obtaining the flight manifests he needed from United Airlines, but time had moved on and he hadn't met the present incumbent. However, the Deputy DG of the SIS was required to maintain very close links with the CIA chief and he had simply routed the request through Clifford Peachey.

Securing the airline's co-operation had been easy; deciding over what period he wanted United to provide copies of their flight manifests was the difficult part. No matter how many times Lal had changed his story, he'd always maintained he didn't know exactly when V. J. Desai had left the country. The decision to eliminate Wilks had undoubtedly been taken by Desai, and the private investigator had been killed on Monday, 16 October, thirteen days after Dr Ramash had been murdered. However, unlike the good doctor, it was evident that Wilks had continued to be a threat after his death. Desai had therefore decided to leave the country as soon as possible, which probably meant within twenty-four hours. Acting on this assumption, Ashton had asked United Airlines at Manchester for all their flight manifests from Tuesday, 17 October to inclusive Saturday, 21st. The printouts, which had been collected from the American Embassy that morning, ran to 315 pages. Ashton had scrutinised only a fraction of them when Jill Sheridan walked into the office.

'Can you spare a minute?' she asked, and then plunged straight in without waiting for an answer. 'I want to pick your brains.'

'What about?'

'The arms drop on Udhampur. The weapons had apparently been purchased by the Rao Corporation, Karachi but the down payment to Marchukov appears to have been raised in Delhi. To me that's a a contradiction. I mean, those weapons were designed to be used by the Kashmir Liberation Front against the Indian Army so why was the contract for the air drop finalised in Delhi? And another thing, most down payments represent fifty per cent of the total amount and a quarter of a million dollars doesn't strike me as being overgenerous. How many Latvians were there in his crew?'

'Six,' Ashton told her.

'Six.' Jill perched herself on his desk, her feet still firmly planted on the floor. 'Half a million dollars split seven ways less the cost of fuel and landing charges at Larnaka and Bahrain. It doesn't seem a good return considering the risks which were involved.'

'Maybe it was just money in Marchukov's back pocket?'

Jill looked at him thoughtfully. 'What are you suggesting, Peter? That it was a double-cross?'

'Yes, I think Marchukov had two paymasters.'

'Have you any proof?'

'Come off it, Jill. You know very well that most of the time we are trying to find out what we don't know by what we do.'

'Sounds familiar.'

'Wellington said it originally, he called it guessing what was the other side of the hill.'

'So guess.'

Ashton believed you had to go right back to when Inter-Continental Arms had purchased the surplus arms and ammunition from the Ordnance Depot in Cyprus, only to find the prospective clients had changed their minds. While trying to find another buyer for their merchandise, Inter-Continental Arms had been approached by representatives of the Ananda

Marg who had offered to purchase the whole stock on one condition.

'The world and his wife had to believe the arms and ammunition had been bought by agents acting on behalf of Pakistan. Now we know the weapons and ammunition became the property of the Rao Corporation, at least on paper. I think those people in Hong Kong persuaded them they had purchased the hardware on the instructions of the Kashmir Liberation Front, but of course they can't show that on the export licence, and would Rao consider acting as a front? Pakistan has always regarded the Indian occupation of Kashmir as illegal so I don't imagine they needed much cajoling.'

'Then what does Inter-Continental do? Involve the Pakistan Government?'

'I doubt the conspiracy went all the way to the top but it's likely more that one highly placed official with a misplaced sense of patriotism was drawn into the plot.'

The officials would have been shown the flight plan Marchukov would file with the Indian Civil Aviation Authority and then told how the clandestine mission was to be executed. They had also received assurances that no matter what happened, there was no way Pakistan could be implicated.

'Bryce and Bryce were the major players in the deception plan,' Ashton continued. 'Before they could be air dropped, the weapons and ammunition had to be made up in pallets which couldn't be done in Larnaka. Bryce and Bryce obviously arranged for the material to be moved to their warehouse in Bahrain where the work could be carried out. If you want proof, get your whistle-blower inside the firm to check out the shipping movements.'

'I'd like to hear the rest of the story first,' Jill told him.

'The whole operation was conceived and controlled by the Ananda Marg. When Marchukov dropped those pallets in Udhampur, he was following their instruction to the letter. Same applied to the navigational hazard he reported to Air Traffic Control, Delhi, and his decision to make for the nearest airfield. They had told him to land at the Pakistan Air Force base, Lahore and suddenly the Government finds itself involved in a major diplomatic row which is not of its making. Small wonder the officials who were drawn into the conspiracy couldn't wait to put Marchukov on the first available flight out of the country.'

'It's almost too neat, Peter.'

'It's all of that but once in a blue moon an operation does go like clockwork and this one was masterminded by V. J. Desai.'

'I don't get it,' Jill said. 'Can you explain to me what he hoped to achieve?'

'He wants to start a war between India and Pakistan,' Ashton told her, 'and he isn't finished yet.'

Like a burglar going about his unlawful business, Calthorpe sneaked into the British High Commission and went upstairs to his office in the secure area. He had been up all night with Sumitra, sitting outside her private room at the Safdar Jang Hospital. Since he hadn't washed, shaved or changed his clothes, he didn't want to run into the High Commissioner or his deputy.

Sumitra had taken an even worse beating than he had imagined. Apart from the most visible injuries which he'd noted, the doctor who had examined her had told him that two of the upper ribs on the left side had been broken as had the jaw and both little fingers. By the time he had summoned an ambulance and shown the crew the way to the bungalow, it had gone 8.00 p.m. when Sumitra had been admitted to hospital. He had immediately telephoned Choudhury at home, explained what had happened and asked him to arrange for at least one, preferably two, armed police officers to protect her while she was in hospital.

Although Calthorpe had been told he wouldn't be allowed to see Sumitra for a minimum of twelve hours, he had stayed on at the hospital, waiting for the police to arrive. At ten o'clock when there was still no sign of them he had rung Choudhury again. After making enquiries, the Deputy Chief of the Intelligence Bureau had returned his call to inform him that the officers had been sent to the wrong hospital but were now on their way to the Safdar Jang. At midnight he had disturbed Choudhury a third time to express his concern at the lack of urgency shown by the police. At half-past midnight Choudhury himself had turned up at the hospital to be followed twenty minutes later by an unarmed police constable on a bicycle. Finally the Deputy Chief of the Intelligence Bureau had contacted Headquarters Delhi Military District and the army had furnished two NCOs from the Provost Marshal's department in double quick time.

Calthorpe could have gone home once the NCOs were on guard outside Sumitra's room but he stayed on because there had been things he'd wanted to air with Choudhury. The day before yesterday, when he had called at the bungalow, the Hindustan Ambassador had been missing. Nevertheless he had checked to make sure Sumitra was not at home and would have noticed had the front door shown signs of being forced. Approximately twenty-four hours later, the car was back, the bungalow had been wrecked, and Sumitra was at home battered almost beyond recognition. As far as he was concerned that meant Sumitra had been abducted, taken to some unknown place and interrogated with the utmost hostility. Furthermore, he also believed the men who had kidnapped Sumitra, had been known to her and she had willingly let them into the bungalow.

'So why hadn't they killed her? Surely she was too dangerous to be left alive?' Choudhury had asked, and Calthorpe had had to admit he couldn't think of an explanation.

Choudhury had had no such difficulty. When Calthorpe had called on Sumitra the first time, she had been out visiting friends and he had simply missed her. However, sometime yesterday two or more robbers had broken into the bungalow and had tortured Sumitra to make her reveal where she had hidden her money. The bungalow was in an isolated position, at least four hundred yards from the nearest neighbour and nobody would have heard her screaming. So what if her telephone had been out of order for over two days? The telephone engineers were on strike but of course that inconvenience would not have affected the diplomatic community, the Government Secretariat or the cantonment.

Choudhury had also been able to excuse the lack of urgency shown by the police. Feelings had been running high against the Muslim community of Delhi and the police were still out in force, patrolling the streets to prevent intercommunal violence. Sumitra Bannerman had obviously been low down on their list of priorities.

Calthorpe opened his safe, took out the filing trays and placed them on his desk. Top of the pile awaiting his attention in the pending tray was the Op Immediate signal from Bill Orchard. Of the questions raised by the Head of the Asian Department, there wasn't a single one he could answer with any authority. Although he and Choudhury had been allowed to see Sumitra briefly before they left hospital, she had become so agitated when they'd walked into her room that the intern had requested them to leave at once. Back in his office, Calthorpe was unsure who had alarmed her the most, himself or the Deputy Chief of the Intelligence Bureau.

Ashton was tempted to dump all 315 pages of flight manifests into the wastebin and give the whole thing up as a bad job. He had looked for two men seated in the same row whose family names suggested they were Indian nationals and had drawn a blank. He had then gone through the lists again looking for two obviously unattached men on the same flight and hadn't found a matching pair. There was no shortage of Indian nationals on the flights but the vast majority were accompanied by their families. Although the airline had indicated the ticketing agencies where known, none of these had been in the London area and in the end, he had been left with the names of four unaccompanied men who had departed for New York between Tuesday 17 October and Saturday 21st, which didn't look at all promising.

Lal was a proven liar many times over but the man had been too concerned to save his own skin when Ashton had bearded him at his head office in Cricklewood. Unfortunately V. J. Desai had anticipated that when push came to shove, Lal wouldn't hesitate to betray him. Knowing this, he had used Lal to put up a smokescreen. Chances were he hadn't flown out from Manchester and he'd travelled alone, not with R. S. Joshi.

What was it Choudhury, the Deputy Chief of the Intelligence Bureau, had said of him? If V. J. Desai had stayed in the army he would have made one-star, possibly two-star rank? A major general? That had to be a conservative appraisal; when it came to the major principles of war the man was a master at deception. He probably had a whole briefcase stuffed with false passports. Ashton looked up from the list of names. That wasn't quite so ridiculous as it sounded. At the beginning of August when Desai had wined and dined Lorraine Cheeseman at the Bristol Hotel Kempinski in Berlin he had registered as V. J. Ramash.

The way forward was to give the four names culled from the flight manifests to Bill Orchard and get him to run them past Hugo Calthorpe a.s.a.p. What he wanted to know from Central Bureau of Investigation in Delhi was if any of them had ever been used as an alias by V. J. Desai. He also wanted a list of names that Desai was known to have adopted in the past. Meantime, he would get the Bundesnachrichtendienst to check whether a Mr V. J. Ramash, who could be travelling on a British passport, had resurfaced in Germany. Specifically he wanted the BND to try the name on every carrier operating out of Berlin, Cologne, Düsseldorf, Hamburg, Frankfurt and Stuttgart International Airports.

V. J. was driving a yellow cab. Visitors to New York were always telling him that nearly every taxi driver in Manhattan seemed to have come from either India or Pakistan. There were, of course, a large number from the subcontinent roaming the streets looking for a fare, but there were a hell of a lot more who hailed from the Caribbean and Africa. There were even some Afro-Americans who spoke a brand of English that was almost unintelligible. A white, native New Yorker behind the wheel was becoming a rarity, which wasn't too surprising. You never knew from one day to the next how much you were going to earn. You rented a cab from the company, filled it up with gas out of your own pocket and could end up working through five hours out of an eight-hour shift before you began to show a profit. There was, however, nothing to stop you working ten, twelve, even fourteen hours at a stretch.

For a white, native-born American there were better and easier ways of making a living, but not if you were an alien with just a work permit and no particular skills to offer. All you needed to become a cab driver in New York was a valid driving permit, the ability to understand basic English and enough cash to pay for the licence. To obtain a licence the applicant was required to produce four passport-size photographs of himself. One was retained by the city office, the second went to the Yellow Cab company, the third was displayed inside the cab where the fare could see it, and, by Law, the fourth had to be carried on the driver's person. The licence showed that Desai was now masquerading as V. J. Patil.

Desai headed uptown on Eighth Avenue, made a right on West 42nd and stopped outside the deli below the New Amsterdam Theatre. He switched off the external light on the roof, picked up his mobile and got out of the Ford. The time was ten after seven and so far he had put in nine hours making three runs out to JFK, a couple to La Guardia and racking up another 135 miles around Manhattan. Another hour, an hour and a half at the most, and if the man hadn't contacted him by then he would call it a day, turn the cab in and ride the subway home to the rooming house in the Bronx.

He walked into the deli, bought a cup of coffee to take away with him and a tuna club sandwich and returned to the cab. The mobile rang before he could unlock the doors; switching to send, he asked the caller to hold, then got into the cab.

'My apologies,' he said.

'That's OK, Mr Patil. If you're free, I'd like you to pick me up from 254 East 72nd Street.'

No need to ask who was calling. He had picked up the English-speaking Russian often enough the last time he was working in New York back in February to know his voice anywhere.

'How long will it take you to get here?'

'No more than fifteen minutes if I'm lucky,' Desai told him.

Whether or not the Russian had recognised his voice was immaterial. He simply wouldn't get into the cab unless the driver had a swarthy complexion, a pockmarked cheek and a black bushy moustache.

Chapter Twenty Six

———————————⟫•◦•⟪———————————

It took the BND less than seventy-two hours to complete their enquiries and ascertain that no airline had carried a Mr V. J. Ramash between 17 and 21 October. By then, Hugo Calthorpe had also heard from the Central Bureau of Investigation that none of the four names that Ashton had culled from the flight manifests had been used by V. J. Desai so far as they were aware. However, when he had subsequently disappeared after delivering a lecture on Hindu Nationalism at the University of Mysore on 15 February, he was rumoured to have flown to Sri Lanka travelling under the name of V. J. Mackajee. Another unreliable source had placed him round about the same time in Vancouver where he was said to be masquerading as V. J. Patil. The bureau further stated that Mr R. S. Joshi had never come to their notice.

Based on this information Ashton had drafted a Terrorist Alert for the attention of Intelligence agencies in Belgium, Eire, France, Germany, Holland, and Italy. The text described the physical characteristics of V. J. Desai also known as V. J. Ramash, V. J. Makerjee and V. J. Patil, and gave the probable date of his departure from the United Kingdom. Addressees were further informed that the subject was believed to be in transit by air for New York and were requested as a matter of urgency to check all departure flights and report any sightings.

The draft had been considered by Clifford Peachey, who had inserted an additional paragraph exclusive for the Bundesnachrichtendienst stating it was appreciated that the BND had already conducted a search for V. J. Ramash with negative results. As a matter of routine he in turn had referred the draft to the DG for comment. Desai was wanted for murder and Hazelwood had made the point that perhaps the request for information should be directed through Interpol Headquarters at St Cloud outside Paris. After conferring with the Assistant Commissioner (Crime) he'd learned the case against Desai was not yet sufficiently advanced to issue an international arrest warrant. As a result the top priority signal had been sent to the addresses Ashton had originally suggested. The delay had, however, cost the better part of a working day.

The crypto-protected transmission from the *Direction de la surveillance du territoire* was received on 7 November. Some twenty-two days had elapsed since the body of Basil Wilks had been found on the railway line a mile from the station of South Kenton. Ashton learned of the development shortly before noon when he was summoned to the DG's office.

'We've had a stroke of luck,' Hazelwood announced, then handed him the signal to read.

He thought Victor was right, they had been lucky. When dispatching the Terrorist Alert, they'd had absolutely no proof that Desai was in transit to New York. The man had lied to Hakkison Lal about departing from Manchester on a United Airlines flight and disclosing his ultimate destination could so easily have been part of the deception. But for once in his life he had slipped up and had failed to conceal his tracks. On the evening of Wednesday 18 October, a Mr V. J. Patil who answered to the description of V. J. Desai had flown Air France to JFK New York.

'Rowan Garfield thinks he may have travelled to Paris on the Eurostar from Waterloo International.'

'Yeah, well, however he got there we're lucky Air France hadn't put that particular manifest through the shredder.'

'Even if they had, I believe they would have kept Mr V. J. Patil's details on record.'

Paris had been on the receiving end of a number of terrorist outrages committed by Islamic Fundamentalists from Algeria. In view of this, Hazelwood was damned sure the *Direction de la surveillance du territoire* would want to keep tabs on people whose appearance suggested they could be of North African origin.

317

Ashton looked at the signal again. 'I see Desai was using an Indian passport.'

'So?'

'So have we advised the Americans they've got a cuckoo in their nest?'

'Clifford will be talking to Director Freeh of the FBI in just under an hour's time. He'll give him the good news. Meantime you'd better get off home and throw a few things into a bag. With any luck we'll get you on the evening flight to New York.'

'What am I supposed to do over there?'

'Liaise with the FBI and get to Desai before some good lawyer does. I don't want him doing another vanishing act.'

'What makes you think he hasn't already done so?'

'Call it intuition.' Hazelwood raised the carved lid on the ornate cigar box and helped himself to a Burma cheroot. 'That plus the fact that your old sparring partner Pavel Trilisser took up the appointment of Russian Ambassador to the UN yesterday,' he added.

The *True Volunteers* was an English language, bi-monthly organ which supported the Irish National Liberation Army and other breakaway factions. It was printed in Dundalk and boasted a circulation of twenty-five thousand, a figure that owed more to wishful thinking on the part of the editor than established fact. The true circulation was under two thousand. The paper had reached Cathal via Richard, the fourth member of the active service unit, whose elder brother was a staunch Republican living in Louth approximately ten miles southwest of Dundalk. Elder brother liked to think he was security-minded because he made sure the *True Volunteers* was always dispatched rolled up inside back copies of the *Irish Independent*. However, in Cathal's opinion, this precaution was next to useless and he had lost count of the number of times he had told Richard to put a stop to it. The only saving grace about the present arrangements was that the newspapers were always sent to a poste restante to await collection. Even so there was still the risk that in time the Brits would cotton on to this and Richard would inadvertently betray the rest of the unit. But today was the first occasion when Cathal hadn't reminded him of this possibility.

The latest bi-monthly of the *True Volunteers* was dated 3 November and was nearly a week old. Mairin was still employed as a hospital cleaner at the Rechts des Isar Clinic and she had already left for work when Richard had walked the newspaper round to their flat in Mitter Sending. When she finished work at 13.00 hours, Cathal was waiting for her outside the clinic. Without saying a word, he led her down the road to Max-Weber-Plaza and into the nearest *Gasthof*. Signalling a waiter, he ordered a glass of hock for Mairin and a beer for himself, then steered her to a quiet corner table well away from the bar.

'Something's wrong,' she said in a low voice. 'Don't deny it.'

'I wasn't going to.'

'So what's happened?'

'Be patient, you'll know soon enough.'

After the waiter had served them and returned to the bar, Cathal reached inside the donkey jacket he was wearing and brought out the latest edition of the *True Volunteer*. 'Page two,' he told her.

The headline read 'Cold Blooded Murder at Castlegreenore' and in smaller type underneath – 'Commanding Officer South Armargh battalion and wife shot to death in bed'. He had read the succeeding paragraphs so many times he could have recited them word for word. On Thursday 26 October at two o'clock in the morning, four masked men had broken into Barry Nolan's cottage on the outskirts of Castlegreenore. He and his common-law wife, Caitlin, had three children a girl aged seven, a hyperactive boy of six and his younger brother aged three. All three children had been herded into one bedroom and locked in. The girl had told reporters that she had heard her mother pleading with the intruders before she was killed. Nolan himself had died cursing his murderers who had shot him four times in the legs, chest and stomach before delivering the *coup de grâce* in the head.

'There's an editorial on page five,' Cathal informed her.

The editorial was a twenty-six line denunciation of the Provisional IRA, the Army High Command, and Lenihan in particular, who was described as a cowardly traitor with the blood of Irishmen on his hands. When Mairin looked up from the broad sheet her eyes mirrored the hatred she felt after reading the report followed by the editorial.

'That's right,' Cathal said in a low, venomous tone of voice, 'the Brits demanded his head and the big man from Dublin couldn't wait to oblige them. Nolan was a hero; he wasn't going to disarm his battalion to please those bastards in Dublin and in London.'

'And we helped to kill him,' Mairin said angrily. 'We could have prevented that meeting from taking place.'

'The decision was Lenihan's. Anyway, it's too late for regrets.'

'But not for revenge,' Mairin said.

'We'd be playing into the hands of the Brits. I'm not saying Lenihan doesn't deserve it.'

'I wasn't thinking of him, Cathal. I meant those jackals from the SIS.'

'Messenger.' Cathal shook his head. 'You heard what Kennedy said, it's just a codename used by all and sundry, doesn't tell you who he really is.'

'I've got a real name and an address.'

'Yeah?' Cathal reached for his beer and drained it in one go, then wiped his lips on the back of his hand. 'Like who, for instance?'

'Like Mr Eric Daniels of 147 Inkerman Road, Camberwell, the driver of the VW Passat. We could make a start with him.'

'That we could,' Cathal agreed.

Calthorpe left the diplomatic enclave and picked up the now all-too-familiar Sardar Patel Marg. Sumitra Bannerman had spent twelve days in the Safdar Jang Hospital and would presumably still be there now if the Bureau Chief of Reuters hadn't insisted she convalesce at his residence in the cantonment. Remembering how Sumitra had reacted the last time he had seen her, Calthorpe wondered what sort of reception he would get this afternoon.

The residence was on the edge of Subroto Park where Sardar Marg suddenly became Parade Road. The drive was off to one side of the property and swept in between two large white pillars, which would have looked even more imposing had there been a pair of wrought-iron gates to go with them. The monsoon had brought the lawn to a lush green but the grass would begin to lose its freshness by Christmas and come next May the turf would have reverted to the usual dusty patch.

Calthorpe had phoned the Bureau Chief to ask if he might call on Sumitra and had hoped Mary, his wife, would be at home but it was evident she had taken herself off somewhere. Clutching the bottle of scent he'd brought as a gift, Calthorpe followed the bearer through the bungalow to the water garden at the back.

Sumitra looked only marginally better than the last time he had seen her. Although her eyes were no longer closed to narrow slits and the swellings had gone down, the bruises on both cheeks were the colour of ripe bananas tinged with purple. The little finger on each hand was taped up and splinted and there were bruises on both legs extending from the ankles to just below the knees which hadn't been apparent when he'd found her.

She was sitting in an armchair with her legs up on a pouffe and wearing a pair of slippers that would have been several sizes too large for her but for the dressings on her feet. On a small table to her right there was a pitcher of lemonade, two glasses and a bell. Calthorpe assumed the upright chair had been moved from the dining room to the terrace for his benefit.

'May I sit down?' he asked.

'Please do,' Sumitra told him with a noticeable lack of enthusiasm.

'The scent's a small present for you,' Calthorpe said awkwardly. 'Mary helped to choose it.'

'Anaïs Anaïs.'

'Yes. I can always change it if you would prefer something else.'

'No, it's very sweet of you both.' Sumitra dabbed some on her wrist and raised it to her nose. 'And it smells lovely.'

'Oh good. I'm so glad you like it. Mary will be pleased too.' Calthorpe cleared his throat. Now comes the tricky bit, he thought, and didn't know how to proceed. 'I've read the statement you gave to the police,' he said presently.

Statement? It read as though Choudhury had put the words into her mouth. She hadn't been abducted; masked robbers had broken into the bungalow and tortured Sumitra to make her reveal where she kept her money and valuables.

'I'm afraid I didn't believe a word of it,' he added.

'I think you had better leave, Mr Calthorpe.'

'Why were you so alarmed when Brigadier Choudhury and I walked into you room at the hospital?'

'I've asked you politely to leave. If you continue to ignore my request, I shall be forced to ring for the servants.'

'You recognised his voice, didn't you? Brigadier Choudhury was one of the so-called masked robbers who broke into the bungalow and abducted you, wasn't he?'

Sumitra didn't say anything. Instead, she reached for the bell on the table and rang it, but not so loudly that the sound carried to the servants inside the bungalow.

'I'll tell you what they were looking for; it wasn't money, jewellery or valuables or anything like that. They had read the journal which Logan had taken with him to Ranikhet and they wanted to be sure your husband hadn't secreted something even more damning at home. In short, the men who tortured you belonged to the Ananda Marg.'

Sumitra told him he was being silly, her voice a nervous whisper. Although she was still clutching the handbell she made no attempt to ring it. Very gently, Calthorpe removed the bell from her grasp and set it down beside his chair.

'Who told Logan the leaders of the Ananda Marg were holding a secret meeting up at Ranikhet? Was it the Brigadier?'

'No.'

'I don't understand you, Sumitra. This man had your husband murdered. Why are you shielding him?'

'You're so wrong, Mr Calthorpe. Logan received a hand-written note inviting him to meet V. J. Desai who wished to correct some of his misconceptions about the Ananda Marg.'

'Who was the author?'

'It was unsigned.'

'Logan wouldn't have taken off for the hills on the strength of an anonymous note.'

'But he did.'

'Then the note must have complemented something he already knew. Logan didn't always come straight home from the office, did he? I bet sometimes your husband stopped off for a drink at the club? Who did he meet there? The Brigadier?'

'I don't know.'

Sumitra was lying; Calthorpe knew that as surely as there would be a tomorrow.

'Keeping silent isn't going to save you. They may have spared your life once but you are a threat to them and one day somebody is going to have second thoughts about you.'

'Choudhury. Logan used to see him occasionally. He was one of his sources.'

'We're talking about the Deputy Chief of the Intelligence Bureau?'

Sumitra shook her head. 'No, I mean Vasani Choudhury, the younger brother. He's a junior government minister responsible for science and technology. He will be attending a convention on nuclear energy in Moscow during early December. Logan told me he was fairly sure Vasani Choudhury supported the aims of the Ananda Marg and was prepared to assist them in any way he could.' And posthumously Logan had been proved right. Vasani Choudhury had been one of the men who had kidnapped Sumitra and had been present the whole time she was being tortured. He had in fact interrogated her at length.

'I never saw him, Mr Calthorpe, but I recognised his voice.'

'Then why did he spare you?'

'Because we had never met. Logan had secretly taped an off-the-record interview with him and I'd listened to it. The tape still exists; it's in our deed box at the Bank of Baroda. I knew that if I told them about it, I would be dead.'

'What about Brigadier Choudhury?'

'I mistook him for his younger brother; that's why I was so frightened when you both walked into my room at the hospital. When he returned the following day he more or less suggested what I should say to the police. I think he was trying to protect Vasani.'

Although Calthorpe made all the right responses at the right time, his mind was elsewhere, busy formulating the arguments he would put to Sumitra which would convince her that releasing the tape to him was the only sensible thing to do. He wasn't sure yet how many copies he would make but certainly the Choudhury brothers would each receive one. The idea of exerting a degree of control over the Deputy Chief of the Intelligence Bureau rather appealed to him. Life, he thought, was getting to be quite like old times.

A few minutes after the cabin staff had finished serving dinner, Ashton had tipped his seat right back and had made a determined effort to snatch a few hours' sleep. You caught a flight departing Heathrow in the early evening and found yourself in New York at nine thirty with the rest of the night before you. Unfortunately by then you'd already been awake for over nineteen hours and your body clock wasn't in sync with Eastern Time. However, try as he might, sleep evaded him and he was still wide awake when British Airways Flight 177 began the final approach into JFK. Trying to unwind had been his problem. Everything had happened in a hell of a rush. Home to throw a change of clothes into a bag then back to the office again for a briefing from Clifford Peachey that had gone on forever, followed by a session with Roy Kelso and Ken Maynard from the pay branch. By the time he had checked in at Heathrow, he'd had a mere five minutes in hand to call Harriet and say goodbye.

On reflection Ashton thought it was probably just as well he had been pressed for time, otherwise a difference of opinion might have developed into a full-scale row. While he was being briefed, Jill Sheridan had telephoned Harriet to inform her that Frank Warren had submitted his resignation and would be leaving on 31 December. She had wanted to know if Harriet would reconsider her decision and apply for the job when it was advertised internally. And he'd had to explain to Harriet why he hadn't told her about the vacancy, and it was no use him telling her it wasn't in Jill's gift or that it had never occurred to him Frank would quit. So he'd told Harriet the truth, which was that he had assumed she wouldn't be interested and had turned it down out of hand. He had been right in one respect; Harriet wasn't interested but she had made it crystal clear she should have been consulted.

At 21.30 hours local time and right on schedule, BA Flight 177 touched down and taxied round to the designated terminal. As soon as the trunk was in position, Ashton lifted his overnight bag down from the bin above his head and joined the throng heading towards the exit. Not having to wait for your baggage to appear on the carousel was one of the advantages of travelling light. Unless you were among the first off the plane, how fast you went through Immigration was a matter of luck. As was becoming a habit, Ashton contrived to join the slowest queue. Eventually he reached the window, handed over his passport and landing card and waited while the Immigration officer clipped the bottom section of the entry form to a blank page, then passed through Customs into the arrivals hall.

The agent who'd been sent to meet him looked young enough to have just graduated from the FBI Academy. He was wearing a dark grey single-breasted suit under an equally funereal overcoat which he had left unbuttoned. He was holding a strip of cardboard across his chest with Ashton's name printed on it with a purple, felt-tipped pen.

Ashton went over to him, introduced himself and was immediately asked for some sort of ID.

'My name's Voce,' the agent told him after examining his passport. 'Alan Voce. My partner's waiting for us outside. We're going to run you into town.'

'That's very good of you.'

'You're welcome, Mr Ashton. Where are you staying?'

Ashton dipped into his jacket pocket and pulled out the memo Kelso had given him. 'Loews, 569 Lexington Avenue at East 51st Street,' he said, and followed Voce out of the terminal.

The partner's name was Quinn which had a nice Irish ring to it. He wasn't over-friendly and Ashton wondered if he'd heard what had happened to Barry Nolan and blamed him for it.

'Is this your first time in New York?' Voce asked as they pulled away from the kerb.

'Yes, it is.'

'But not Stateside I hear,' Quinn said.

'No, I've been to Chicago, Washington DC, Seattle, St Louis, LA, Lake Arrowhead.'

'And Richmond, Virginia. Let's not forget that.'

'You're well informed.'

'Let's say your reputation has preceded you,' Quinn told him.

'And?'

'The bottom line is we don't want you setting fire to Manhattan while you're looking to find this V. J. Desai or whatever name he's using right now.'

'He arrived in New York as V. J. Patil, flew Air France from Paris on October the eighteenth.'

'We're already on to that,' Voce said. 'The Immigration Service is checking their records. His visa application will be on the database and that will show the address where Patil is staying while he's over here—'

'How many people has he murdered in your country?' Quinn asked, interrupting his partner.

'Four,' Ashton told him.

'Four. Why the hell would he stay in New York waiting for you guys to catch up with him? Take it from me, he'll have left town long ago.'

'Don't take any notice of Mick,' Voce told him. 'He's a born pessimist.'

Nobody said much after that. Ashton passed the time looking out of the window at the road signs. Rockaway Boulevard, Woodhaven, Queens Midtown Expressway – none of which conveyed anything to him.

'We're going through the Midtown Tunnel,' Voce said. 'Takes us under the East River into Manhattan.'

They emerged from the tunnel on East 37th Street and headed uptown on Third Avenue to make a left at East 51st. Quinn then made another left into Lexington Avenue and pulled up outside the front entrance to Loews.

'This is it,' Voce said a little unnecessarily. 'I don't know what your plans are for the rest of the night but . . .'

'I'm going to take a long, hot bath and then turn in,' Ashton told him.

'A great idea. We'll pick you up tomorrow at eight thirty if that's OK?'

'Fine.'

'Of course if anything should happen before then, you'll be the first to hear.'

'Don't wait up,' Quinn said, 'nothing is going to happen.'

'I told you he was a pessimist,' Voce said cheerfully, and they drove off.

Chapter Twenty Seven

<hr />

In accordance with the instructions he had received on his mobile, V. J. Desai turned off Central Park West at West 65th Street and cut through the Park on the transverse. Leaving Central Park, he crossed Fifth Avenue into East 65th Street and headed north on Madison. Along the way a couple of fares tried to flag him down but the illuminated sign on the roof wasn't showing and he happily ignored them.

The fare Desai was going to pick up was waiting for him outside the IRT's East 86th Street station on the Lexington Avenue Line. His name was Pavel Trilisser and the last time they had met was 24 February in Geneva. Photographs of the Russian were misleading and didn't give a true likeness. Meet him face to face and he became unforgettable. Pavel Trilisser was fifty-six, going on fifty-seven, but his age didn't show. He was a tall, lean, ascetic-looking man who put one in mind of a high-ranking judge or distinguished physicist, until you saw his eyes. They were the colour of an aquamarine gem yet burned with the intensity of an oxyacetylene torch.

Some fifty yards from the rendezvous, Desai switched on the illuminated sign which indicated the driver was plying for hire. For good measure he was about to kill the main beams and put them on again, but the Russian had already spotted his cab and had moved up to the kerb, one arm raised aloft as if to flag down the taxi. Desai checked the rear-view mirror, flicked the trafficator, then drifted close to the kerbside and stopped opposite Trilisser. The Russian got into the back, slammed the door and moved across the bench seat to sit directly behind him.

'Where to?' Desai asked.

'Head for midtown where there is more traffic and just drive around.'

'Certainly.' Desai switched off the taxi sign, shifted into drive and moved off.

'After all we don't want another coincidence like Geneva, do we?' Trilisser added.

Desai said nothing. Trilisser had chosen the venue because he had been a member of the Russian delegation which had attended an extraordinary general meeting of the World Health Organisation on the resurgence of tuberculosis in developed countries. Unfortunately at precisely the same time there had been a seminar on violence in the home which had been attended by some of the foremost clinical psychiatrists in the field. He'd had no idea that his former sister-in-law would be attending the conference. Worse still, when Trilisser had suggested they conducted their business over dinner at the Hotel President-Wilson on the Quai Wilson, neither of them had known that a number of the psychiatrists were staying at the hotel.

There had been few worse moments than when he had spotted her at a window table on the far side of the restaurant. Although he'd immediately looked away, she had sensed somebody had been watching her and looked round in their direction. Desai had hoped she hadn't seen them but Trilisser had wanted to know why the attractive Indian woman across the room was taking such an interest in them. And that had been the start of an unwelcome diversion because the Russian had demanded he ascertained how much of a threat she presented and take whatever action was required.

'Do you have the statement?' Trilisser asked now.

Desai took one hand off the wheel, reached for the envelope in the glove compartment and passed it back over his shoulder.

'Do you have the first consignment, Mr Trilisser?' he countered.

'All in good time.'

The statement was a printout showing the transfer of one hundred and fifty thousand pounds from the Chartered Bank of the Caymen Islands to a numbered account with the Bank of

Landschaft Aagau in Berne. The transaction had been initiated by R. S. Joshi five days ago on 2 November. The money could not be moved to a bank of Trilisser's own choosing without the executive codeword and Desai was not going to disclose that until the Russian had delivered the first consignment. This was a 250 millilitres plastic dispenser containing Anthrax spores, one of the most deadly agents for waging germ warfare. A hundred per cent lethal, the decay rate of Anthrax was measured in years not days. On a remote, deserted island in the Orkneys, where experiments to determine the effectiveness of biological weapons had been conducted by the British Government during World War II, the soil was still contaminated and life-threatening fifty-five years later.

'The consignment,' Desai repeated. 'Where is it?'

'Not so fast. I want to know how you propose to use it.'

'That's none of your business.'

'You're wrong. It is my business when the Ananda Marg is obviously riddled with informers. You have powerful enemies, Mr Desai. Years after the assassination of Lieutenant General Rao Narain Singh, the former Commander-in-Chief, Eastern Command, an informer telephoned the Central Bureau of Investigation and named you as the man who'd planned it. He must have provided evidence to support the allegation because you have been on the run ever since.'

Desai turned off Lexington Avenue and headed west on East 57th Street. Trilisser was right, of course; there were people within the movement who were jealous of him. He had been driven out of the country and made less effective.

'The agent will be used in Kashmir,' he told Trilisser.

'Naturally – that's the flashpoint. But how?'

'The attack will be launched from inside the Pakistan-occupied zone. It will be directed against the Hindu village of Kandwara two thousand metres beyond the so-called border accepted under the terms of the disgraceful Simla Settlement of 1973.'

Desai made a left turn and headed south on Fifth Avenue.

'The agent will be delivered by means of an 81mm mortar.'

In all seven bombs would be fired at the target, six high

explosive and one parachute illuminating bomb specially adapted to deliver the Anthrax. The mortar had been manufactured in China and had been captured from a guerrilla band belonging to the Kashmir Liberation Front operating in the Karakoram Range. So had the ammunition.

'Can you get your people in and out of the Pakistan zone without them being intercepted?'

'I wouldn't have sanctioned the operation if there had been any doubt in my mind about that.'

'There must be no Russian involvement. If Marchukov had been detained by the authorities in Lahore the situation would have become very ugly.'

Pavel Trilisser had lost faith, that was the trouble with him. He was now a businessman pure and simple. The future of his country had ceased to concern him.

'You needn't worry,' Desai told him. 'No one will point an accusing finger at you. There will be no Russian involvement. Are you satisfied now?'

'Yes.' Trilisser leaned forward and tapped him on the shoulder. 'Give me your right hand, palm uppermost.'

'What childishness is this?'

'Just do as I say.'

Desai took his hand off the wheel and reached over his shoulder.

'This is one key to a safety deposit box lodged in the vaults of the Huber Bank in Geneva. The other key is held by my associate, Leonid Zaytsev. A reservation for the twenty-second and twenty-third of November will be made at the Hotel California for your representative. Naturally we need to know his name?'

'Joshi. R. S. Joshi.'

The arrangements were simple enough. Leonid Zaytsev and R. S. Joshi would meet at the Huber Bank on the morning of 23 November. Together they would go down into the vaults and open the deposit box. As soon as Joshi had taken delivery of the Anthrax, he would accompany the Russian to the Bank of Landschaft Aagau in Berne and effect the transfer of the hundred and fifty thousand pounds.

'I trust this arrangement is acceptable?'

'We shall be pressed for time,' Desai told him. 'Vasani Choudhury leaves for Moscow on December the fifth.'

'You can drop me at Penn station,' Trilisser said, interrupting him.

Desai calculated they must be approaching 47th Street because they had passed the Rockefeller Center and Saks a few minutes ago. Coming up to the next intersection, he discovered they were several blocks further south than he reckoned. At 42nd Street, he turned right and headed for Seventh Avenue.

'There will be no second consignment,' Trilisser announced.

'What?'

'Choudhury is not to be trusted. He considers you to be a danger to the movement.'

'How would you know?'

'Because I make it my business to find out all I can about the people I am dealing with.'

There was no budging Trilisser. No matter what arguments he put forward or how angry he became, he could not persuade the Russian to reconsider his decision. When they parted company at Penn station, Desai was in a murderous rage. Seeking to exorcise his anger, he cut through to Eighth Avenue and headed north, a heavy foot on the gas pedal. The lights were in his favour all the way from West 31st for ten blocks. He was doing over sixty when he caught a red at 42nd Street and shot the lights. A rig heading west to Ninth Avenue smacked into the rear nearside door and spun the Ford across the centre line into the path of an oncoming bus.

After lying awake for hours on end and metaphorically counting millions of sheep, Ashton had been asleep for under an hour when the distant sound of a bell woke him. Totally disorientated, he was slow to connect the noise with a telephone. He was lying in the middle of a king-size bed, and in his still befuddled state it seemed only sensible to get up when he physically couldn't reach the phone. He pawed the air, bumped into the other bed, turned about and felt his way slowly and surely to the bedside table and the telephone. Lifting the receiver

332

with one hand, he wiped his mouth with the other and said hello.

A triumphant voice said, 'Hi, it's me, Alan Voce. I thought you'd like to know we've found V. J. Desai. Or to be more accurate he found us.'

'That's terrific news. Where is he being held?'

'St Clare's Hospital. He was involved in a traffic accident. Of course he has still to be formally identified.'

'When will that happen?'

'We're on the way to the hospital now.'

'I'd like to come with you.'

'There's no need. We have copies of his photo which you people faxed to Washington.'

'I'd still like to come with you,' Ashton told him.

Voce didn't say anything. From the unintelligible mumble he could hear in the background, Ashton guessed the American was consulting his partner.

'Can you meet us at reception in five minutes?'

'I can be there in less,' Ashton said, and hung up.

He switched on the table lamp, stripped off and went into the bathroom for one of the quickest showers of his life. Shaving was out but he found time to brush his teeth before pulling on his clothes. He combed his hair on the way down to the lobby.

'Four minutes,' Voce told him. 'Not bad going.'

'So what are we waiting for?' Quinn growled. 'Let's move it.'

Ashton followed them out of Loews Hotel into Lexington Avenue. It was five thirty on a pitch-black morning, the temperature didn't feel much above freezing, there was a chill north wind that cut through to the bone and he had neglected to bring his Burberry trench coat which would have kept him moderately warm. But there was no turning back now; anxious to get out of the wind, he scrambled into the rear of the car and slammed the door.

Quinn meant what he'd said about moving it. Before Voce had time to fasten his seat belt, he had pulled away from the kerb and was nudging the thirty-mile-an-hour speed limit.

'You could say Desai is lucky to be alive,' Voce observed. 'According to the cops he should be lying in a morgue. The taxi he was driving was reduced to scrap metal but the only injuries he suffered were a sprained wrist and a nasty gash above the left eye. Seems he was hit by two vehicles travelling in opposite directions, and the seat belt was torn loose under the double impact. Anyway he was knocked unconscious.'

At first Desai had tried to refuse hospital treatment but had changed his mind when the police were going to take him in for questioning. The intern on duty in casualty had put eight stitches into his head and had had the wrist X-rayed to make sure it wasn't fractured. Aware that the patient had been knocked unconscious and needed to be treated for shock, the intern had also decided he should be detained overnight in hospital because he was displaying all the classic symptoms of concussion. The only reason why Desai hadn't carried out his threat to discharge himself had been the presence of the cop who'd accompanied him to the hospital.

'She wasn't going to stand for that,' Voce continued. 'She made it damn clear to Desai that if he discharged himself from hospital, she was going to run him straight into the 18th Precinct.'

Before leaving the scene of the accident, she had transmitted a preliminary report which had included the names of the injured. Earlier that day, the 18th, like all the other precincts in New York, had received a copy of the wanted bulletin on V. J. Desai aka V. J. Patil.

'They didn't make the connection straight off the bat,' Quinn said. 'Matter of fact it wasn't until the graveyard shift was taking over and the relief commander was going through the log that they spotted the taxi driver's name was V. J. Patil. So they contacted the officer at the hospital and asked her to describe the cab driver and that was that.'

Desai had been moved from the man's medical ward to a small room with no windows and a reinforced door where he was in solitary confinement. Ever mindful of the horrendous cost of litigation, the medical staff would not allow the police to question him. There was, however, one officer on guard outside his room at all times.

'This guy Desai,' Quinn said abruptly, 'he's murdered four people. Right?'

'Yes.'

'You got a warrant for his extradition?'

'Not on me,' Ashton said.

'That's what I figured.' Quinn pulled up outside a grey-looking building on West 51st, six blocks from Loews Hotel. 'This is it,' he added. 'St Clare's Hospital.'

'So how are we going to play this?'

'That's easy, Mr Ashton. We'll take you into his room where you will formally identify V. J. Desai before giving us a statement. After that, he will be held in custody, probably by Immigration since he entered this country illegally under an assumed name. NYPD would also like to get their hooks into him but they will have to stand in line.' Quinn released his seat belt and opened the door. 'Now let's go see the man.'

Ashton had never liked hospitals and he'd seen a fair number of them around the world. There had been St Thomas's on the Mittelhofstrasse in Berlin where Harriet had been taken after her skull had been fractured by a stone, the Passadena General whose surgeons had removed a bullet from his shoulder. Some were grimmer than others like the Piragow Hospital off Lenin Prospekt in Moscow where Elena Adrianova, who'd worked for the Commercial Attaché in the British Embassy, was lying on fracture boards in a ward with seventy-nine other patients. St Clare's was probably the biggest and the best equipped he'd seen but it still had that familiar smell of disinfectant which always turned his stomach.

Desai was on the fourth floor in a room midway between the lifts and the emergency exit. The athletic young woman seated outside the door was, he learned, the same officer who had accompanied Desai to the hospital, and had elected to remain on duty.

'Are you on your own?' Quinn asked, and produced his badge.

'No. My partner's getting two cups of coffee from the vending machine on the third floor.'

'OK.' Quinn nodded as if he approved of the arrangement. 'This gentleman here is from England,' he said, pointing to Ashton. 'He's going to identify the prisoner.'

'Well, I don't know about that. My instructions from the doctor were to admit nobody without his permission.'

'What's your name, officer?'

'Yakunin. But—'

'This isn't going to take a minute, Officer Yakunin. We'll be in and out of there quicker than you can blink.'

'I'm sorry, sir, but—'

'You've got a key, haven't you?'

'Yes, but you still need to—'

Quinn put his face close to hers. 'Let's get this straight,' he snarled. 'I'm not asking anybody for permission. Now take the key out of your pocket and open this goddamned door.'

Yakunin opened her mouth as if to continue the argument, then thought better of it. She took the key out of her pants pocket, moved the chair aside and looked through the small reinforced window in the door. 'Desai seems to be asleep,' she muttered.

'Well, that's just too bad,' Quinn said.

It happened fast. Yakunin opened the door, walked into the room and was immediately grabbed by Desai. The figure she had seen on the bed was a pillow carefully rearranged under the blankets.

Voce was the first to react. Pulling a short barrel .357 revolver from his hip holster, he charged forward, then screamed in agony as his right arm was trapped between the door and the jamb. The bone snapped like a dry twig and he dropped the revolver inside the room.

'Take it easy,' Yakunin shouted hysterically. 'He's got my pistol.'

'Don't worry,' Quinn told her in a soothing voice. 'Nobody's going to do anything rash. Isn't that right V. J.?'

'I'm leaving,' Desai said in a loud voice.

'Sure you are. So let's calm down and talk about the arrangements. OK?'

'I mean this very minute.'

'What about transportation? You thought about that?'

It was the classic hostage situation and it was obvious to Ashton that Quinn was a trained negotiator. But in this instance he was pitted against a fanatic who wasn't prepared to listen to him. The first shot came through the door at an oblique angle, missed Quinn by a matter of inches and ricocheted off the opposing wall. The door opened wide and Yakunin appeared in the entrance, her wrists handcuffed behind her back, a pistol to her head. Still playing it by the rules, Quinn dropped his revolver, raised his hands and backed off.

'Don't do anything stupid,' he said calmly. 'You can walk out of here. Nobody is going to stop you.'

But somebody was about to. Ashton heard the lift ascending and knew it was going to stop at the fourth floor. Voce was facing him across the corridor nursing his broken arm, and right in the line of fire if Desai suddenly went ape. Using Yakunin as a human shield, Desai began to sidestep down the corridor towards the lifts, his back to the wall.

The lift stopped; there was a faint hissing sound as the doors opened and moments later Yakunin's partner appeared in the corridor, a polystyrene cup in each hand. He needed only a second to realise what was going on. As he dropped both cups and went for the .38 in his holster, Voce shouted at him to hold it.

Desai had no such intention. Still using Yakunin as a shield, he fired at her partner and hit him in the right leg, then wheeled half left and shot Voce in the face at point-blank, spattering the wall behind the FBI agent with blood, fragments of bone and brain tissue. Quinn threw himself flat on the floor, one arm outstretched towards the revolver he had dropped. The only help Ashton could give him was to act as a decoy. He backed slowly away from Desai talking nonstop about Hakisson Lal and R. S. Joshi in an effort to capture and hold his attention while Quinn inched towards the Colt .357. Unable to see where he was going, Ashton blundered into a wheeled stretcher that had been left in the corridor. Then Yakunin's partner took it into his head to call Desai a murdering son of a bitch and the shooting started again.

Ashton grabbed hold of the stretcher, swung the trolley around and pushing it in front of him, charged at Desai while he was still firing at the wounded police officer on the floor. An Olympic-class sprinter could not have made a quicker start than Ashton and he was going like the wind when he rammed the

Indian terrorist in the back. The impact bowled Desai over and cannoned into Yanukin and sent her flying. The stretcher ran into the two bodies on the floor and tipped over sideways. Unable to stop in time, Ashton dived over the obstruction. Breaking his fall with one hand, he rolled over on his right shoulder. When he started to get up on hands and knees, he found himself looking straight into the mouth of a .38 pistol which Desai had somehow managed to retain.

He saw the cylinder slowly revolve to bring the next round up into the chamber and threw up his left arm to knock the barrel aside, only to feel a searing pain from wrist to elbow. In that same instant there were three deafening explosions and his face was suddenly splattered with a lot of grey matter.

Somebody Ashton couldn't see at the other end of the corridor was screaming and Quinn was yelling it was all over.

Ashton slowly got to his feet nursing his injured arm. With Voce, Desai and the uniformed police officer all dead and Yakunin in a state of shock, the corridor resembled a battlefield. Somehow he managed to unbutton his bloodstained jacket and slip out of it.

'Are you OK?' Quinn asked him.

'I think I've been shot.'

'Yeah?' The American produced a pair of scissors from somewhere and cut the sleeve out of the shirt, and examined the furrow. 'Nah,' he said, 'you're OK, it's just a scratch.'

'That's what I like about you,' Ashton told him, 'you're all heart.'

Chapter Twenty Eight

The scratch turned out to be a chipped bone which, although painful, would not ultimately be debilitating, or so the Harley Street specialist had assured Ashton. Since he was the same man who two years ago had supervised his postoperative rehabilitation, after the surgeons at Passadena General had removed a bullet from his left shoulder, Ashton had a great deal of faith in his prognosis.

The NYPD traced the rooming house in the Bronx where Desai had been staying a lot quicker than most people in the law enforcement business had anticipated. Routine police work had had little to do with it. The gun battle in St Clare's Hospital had made headlines in all the papers but the *Daily Post* had carried a photograph of V. J. Desai taken from his taxi licence on the front page and the owner of the rooming house, in a rare example of civic duty, had come forward. Nothing of interest had been found in his room. Contrary to what Ashton had surmised, there had been no briefcase stuffed with false passports and Desai had left nothing behind in the way of notebooks or a diary which might have indicated what he was planning. From first to last he had shown a remarkable talent for preserving his anonymity.

The only tangible thing Ashton had brought back from New York was a key to a safety box which he and Quinn had found when going through Desai's personal effects at the hospital. Quinn hadn't wanted to part with it and even though the engraved number on the key had included a continental 7, Ashton had been unable to convince him the bank or company renting the box had to be in Europe. In the end they'd had a locksmith cut a duplicate which Ashton had switched when Quinn hadn't been looking. The Swiss bank which owned the relevant box had been identified by the Foreign Exchange division of Lloyd's.

Swiss banks had enjoyed a reputation for being the most secretive in the world and hitherto a numbered account had been regarded as sacrosanct. However, of late the Swiss Government, as well as the banks, had come under fire for the way they had hung on to large sums of money which rightfully belonged to survivors of the holocaust. With a little pressure from the Foreign and Commonwealth Office, the Swiss Government had ordered the Huber Bank in Geneva to open Box number 127. The discovery that it contained 250 millilitres of Anthrax had given everybody a nasty turn, no one more so than Bill Orchard, who had begun to wonder what other unpleasant surprises might emerge in two years' time when India and Pakistan celebrated the fiftieth year of Independence.

One month before his date of retirement, Frank Warren's appointment was duly advertised internally but this was really for the sake of appearances; Hazelwood had already decided that ex-Detective Chief Superintendent Brian Thomas from the vetting section would take over from him. A collection for Frank's leaving present had been started at the same time, though precisely what they should give him was a problem that had exercised everybody at Vauxhall Cross. It had been Harriet who had known what Frank would appreciate. Although she had only worked alongside him for a few months at Benbow House, she had learned more about his personal life, his likes and dislikes than all his other colleagues put together. Even though he was addicted to the game, there were a few who thought presenting him with a golf buggy was going a bit far, popular though Frank was. Ashton supposed that in the circumstances, it was almost inevitable that he would be landed with the job of organising the collection. The most generous donation was given by Roy Kelso, the meanest by Jill Sheridan, which hadn't surprised him.

At the beginning of December Jill Sheridan had produced her paper on the suggested reorganisation of the SIS in the certain knowledge that it would be well received in some quarters. She was, however, careful to ensure that Ashton wasn't included on the distribution list in case some of her arguments seemed familiar to him.

The Peacheys were still feeding two Special Branch officers as the year was drawing to a close. Although the threat posed by Barry Nolan had been defused and the ceasefire was still holding, it had been decided to maintain maximum security until he retired in early January and moved house to Yorkshire. The officers assigned to this duty were however rotated much more frequently and O'Meara had even filled in for twenty-four hours on one occasion.

Ashton had tried to contact O'Meara a couple of times because he'd heard she had been hauled over the coals for withholding information about Hakkison Lal. But she had always been out or otherwise engaged whenever he'd called and after a time he had given it up as a bad job. Eric Daniels had shown greater persistence in that respect.

O'Meara thought she must have been crazy to get into a relationship with him when she already had enough problems to cope with. She was thirty-seven years old, had a son now going on her age when she had married at eighteen, and a daughter of fourteen who was being difficult, something that had started way back when her husband had walked out on his family in 1989 If there were two things her children had in common it was hatred of the police and a strong aversion to all white people. They had reluctantly made an exception in her case though whether they would ever accept Eric Daniels was another matter. She wondered too if his children would accept her but of course Eric was forty-six and both his children were married and had families of their own.

O'Meara had lost count of the number of times she had resolved to end their relationship before it got too serious, but it was easier said than done because she was genuinely fond of him. He had turned up on her doorstep with a large bunch of flowers and invited her to dinner when she had been feeling particularly low. How he had learned she had been officially reprimanded by the Assistant Commissioner, Special Branch that afternoon was a mystery. How many times had he dated her since then?

Whenever she hadn't been on night duty was the short answer. And how many times had she been to his place at 147 Inkerman Road? Five? No, six. And what could be nicer on this wet December evening than to sit back with a glass of wine, listening to the *Best of Frank Sinatra* on the CD player while Eric slaved away in the kitchen cooking spiced prawns with tomatoes and pilau rice according to Delia Smith? Then the doorbell rang breaking the spell.

'I'll get it,' she yelled and put her glass down.

The two young people on the doorstep were only about five six, slender and dark, especially the girl, whose shoulder-length hair was black and glossy like a raven.

'We've come to see Mr Daniels,' the man told her. 'He's expecting us.'

Despite the efforts to suppress it, the brogue still came through.

'You got the wrong address, man,' O'Meara said, putting on a West Indian accent. 'Ain't no Daniels here.'

'That's funny, he answered the phone last night,' the girl said, and got a foot in the door.

The girl was real bad trouble. She was nasty, ruthless and her hand was creeping towards the pocket of her anorak. O'Meara knew what was coming and acted, smashing the heel of her palm upwards into the girl's nose. There was a crunching noise as it broke and she didn't give a damn if the shattered bone had penetrated the brain and killed her. The man was still gawping when she slammed the door in his face and went down fast. As she crawled on her belly towards the kitchen, O'Meara heard the hollow cough of a pistol fitted with a noise suppressor.

'What the hell are you doing on the floor?' Daniels asked her.

'For Christ's sake, get on the phone and hit 999,' O'Meara told him. 'The bloody war's started again.'